Advanced
Dungeons&Dragons®

The Rod
of Seven Parts

Douglas Niles

For Fred Schroeder,
brother, uncle, and friend

The Rod of Seven Parts

Random House and its affiliate companies have worldwide distribution rights in the book trade for English language products of TSR, Inc.

Distributed to the book and hobby trade in the United Kingdom by TSR Ltd.

Distributed to the toy and hobby trade by regional distributors.

Cover art by Jeff Easley

First Printing: February 1996
Printed in the United States of America.
Library of Congress Catalog Card Number: 95-62073

9 8 7 6 5 4 3 2 1

ISBN: 0-7869-0479-8

8040XXX1501

TSR, Inc.
201 Sheridan Springs Road
Lake Geneva, WI 53147
U.S.A.

TSR Ltd.
120 Church End, Cherry Hinton
Cambridge CB1 3LB
United Kingdom

Books by
Douglas Niles

The Moonshae Trilogy
Darkwalker on Moonshae
Black Wizards
Darkwell

The Maztica Trilogy
Ironhelm
Viperhand
Feathered Dragon

The Druidhome Trilogy
Prophet of Moonshae
The Coral Kingdom
The Druid Queen

DRAGONLANCE® Novels
Flint, the King
The Kinslayer Wars
Emperor of Ansalon
The Kagonesti

The Quest Triad
Pawns Prevail
Suitors' Duel
Immortal Game
(February 1996)

PROLOGUE

The wind changed suddenly, in the space of a heart-beat. Arquestan discerned the subtle alteration and knew that the creature of chaos, his quarry, must be near.

The outcast wind duke halted, standing as rigid as any of the gnarled willow trunks that surrounded him. The trees jutted from the rancid swamp water for as far as Arquestan could see—though on this bleak, fog-bound world, that distance was not terribly great. In such a misty landscape, the motion of air was so faint that no ripples disturbed the placid water, but still the hunter sensed the change in the ephemeral current.

Arquestan's ink-black skin glistened like oil in the murky haze that passed for daylight here, the slick darkness of his body contrasting sharply with the muddy brown of lifeless trees and putrid water. The wind duke remained as still as a rock as he listened and looked and waited for the next motion of the thick, rot-infested air.

Douglas Niles

Brackish water rose to Arquestan's knees, concealing a bed of twisted roots intermingled with pockets of soft silt. The willows rose from the water like frozen ghosts, their supplicating limbs draped in ragged foliage and moss. Nearby, the trees loomed in clear detail, though those in the middle distance vanished like ghosts into the thick gray air.

No noise rippled through the heavy mist as the tentative wind, barely a feathery wisp of motion, again brushed Arquestan's bare back. Centuries of decay masked the air in thick, heavy perfume, cloying vapors that coated the wind duke's nostrils with each breath. Arquestan's dark chest, a coil of wiry sinew, rose and settled only slightly as the outcast hunter waited for thirty heartbeats, probing the unknown, mist-shrouded distance by sight and sound and smell.

Momentarily satisfied, Arquestan advanced, stepping so slowly that no sound, no single careless splash of water, signaled his movement. With long strides, he parted the oily liquid, moving toward a rise of tree-studded land that broke the monotony of the apparently eternal swamp.

A bubble of pale light drifted nearby, a floating sphere nearly as large as the wind duke's head. Brightness diffused across the entire silken surface of the globe, though the light source itself was visible as a tiny spark of vitality floating inside the filmy ball. The sphere floated gently, glowing softly, following the tall black figure through shallower water as he finally emerged onto the small circular island.

Once on dry land, the wind duke again froze, repeating his patient, multisensory probe of the surroundings. Finally he was satisfied that nothing moved in the murky distance.

"Stay here, Bayar."

Arquestan's voice was deep, but even more soft than the rustle of wind through distant willows. The globe halted, poised over the outspread branches of a low, gnarled willow. Craggy limbs formed a cradle of sorts, as if to seize the sphere if it should drift too low.

Again came a whisper of air, a mere touch of moisture against the wind duke's skin.

Now Arquestan was sure—the wind direction *had* shifted. For the last three days, since his arrival on this hellish world, he had steadfastly maintained his progress into the barely perceptible current of sluggish, stagnant air. A faint scent, and the instinct of deeper senses, had driven the outcast after his elusive quarry. During all that time the feeble sun, a spot of brightness against the eternal gray haze, had never moved. The orb remained barely visible through the misty stratus, providing the ranger with a steady reference for his bearings.

Together with his faithful hound, the wind duke had followed the subtle spoor of the lycosyd through this forsaken waste. It was a feat of tracking that no other ranger, human or half-elf or vaati, could have accomplished, the product of knowledge that was present without arrogance in Arquestan's mind. Instead, it merely underlay a truth: There was no other mortal in all the planes who could perform the tasks that the outcast vaati had made a way of life.

A sound disturbed the swamp some distance away, and Arquestan turned his head slowly. Bayar's dim glow faded almost to nothing as the hound swooped behind the wind duke's angular shoulder, the glowing sphere waiting and watching as patiently as her master.

Another ripple of noise came to the outcast's ears, and

3

he knew that the deadly lycosyd was near. This time, Arquestan vowed in grim silence, the beast would not escape. The spyder-fiend had been sorely wounded during their first encounter three days ago. With one of its eight legs sliced off and a deep stab into the abdomen, the monster had teleported wildly, unable to return to its hideous mistress, the Queen of Chaos. Yet the tanar'ri had still escaped through the planes, seeking refuge in this nether world. Arquestan had tracked it here, following the faint spoor through ether and air, finally trapping the beast in this seemingly eternal fen.

The lycosyd was a powerful foe, fanatically loyal to the Queen of Chaos and, together with all the spyder-fiends, a sworn enemy of the wind dukes. Traveling among the planes even more freely than the vaati outcast, the queen's tanar'ri were vicious and implacable foes. The antipathy between vaati and spyder-fiend alone would have been enough to compel Arquestan into his grim pursuit.

Yet this time there had been an even greater inducement, a thing no vaati, whether an outcast like Arquestan or a loyal and lawful dweller of Aaqa, could dare to ignore. This lycosyd had reeked of a spoor that the hunter had not sensed for more than seven centuries, a magical essence that compelled him unquestioningly into this deadly chase.

The wind duke was certain that this tanar'ri spyder-fiend had, very recently, held a segment of the sacred rod. That certainty was a tiding of both hope and fear, a portent that the outcast must do everything in his power to confirm, for if the rod was again scattered upon a world of mortals, the great war of law against chaos would once again rage into open battle. spyder-fiend and vaati would

4

again strive for the ultimate victory, a triumph that had eluded both sides upon the ancient and bloody field of Pesh.

Again came the faint sound, rippling water caused by something moving through the swamp with insufficient caution. Carefully Arquestan edged to the side, patiently shifting his stance in the water, too slowly to make even a hint of splash. Though his feet were bare, they were well toughened, inured to the barbs and branches that lay tangled across the floor of the stagnant swamp. Likewise, his naked skin was slick and perfect, unaffected by elements or abrasion. Unlike a human, the wind duke lacked the apparatus of either sex; in battle, he was spared the need to protect what would have been an exceptionally vulnerable part of his body.

Arquestan held a vaati blade in each hand. The swords were keen, double-edged weapons, far stronger than any normal steel. One blade was long, the other short, both mounted in hilts especially formed to fit the outcast's long-fingered hands. Forged in the Valley of Aaqa, the weapons had been given to Arquestan by the vindeam Xathwik, one of the few vaati who would grudgingly acknowledge the worth of his outcast cousin's endeavors. Of course, even Xathwik deplored the chaotic impermanence of Arquestan's life, the whirlwind of places and companions that were the outcast's lot. Xathwik, vindeam sorcerer to the core, had spent all the centuries of his life in the rigid world of Aaqa, and would no doubt remain in the wind dukes' precisely ordered homeland until the end of time. To Xathwik, and to most of his kinsmen, the wendeam outcasts were mysterious and frightening.

For the briefest of moments, the outcast envied his

cousin, longed for the precise security that was the wind dukes' homeland. Then came another trace of movement through the stagnant water, and all longing, all regrets, gave way to pure, taut alertness. The spyder-fiend approached, and it was time for battle.

Even wounded, the lycosyd would be a formidable foe. Arquestan pictured the vicious, wolflike head, upper and lower jaws bristling with fangs and dripping with potent venom. The arachnoid body, the tanar'ri's most vulnerable area, was protected by a carapace of steel-hard shell. Two muscular humanoid arms grew from the shoulders, and each terminated in a powerful hand of flexible, taloned fingers. During the fight with Arquestan, the monster had kept those hands hidden beneath its belly, where, the wendeam suspected, the lycosyd had clenched a portion of the Rod of Seven Parts. The essence of that ebony shaft, the lost artifact of the wind dukes, had been a clear spoor in the air.

The vaati and the spyder-fiend had waged a brief fight on a remote desert world. It was the outcast's ambush that had allowed any battle to occur at all. The spyder-fiend had tried to teleport immediately, to escape to the fortress of its queen, but Arquestan's attack had been too swift, too deadly. Even then the wendeam had sensed the spoor of the rod, knew that at least a portion of the sanctified artifact was within reach. He had pressed his assault until the tanar'ri fled in desperation, seeking refuge here until its strength could be restored.

But the implacable wind duke had followed, and now, once again, the ranger's quarry was close. Breathing easily, hefting the twin blades in his hands, Arquestan made ready to fight. Creasing his forehead, shifting the tight curls of his hair, Arquestan concentrated upon the power of the wind dukes, the inherent magic that allowed him to exert the force of law over surrounding chaos. Responding to his will, the temperature began to fall. Immediately the vaati's skin was coated with a glistening layer of dew, shimmering droplets of water condensing from the air. The outcast held utterly still, feeling the specks of water turn to frost, grateful that much of the odiferous rot in the air sifted downward with the moisture. Arquestan watched as a film of ice formed across the swamp nearby, growing thicker and expanding as he maintained his concentration.

The bubble that was the Hound of Law floated to the ground near the shore of the small island. In a blink of transformation, Bayar stood there, all flopping jowls, melancholy eyes of brown, and a cloak of skin that seemed several sizes too large for the lanky canine body. Her dark eyes glowed with intelligence and anticipation as Bayar stared into the mist. The dog's nostrils twitched slightly, and Arquestan knew that his hound monitored, by scent, the approach of their enemy.

Then the fog seethed and the lycosyd burst into view, splashing through murky water with quick, lurching leaps, moving with alacrity on its seven good legs. Ducking around stooped willows in a brown froth, wolflike jaws curled into a vicious snarl, the monster attacked.

Arquestan saw that the lycosyd's bulbous body had regained its bright green color, a sign of restored health. The wolf head was flat-skulled, covered in black fur, but emerald plates of armored chitin lined the abdomen and bristled in a wide collar behind the snarling head. The two humanlike arms were visible, growing from the lycosyd's shoulders, but these limbs were clasped out of sight beneath the creature's belly.

The wind duke waited at the edge of the island, bracing his feet against stout trunks. The tanar'ri raced closer, until its forelegs struck the frozen water and the beast skidded. Ferocious jaws snapped at the wind duke as Arquestan slashed with his right blade, deflecting the bite with his short sword. Barking in challenge, Bayar leapt at the fur-covered abdomen, chomping hard. The dog's white fangs, no longer concealed by the deceptively harmless jowls, drove deep into the monster's body, tearing free a chunk of gory flesh.

The lupine head lashed around, seeking the hound's spine, but Arquestan was ready with his long sword, chopping a lethal slash to the back of the monster's skull. The lycosyd leapt away, skittering to the edge of the ice and splashing into the shallow water as ichor streamed from the gash in its head.

Growling, baring her long white teeth, Bayar crept after the monster. Arquestan, too, approached the motionless form, studying the once hateful visage. The wolflike head glistened with smooth black fur, evilly handsome now that the hooded lids were closed over the infernal, fiery eyes. The two arms, knotted with muscle and covered with patches of coarse black hair, curled downward, the hands still clenched beneath the green-plated body.

Again Arquestan caught that tantalizing spoor—the rod! He stiffened, leaning down, trying to see underneath the massive arachnoid body.

The red eyes opened suddenly, and the wind duke sprang back, both swords raised in defense. But the lycosyd didn't attack. Instead, it snarled once, then vanished.

A less experienced warrior might have thrust forward with his sword, angrily striking the space vacated by the teleporting spyder-fiend. Arquestan merely froze in place, listening, and was quickly rewarded by a rustling sound.

The tanar'ri, still wounded, had not traveled very far. Now it limped through the woods, still on this very patch of ground! Stalking silently, moving like a shadow between the trees, Arquestan approached the center of the island. He worked his way between gaunt willows, drawing ever closer to the source of the subtle noise. Soon he discerned a large hummock of ground rising from the mist. At the base of the hill was a dark aperture, and the wind duke's keen nostrils told him that the wounded lycosyd had sought shelter within this shallow niche.

Once again came that other, seductive spoor, an aura of magic that tingled along Arquestan's scalp. Surely a piece of the rod was near!

The lycosyd lay just inside the shallow niche, legs coiled beneath the bloated belly. The green-plated flanks heaved as crimson eyes glared hatred at the approaching wind duke. Arquestan raised his long sword as the creature's eyes flashed wickedly, though the glare of hatred had dimmed like a suffocating coal.

"You fail, vaati wind duke. Even as you slay me, you and your kind are doomed!"

The lycosyd spoke in a tone of smooth, cultured elegance and a deep and abiding confidence that brought Arquestan to a halt.

"You smell of the rod, spyder-fiend. Speak to me—tell me what you know."

"You wendeam roam the planes seeking word of the rod, do you not?" pressed the wolf-head with a sneer of contempt. "Outcast even by your own, you perform a fruitless quest!"

"What could a weakling such as you know of the pride

that drives a wendeam?" the wind duke asked calmly. "Our quest has borne fruit in the past. No doubt it will do so again."

"Proud words . . . but do you know that pride is merely a useless outgrowth of law?"

"Only a servant of chaos could make such an assumption. The loss is yours."

The tanar'ri chortled a wicked laugh. "I do know of the rod. I know, too, that your will shall be thwarted. The artifact has already been discovered—by agents of the queen!"

"It has been many centuries since any piece of the rod has appeared on a world of mortals," Arquestan remarked cautiously.

"Yet it has done so again." The lycosyd spoke sneeringly, cruel arrogance loosening its tongue. "The seven segments came to rest upon a place of humans and ogres, halflings and dwarves. Already we have claimed two of them!"

The spyder-fiend shrilled with laughter, the sound tainted by the madness of imminent death. "And still the tanar'ri gather, waiting at the gates for signs, for the command to embark upon the ultimate quest! At the word of our queen, we strike across the planes, sweeping forward with a wave of chaos like the worlds of life have never known!"

Gasping, its long tongue trailing from foaming lips, the wolf-head flopped forward onto the ground. The light of cruelty still blazed from the twin embers of its eyes.

"The tanar'ri gather . . . but they wait? Why?" Abruptly Arquestan knew what the spyder-fiend meant—and that the creature had revealed more than it intended.

"You may have two of the segments," the wind duke

declared with sudden insight, "but they must be only the largest, the sixth and the seventh, else you would know the way to the remainder!"

The tanar'ri coughed, but there was a glimmer of realization in its pain-wracked arrogance. With a clenching of jaws, the spyder-fiend spasmed, spewing a stream of black bile. Arquestan stepped back warily, watching the monster's death throes. Then, with a gurgling sigh, the tanar'ri collapsed into a motionless tangle of twisted limbs and fur-covered body.

Bayar's growl was the only warning, and it came nearly too late. The outcast heard the noise and spun on his heel as a second spyder-fiend burst from the shadows in the corner of the lair. This tanar'ri had a torso of rust red, considerably more sleek than the lycosyd's bloated abdomen. Even in the instant of reaction, Arquestan recognized a raklupis, the most powerful of the queen's tanar'ri, the potent master of the cruel lycosyds.

Brandishing a long halberd in its knotty human hand, the spyder-fiend swung the weapon in a deadly strike toward the outcast's head. Arquestan blocked the attack with his long sword, staggering to the side under the force of the blow. Crouching, both swords held ready, he prepared to meet the monster's follow-up attack.

But instead, the raklupis, with a single powerful spring, pounced over the body of the lycosyd and spun to face Arquestan. The tanar'ri growled viciously while its free hand groped under the slain spyder-fiend.

Understanding came instantly, and Arquestan flew into the attack, knowing that he was so close. His two swords whirled, driving the raklupis back, but already the tanar'ri clutched a black stick in its hand.

With a snarl, the raklupis snapped at him, but the out-

11

cast bashed aside the attack and lunged. Arquestan's heart pounded, desperately inflamed by the sight of the ebony stick clutched in the tanar'ri's fist. He had to stop the monster before it could teleport away.

The wind duke stabbed, dodging away from the crimson, hate-filled eyes. Teeth snapped shut just beyond his arm, and the spyder-fiend reared back. Hacking in a savage blow, Arquestan nicked the twisted hand with his long sword, but, abruptly, the outcast's opponent was gone.

A wisp of acrid smoke, fouled by a being of great power, lingered in the air as Arquestan gasped for breath. A stench wafted through the gate, and the wind duke knew that the raklupis had returned to its mistress. This time there would be no pursuit through the planes.

Bayar growled, pawing at the corpse of the lycosyd, and only then did the wind duke realize that there was another spoor, an aura suggesting that the raklupis had not been entirely successful. Gingerly, using both of his swords, the wind duke flipped the gory body of the lycosyd onto its back.

There, clutched in its other hand, was a telltale gleam of blackness—another segment of the precious shaft! Carefully, reverently, the wendeam reached down and took up the segment, knowing that he was the first vaati in over seven hundred years to handle this rare treasure.

Arquestan could scarcely believe his eyes as he looked at the shaft of ebony. The stick was perhaps a foot long, with a geometric pattern carved into each end. That pattern, he knew, was part of the key needed to link the piece to its neighboring segments. Careless attempts would cause the segment to become lost again, perhaps for centuries. Remembering the way the monster had carried the pieces, the outcast suspected that the lycosyd had been aware of the danger. That was why it had held one segment in each hand, and taken care to keep them well separated from each other. Doubtlessly, after its critical wounding, the lycosyd had gated in the mighty raklupis, intending to pass the treasures on to the Queen of Chaos with its last gasp of life.

Yet the raklupis had arrived too late to claim both pieces; the presence of the outcast vaati had seen to that. Arquestan deeply regretted his inability to slay the second tanar'ri, the raklupis. At the same time, Arquestan possessed a segment of the scattered artifact, something no wind duke had done for hundreds of years. He knew by its size that the piece he held was one of the largest, undoubtedly the sixth, since the seventh and longest piece had the geometric locking pattern on one end only.

And because of the guiding power in each segment, with the sixth piece, he would be able to locate the seventh when the time was right. He knew of the great powers imbued into the Rod of Seven Parts. Among these was a minor function: Each segment of the rod possessed an arcane directional sense that gave its bearer unerring guidance to the next larger piece. Since she held only the largest piece, the queen and her agents would not be able to find the rest of the rod!

Delaying only long enough to clean his weapons on the lycosyd's fur, Arquestan turned from the corpse and faced the brackish, eternal waters. His lips mouthed a silent command, and immediately a wind surged through the trees. Nearby, the swamp water rose into a sheer spray, funneling upward, whipped by the swirling whirlwind. In a heartbeat, the vaati's chariot materialized, two ghostly horses of white wind prancing eagerly above the frothing, fetid water.

The hound, Bayar, once again floating as a bubble of soft light, rose to the edge of the compartment as Arquestan climbed into his chariot and took up reins of air. With a twist of his wrist, the wind duke urged the whirlwind into the sky, into realms of gray fog and ether.

The words of the lycosyd remained in his mind, wrapping his thoughts in a shroud of apprehension. The rod was adrift among mortals. It was a development fraught with peril, but hopeful as well. Indeed, this seemed to be the best opportunity in many centuries. Perhaps, with the aid of those mortals, the segments of the potent artifact could be gained.

Still thinking, Arquestan turned toward the globe that was his hound. "Bayar, my faithful one, you shall have to seek this world where the rod has been scattered. I commend you to the planes, onto the spoor of foul tanar'ri. You must strive to pass the gates before them, giving warning at least to the mortals who may encounter the rod."

The bauble of brightness flickered and disappeared; already Bayar was intent upon her mission. Arquestan turned through the featureless fog, reluctantly contemplating his own task, a thing he had postponed for too long.

Now, with the trail of the artifact fresh before him, it was time for the outcast to return to Aaqa.

CHAPTER 1

GOOD LIVES
DOWN THE DRAIN

Calm . . . cool . . . collected . . .

I reminded myself of these desirable traits, tried to concentrate on the slender wires of my picks working through the keyhole of the massive, iron-clad lock. Shifting my feet, I sought to avoid the spreading pool of blood on the floor, but the corpse of the damned ogre just kept bleeding. Resigned to getting my boots wet, I probed for the workings of this crude but effective clasp.

"Hurry!" Barzyn hissed. The dwarf's beard tickled my ear as he leaned over my shoulder, taut with urgency. His breath reeked of stale beer and the raw garlic he so enjoyed, but the stench was just one more distraction I tried to shrug away.

A twist and another probe, and suddenly there was resistance—the wire had snagged on the lock's tumbler. Gingerly trying to retain that precious catch, I started to bend the pick.

15

"C'mon!" Barzyn repeated.

"Shhh," whispered Saysi sternly, laying a comforting hand on my other shoulder. The touch of her delicate fingers soothed me, helped me focus on the lock. Barzyn and my other companions, plus the dead ogre and the strewn bodies of his goblin pals, the whole vast, stinking lair of ogres and goblins, ceased to exist. My life became this lock, these wire tools, and the gentle priestess who silently, calmly urged me to proceed.

The *snap* of the catch echoed like a thunderclap through the silent corridors. Instinctively I froze, expecting goblins, ogres, or worse to charge toward the sound. Instead, the dungeon of Scarnose Ogre and his band of cutthroats remained quiet around us.

"Good work," declared Barzyn, squeezing my shoulder and reaching for the door.

"Wait! I didn't check for—"

My warning was interrupted by the sound of about a million bells going off at once. Jangling in an unmelodious cacophony, the noise crushed my eardrums like a physical force, echoing with dissonant volume that must have been audible for miles—or at least into every corner of the teeming ogre den.

"—alarms," I finished lamely, the word swallowed in metallic resonance.

Even the clanging couldn't overwhelm the noise of heavy footsteps—*ogre* footsteps—pounding toward us. Or maybe I just felt the floor vibrating underfoot. In any event, we all knew that our once-surreptitious party had just called a lot of attention to itself.

"Which way?" demanded Hestrill. I knew the scrawny wizard wasn't lacking in courage, yet the quaver in his voice matched the terror I shared with him.

"Not there," Saysi shouted over the bells, pointing along the wide passageway we'd followed to this door. Already I could see torches, a dozen or more of them, rushing toward us like very deadly fireflies bobbing through the darkness.

"This way's no good either," Dallzar, the other dwarf, snorted. He'd been guarding the approaches from the opposite direction, and now he trotted up to us, shaking his head grimly. "Unless you want to fight a hundred ogres."

"Through the door!" I snapped, grabbing Barzyn and trying to shove him ahead of me. Of course, when a halfling tries to push a dwarf, not much of anything happens, and for a second or two, we were all jammed in the portal.

Barzyn made the decision and plunged ahead, the haft of his battle-axe held in both hands, the blade raised menacingly over his head. "Follow me—*damn!*"

The dwarf tumbled headlong, armor clanking and helmet clattering as he plunged down a steep flight of stone steps. His shield banged loose, adding another dissonant note to the ringing of the bells, which had finally begun to fade. It seemed as though they'd been jangling for the last several years, but I guess it was really more like five or six seconds—just enough to attract every killer monster in the dungeon.

Grabbing Saysi's hand, I pulled her after Barzyn, squinting through the darkness and picking out the dank steps of stone. Hestrill came next, then Dallzar and Benton, the strapping giant of a barbarian, who pulled the door shut behind us.

"Kip!" shouted Benton, his voice a growl that rumbled as deeply as the ogre footsteps. "How do you lock this thing?"

"Go on!" I urged Saysi before turning back to the door. Dallzar slipped past, giving me room to work, while Benton leaned against the metal surface. The big fellow was obviously determined to hold it by brute force if I couldn't lock it in time. Heavy boots pounded the floor beyond the iron barrier as I reached for the bolt—luckily it didn't need a key—and slammed it into the socket in the stone doorframe.

A thunderous *clang* nearly knocked me off the landing as the door vibrated under the smash of a heavy body. The ogres pounded against the stout sheet of iron with furious force. For Benton and me, it was like being trapped inside some kind of huge, thundering drum.

"Down the stairs!" I shouted at the barbarian, though my words vanished into the general dissonance of fading bells, pounding ogres, and the deafening thumping of my own heart. Surrounded by dark shadows, I smelled, acutely, the raw stench of my own fear and that of my companions.

Fortunately Hestrill chose that moment to bring out his magical light gem. Stuck into a claw on the end of his wand, the stone flared into bright illumination, casting shadows up the narrow, stone-walled stairwell and showing that our companions had progressed far down the narrow flight of steps.

Beyond Hestrill and his glowing gem, the mightily cursing Barzyn picked himself up on a landing maybe thirty steps below. The fuming dwarf, his long red hair whirling wildly, dusted himself off and glared upward as Hestrill, Dallzar, and Saysi slipped past him. With a curt gesture, he summoned Benton and me to follow—not that we needed the suggestion.

Even my short legs covered three or four steps with each downward stride as the barbarian and I plunged after our companions. Naturally we had no way of knowing what was down these stairs, but we knew what was at the top, and that was enough to propel us along.

A long, long time ago—it was at least a minute and a half—we had thought that the heavy iron door must guard the entrance to Scarnose's treasure room. After all, the barrier had been heavily locked, guarded by a strapping and unusually alert ogre, and was far more solid than the doors of rotted planking that had been the norm throughout the rest of Scarnose's lair.

Of course, just because we'd found a stairway didn't mean that there wasn't a treasure room down here. Still, my heart sank even faster than the rest of me as Benton and I raced over the first landing and started down the next flight. After all, there was a lot of truth to the old saw about gold: No matter how much of it you possessed, it was never more useless than when you were spending it on your own funeral.

The glimmer of Hestrill's light was a beacon in the darkness, drawing us after the others. Gasping for breath, flinging ourselves down more flights of stairs, Benton and I finally caught up to Saysi, the wizard, and the two dwarves. The pounding on the door above us had faded slightly with the distance, but still thrummed in a menacing cadence.

"They've got a ram," Barzyn noted, remarking on the steady rhythm that had replaced the earlier stuttering bashes against the door. "Won't be long before they smash it down."

"Why'd you stop?" I panted, leaning on my knees and drawing ragged breaths.

" 'Nother door," declared the burly dwarf.

For the first time, I noticed the metal slab blocking passage along the subterranean corridor. This barrier was even larger than the door at the top of the steps, and the black iron surface was studded with bolts the size of my fist. There was no keyhole to be seen, though a small grate blocked off the portion near the floor with steel mesh fine enough to stop a good-sized rat.

Several metal brackets were mounted on this face of the door, but I wouldn't figure out the purpose of those for another few minutes. By then, naturally, it would be too late.

With no lock visible, I reached out and pushed on the barrier. Shuddering and creaking, it moved a few inches inward—until my bare feet skidded off the damp paving stones and I smashed, face first, to the floor.

"It's not locked," I muttered, crawling to my hands and knees as Barzyn and Benton put their shoulders to the task, swinging the door inward with a groaning, shrieking protest of rusty hinges.

A clang loud enough to force all other thoughts from our minds suddenly resounded from above, and we all knew that the upper door had been smashed inward.

"Through here!" hissed Hestrill, following the dwarf and the barbarian into the shadows beyond the second door.

"Are you all right?" Saysi asked, helping me to my feet. Her eyes, as soft and liquid brown as melted chocolate, looked at me with concern. Though a fellow halfling, she hailed from the Tallfellow clans and thus stood a trifle higher than I; still, her gaze met me evenly, reassuring and hopeful and appealing in that way that no one else could ever hope to match.

"Just a scratch," I grunted, wiping my nose—and bringing away a hand covered with blood. The gesture sent pain stabbing across my face, and I knew that my nose was broken. "However, I might have lost my boyish good looks," I groaned.

Through teary eyes, I saw her reach forward, touching my nose with her own dainty hand.

"Patrikon . . . my lord, benign god of law . . . please mend Kip's nose . . . cease his bleeding—and restore unto him his boyish good looks, such as they were."

She smiled, her round face warming enough to take the sting out of her words even as her cure spell washed the pain from my face.

"Thanks!" I whispered, taking her hand and pulling her through the big doorway after the others.

"Hurry!" urged Hestrill as Benton leaned against the iron slab, pushing the doorway shut with renewed creaking and groaning of poorly lubricated hinges. Already the pounding footsteps of our ogre pursuers thundered from the stone steps. The mob of infuriated humanoids howled and bellowed toward the bottom of the shadowy stairway.

"Double damn and feed me to the buzzards!" growled Barzyn, frantically groping over the smooth portal of metal. "There's no way to lock this thing!"

My heart sank as I saw, in the reflected light of Hestrill's spell, that the dwarf had spoken the truth: The interior surface of the door was studded with bolts to match the giant nuts on the far side, but there was no latch, no lock or hasp or fastening of any kind.

It was then that I realized the purpose of the brackets on the other side of the door. They were latches to hold a bar, preventing the barrier from being opened from our side. It seemed a bad time to mention my deduction, but

I began to feel a little sick to my stomach.

"They won't be coming through!" declared Benton, grimly. The strapping barbarian leaned against the iron slab, and I could see the sinews tightening in the tree trunks that were his legs. "The rest of you go on—flee!" he spat.

Spinning on my heel, I started for the darkness beyond. It was Saysi's voice that brought me up short.

"No! We'll all stay with you! That's the only way we have a chance of keeping them from coming through the door."

Though the little cleric didn't come as high as Benton's waist, the barbarian reached out and touched her shoulder with a massive hand. "Thanks," he said thickly. "You always were a brave one for a wee lass, but there's no point in wasting more lives than one. Now, hurry!"

"Come on!" I urged, holding out my hand to Saysi, acutely conscious of heavy footsteps thundering down the stairway beyond the door.

A jarring *bang* sounded against the iron slab, but this was not the sound of a ram. With a curse, Benton grabbed one of the bolts and tried to pull the door open. It refused to budge, and I knew that my suspicion about the external brackets had been correct.

"We're locked in," confirmed the barbarian, glowering at the door as if his own bluster might force it open.

"But why would they—?" Saysi started to ask, then swallowed her words as the answer became clear even to her. "We're trapped," she gulped.

She was a real sweetie, but at times like this, I wanted to grab her shoulders, shake her firmly, and yell "Of *course* we are!"

Instead, I tried to distract myself by having a look

around at our surroundings. The dank, stone walls of the dungeon were cracked, mossy, stained, and wet—the same as they'd been in the stairway and the upper corridors. The passageway beyond the door was somewhat wider than the stairwell, however, and extended inward for a dozen or so spaces before making a sharp turn to the left.

"Let's have a look," Barzyn declared. Dallzar fell into step beside his fellow dwarf, with Hestrill following. The mage raised the wand and its glowing gem of light overhead, though now the spot of illumination seemed dim and futile against the enclosing darkness.

Saysi and I followed a half dozen steps behind the magic-user, and Benton brought up the rear. The barbarian kept his eyes toward that ominously silent door, as if he expected it to leap off its hinges at any moment to join the legion of enemies ranked against us.

The dwarves reached the bend in the corridor and, since the glow of the light spell cast their shadows before them and canceled any chance of surprise, charged around the corner in tandem. I heard them skid to a halt as Hestrill followed. The fact that they didn't cry out in alarm I took as a good omen as Saysi and I hurried after.

The corridor debouched into a large, square chamber. In the center of the big room stood a raised stone hearth, with a brazier of coals resting atop the flat platform. I knew the fire was hot because the room was warm, and a glow of cherry red seeped upward from the iron mouth of the kettle, clearly visible even in the brightness of Hestrill's spell.

The corners of the room remained shrouded in shadow, but the lanky wizard raised his wand high, and the light revealed a bare floor and smooth walls utterly lacking any suggestion of alcove or doorway. The only obvious feature of the chamber was that high, blocklike hearth. An air of reeking mustiness, like ancient carrion, pervaded the place, and suddenly I wanted very desperately to be someplace—*any*place—else.

"Stay here," muttered Barzyn to the rest of us as he and Dallzar started forward. The dwarves split up, one going to either side of the hearth, which rose to about my eye level from the floor.

Suddenly Dallzar stumbled violently backward, choking out a surprised curse as he smashed to the floor. The dwarf's back arched and he clutched at his throat, making horrible gurgling sounds. With a shuddering exhalation, he relaxed abruptly, stretching utterly still on the floor.

The little cleric darted forward, but I seized her arm, pulling her back as a face materialized from the shadows beyond the brazier. The visage was somewhat human, yet beastly and unspeakably hateful. Cruel yellow eyes, slitted like a snake's, reflected brightly in the light of the spell.

Saysi and I tumbled to the floor as I barely caught a glimpse of red stripes and a long, whiplike body. The monster's leap at Saysi was foiled by my grab, though wicked fangs gleamed a few inches from the terrified priestess's face as a snakelike form gathered again into a seething coil.

"Naga!" cried Hestrill, swinging his wand downward.

The snake body writhed, supple coils slithering sideways across the floor. The crimson lines were formed of blood-red scales and rippled the length of a sinuous body that was otherwise inky black. The snake's body was as thick as one of Benton's thighs, merging into the humanlike head and face, with no suggestion of a narrowed neck.

The naga coiled like a cobra, rearing high, and only then did I get a clear look at the awful visage. The mouth gaped, revealing twin fangs more lethal than any viper's, the tips still crimson with Dallzar's blood. Strings of dark hair plastered across a scalp so pasty white that it might have been bleached bone. The naga hissed a sibilant cackle, sending the stench of death wafting through the room, a putrid stink that made Barzyn's garlic-tainted halitosis seem like the first breath of spring.

Hestrill started to chant something, but the naga made the next move. The monster spat a word that plunged the entire chamber into darkness. I grabbed Saysi's arm—or maybe I'd never let go; I wasn't entirely sure. In any event, I pulled her away from the snakelike horror, stumbling across the smooth floor, striving to place the blocky hearth between us and the monster.

I heard a heavy smash, recognizing the resonance of Benton's mighty broadsword bouncing off stone after a missed blow. The barbarian cursed in a low voice, then grunted something inarticulate between his clenched teeth. He dropped his treasured blade with a sudden clash of metal, and the echoes still rang through the room as a heavy *thunk* followed the sound of the fallen sword. Without a shred of doubt, I knew that Benton's poisoned body had slammed into the floor.

More sounds jabbered through the room as Hestrill tried another spell. Bolts of crackling light sizzled as a series of sparking magic missiles seared from the wizard's fingers into the naga's body. The monster hissed furiously—and abruptly the arcane arrows spattered against an invisible barrier, fizzling into cascades of sparks just before the naga's face.

In the glow of the fading spell, I reached up and knocked the iron brazier off the hearth. The basin tumbled to the floor with a resounding crash, scattering glowing coals across the stones. As the last missiles sputtered out, the crimson glow filtered upward, providing minimal illumination.

Barzyn rushed around the hearth, charging the naga with upraised axe. The monster slashed forward, and the dwarf hacked, almost connecting, but the supple snake writhed out of the way before coiling again in the mouth of the corridor where we'd entered. I saw Benton's body, as limp and still as Dallzar's, sprawled on the floor.

Hestrill tried to chant another spell, but I watched in horror as the wide, glowing eyes of the naga settled onto the magic-user's face. His words trailed into an incoherent mutter, and his arms dropped vaguely to his sides.

"Hestrill!" cried Saysi, who would once again have rushed into the jaws of death except for my firm grip on her arm.

"Let me go!" she demanded, twisting with remarkable strength for her small size. Her tone lacked any sense of gratitude for my role in saving her life, but I merely held tighter, pulling her behind the stony hearth. I wanted to attack, but my own short sword, a keen enough blade that I had dubbed Goldfinder, seemed puny and useless against this scaly, coiling horror.

I raised my eyes enough to see the naga spring forward, driving those wicked fangs into Hestrill's gut. With a depressed sigh—as if he'd just learned some very bad news, which was a pretty accurate assessment of his circumstances—the skinny young mage sank to his knees, then sprawled like a rag doll, face first onto the floor.

"Die, snake!" cried Barzyn, once more rushing the naga, his body tense with fury.

"*Do* something!" Saysi hissed, finally twisting free from my grip. I could only watch, horrified, as the dwarf slashed and swiped at the snakelike horror.

The naga twisted out of the way, glaring at Barzyn, trying to entrance him with those wide, luminous eyes. The dwarf thwarted the monster as Barzyn kept his own glowering gaze focused on the naga's thick, scaly body, slashing again and again with his broad-bladed axe.

"Look out!" I shouted, seeing the lashing tail whip toward Barzyn's legs. Scrambling onto the hearth, I clenched my short sword with aching fingers and squatted amid the scattered coals. Terror threatened to paralyze me, but I knew that I had to strike now or Barzyn would be killed and the naga would be left in here with just the two of us halflings. Miserably I looked for a chance to attack.

The dwarf skipped backward, barely avoiding the tail that whipped past his shins. Hissing with a sound like a roaring fireplace, the naga twisted away from his slicing axe blow. Once again the creature's fetid breath filled the room, a gagging cloud of filthy vapor. The serpentine body flowed quickly, evilly, into a monstrous coil, head rearing and mouth agape.

Barzyn retreated until he was trapped in a corner of the room. I heard Saysi scuttling behind me and felt pretty certain that she was going to do something stupid, like charge the big snake and get herself killed in the process. Stifling a groan, I knew I couldn't let that happen.

The naga's head whipped back, like a bowstring tensed for the shot. Swaying back and forth, the monster fastened its eyes upon the dwarf, waiting for an opening.

When the scaly neck reared close to the hearth, I knew I wouldn't get a better chance.

I sprang from the stone platform with Goldfinder extended before me, aiming for that black-scaled neck. With agonizing slowness, I flew through the air, until the tip of the weapon pierced the monster's body and the naga shrieked in rage and pain. Consumed by panic, I tumbled to the floor, feeling the hilt of my sword slip from my grasp.

The weapon remained wedged in the wound as I fell into those hideous coils. A scaly tail curled around my legs, pinning me, and I flailed blindly with my hands in deadly fear of those killer fangs. The stench of death surrounded me, and my mind flashed a gruesome thought— the sensation that I was smelling my own corpse.

Something heavy fell across my chest, and I grasped the naga around the neck, desperate to hold the venomous bite at bay. The snakelike body shuddered, and I felt the pressure pinioning my legs relax. Still my jaws remained clenched, my eyes squeezed tightly shut, as I waited for the deadly touch.

Gradually I realized the naga wasn't squeezing, wasn't moving at all. I squinted through one eye and saw that I held the scaly body well down from the neck. If it had been able to move, the monster could have bitten me without any regard for my frantic defense. The snake, however, was never going to bite anyone again.

"Thanks, Kip," Barzyn grunted, limping over to me. He kicked at the scaly neck, flipping the horrid face onto the floor. My short sword, buried to the hilt, jutted from the back of the creature's neck. With a shudder of revulsion, I twisted free from the cold coils, still shivering as I watched the dwarf place a heavy foot on the naga's head and give Goldfinder a pull.

The weapon came free, and Barzyn wiped the black blood on the body before holding it, hilt first, toward me. I took it automatically, scrubbing the shiny steel against my own tunic before I was willing to slide the blade back into my scabbard.

Saysi, meanwhile, checked Dallzar, Hestrill, and Benton. Her eyes were wet with tears as she knelt beside the big barbarian, then rose to her feet and shook her head.

"What do we do now?" I asked, trying not to look at the bodies.

"Let's have a look around," Barzyn said. "Maybe there's another way out of here, or something we can use."

I kicked the embers from the spilled brazier into a small pile against the hearth. Like most halflings, my feet were tough, protected by fur and calluses. Though some of the coals were still hot and glowing, even hissing against my skin, I suffered no burns. Fortunately the embers still cast enough light for Saysi and I to see; Barzyn's keen dwarven eyesight would have functioned even in utter darkness.

For a few minutes, we went around the walls of the room, feeling for a niche in the bricks, or any kind of irregularity that might have indicated a secret door, concealed passage, or anything else that might offer some hope. The dwarf went into the short, L-shaped entry corridor where the light from the coals didn't penetrate, while Saysi looked around the base of the squat, squarish hearth.

When we didn't find anything but cold, impervious stone, we started looking over the floor. Crossing the place I had just cleared of coals, I was startled by a small chip of darkness—something separate from the smooth stone. Curious, I bent over, then saw that it was only a stub of stick, shiny black on the surface but no more than a few inches long. Wondering at first if it was a remnant of coal, I realized on second thought that it seemed too regular and had a noticeably shinier surface than any of the embers.

"Was this here a minute ago?" I asked Saysi as she came around the hearth. "I thought I kicked all the coals off of this part of the floor, but then I turned around to find it."

"It doesn't look like anything that could help us," Barzyn declared sourly, clumping back into the large room. He shook his head, grim-faced. "I tried the door out there. It's still barred, but I couldn't hear anything on the other side. It's like they locked us in here, then climbed back up the stairs and left us to rot."

"Good plan," I declared disgustedly. "I don't see that we've got much choice."

Already the dark chip of wood was forgotten as I entered the short corridor, feeling with my hands when I turned the corner into utter darkness. The door was cold and firm, as immovable as before. I pressed my ear to the chilly iron and listened.

Barzyn was right—there was no sound, not even the surreptitious breathing of a lone ogre sentry. Then my heart caught, almost ceasing to beat as I heard something. Trilling musically along, the sound was clear and bright, suggestive of a mountain stream, perhaps, or splashing brook.

I reached down and touched the floor, confirming my worst fears as water spilled under the iron door, quickly washing over my feet. Now I knew why the grate was down there. By the time I trotted back to the large room, surging liquid flowed the length of the short hallway, rushing across the floor. Thinking fast, Saysi used her buckler to scoop the remaining embers into the iron brazier, barely saving our light source before water swirled across the room to cover the entire floor.

The sound of the flow rushing under the door increased to a rumble, filling the damp air with hissing sound and mist. By the time it had risen to our ankles, I had a pretty good idea why there were no ogres hanging around at the bottom of the stairwell.

And the water continued to rise.

CHAPTER 2

HALFLINGS AFLOAT

The water swirled around my thighs as I helped Saysi onto the stone platform that had supported the brazier. Wide-eyed, she held her hand to her throat. I knew that her tiny fist clenched the jade amulet of her holy symbol, the hollow octagon ring of Patrikon.

"Can't budge the door," Barzyn declared grimly, sloshing back to join us. By this time, water reached my torso and still splashed upward. I leaped and kicked, sprawling half atop the hearth. A hand groped mine, and Saysi pulled me fully onto the solid block of stone.

Lying on my back, I wiped my eyes and sputtered, trying to draw a full breath. A shadowy outline darkened the ceiling over my head. I blinked and stared, realizing that—though the embers in the brazier continued to glow—the black square marked a gap in the ceiling where no light could be reflected.

"A chimney!" I muttered. "Of course! The smoke from

the brazier has to go someplace!"

"Eh?" Barzyn pushed over to the hearth and climbed up beside us, wringing out his beard with both hands as he turned his dark-sensitive eyes upward. "Yer right!"

"A way out?" wondered Saysi, standing and probing upward with her stout stick. The club clanked heavily against something metal and my heart sank.

"Bars," grumbled the dwarf, his shoulders slumping in resignation. "There's a grate across the chimney."

"No!" I didn't want to believe it, but it made perfect sense. No self-respecting goblin would have left such an easy way into, or out of, his lair.

"Let me have a closer look." Stretching upward, Barzyn reached into the darkness. The water swirled and frothed just below the level of the hearth as Saysi and I stood to either side, helping the dwarf balance.

I could see the grate now: a series of rusty bars, no more than a handspan or so apart, running from one side of the chimney entrance to the other.

Grunting, Barzyn grasped one of the bars and yanked. "Damn!" he muttered, quickly releasing that rod in favor of a neighboring shaft of iron. My heart quickened at the sound of a rasping scrape, and I could see the dwarf twisting and tugging, moving the bar very slightly.

"Can you get it out?" I asked as water rushed across the surface of the hearth. Now the iron kettle and the three of us were the only features sticking above the tempestuous surface. The flow through the hallway continued unabated, more and more water flooding into our dead-end room.

"Here!" shouted the dwarf in sudden triumph, pulling downward. One end of the bar came free, and the sinews in Barzyn's strapping forearms stood out like steel cords

33

as he twisted. Gritting his teeth, he slowly bent the shaft out of the way, one bar sticking straight downward, jutting from the shadowy chimney.

The opening still looked terribly narrow. I could only hope that Saysi, at least, could squeeze through. "Bend another one!" I urged, as if Barzyn wasn't doing enough on his own.

Again the burly dwarf seized a bar, and once more his teeth clenched and his muscles knotted in tension. Jaw set firmly, red beard bristling, Barzyn pulled. Rivulets of moisture trickled from his brow, streaming through the furrows of his ruddy skin. Even the veins in his forehead bulged, until abruptly he let go, slumping backward. Frantically I grasped his shoulder as the dwarf sank to one knee and drew ragged gasps of air.

Sudden hissing signaled further bad news as the water slopped over the top of the brazier and our feeble illumination was doused. In the sudden blackness, I felt a complete blanket of despair and was on the verge of giving up when I felt Saysi's hand on my shoulder.

"Help me," she said, in a voice that was remarkably composed for the circumstances.

"Do what?" I grunted, still despairing.

"Maybe, at least, we'll be able to see something—just don't let me fall."

I grabbed the tiny priestess around her waist and held firm against the force of the current washing across the hearth. Even on the platform, we were already waist-deep in cold water, and it rose higher with each passing heartbeat. The stone block seemed perilously small—a single false step, a tiny slip, could plunge us into deep, churning water.

Saysi started to chant something—a prayer to

Patrikon, I recognized, though I've never been able to tell one of her incantations from another. Whatever the spell, it could only help.

"Come on," I whispered inaudibly. "You can do it!"

I believed it, too. Throughout our year together, Saysi had proven herself a halfling of courage and steady nerves. Although she was a trifle rigid about some—well, *most*—aspects of morality, that was only to be expected in a priestess of law. And even her strict code of morals was softened by a bright sense of humor and refreshing enthusiasm. Now, her slim hips warm and firm under my hands, I regretted the strict code of behavior that had prevented this delightful maiden from yielding to my usually irresistible advances. Not that I hadn't tried . . .

Light suddenly washed through the room. The rounded and worn head of Saysi's mace now glowed like an enchanted crystal. Clear illumination spilled up the chimney, which proved to be a straight shaft leading upward. The grate still blocked entry, but otherwise the soot-lined passageway was open and led as far as we could see.

Looking back across the room, my heart sank as I saw how close to the ceiling the water level had risen. Waves chopped all around, and with our increasing buoyancy, it was hard to remain standing on the hearth.

"Here—Saysi." Barzyn suddenly pulled her away from me.

"What?" she squawked in surprise as he tugged at her backpack.

"You'll have to get rid of this or you'll never fit through."

Her eyes widened in comprehension—and fear. Nevertheless, she nodded grimly and shucked out of the straps, letting the knapsack float away as the dwarf wrapped his hands around her and hoisted her onto his shoulders.

"Grab the bars. Let me give you a push."

Immediately I saw what he had in mind. The gap where the dwarf had bent the bar looked perilously narrow, but there was clearly no other choice. Saysi took hold of the metal rods, steering carefully around the downward-jutting spike of the dislodged pole.

With a grunting heave, Barzyn pushed. I heard Saysi cry out in sudden pain, and then she was gone, popping upward like a cork exploding from a bottle. She squatted on the grate, balancing on her small, bare feet, holding her glowing mace down to shed its light into the room.

"Yer next," Barzyn said, clapping a hand on my shoulder.

Dubiously I examined the narrow gap. It looked as if I'd have to scrape off an inch or two of flesh in order to get my shoulders between the remaining bars. Still, I dropped my own backpack. Moving my scabbard around to the small of my back, I let Goldfinder hang loosely as I tried to make myself as small as possible.

"Up you go." The dwarf hoisted, and I extended my arms, slipping into the gap and kicking and squirming as my shoulders jammed against the metal rods.

"Breathe out," Saysi urged. "And relax."

Easy for her to say, I thought grimly. Still, I exhaled, feeling Barzyn pushing hard from below. Bracing my feet on the dwarf's broad shoulders, wriggling back and forth, I felt one of my shoulder blades scrape through the grate. Saysi seized my wrists and pulled, and in another instant, I squirmed through the narrow gap.

Only then did I fully comprehend the nature of

Barzyn's sacrifice.

Water swirled around the brawny dwarf's shoulders as Saysi and I perched on the grate. "C'mon!" I shouted. "Reach up—we'll pull!"

"Thanks, friends," he said, with a remarkably cheerful grin. "But I think this is where the trail ends for me."

Saysi reached through the bars and took one of Barzyn's hands in hers. "Kip's right—you've got to try!" She pulled courageously, choking back her sobs, but it was clear that the dwarf's burly physique was far too broad for the narrow gap in the bars.

"Try to tread water as it rises," urged Barzyn, tilting his head back as the churning liquid sloshed over his shoulders. His long red hair floated in rusty tendrils, beard spreading from his chin like a long, stringy napkin. He was floating now, his face lifting through the gap as the water reached the ceiling of the room.

"Good luck!" he shouted as that upraised face was buried by the rising tide.

"Barzyn!" cried Saysi, reaching down, seizing the dwarf's muscular hand. I saw those blunt fingers close once around her fingers, squeezing; then he let go, and the rapidly rising water quickly overwhelmed our courageous companion.

"You've got to help him! We can't just let him drown!" cried the priestess, grasping down through the water, turning her soaked face to me with a look of blazing accusation. She waved the glowing club as if it were some kind of magic wand, but all I could do was shrug helplessly.

"He's gone, Saysi," I shouted, acutely aware of water spuming upward from the grate, chest high and rising fast. "There's nothing we can do!"

"No!" She turned away, plunging face first into the churning torrent. The glowing head of her mace shed its brightness through the flow, but I could see no sign of the heroic dwarf. Suddenly buoyant, I felt my feet lift from the metal bars. Treading water with one hand, I reached for Saysi with the other, grasping her sodden tunic and pulling her upward with me.

Her face broke the surface, and I couldn't tell if she was choking or crying. Crooking an arm around her neck, I supported her face above the water—until her elbow jabbed me in the ribs. I released her, drawing a deep, ragged gasp that included far too much spray.

"I can swim!" she insisted forcefully, treading water beside me as we continued to bob upward. "I don't need your help!"

"Fine," I groaned, leaning away from her and turning my own face upward, both to keep my mouth out of the water and to try to get a look at the upper portions of the chimney. I saw nothing except the enclosing walls of darkness, though by touching the sooty surface, I knew that we still rose steadily.

"Hey!" I cried, smashing my fist against something that brushed past my face. Remembering the bodies floating in the room below, I had a panicky vision of the naga slithering after us, wrapping a scaly coil around an ankle or waist.

But as my hand splashed through the water, I knew immediately that this was not the naga or any other body. Instead, it was something much smaller, and as my fingers brushed the bobbing chip, I realized that the shiny piece of wood I'd noticed on the floor was floating upward with us. Relieved, and irritated with myself for admittedly childish apprehension, I forgot about the stick and resumed looking upward.

It seemed much darker in the chimney now, and I realized that Saysi's club was once again under the water.

"I—I can't hold it up any longer," she gasped, sputtering and coughing.

"Here." My own hand fumbled for the weapon. She let go, but it slipped from my hand, sinking through the water that quickly swallowed our light source.

Yet I could still see! A grayish illumination spilled softly from the side a short distance overhead. Another shaft linked to the chimney, and somewhere not too far away there was a source of daylight!

The rising water quickly carried us to the juncture, where the current spilled into the side passage with an onrush of white spray. Kicking and wriggling, Saysi turned the corner and disappeared into the shaft. I bobbed after, kicking hard to propel myself into the horizontal pipe.

"Turn around—feet first!" I shouted to Saysi, who skidded helplessly before me. My mind recoiled from a grim fear as I imagined her smashed against some unforgiving brace. At least, if she absorbed the impact with her feet, she might have a chance to spare herself serious injury.

But that was a futile hope, as more and more water rushed along the shaft. The circular pipe was not quite high enough for a halfling to stand, even if we could have tried, and now it was about half full of water. Of course, it was half full of air, too, but this was hard to remember as I gasped and choked on the thick spray that filled my lungs with each breath.

The brightness I had noticed earlier continued to grow, and finally I saw a haze of daylight up ahead somewhere. The circle of gray light expanded, though it was hard to see details through the mist and spray. Abruptly there was brightness all around, and a disorienting sensation of weightlessness as the shaft ended. The feeling lasted less than a heartbeat before I smashed to the ground in a muddy ravine, skidding and plummeting downward amid a strong current.

"Kip—here!" Saysi's voice cut through the churning noise, and I reached out to feel her strong fingers grasp my wrist. With a grunt, I came to a halt, my arm nearly jerked from its socket. But we were outside, with wonderful air all around us and an apparently limitless sky overhead!

Scrambling up the muddy bank, aided by Saysi, I finally perched on a patch of dry ground. It was several moments before I could catch my breath and dry off enough to take a good look around.

The first thing I saw was the little priestess. Concern radiated from her large brown eyes and tightened the corners of her mouth, bringing her round face into a terribly fetching expression of caring attention. Damp curls, the color of pale copper, hung in a bedraggled mess to either side of her plump, frowning cheeks. Only then did I realize that her robe had been torn in the current, and now trailed in ragged tatters down around her waist.

Blushing, she immediately drew the sodden material over her shoulders, and by the time she brushed her hair back from her eyes, her expression of sincere concern had turned to a stern and accusatory stare.

"Well, I guess *you're* feeling better!" she declared.

Her tone was decidedly huffy, but I decided to ignore that for the moment. "We're pretty lucky," I admitted instead. Casting nervous glances across the hillside, I saw a lot of scrub brush and boulders, but no sign of ogre or goblin patrols—another piece of good news.

"Barzyn . . ." Saysi's eyes filled with tears as she stared at the mouth of the pipe. "And Hestrill . . . Benton . . . Dallzar . . . I can't believe they're gone. All dead . . ."

I remembered that Saysi had been new to the adventuring life when she first joined up with us, a year or so ago; this was the first time she'd lost companions in the course of a dangerous quest. In my own experience, I had learned that such occurrences were not uncommon. One had to simply carry on in the face of such setbacks.

"Don't worry. It gets easier after you've gone through it a few times," I assured her. "Just be glad that *we* were able to—"

"How can you say that?" she demanded, whirling to confront me with a glower that made her earlier glare seem positively benign. "Barzyn bent the bar so we could escape. He sacrificed himself for us!"

"Not exactly," I demurred, my feelings hurt. After all, I'd been involved in hair-raising escapades for more than the last decade, and it bothered me that she didn't give my superior experience a little more respect. "I mean, he bent the first bar before he knew that he couldn't bend any of the others. He was trying to get a way out for himself as much as for us!"

"So? Even if he knew there was only room for halflings to get out, do you think he would have left the bar in place just so we'd . . . die with him?" Again tears filled those dark, luminous eyes, and I wanted to comfort her but didn't seem to have the words.

"No . . . Barzyn always was decent that way," I acknowledged. It was true, and I would miss the grumpy old curmudgeon, garlic and all.

I felt a twinge of sadness as I recalled a paladin we'd

been forced to leave to a gelatinous cube some years ago, and the twin warriors who'd held a narrow breach against a mob of enraged trolls, allowing Hestrill and I to escape with our lives. Then there had been that half-elven scout who'd been tortured by hobgoblins, but limped back to our camp to warn us about the impending ambush, and . . .

I forced myself to stop thinking along those lines, since it was getting pretty depressing.

"And all the others . . . poisoned by that—that *thing!*"

"It was a naga," I reminded her, trying to be helpful.

"I know that!" she snapped, still not getting the point.

I took the opportunity to look around. We were sitting on a steep, scrub-covered hillside above the bank of a stream. The outflow from the chimney pipe was splashing through a narrow ravine below our feet. It was from that ditch that Saysi had plucked me, sparing me a long slide into the churning waterway below.

"I guess we came out on the north side of the hill," I suggested, deciding that a change of subject might be the best thing. "If we follow this stream to the east, we should come out in the valley."

That would lead us back to the trail, and the trail would take us down to the valley road to Oakvale town, the only outpost of civilization for a long distance in any direction. The goal seemed like a worthy objective as I got to my feet and tried to wipe some of the drying mud off of my skin and clothes.

Sighing, Saysi, too, stood up and cleaned herself off as best as possible. The torn robe barely provided her with the minimum of privacy, and her shapely legs were in view as far as the middle of her thighs—though I tried not to stare, comprehending that the timing was less than perfect for any amorous attention.

In addition, we'd lost our backpacks, and Saysi her weapon. I removed my short sword and dried Goldfinder as best as I could, while she polished some mud off of her eight-sided amulet and let it flop loosely onto the wet silk between her small, well-defined breasts. Once again I tried not to stare.

"Do you think we can get back to Oakvale from here?" she asked.

For once, I had the answer ready and explained to her my deductions about this stream and the eastward-leading valley we'd find on the other side of the hill.

"What's that?" she asked suddenly, pointing to the ground as we started down the steep hillside, trying not to skid all the way to the bottom.

At first I didn't see what she meant, but then I discerned a flash of bright ebony against the dark brown of the mud. "It's just that stupid piece of stick," I declared bitterly, realizing that the little stub had floated all the way out of the dungeon with us. Somehow, in the course of splashing down the ravine, it must have bounced out of the water to land on the bank beside us.

I picked it up and looked at it with a startling feeling of distaste. The chip was round, blunt at one end and marked with a curious pattern of geometric shapes at the other. It was pure black in color, and harder than any piece of wood I'd ever held.

For some reason, the little thing angered me. If we could have only one item salvaged from that deadly room, why did it have to be something so utterly useless?

With a grimace of disgust, I gave it a toss, watching as it fluttered through the air and plopped into the water that still gushed through the ravine. In a second, the current swallowed it up, though by the time the piece of stick was out of sight, we had already turned our backs, seeking the safest way down this steep, wet hillside and along the bleak road back to Oakvale.

CHAPTER 3

THE RED GARTER

"Are you *sure* you didn't steal this money?" Saysi asked me for about the fiftieth time. "I don't see how you could have earned enough to pay for these rooms and all that food in just one morning."

She was speaking to me in the dressing room of our suite at Oakvale's swankiest inn, an elegant gambling house called the Red Garter. Of course, a lot had happened in the twenty hours or so since we had escaped Scarnose's lair, but was I to blame that Saysi had slept through a good portion of it?

"I told you, every one of these silver pieces I earned, in fair trade with a local money changer," I replied.

It was the truth, as a matter of fact. It *had* been an honest trade. Of course, I neglected to add that I had stolen my goods for barter—a charming necklace studded with gems—from a silver merchant's stall in the Oakvale marketplace. "Why don't you stop worrying about it?"

She huffed, her irritatingly suspicious nature still unmollified. Still, she was forced to admit that a hefty lunch and an afternoon's sleep in real beds—two beds, despite my best efforts to consolidate—had done wonders for both of us. She looked radiant, even in her torn, travel-stained gown and leggings. As I looked in the mirror, I flattered myself with the thought that I, too, had cleaned up pretty well. My longish hair was combed into thick waves of brown, nicely augmenting my eyes of smoldering black. At least, *I* thought that they smoldered; Saysi, on more than one occasion, had referred to them as "beady." Even the tufts of hair on my feet had been combed, and now I felt ready to take on the world—or at least the portion of it that was Oakvale.

We had reached the town only that morning, in a sad and bedraggled state after a long night's dejected march from the ogre lair. Lacking lodging and money, we had made for the public marketplace in the town square, where Saysi had quickly fallen asleep on a bench. That gave me the chance to slip away and work my skills amid the bustling shops.

Quickly I had found a silver merchant. The overfed shyster never saw me slip behind his curtain and crawl under the table. While he haggled with a customer over a few copper pieces, I stealthily lifted a piece worth nearly fifty gold! Trading the goods had been easy, since, from an earlier visit to Oakvale, I had remembered a money changer's shop on a narrow side street. Going there, I had quickly swapped my ill-gotten baubles for a substantial sum of coins. Indeed, my purse was so well filled that I had taken pains to conceal it from Saysi, knowing that it would only arouse her suspicions.

It was damned inconvenient sometimes, her being a

priestess who held the law in such high regard. When she had awakened, I made up a story about trading a silver ring that I supposedly had kept concealed in my boot for just such an emergency. Even so, I had been forced to talk her into accepting the shelter of this comfortable, even luxurious, inn.

"Here—I got you something," I offered, handing her a thin bundle of green silk, which she held up to reveal a small vest I had purchased.

"Kip—it's beautiful!"

I nodded in agreement, certain that the color would perfectly complement her fiery hair.

"Did you steal it?" she asked quickly.

"No. I *bought* it," I asserted truthfully, still ignoring the minor details—ancient history, really—of how I had come into the money in the first place.

Our bedrooms were connected by a well-appointed dressing chamber in our suite on the second floor of the Red Garter. The innkeeper had been delighted to provide us with these splendid accommodations as soon as he saw the number of golden coins I was able to plink into his well-oiled palm. Now night had fallen, and our appetites for food returned. Having glanced into the gaming room earlier, I felt a tingle of anticipation and was more than ready to try my luck after we filled our bellies again.

The smell of roasting meat rose from the kitchens, and for now I was set to dig into a hearty slab of beefsteak.

"Are you sure we shouldn't save your money? I'd be happy with bread and cheese," Saysi suggested after hearing of my dinner plans.

"I might be able to trade something else tomorrow," I assured her, thinking of the gold and platinum coins safely secured in my deepest belt pouch.

"But what if—"

"Stop worrying! If my luck holds, by the next day or two, I'll have enough money that we can even get some new clothes."

As a matter of fact, I was already carrying enough coinage to outfit us both in regal finery, but I knew that if I displayed too much of my sudden "earnings," Saysi's suspicions would grow too strong to ignore. "For now, let's just enjoy supper. I'll risk a couple of silvers at the gaming tables, and maybe that will see us through tomorrow."

"Well, all right."

I took Saysi by the arm and escorted her along the carpeted hallway and down the wide mahogany stairway to the main floor. The headwaiter recognized me, thanks to a tip I'd left earlier, and ushered us to a fine table near the fireplace. We ordered our meat, which was delivered quickly, and washed it down with a bottle of the tart red wine that was quite popular in these parts. Saysi and I ate like the starving wayfarers we were.

Despite the good food and splendid surroundings, I found myself dragged down by a feeling of melancholy. My companion, too, ate with a certain listlessness. We both cleaned our plates with a mechanical quality that prevented enjoyment of the meal.

I realized that the loss of our companions still weighed on me, and I felt a tightening in my throat when I thought of Barzyn's courage, Hestrill's wry sense of humor, the redoubtable strength of Benton and Dallzar. They had been dead for more than a day, and in the past, this would have been more than enough time to grieve for lost companions.

Somehow this time it was different.

My own bleak musings were interrupted by the sight of

Saysi's tear-filled eyes, turned in my direction but obviously looking far, far past me. It was clearly time to do something.

"Let's go into the gaming hall," I suggested. "A little gambling might take our minds off . . . what happened."

She trailed along with obvious reluctance as I passed under the big wooden arch that divided the dining chamber from the gaming hall. Chandeliers illuminated the room in a steady glow, with a few magic baubles shining directly above the tables where the high stakes were waged. I saw matches of thimbles, knucklebones, double-guesser, and other contests I didn't recognize as we walked on the polished hardwood between the gamblers.

In this hall, the walkway was raised to about the level of the gaming tables, with each game played down in a sort of pit. This made it easy for us shorter folk to get a good look at what was going on, and I quickly spotted the game I sought.

"Dragonfire," I pointed out to Saysi. She nodded, still listless, as I took her hand and led her down the steps into one of the pits.

The table before us was circular, with a small indentation for the dealer's stool. This fellow was a young man, clad in a black and silver tunic and perched easily on his raised seat. Several stacks of tiles lay facedown before him, while three players regarded an array of single tiles spread across the middle of the table.

I took in the other gamblers with a casual glance and immediately liked my chances. One of them was a big warrior wearing a loose shirt of chain mail, though, in typical custom, he had left his weapons at the door. The fellow was obviously very drunk, swaying uneasily even in his low chair, with a nearly empty bottle of cheap whiskey standing beside him.

The next player was a matron of some wealth, to judge by the diamond rings on her fingers and the golden chains encircling her throat. She wore a low-cut gown of silk, revealing enough cleavage to swallow a careless halfling, and her overly rouged eyelids narrowed shrewdly as she kept her eyes on the dealer and the tiles.

The last player was a foppish fellow in a feathered hat and silken jacket embroidered with golden threads. I noticed immediately that the plume was tattered, the material of the coat threadbare. The man's beardless face was narrow and pinched, his eyes gleaming with an unnatural glow. A mug of wine rested on the table beside him, and though he took a long swill as he waited for the deal, I got the impression that he wasn't drunk. Instead, he seemed vaguely desperate. There was a sense of hunger in the way he watched the shifting of the colorful tiles.

"Joining the game?" the dealer asked as I took the fourth and final chair at the table. In reply, I placed some silver pieces on the table, careful to avoid Saysi's eyes, though I could clearly imagine her frown as she stiffened beside me. Four coins I set aside, since dragonfire required each player to maintain a standing bet, while the others I would use to wager on each of my turns.

The dealer placed a pattern of twenty-five tiles on the table, arranging them in five rows of five. The drunken warrior pitched a pair of silver coins into the center of the table and gestured at one of the tiles. The dealer flipped it over to reveal an image of a steel-bladed short sword. With a grunt, the fighter pointed to another tile; this one came up to reveal the image of a ruby ring. The brawny warrior muttered something profane under his breath as the dealer gathered in both of the coins.

Next the matron bet, wagering four gold pieces. She gestured, and the dealer flipped over a tile to reveal a rampant stallion's head. The second tile showed the match for the ruby ring revealed by the fighter, and I winced inwardly. This meant that the dealer had to reshuffle ten of the tiles, which he did after claiming the woman's golden coins. I tried to follow his supple fingers without success.

When all twenty-five tiles were again positioned, the dandy beside me had his turn. First he reached into his belt pouch, which I saw from the corner of my eye looked rather flat, nearly empty. He fished out four silver coins and placed them on the table with a certain aggressiveness. His standing bet, a mere two pieces of silver, stood forlornly off to the side. The dealer waited impassively as the man indicated one tile, which was flipped to reveal a proud charger rearing angrily, snorting steam from flaring nostrils.

With a trembling finger, the fop pointed to a second tile. The dealer smoothly turned it over, and I winced sympathetically as the image of dragonfire was revealed: a boiling ball of flame, painted so brightly that it seemed to flicker and rise from the shiny surface of the tile. With a tiny shrug, the dealer reached out and took both of the man's bets, while each of us other players threw in half of our standing bets.

Even with my own loss, I almost felt sorry for the overdressed fop as I sensed him wilting into his chair. The dealer, meanwhile, picked up the dragonfire tile and, with gestures too fast even for my keen eyes, flipped it about with several other anonymous tiles. When the five-by-five pattern had been restored, the disastrous image could have been represented by any of a dozen or so different tiles.

For now, it was enough to know that those twelve tiles should be avoided. My turn came up, and I started cautiously, betting just two of my coins. The first tile was a lucky guess: It was a match for the rearing charger. Immediately I gestured to the other tile displaying the proud stallion, remembering where the fop had found it. When the black horse was revealed, the dealer slid two silvers toward me and looked at me in silent question.

Slowly, deliberately, I nodded. There was a third and a fourth image of a war-horse somewhere on the table, and if I could find either one, my four silvers would rise to twenty in one lucky guess. Showing more confidence than I felt, I pointed to another tile, taking care to avoid the twelve that included the dragonfire. The dealer flipped it over to reveal one of the ruby rings, and I nodded in res ignation as he swept back the two coins he'd awarded me only moments before.

The game went back to the brawny warrior, who bet a hefty four gold pieces and selected a tile displaying a bejeweled shield, but then couldn't find the match. He seemed mainly interested in draining his bottle as the dealer pulled the golden coins into his pile. With a sniff of disdain, the woman repeated her bet of four golds. She drew a match for the shield and pointed to the tile that the warrior had discovered, collecting four more coins for her match. Unlike me, she declined to seek the third match for her set, and play passed to the desperate dandy.

He placed a gold piece on the table, which I sensed was his last coin. The dealer gave him ten silvers, and with a reckless shake of his head, he pushed four of the coins into his standing bet and placed the rest into the wagering circle. Avoiding the rows that included the reshuffled dragonfire, he managed to select a horse and a sword, losing six of his silvers for the mismatch. I made my own bet, this time losing two silvers; even worse, the second tile was a match for the sword revealed by the young man beside me, resulting in all twenty-five tiles being reshuffled.

The game proceeded through several more rounds, until the stern-looking matron was the next to encounter the dragonfire tile. She spouted some very unladylike language as the dealer raked in her ten gold pieces. Of us all, however, she seemed most unaffected by the loss; in fact, as play passed to the young fop, she was already pulling another stack of gold from the purse concealed underneath her dress.

The fop was down to two silvers, and he watched glumly as one of these was taken following his mismatched selection. He looked almost hungrily at the pile of coins across the table as the dealer turned to me.

With a bet of four silvers, I got lucky again, finding a match for the war-horse tile. Once again I took a chance, wagering all eight of my coins, and I heard Saysi gasp with surprise and delight when the third match came up. The dealer passed four gold coins over to me, and I promptly slid three of them into my pouch, knowing that I had won enough to take good care of Saysi and me for the next week or so, without having to explain the rest of the cash reserves buried in my purse.

When the cycle reached the dejected fellow whom I guessed was down to his last coin, the dealer raised an inquisitive eyebrow. The minimum bet for the game was two silvers, and the fellow had but one on the table before him. Hesitantly the man reached into a belt pouch, a different sack than his coin purse. I watched with interest as he pulled something small out of the bag, and my jaw dropped in astonishment as he placed it on the table.

He had a small chip of ebony stick, a piece of wood that I recognized very clearly indeed.

"Sir . . . the gaming is limited to coin bets," said the dealer, his brow crinkling with distaste.

I barely heard him, however. I felt Saysi's fingers tighten on my shoulder as she, too, spied the small stub. There was no way I could be mistaken. This was the same chip of wood that we had seen in the naga's chamber, that had floated up the chimney with us, and that had spilled down the hillside on the current of overflowing water. The regular carving at one end, like the precise cut of some sort of locking mechanism, was unforgettable. Looking at the piece as it lay on the table, I distinctly remembered tossing the vexsome stub into the stream, annoyed that something so obviously useless had displayed such uncanny persistence.

Now I felt a chill as I realized exactly how persistent the little stick was proving. Vaguely I heard the fop speaking, sensing the desperation in his tone.

". . . *not* worthless!" he declared insistently. "It's magic. It has a power!"

"What does it do?" asked the warrior, glowering suspiciously at the chip of wood.

"It—it can *cure* things! I was injured when I found it. I had a broken hand. I picked it up, and before I knew it, my bones mended and my hand was healed!" The fop turned his eyes from the warrior to me, pleading with the desperation I had earlier sensed. "Won't you buy it? I tell you, it's worth a lot!"

Saysi's grip on my shoulder had not lightened, and I was glad for the intensity of her fingers. It gave me a sense of solidity, of reality in what was becoming a very unreal situation.

"Sir, please!" the dealer declared, raising his head to look around for a guard.

"Where did you find it?" I demanded, surprised at the dry, rasping hoarseness of my voice.

"It's a family treasure. My grandmother gave it to me!"

The fellow refused to meet my eyes as he spoke, though I would have known he was lying even without that obvious clue. "How long have you had it?" I asked casually.

"Years! It's been in my family for generations!"

"And you'd sell it just like that?" declared the matron who had been gambling at our table. She looked at the fellow as if he were something discovered on the muddy ground of some darkened alley.

"He would, because he's lying, at least about how long he's owned it." My own voice was light and cheerful, but I fixed my eyes on the human's face with a steady, gently encouraging gaze. "You've only had that stick for one day, if that long. Isn't that the truth?"

Something in my look convinced him that further deceit would be pointless. His shoulders sagged in defeat. "I tell you, it's *magic!* I'm not lying about that. But how did you know that I only found it this morning?"

I shrugged. "Where was it?"

"At the riverbank," the man explained, almost pathetically grateful that he had my attention. "It caught my eye—it's so shiny. You see these odd carvings at the end? I knew it wasn't just a piece of wood that had broken off a stick."

His explanation coincided with my experience. The

ravine behind the ogre's lair had spilled into the stream following the winding valley all the way to Oakvale. At least, it was possible, though the overall collection of circumstances seemed to go far beyond the realm of coincidence.

"Can you *prove* that it heals?" growled the warrior, his suspicious eyes shifting from the fop to me. Abruptly he stood, unceremoniously pulling aside his tunic to reveal a deep gash in his thigh. It looked as though he'd been stuck pretty good with some kind of blade. Though the wound was scabbed over, it remained swollen and angry-looking; I didn't need a lot of imagination to picture him losing the leg unless he did something about it.

"Sure! Sure I can!" The dandy took the piece of wood and touched it to the crusted skin.

I watched in amazement as the swelling immediately melted away. The redness of the skin was instantly soothed, fading to a normal pallor that matched the rest of man's sinewy thigh. The fighter's eyes widened slightly, and he plucked the piece of stick out of the dandy's hand before the fellow could object.

"I'll give you three gold for it," said the warrior.

"I'll make it four," I countered, surprising myself—and, no doubt, Saysi—by my sudden determination. Yet it suddenly seemed important to gain that piece of stick.

"Six." The warrior puffed out his chest and fixed me with a stern glare, as if daring me to challenge him again.

I thought of the four gold coins I had won in this game and the silvers I had shown to Saysi before entering the hall, knowing that the bidding had already passed the point where I could maintain my deceit about my funds and reasonably expect to participate. But this chip of stick had taken a firm grip on my curiosity, and I couldn't pass.

"Ten?" I said, more timidly than I liked.

"Twelve!" growled the fighter, reaching into his pouch and setting a stack of coins on the table. For the first time, I noticed exactly how muscular he was. Sinew rippled along his bare arms, and each of his fingers seemed as big as a good-sized sausage.

I gulped, feeling Saysi's hand relax on my shoulder. I sensed that she was as curious about the stick as I was, but clearly she believed that the bidding had progressed beyond my means.

"Fifteen," I declared firmly. I pulled a platinum piece and five golds out of my pouch, wincing inwardly as her touch was instantly withdrawn. I heard Saysi's intake of breath and started working on an explanation.

With a mutter of disgust, the fighter tossed the chip of wood past the other gamblers; I snatched it out of the air with a reflexive grasp. The fop grabbed at the coins, inspecting them to make sure that they were genuine, and then bobbed his head happily.

"You won't regret it!" he promised. "That's a special little stick, I tell you! Now . . ." He turned his eyes back to the dealer and slid the platinum piece across the table.

A heavy hand clapped him on the shoulder, however, and two brawny guards hoisted him bodily out of the chair.

"Sir," the dealer sniffed, "in the future, you will please conduct your bartering in the marketplace."

"But—but . . ."

Protesting, but helpless in the grip of the guards, the man was escorted toward the door—the *back* door—of the gaming hall. I watched, feeling a twinge of pity, as the guards pitched him into the alley.

I touched the smooth surface of ebony, feeling strangely pleased that I had acquired this mysterious chip of wood. Perhaps I regretted not picking it up when I could have had it for free, but this was a minor consideration. Now it seemed well worth the price I had paid. Then, casting a sidelong glance at Saysi, I couldn't help but wince at her angry glower. She looked down at my coin purse in an expression clearly indicating that we were going to have a serious discussion in the very near future.

Turning my head, I tried to meet her eyes, mutely pleading for a chance to explain, but with a toss of her head, she turned away. The dealer shuffled, preparing for a new game, and my gaze strayed across the room. Abruptly I saw a large figure, familiar enough to cause me a moment's dismay. It was the silver merchant I had robbed! The obese fellow lumbered through the hall, looking down his nose at the various gaming tables.

I recalled the circumstances of my earlier adventure and remembered that the merchant had never seen me. I reassured myself with that knowledge, but just as I was about to turn my attention back to the tiles, I saw a fellow in the merchant's tow and realized that my situation was more serious than I had first suspected.

The silver merchant was accompanied by the scrawny money changer to whom I had sold the pilfered necklace. I gulped as the pair seized a startled halfling by the shoulder, spinning the little fellow away from his game of knucklebones. While the diminutive gambler squawked in protest, the money changer squinted at his face, then shook his head. The merchant released the halfling and craned his neck, looking around the room once again.

Before I could turn away, his eyes fell upon me. Trying to remain casual, I gathered my winnings and placed the stick of ebony into my pocket. I rose to my feet and started up the stairs to leave the gaming pit, but the gaunt money changer was much more agile than he looked.

I found myself looking into the narrowed eyes of the coin merchant, with the huge bulk of the angry silver dealer looming behind him.

"That's him!" charged the man who had been only too willing to buy my bauble.

Before the merchant could grab, and presumably throttle, me, the same two guards who had pitched the fop into the alley seized me by the shoulders and shook me roughly.

"Did you steal a necklace from this man's wagon?" demanded one of the men-at-arms.

"Yes!" I cried eagerly, even as I tried to think of a way to lie my way out of this. My hand flew upward, clapping across my treacherous mouth as I gaped in astonishment, appalled by my involuntary honesty.

"But—" I groped for a way to dispute my confession as my mouth continued to babble away in full betrayal. "I climbed along an oak limb, ducked down into the wagon, and snatched it from below the counter."

I pictured a hangman's noose settling around my neck. The image sent a shiver down my spine, but it wasn't enough to shut me up. "That is, we were hungry, and Saysi wouldn't let me steal anything. But I'm a very skilled thief, and when she nodded off on the bench, this fat fellow looked like the best target."

"Insolent runt!" growled the merchant, lunging.

"Well, you *are* fat!" I retorted, asserting righteously in my own mind that I was only telling the truth. But *why?*

"I know it was wrong," I declared. "And I'm sorry." Turning to Saysi, I continued. "I wasn't going to tell you, and that's wrong, too."

"But *now* you're telling me? Telling *everyone?*" she gasped. To my surprise, and relief, she looked more worried than angry.

"Well, it was wrong," I said lamely. "I see that now."

"A little too late!" declared the guard. "It's off to the magistrate with you!"

"I understand."

Nodding agreeably, I turned to the merchant. "Here's the money," I told him helpfully, pulling out my pouch and emptying the platinum and gold coins into his outstretched hand, though I held on to the chip of ebony stick. "I think I got a pretty good price for the piece. It was a nice necklace."

Scowling suspiciously, the man snatched away the coins, his eyes glittering avariciously as he ascertained the value. When he looked back at me, his expression was guarded, as if he feared he were in the presence of madness. "What kind of a thief *are* you?" he growled.

"A halfling. I'm quiet and nimble—quite good at picking locks, if I say so myself. Let's see . . ."

"Enough! Time to go." The man-at-arm's grip tightened on my shoulder as he jerked me toward the door.

"You come along!" declared the second guard, dropping a heavy hand onto Saysi's shoulder. Still stunned by my confession, she made no move to object.

"I told you she didn't have anything to do with it!" I objected crossly. "She won't let me steal, so I have to do it when I can get away with it, when she doesn't know."

"Yeah—and halflings can fly and turn eight shades of blue!" sneered the second guard.

"I'm telling the truth. I wouldn't lie!" I declared, righteously indignant.

Indeed, the very idea of speaking a falsehood was

unthinkable, though I realized with surprise that this was the first time in my life I'd ever felt that way. More important, I started to fear that I'd placed Saysi in a great deal of danger. The hangman's noose I had earlier imagined wasn't just an idle flight of fancy.

"You just told us you're a thief. In my book, that makes you a liar as well." The guard's logic was impeccable, in a twisted sort of way.

Further protest on my part was interrupted by a shriek of inhuman terror from somewhere—the alley behind the gaming hall, I guessed. Something banged loudly into the wall, then again, splintering the planks and setting all the chandeliers to swinging wildly.

"Earthquake!" someone screamed, diving to the floor. Panic spread through the crowded hall, and I was jostled by a stampede of gargantuan humans rushing toward the door.

Again something smashed into the wall, and this time the barrier caved in. A messy orb tumbled through the gaping, splintered hole, rolling across the floor. More of the gamblers, shrieking and screaming in terror, fled in every direction, scattering tables and even ignoring tumbling coins.

"By the gods, what's that?" demanded the merchant.

I knew immediately. I recognized the thin lips, the small chin, the narrow, pinched nose. Even without the fancy hat, the fop who had sold me the ebony stick of healing was clearly recognizable.

At least, his head was. I didn't have any idea what had happened to the rest of him. The gaping hole flanked by splintered planks in the side of the gaming hall showed only darkness beyond.

More screams, female in tone, shrilled from the alley. I

was forgotten for the moment as the two guards drew swords and charged across the room, far braver than I.

The silver merchant's face had gone pale as he stared at the head of the gambler. The gory object rested upright, and the sightless eyes seemed to study the big fellow's horrified features.

"Do you want to take me to the magistrate, or should we wait for them?" I inquired, gesturing at the guards, who now peered cautiously through the gaping hole in the wall. Once again I was astonished by my own honesty, yet I knew that fleeing would be, well, it would just be *wrong*.

"Kip!" Saysi grabbed me by the shoulder, whirling me around so that she could stare into my eyes. "What's wrong with you?"

"What do you mean? I thought I was doing the right thing!" My feelings were hurt. After all, if anyone should understand this, it was good old straightlaced Saysi.

"Come on. We're getting out of here!" she declared, seizing my hand in a surprisingly strong grip.

"But I'm supposed to go with them!"

The guards, blades extended, were arguing as to which of them should go into the alley first.

"Something is wrong," Saysi said seriously. "But this isn't the place to talk. Come *on!*"

One of the guards suddenly screamed in shock, tumbling backward into the room, his face obscured by a film of blood. The remaining gamblers, who had just begun to creep back to the overturned tables, fled in renewed panic, knocking Saysi and me apart in the stampede.

"Kip—here, take my hand!" The priestess's shrill voice reached me through the mob, and I reached between two burly drunks to grab her. One of the men lurched, knocking me to the floor, and the other plopped his iron-cleated boot onto my ankle. I heard the snap of bone at the same time rivers of agony coursed up my leg.

"Damn!" I cried, biting back further expressions of pain. I heard Saysi scream nearby, lost somewhere amid the stampede of legs and feet. Catching a glimpse of copper curls, I limped through the throng, helping her to her feet.

Stumbling desperately, I let Saysi pull me along with the crowd of fleeing gamblers, and we finally broke from the press of the fleeing bodies. I rose to my feet, hobbling on my good leg, and together we stumbled into the cool night of Oakvale's main street.

"This way!" she urged, pulling me along the avenue, away from the inn. Limping for a few steps, I shook my head in confusion, then came to a halt.

"I don't know," I balked, surprised at her behavior. "Don't you think I should wait here for the guards?"

CHAPTER 4

STALKERS OF CHAOS

"I *knew* you stole that money! I confess I was surprised by how much, but how could I not know how you got it?"

"But—but—" I gaped, probably somewhat stupidly, at Saysi. "How did you know?"

She confronted me with an expression that seemed, surprisingly, more concerned than angry. "You really don't get it, do you? I'm your *friend*—I know you. I even think I understand you."

We were back in the central square of Oakvale, sitting on the bench where I had left her sleeping just a half day before. My broken ankle had been cured, patched up like new, by Saysi's healing spell. The plaza was mostly dark, illuminated only by the flickering torches and lanterns set outside the dozen or so inns and gaming houses that lined the three sides of the great marketplace. On the fourth, where the river flowed softly, all was darkness, as if in dire warning of the bleak wilderness of ogre lairs and worse stretching beyond the watercourse.

Because of the huge oak trees, the torchlight in the square was sporadic at best, and our bench was almost completely screened by shadow. A few people drifted here and there—lovers out for a private walk, others with more sinister purposes, perhaps—but we had the nearby area all to ourselves.

"I knew because that's how you *always* get money when we need it. You didn't think I believed that you'd actually *worked* for it, did you? Do you think I'm *stupid?*"

Something in her tone suggested that I had better tread very carefully, but that wasn't enough to shut my newly honest mouth.

"Yes. That is, I thought you believed me." Her sharp intake of breath was her only reaction as I blundered on. "Not that you're stupid; I wish I was half as smart as you. It's just that I know how you feel about stealing, and I thought you'd leave me, go away somewhere, if you thought I was a thief."

"I *know* you're a thief!" she snapped, though she didn't sound as angry as she could have. "It's what you do! Or at least, it's what you *did.*"

She looked along the street, toward the wide avenue leading to the Red Garter, then turned back to scrutinize me. There was that soft look of concern again, melting my heart like the liquid chocolate color of her eyes. Of course, I had always known she was pretty, but it was shocking to think that I had never understood the full extent of her beauty. Now she took my breath away, set my heart pounding like a blacksmith's hammer.

"I have to confess," she concluded with a wry smile, "you could have picked a better time to reform."

For the first time since I'd pulled out the money to pay

for the ebony stick, her tone softened slightly. "You did change, didn't you? Did you do it for me?"

Lie, I told myself. She's going to forgive you! Tell her you did change for her!

"No." I sagged miserably, listened to her sigh in resignation. "I—I don't know why I felt I had to be honest in the gaming hall, or even right now, with you. But if I told you I changed because of you, it wouldn't be the truth."

Another thought occurred to me, once again compelling my mouth to move in directions that I wasn't sure the rest of me wanted to follow. "You *knew* I stole to get us money? But you let me take you to an inn, buy food and lodging. Isn't that against Patrikon's doctrine?"

"Patrikon's rules are good ones," she said after a moment's thought. "But he is an understanding god, and a forgiving one. I think he knows that you weren't trying to hurt anyone. If anything, you were trying to help me, to take care of me. I guess I make that kind of difficult sometimes."

I shook my head in amazement, wanting to ask her about other times. She had hinted, after all, that she knew this wasn't the first time I had deceived her. Still, the words were hard to form. Turning to the little halfling maid beside me, I wanted only to tell her the truth, let her know that I had changed, my thieving days were behind me.

But I still didn't know why.

I took her hands, seeing the luminous pools of her eyes even in the thick darkness. "Saysi, you're the most important person in the world to me. I hate the thought of you going away, of having to live without you. But I've always been who I am. I don't know what made me stop being that person!" Squeezing hard, I started to draw her close,

66

wanting very much for her to understand.

Saysi winced and pulled one hand away—not because of reluctance, I sensed, but because she was hurt. I couldn't see her face as she turned away from me in the shadows.

"What is it? What's wrong?"

She grimaced and raised her left hand. "When we fell down outside the inn, someone stepped on my wrist. I think it might be broken."

"You should have told me!" Now guilt rose anew. Here I'd let her haul me along as if I were some kind of helpless idiot, healing me with her magical curing, and she herself had suffered a broken bone!

"Let me see," I added gently.

She extended her arm, and I heard her gasp when I touched a fingertip to her wrist, which was swollen and quite warm to the touch. I saw that her whole wrist was inflamed, discolored to an angry red. Despite her brave stoicism, I knew that she must be in severe pain.

"My curing spell will return after I get a good night's sleep. . . . Patrikon will give me the power after my morning prayers. I'll be all right until then."

"The chip of wood! It can heal you right now!" I said excitedly, reaching into my pouch for the ebony stick. Gingerly I placed the thing against her arm, as I had seen the fop do for the cut on the fighter's thigh. A buzzing sensation pulsed through my hand. I didn't see or hear anything, but I felt the power in the little chip of wood and watched in wonder as Saysi's throbbing limb quickly shrank back to its original delicate proportions.

"Your wrist—how does it feel?" I asked.

Saysi touched her skin in wonder, bending her hand back and forth, raising it to inspect the formerly angry-looking wound. "It feels fine. The pain is gone."

"I guess that poor fellow was telling the truth after all," I admitted, dropping the wooden curing stick back into my pouch. I shuddered at the memory of the blood-spattered head, face locked in an expression of supreme horror, tumbling through the hole in the wall and rolling across the floor.

"Now what do we do?" Saysi wondered, sitting up and stretching. Though pale dawn had begun to glimmer in the east, Oakvale was still hours away from daytime activity. Even the lovers and lonely strollers who had drifted around the plaza in the midnight hours had apparently gone somewhere to sleep. We were the only people in sight.

For the first time since our encounter in the gaming hall, I gave some thought to the immediate future. We had no money, hardly any possessions—just Goldfinder, the keen short sword I still wore at my side, and the shiny black stub of a curing stick, and we shared an unspoken reluctance to return to the Red Garter, where I had paid for three nights in advance.

"I . . . I guess I could look for a job—I mean, a *real* job," I suggested hesitantly. It was the honest thing to do, though the prospect sounded startlingly bleak when I heard it from my own lips.

"Or I could," Saysi said quickly. "Or we could find a temple, maybe one in a larger town, and ask the high priests for suggestions. I'm a full-fledged priestess, you know. My skills are worth something."

Sadly, I reflected that, to an honest human or halfling, my skills weren't good for much at all. Stealth, lockpicking, pilfering, and such had little place in the sweaty, bustling world of honest work. As I ticked off these considerations, another thought came to me. "That silver merchant's still going to want me in irons. He'll probably be along sometime today. . . ."

"No! I don't want to you see him!" Saysi said with surprising forcefulness.

I stopped to consider the situation. Turning myself in was still the right thing to do, I realized, but it had become a little more complicated. Did I just abandon Saysi to her fate, leaving her alone in a town full of humans, with no friendly temple for miles? That most definitely did *not* seem like the right thing to do.

The greedy fellow had seemed all too willing to include Saysi in the punishment for a crime that had been mine alone, and that was a clear and obvious wrong. I knew immediately that I couldn't allow that to happen.

"Maybe we should leave Oakvale, go to another town," I said hesitantly.

Before Saysi could reply, we heard the urgent noise of an animal whining behind us. We whirled to see a large hound creep toward our bench. The animal's tail and head were low, more beseeching than threatening. Advancing cautiously around the bench, the dog placed its head on the boards beside me.

"What is it, hound? Are you hungry?" I asked, feeling immediate and intuitive sympathy for the animal. "I wish we could help you."

The question made perfect sense, I realized, noticing that I was getting pretty hungry myself. My words reminded me that I had to do *something*.

The animal made a chuffing sound and raised its head, looking at me with eyes of melancholy brown, moist orbs that gleamed with startling urgency, as if the dog were trying to communicate something of great importance.

"Is she hurt?" asked Saysi, kneeling beside the hound

and looking at each of its forepaws. "Nothing's wrong that I can see."

The dog's coat was scruffy, with several burrs matted along her shoulders. Still, when I stroked her head and neck, I felt solid muscle. This was no scrawny, starving mutt, nor was the pleading manner a sign of meekness. The animal's broad face rose, loudly snuffling the air, the gaze of the bright brown eyes was bold and alert.

Abruptly the dog cocked her head, turning penetrating eyes across the plaza, toward the row of buildings on the near edge of the square. I felt bristling hackles rise beneath my hands, saw the dog's tail stiffen and lash in obvious tension.

"Kip—what is it?" There was real fear in Saysi's voice, and in her fingers, which suddenly came to rest around my arm. I blinked, uncertain in the dim light of exactly what we were seeing.

My gaze focused on the brown planks of a warehouse. They seemed to be moving, slowly melting before my eyes. A warm glow suffused the wall, or, rather, a large portion of it. A circular shape took form there, about the size of a wide set of double doors.

But there *was* no door there. The entrance to the warehouse was clearly visible, barred and bolted, several feet to the side of the strange distortion. Moments earlier, I felt certain, the planks there would have been as warped and weathered as the rest of the old building's wall.

I had a peculiar, frightening realization: The place on the other side of that shimmering barrier was not the inside of this mundane storage building, was not like anywhere or any place that we had ever seen.

Cream-colored light spilled between brightening chinks in the plank walls. It was not the illumination of the sun, but neither was it cast by any lamp, lantern, or fire. The hound, legs stiff, growled like a rumbling bear and stepped protectively in front of Saysi and me. The dog's hackles bristled, and her black lip curled back to reveal sharp, white fangs.

My eyes remained fixed upon the shifting, surreal brightness. The outline of mundane boards faded, pale light washing away any resemblance to a solid surface. Glowing, the power surged like an unrestrainable force seeking, growing toward, an explosive release.

Then it was as if the wall disappeared entirely. Bright columns of white stone formed the borders of a supernatural tunnel leading into the distance, while a sky of flat white glowed overhead. Blinking in astonishment, I rose from the bench and took a step forward, conscious of the great hound advancing before me.

"Kip . . ." Saysi's voice was tremulous.

My apprehension grew, though I didn't—yet—feel a sense of terror. Perhaps I was hypnotized with wonder or awe; I found it impossible to do anything except stare, my heart pounding hard in my chest.

The alabaster spires, jutting upward like crags of white quartz, were not in fact stone columns, but the smooth and straight trunks of very unnatural trees. They merged into an overhead canopy, the whitish glow above them actually a blanket of dense foliage, with radiant leaves, as if brightened by an internal flame. The bizarre growth merged together to form something like a pale overcast brightened by a high, midsummer sun.

But whatever the sun that was lighting this scene, it was not the same fiery orb of my own world.

"Kip—look! What's that?" Saysi's voice, tight with panic, came from beside my shoulder. I saw her finger pointing straight ahead.

Only then did I see the things racing along the ground, lurching between the trunks, galloping toward the opening that had now stabilized in the warehouse wall. Shaking my head in astonishment, I tried to focus on an image that my mind refused to comprehend.

Something moved there, creatures—monstrous, grotesque beings—that were *alive*. I blinked and shook my head again, wondering if some viciously prankful wizard had created a bizarre and frightening confluence of evil.

Three creatures charged with shocking speed. I wanted to say that they were running, but their movement was too unnatural, too grotesque to be described by any such mundane term. It was more as if they scuttled like gigantic spiders, but they traveled with the speed of a charging war-horse. The monsters had eight legs and propelled themselves forward in a series of bursts, striding with four legs at a time. The huge, bulbous bodies looked like grotesquely oversized tarantulas.

But the most horrifying features were the heads, which were cast in the exact images of ravenous, drooling wolves. Jaws gaping, they howled a beastly refrain mingled with wet, snarling growls. Bristling fur jutted from brown shoulders, and the lupine mouths brayed on, uttering unworldly howls and yelps that further heightened my fear. On each head, I saw long yellow fangs, slick with drool, and red, hungry eyes.

The stray hound bayed loudly, bounding toward the edge of the street and barking furiously into the otherworldly opening. The trio of beasts raced in that scuttling gallop between the pillars, rapidly approaching the circular aperture in the warehouse wall, the hole that I knew linked this place with . . . with wherever *that* was.

"Let's go!"

Saysi touched my arm and I whirled, fully propelled by fear now, ready to follow her across the tree-studded grounds of the market plaza.

"Dog—this way! Come!" I shouted over my shoulder, feeling oddly responsible for the hound that had so bravely advanced to face these menacing intruders.

With a final bark, the animal spun about and raced after me, following just behind us as if she wanted to herd us to safety, to protect these two halflings from an unspeakable menace. I cast a single look backward, saw the three spider-wolves spill from the glowing opening and speed across the street and onto the grassy plaza. As soon as the monsters emerged, the glowing circle began to fade. Once again the brown planks of the warehouse wall materialized, apparently as solid as they had been a few moments before.

"This way—into that alley!" I shouted between my gasps for breath, touching Saysi on the shoulder. She sensed my intent without looking, veering around a sturdy oak trunk and sprinting for a shadowy gap between two dark buildings.

I skidded around the same tree, drawing Goldfinder as I followed her toward the alley. Even without looking, I knew that the monsters were gaining on us, and the memory of those slavering jaws, the hideous and swollen bodies, gave me very little hope of a successful fight. Still, for once I was determined that I would give my own life to see that a companion had the chance to escape.

The chorus of snarls and growls roared in combative fury, frighteningly near, and I knew that the stray hound had thrown herself against the monstrous attackers. I didn't turn to look, but I heard the savage barking of the dog mingle with the yelping howls of the unnatural creatures.

"Run!" I gasped to Saysi quite unnecessarily. Only then did I halt and spin to face the galloping pursuers, my keen steel gleaming coldly in the early dawn light.

I couldn't believe how close the damned things had gotten. A few paces away, the hound whirled through a tight circle and charged at the flank of the leading spider-wolf, leaping with a roaring, furious bark. The monster tumbled, rolling along on the ground, and I heard the clacking of its drool-spattering jaws as it grappled with the brave dog.

The next beast sprang toward me with unbelievable quickness. My eyes registered an expanding mouth of bristling teeth and drooling tongue. Fetid breath reeked all around as I slashed blindly with Goldfinder, thinking that the steel blade seemed a pathetic counter to those fangs, that powerful body.

The creature darted away from my blow, pouncing onto all eight of its feet before scuttling around to face me. I darted behind the nearby tree trunk, feeling staccato footsteps through the soles of my feet as the monster raced after me. Before it completed the circle around the gnarled bole, I spun back and slashed, bashing Goldfinder into the wolfish head that suddenly snarled right in my face. Recoiling from an image of glaring eyes and snapping, drooling jaws, I nevertheless sliced once more, this time into the side of the lupine head. The creature whirled, screeching like a banshee, driving me back with an exhalation of foul breath.

Chopping again, I cut deeply into one of the beast's legs before stumbling backward. Slowed, the creature limped toward me, giving me enough time to scramble to my feet. It leapt with a triumphant howl, but not until I was ready. This time my blow was precise and well aimed, cutting deeply into the bristling neck and killing the beast instantly.

I saw Saysi disappear into the alley with the third spider-wolf racing in pursuit, and fear drove me into desperate haste. From somewhere nearby the snarls of the second monster mingled with those of the courageous hound. I could only hope that the dog could hold her own.

Again I sprinted, fear rising like bile in my throat. If only I could get there in time . . . but these monsters were unbelievably fast, viciously cruel, and deadly—and Saysi didn't even have a weapon! I remembered the gambler who'd been ripped to pieces earlier tonight, wondering if these same hideous attackers might have been behind that violence as well, a suspicion I didn't have any trouble believing as I raced across the cobblestone street.

Charging around the corner, I saw a sight that brought fear and despair forth from my throat in a tangled, wailing snarl. The third spider-wolf crouched facing me, jaws slick with fresh blood—*Saysi's* blood—and eyes boring hatred. I skidded to a halt, waving my sword in an effort to hold it at bay, frantically searching the shadows beyond. Again I groaned aloud, a wrenching cry of anguish. The alley was a dead end, and there was no sign of Saysi anywhere within.

Turning my murderous gaze onto the crouching monster, I was only dimly cognizant of a torn wisp of green silk dangling from the hideous jaws. Through the dim haze of my grief, I recognized the emerald sheen of Saysi's vest. A bright crimson stain outlined the edge of the torn segment, and it was this garish remnant that drove any semblance of rationality from my mind.

I flew at the spider-wolf, my body possessed by a determination beyond logic. Perhaps it was the suddenness of my reaction, or the fact that the monster had been sated by its recent feeding, that gave me a fraction of a second's surprise. The creature reared back in the face of my assault, but not quickly enough to avoid the bloody tip of my short sword. The weapon carved into the bristling, hairy throat, and the lupine head flopped loosely as blood and air gurgled outward.

Kicking reflexively, all eight legs splaying wildly, the creature flopped to the ground and lay still in a spreading pool of dark, inklike blood. I saw that the neck was sliced more than halfway through, knew that the monster was dead—yet these were secondary concerns.

Whirling, I stumbled around the small alley, kicking over several empty boxes, staring numbly at the three barren walls. I barely noticed the trembling in my arm, or was aware of my gory weapon shivering unsteadily in the air. I could see no sign of Saysi except for a few spots of fresh blood.

Finally I collapsed, sobbing wretchedly, horrified at the thought of my beloved priestess devoured in such a terrifying onslaught.

A cautious whine drew my attention. I raised my head to see the slack-skinned hound limp into the alley. The dog came over and placed her head on my lap, snuffling tiredly. Then she stepped away, shambling back to the street before turning and looking back to me.

I sensed a plea, both urgent and sad, in those mournful eyes. The animal knew that I shouldn't stay here, which was more than I could say for myself.

"Why?" I challenged, my voice a choking rasp. My tone

grew firm, solidified by increasing anger. "Where should I go? What do I have to live for?"

The dog, of course, made no answer. Instead, she fixed me with that distressingly understanding stare. She sat on her haunches as if to say that she, too, could be stubborn and irrationally patient.

Gradually I came to understand that I couldn't do anything more here, that in fact I might be in danger of a repeat attack by those horrific arachnoids. Rising to my feet, I kicked listlessly at the dead monster, a gesture that did nothing to make me feel better. The hound trotted into the street, then turned to look back at me.

"All right. I'll come with you," I whispered, as if a loud noise would be an affront to my slain companion.

Tears blurred my vision as, with a ragged sigh, I shambled out of the alley and followed the dog into the dawning day.

CHAPTER 5

AAQA

Thirty-two mountain peaks ringed a green and verdant valley. Each of the summits was a narrow spire of gleaming rock, some of them black, others red and gray and white, and a few of the lofty crags even gleamed with a smoothly mirrored surface of burnished silver. The perimeter of mountains formed a perfect circle, and the valley sheltered within that ring mirrored the immaculate and beautiful regularity of the heights.

In places around the pastoral vale, ponds and lakes sparkled, reflecting the azure purity of the sky. Eight mighty waterfalls, evenly spaced around the circumference of the valley, spumed from between the summits, feeding rivers of deep aquamarine, gathering in a crystalline lake located in the exact center of the valley. That great body of blue water was itself a perfect octagon, enclosed by a precise shoreline of eight straight sections.

Winds stroked the needle-like peaks, touching the

spires like precise fingers plucking at the strings of a harp. The keening of the air currents drew forth chords of exquisite, almost heart-stopping beauty. The songs changed constantly, rising through joyous chimes or sinking into minor bass, depending on the directions of the winds and the force of their gusts.

Across the valley floor, the pavilions of the vaati wind dukes stood amid lush groves of pine and cedar, or within rings of mighty oak and mahogany. Animals of many varieties grazed among the flowered meadows or lapped at the clear water bubbling from the frequent springs. There were carnivores here as well, mighty lions and bears among them, but these voracious creatures subsisted exclusively on the bodies of prey that perished naturally. In the Valley of Aaqa, nature enforced the rule of aging, which was the immutable law of all living things everywhere.

A trio of vaati stood upon the raised watchtower at the greatest pavilion, a marble structure located on a rounded hill near the central lake. The dukes were tall and handsome warriors, almost utterly naked, with skins in shades of black that varied slightly between the three individuals. Colorful sashes of brilliant colors—blue, green, and red—further differentiated each. Though their valley was a place of peace, each wore his weapon ready at his side—scimitar, rapier, and silver-springed crossbow. The three wind dukes stood in silent communion, looking toward the ring of summits on the far side of the lake.

"Do the other vaati suspect that Arquestan is coming here?" asked the one called Farrial, bearer of the scimitar. A ribbon of gold-trimmed blue was draped over his broad shoulders, extending to one side of his waist. A flat nose was centered in his handsomely chiseled head, flaring back between high cheekbones and piercing eyes of anthracite black. The tallest of the dukes, Farrial spoke in a deep voice that commanded the attention of his fellow lords.

"None has spoken of it," said another, Xathwik. Xath was shorter than Farrial, his torso more filled out, though still far from fat. He had a complexion of almost bluish-black, and his skull was clean-shaven, while his taller cohort had a crop of tightly curled black hair. Xathwik's symbolic color was green, and a viridescent shimmer of silken ribbon outlined his brawny physique. Emerald rings glistened from the four fingers of his hand as he raised his palm to shade his eyes from the bright sunlight.

As a vindeam, one of the most powerful wizards among the wind dukes, Xathwik was well versed with the plans and intentions of his fellows. "I have spent time in study of all the orders; nowhere have I seen the threat of discovery."

"What fools they can be!" snapped Balka, the other wizard, of the order rudeam. Balka's body was compact and powerful, full of barely contained energy, and now he paced back and forth like a caged cat. "Don't they know that Arquestan offers us our best hope of thwarting the queen?"

"Perhaps they do," Farrial, the grideam tree tender, agreed calmly in his deep and measured tones. "But they know, too, that he is an outcast, and as such, his presence in the valley is a thing to be feared."

"Let them fear the Queen of Chaos!" Balka retorted, clenching his red-colored sash in agitation.

"There. He comes," declared Farrial, pointing with a

long finger of chocolate brown.

"Of course. It is the appointed time, and even an outcast would never be late," murmured Xathwik.

The song of the wind rose to a triumphant chorus as Arquestan's chariot spun low between two peaks of silver. Gusts whispered through the columns around the pavilion as the glowing spiral of air swept just above the ground, circling that grand structure once, airy chargers rearing eagerly on the swirling gusts. The wendeam swept between the lofty pines before guiding his whirlwind to the marble flagstones of the pavilion's courtyard.

Arquestan stood tall in the back of his chariot. His hands were free—he had no need of reins—and he waved casually to the three wind dukes as the spiraling cloud settled. Winds gusted and swirled through the pavilion, until Balka raised a hand and muttered a low-voiced command; immediately the air became still.

"You never did care for my winds, did you?" Arquestan asked, stepping forward with a hearty chuckle.

"Winds can become chaotic, if left to blow unchecked," retorted the rudeam stiffly. "Nevertheless, you are welcome here, my old friend."

The dark, lanky wendeam, as naked as the waiting lords, strode across the plaza on his long legs. A belt of royal blue gathered around the waist of his lean and sexless form. His proud face was etched in a black beard and mustache and surrounded by a mane of shaggy curls that grew long from his scalp, dangling past his shoulders to either side.

Golden eyes, as sharp as a hawk's, met the curious looks of Xathwik, Farrial, and Balka. "I come in good humor, my friends, but this is not to mock your courage. I know the danger to you all for accepting an outcast into the valley—and into your pavilion."

"Courage is a thing in plentiful supply," said Xathwik. "What we need is knowledge—gained from all corners of the planes."

"And even from those that have no corners," added Balka with a shudder. Like all the wind dukes, he despised shapes and forms that lacked precision and regularity.

"You have journeyed to the wildest realm?" asked Farrial, his dark brow furrowed with apprehension.

"Aye, my friend." Arquestan's eyes clouded with memories of Pandemonium. "Miska remains imprisoned within the fortress, but the violence of his temperament is unabated. He paces ceaselessly, destroying parts of the castle as quickly as new structures can be raised. It is only the Barrier of Law that holds him within."

"And the rod . . . ?" Xathwik's tone was tremulous.

"There I have news . . . rather dramatic news, in fact."

"There is word . . . *real* word?" Farrial echoed the vindeam's excitement.

"Even better. I have a piece, held it in my own hands for a time. Now it is hidden where only I can reach it."

For a moment, though the silence was absolute, the emotion of the four vaati formed an almost physical bond between them. It was a heartbeat's time of reverence and worship and of hope for ultimate triumph, which warmed each soul even though it registered as merely a flickering expression across the four dark faces.

"The segment I have is the sixth. Unfortunately, the queen's minions have the seventh," Arquestan explained, breaking the silence and immediately sobering the elation of his fellow wind dukes.

"And the other pieces?" Xathwik quickly asked.

"They have come to rest upon a world—where exactly, I don't know. But we shall learn very soon, for the queen's spyder-fiends are not the most subtle of tanar'ri. When she sends them through the gates, I or one of my hounds will know."

"Quite," muttered Farrial, his bass tones underlying the melodious chiming of the background. "And you will continue the search?"

"Of course. After a meal and a rest, I will be off again. I have come, in part, to gather my pack."

"Your hounds await you," Xathwik said. "They have grown bored of my ministrations. No doubt they will be delighted to chase once more among the planes."

It was good, Xathwik thought, that Arquestan was the one who rode the ether. Xath knew that there were dangers and discomforts galore lurking beyond the Valley of Law, and he was content to remain here and offer judgements on the dangers of chaos without being forced to confront those challenges firsthand. He shuddered again at the thought of the outcast's lonely and disordered existence.

"But what of Bayar?" Farrial questioned, looking toward the place where the wendeam's chariot had landed. "Was she not already with you?"

"Aye. I have stationed my most faithful hound on the crossroads of chaos beyond the queen's palace," Arquestan declared. "Should she send her tanar'ri on another mission of attack, Bayar will precede them through the gate. It is my hope that she might be able to warn the next target."

"Good. We must make every effort to see that the pieces of the rod stay out of the queen's hands. I need not remind you of the costs. . . ." Balka's voice was hard, his eyes glinting like steel as he raised his head.

The others, unbidden, followed the direction of his gaze. The Valley of Law was dotted with many grand pavilions, mighty houses of dukes and captains that rose into the foothills standing at the bases of the thirty-two summits. Glimpses of marble facades, of obsidian walls and roofs of gray slate, showed everywhere among the verdant greenery.

But many of those pavilions were empty, their former masters slain on the plains of Oerth, never returning from a battle that should have attained ultimate victory. The legends of that bloody day, millennia ago, were vivid memories to the long-lived vaati. All four of them had fought on that gory field, had tasted the imminence of near-victory and seen the bitter frustration of an incomplete triumph.

More than half of the wind dukes had died on that plain, slain during the Battle of Pesh, sacrificed in order to banish the menace of Miska, the Wolf-Spider. They had died in victory, their enemy pierced with the potent Rod of Law, and that powerful artifact had driven Miska into his fortress prison.

Even so, chaos had exacted a price upon the sacred rod: The artifact had shattered in its ultimate victory. The vaati keenly recalled the bitter taste of that moment, as Miska had been banished into a Fortress of Law, yet still lived. The Rod of Law, tainted by the essence of its enemy, had been scattered to the far planes. It remained a potent tool for good or evil, hard to wield and dangerous to master. Perhaps more importantly, it was the only key to parting the barrier that imprisoned Miska, and the only tool that might have hope of killing the wolf-spider permanently.

The Queen of Chaos, Miska's mistress and lover, would not rest, they knew, until she gained the rod. Therefore, it was incumbent upon the wind dukes to gather the pieces of the artifact first.

"And now, fellow dukes, allow me one night of comfort and fellowship, of food and good conversation," Arquestan suggested, gently breaking the pensive mood. "For tomorrow, once again I ride among the realms of chaos."

The three hosts shuddered at Arquestan's words, regarding the wendeam with sympathy and more than a little awe. Then, in unison, they turned and escorted their guest into the well-ordered hospitality of the pavilion.

CHAPTER 6

MELANCHOLY FLIGHT

Somehow my boots had gotten wet. In fact, all my clothes were soaked. When I finally sat down and tried to reconstruct the last few hours, I recalled that I had fled right through the stream when I departed Oakvale. A big log had extended halfway across the water, giving me a start, and when I reached the end of the makeshift bridge, I simply threw myself into the river and paddled the rest of the way, ultimately crawling like a drowned rat into the underbrush on the far side.

The hound been there, on the far side of the stream, and she quickly regained her strength, apparently content to follow me. Ripples of her loose skin flopped as she plodded quietly at my heel, waiting patiently whenever I stopped to rest. Soon I was up again, blundering through thickets, blindly driving forward.

I had with me only my short sword, Goldfinder, which I dried off as best I could by using the large fern leaves that grew in these shadowy depths, and the little piece of black stick that offered the power of healing. That ability seemed like a cruel mockery now—power enough to cure Saysi's sprained wrist, but useless against voracious monsters that had charged from nowhere to shatter the predawn peace of a quiet town.

She's gone! The knowledge kept surging, unbidden, into my mind. I couldn't, I *wouldn't*, believe it, but despite my firm intentions, rational memory inevitably intruded, bearing my spirits again into a miasma of hopeless despair. Pushing hard, I tried to exhaust myself, craving only numbness. Perniciously, my mind refused to stop thinking, remembering, feeling.

Through the years, I had lost many companions to sudden and violent misfortune; it was a constant risk in my chosen field of endeavor. Yet the peculiar sense of devastation I felt right now was a new and violently unpleasant experience for me. Grief rose from the pit of my stomach, grabbed my heart and lungs in a vise of enveloping pain, stabbing into my brain to beat against the inside of my skull like some dwarven miner striving to dig himself out of a cave-in.

I stumbled onward, pushing through the woods in a straight line, not bothering to seek a trail or mask my tracks. Pressing ahead, I was directed by some mysterious instinct that lurked below the surface of my awareness. I was vaguely aware of the fact that my course took me well away from the direction of Scarnose's lair. Still, I didn't stop to wonder why I made my path through trackless wilderness, rather than to follow one of the good roads leading out of Oakvale to the east or south.

Rough, craggy foothills rose to block my path, but I was reluctant to avoid the obstacles. By midday, I found myself scaling cliffs of loose, rotting rock, just so that I could continue to travel in a straight line. While I had no idea of what lay ahead of me, I never questioned that I was going the right way.

Numbly plodding, I barely noticed the coming of night. I tried to sleep beneath a bush in the trackless wood, but tossed and turned uncomfortably, thoroughly soaked by a heavy dew. This gave me a good deal of time for reflection, something I usually try to avoid. On this miserable night, however, there was nothing else to do.

At first, I forcibly resisted memories of Saysi, though this only encouraged my mind to drift to even earlier memories. For the first time in many months, I thought of Colbytown, the peaceful little halfling village that was my original home. Surrounded by green and fertile pastures, centered around a placid millpond, the snug community had been eternally peaceful, quiet, and pleasant—deadly dull traits to a halfling who longed for adventure. As a youth, I couldn't wait to make my escape.

Of course, I tried to get back there every now and then. My two sisters, Hallie and Berdeen, missed me and welcomed me gladly on every visit. They were bright and vivacious maids who had married well, and each had given birth to innumerable nieces and nephews. Seeing the little ones again was a bright point of my return visits, for they never tired of listening to my tales of danger and excitement on the road. Once I had thought of taking Saysi there, introducing her . . .

No! I had to think of other things! With wrenching force, I moved my memories along, found myself recalling good times with Barzyn and Dallzar. Of my previous companions, I had known these two brothers the longest. As a trio, we had lived well for all of a decade. Their brawn and courage, coupled with my own knack for stealth and, if I say so myself, keen intellect, had enabled us to reap rewards wherever we traveled. Often we'd done good work, like the rescuing of a helpless prisoner for a substantial reward, or the slaying of a bullying monster in return for its plundered wealth.

But these deeds weren't like a religion with us. Just as often we had plundered the mansion of some rural warlord or robber baron. We had swindled from the foolish rich and spent our gains freely for the benefit of the poor—namely, ourselves.

My mind drifted to our first meeting with the redoubtable Benton. The dwarves and I had watched him dismantle a patrol of guards in the thriving coastal city of Argenport. Realizing that he'd be a real asset to our party, we aided him to escape through the gates in the guise of a beggar woman. The disguise had been my idea, though the lunkhead of a barbarian hadn't grasped the brilliance of the scheme until some time after its success. Now I got a lump in my throat as I recalled how he had bristled every time I mentioned the episode, which I had made a point to do frequently.

Hestrill had been with us for the last three or four years, another brave soul that the dwarves and I had rescued from a life of drudgery. The magic-user had been responsible for the security of one of our robber baron targets, and his magical traps almost snared Dallzar and Benton when we at last broke into the treasure rooms. We were impressed by his spells, and he was depressed by his failure—not to mention the prospect of inevitable execution when the lord found out about his depleted cash reserves. A few simple arguments had convinced him that the life of an adventuring mage was certain to improve his spirits.

These thoughts led inevitably to my first meeting with Saysi. She had come along barely a year ago, and quickly proved herself to be an invaluable member of our group. Her presence had added a special spark to my life as well, a spark that I felt certain would never be rekindled. I still remembered the first time I saw her, as vividly as if it had been yesterday.

We had arrived in a city—I think it was Argenport—with plenty of money to spend and powerful thirsts in need of quenching. In a crowded inn, among musicians and splendid food, I had been flirting with one of the waitresses. She was human, but petite enough that I could hold her on my lap. In fact, an occasional waiflike daughter of man has found my guileless smile to be irresistible; several of these instances have led to some very memorable affairs. This barmaid might have been another, but I was never to find that out.

The door to the inn opened, and I looked across the crowded room to see the most beautiful face I had ever beheld, despite the fact that the poor girl had recently been crying. Her chocolate eyes were almost too big for her dainty chin, her rounded cheeks, and full mouth.

Long, silken lashes of finespun copper seemed to give her dark eyes a perfect framework. Curly hair of the same color fell in boisterous cascades over her forehead and down past her shoulders. Though the lustrous mane was tangled and sodden, her beauty remained undiminished. Even her obvious distress served only to enhance her allure, and made me want to offer her comfort and protection.

So striking was her face that it had taken me several moments to make my inspection of the rest of her figure. The loose, traveling vest could not conceal the voluptuous swell in the front, unusually prominent for a halfling maiden, but no less delightful for its rarity. Her waist was tiny, encircled by a black leather belt, and mud-stained boots and leggings showed the tight outline of delicately curved calves. The only article of jewelry she wore was a jade amulet, an eight-sided stone dangling around her neck on a leather thong. I would soon learn that this was her holy symbol, a talisman of Patrikon, the god of law she had apprenticed to in the years since her coming of age.

At first glance, however, nothing about her appearance indicated that she was a priestess. The waitress on my lap noticed my wandering eyes and rose in a huff, but I didn't even care. Instead, I started for the door, intending to flash this newcomer my most winning smile.

Before I took two steps, however, she turned and vanished into the night. Strangely agitated, I hurried after her, ducking out the door to see her disappear around a corner of the street. I followed so rapidly that my footsteps attracted her attention, and she turned with an expression of alarm, reaching for the metal-headed club she wore at her belt.

"Wait!" I said hastily, holding up my hands to show her that I meant no harm. "I—I saw you back at the inn. You looked as if you were in some kind of trouble. Can I help?"

"Who are you?" she asked suspiciously, still holding the haft of her weapon, though at least she didn't pull it out and wave it at me.

"Kip. Kip Kayle." For lack of anything else to say, I was about to announce that I was a fellow halfling, but fortunately I bit back this self-evident remark before it left my lips. "Is something wrong?"

"I'm Saysi Formillay," she said, instinctively clutching the jade amulet I had noticed earlier. "I'm . . . a pilgrim, part of a caravan to the Altar of the Diamond Father. We were attacked just outside of town—"

Those chocolate eyes teared up again, and I had a grim premonition. Bandits preying on religious caravans had recently performed acts of extreme brutality, and I could easily picture the tragic fate of her party. "And your companions . . . ?"

"All dead," she sniffled. "I tried to help Patriarch Donwell. He is . . . *was* . . . my mentor. He—he was shot through, but not until he hid me in a ditch. I crept out again, but all my curing wasn't enough to bring him back!"

"I'm sure you did everything possible."

"But now what do I do?"

Even if I hadn't already planned an answer to that question, the plaintive note of her voice would have gone far to persuade me. As it was, I was fully prepared.

"Why don't you join me and my friends?" I suggested. "We've got rooms in town here—"

Her eyes widened in alarm, and I hastened to reassure her. "You'd have your own, of course. We've just come into some funds, and the only gold we carry is the kind that's anxious to be set free. When we're rich, we try to accommodate that desire."

"You're rich?" Her tone became openly skeptical as she looked at my patched breeches, the stains on my scuffed tunic, and the long, unkempt mane of hair spraying down to my shoulders and beyond.

"Well, this week we are," I explained—a little defensively, she later claimed. "We just came into some money, and we're kind of glad to be here alive and intact."

"You keep saying 'we.' Who do you mean?"

I explained about Benton and Hestrill, Barzyn and Dallzar. "They're all pretty good folks—for humans and dwarves, I mean. And I can testify that each of them is a handy ally in a fight."

"Do you fight . . . a *lot*, I mean?" she asked, somewhat nervously.

"Only when it's necessary," I answered breezily. "This last time, we had to battle a giant. He wasn't too pleased with us trying to open his treasure chest."

"You fought a giant?" she asked skeptically.

"No!" I hastened to dispel any notions she might be forming about my heroic tendencies. "The very idea terrifies me. I picked the lock on the chest after the others took care of the giant. Benton took a pretty good whack on the shoulder during the battle. That's when we could have used you, or someone like you. He was in pain all the way down from the mountains, till we could get him to the temple here in town and have a cleric patch him up."

This didn't seem like the best time to tell her about our last cleric, Patchel, and his unfortunate encounter with a basilisk. Someday, perhaps, I could *show* her. Patch had been turned into a stone statue and, so far as I knew, was still languishing in a very dark and unpleasant lair.

"I—I guess I don't have anywhere else to go," Saysi said, drying her eyes. "It's kind of you to invite me. . . ."

I felt a twinge of guilt, remembering how my gaze had first latched on to those chocolate eyes and the delightful curves of her demure outfit. Reassuring her, and myself, that the offer was genuine, without conditions, I escorted her back to the inn and made the introductions. At the time, I figured I could be patient; in a few weeks, she would yield to my charms, and more weeks, perhaps even months, of bliss would be the inevitable result.

That had been just about a year ago, but the anticipated intimacy never developed. Saysi and I became friends, of course, and the little priestess had demonstrated herself on several occasions to be a cleric of faith and skill, and a courageous and loyal companion as well.

At last I drifted off to sleep, slumbering very briefly. Stiff and cold, hungry and depressed, I was nevertheless grateful at least to dream of Saysi for a while—and to forget about the fact that she was gone.

CHAPTER 7

BADSWELL LUMMOFF

Misty tendrils of a sticky dawn stroked my face, slowly awakening me. Sitting up to a symphony of aches and pains, I nevertheless felt a strange urgency to move. I crept out of concealment and stiffly stood, flinching as several birds fluttered away. Dusting the dried leaves and twigs from my clothes, I reflected that their flightiness meant that no immediate threat lurked in the area.

Thoughts of danger brought back the full horror of the previous dawn—the unnatural invaders of Oakvale and Saysi's horrible death. The bleak morning immediately felt more oppressive, and for a moment, I longed to return to the oblivion of sleep.

"Dog? Hound?" Remembering the loyal mutt that had followed me from Oakvale, I called aloud, turning hopefully around, looking through the surrounding underbrush.

Nothing stirred. A lump rose in my throat, and I

rebuked myself angrily, thinking that, with all the losses I had suffered in the last days, this was no time to get sentimental about a stupid dog. Nevertheless, the animal's absence left an aching pain as I started through the woods. Hopping across a brook on a series of raised boulders, I pressed into the woods on the other side and started along the side of a sloping hummock of rock.

Again I felt that strange urgency, a guiding sense that led me in a straight line through the forest. Now, at least, the floor of the woods was open. The forest was generally clear of underbrush, thanks to a dense canopy far overhead, and I found the walking, if not pleasant, at least somewhat distracting.

It didn't take long for my thoughts to return to Saysi. I'd never been a religious fellow, but in that wilderness, I prayed to Patrikon long and hard, hoping that her last moments had been quick. The fact that I had slain the beast that killed her was no consolation to my wounded spirit. The memory of those hateful jaws, the bulbous and unnatural body, brought my anger to a fever pitch again, and I fantasized about meeting another of the creatures, solely for the pleasure of bringing about its painful and violent demise—as if more killing could bring my beloved companion back. Still, my fist clenched around Goldfinder's hilt and I learned that anger was a much less painful emotion than grief.

It was with a start that I noticed the lengthening shadows of twilight. I had entered a deep cut in the foothills, a gorgelike depression that fortunately ran along the course of my strangely guided journey. Picking my way along the valley floor, I stayed to the right of a splashing brook that tumbled from some unknown height before me.

With nightfall imminent, I decided to look for shelter against the near wall of the gorge. Turning from the stream, I made my way toward the moss-covered cliff that occasionally showed between the boles of the mighty trees. Maybe I could find a cave or some kind of overhang that might help to keep me dry.

It wasn't until the splashing sound of the brook was muffled by intervening trunks that I heard the groan, a rumbling gasp of pain resonating from a massive chest. Instinctively I took cover, worming between gnarled roots, pressing closer against the cliff.

The groan was repeated. Clearly the sound originated some distance away, near the base of the cliff that rose in a tangled mess of cracked limestone and thick, thorny brush to my right. Creeping with all the stealth I could muster, I advanced along the base of the precipice, cautiously seeking . . . what?

Shadows thickened around me, but I heard no further sounds of pain. My hand went instinctively to the hilt of my sword, but I didn't draw the weapon; instead, inching closer to the source of the noise, I tried to look in every direction at once.

The wind had died away completely, and the birds, too, became strangely still as I crept around a massive, twisted tree trunk. Peering past the rotten, punky wood, I observed a region of mossy talus at the bottom of a steep section of the gorge wall. Once again there was a noise—the deep, rasping sounds of something very large straining to draw a breath. Though no words were articulated, the very intensity of the respiration indicated a creature in severe pain.

I inched up to the first of the fallen boulders, and it seemed as if the panting came from very nearby.

Cautiously I peered over the rock—and confronted a broad, tusked face, barely an arm's length away from my own.

"Ogre!" I yelped, tumbling backward to sit heavily on the ground.

Hearing nothing in reply, I rose cautiously, peering around the corner of the rock, ready to flee at an instant's notice. The rounded muzzle, yellowed fangs jutting upward from the protruding lower jaw, the dark, piglike eyes staring at me with unblinking appraisal, all confirmed my original conclusion. Scrambling to my feet, I drew my sword and took a hesitant step toward the imagined safety of the woods.

The ogre groaned, a piteous expression of pain, and I realized that he wasn't about to leap up and give chase. Or at least, if he was faking his injury, he was a lot more clever than any of the hulking humanoids I'd encountered before. Too, his face seemed less threatening than other ogres I'd seen, even vaguely benign, in a dull sort of way.

Cautiously I crept around the rock, finding another vantage where I could climb up and get a look at him while remaining ten or twelve feet away, enough distance that I could make a quick getaway should the need arise.

"Hello," grunted the ogre, his speech startlingly clear. The tone was deep, the articulation better than that of any of the ogres with whom I'd had the previous misfortune to converse.

"I'm Badswell Lummoff," he added helpfully.

"Kip. Kip Kayle," I replied with a nod. I saw that one of the ogre's legs jutted sideways at a brutal angle, and with a quick look upward, I deduced that he must have fallen from the height of the gorge wall. "Looks like your leg is broken."

" 'Fraid so," he replied sadly. "Guess I'm dyin' here. Not much to do about it, though. Still, Mum's goin' to be sad."

Again he spoke more clearly, and with unogrelike passivity. I guessed that he was a youngster; he certainly didn't loom to the gargantuan proportions of most of the bull ogres I'd encountered. At the same time, I noticed that his muzzle was less protuberant than typical for his breed, and there was an undeniable spark of intelligence—relatively speaking, of course—and even the potential for humor in those dark eyes.

Intelligence and humor were two characteristics I'd never associated with any ogre before, and my curiosity was aroused. Given the distance I'd traveled, it seemed unlikely that the injured brute was a member of Scarnose's band. Yet there were probably others of his ilk around, since I knew that ogres rarely lived alone. Apparently it's too much work to tend to the necessities of daily life when goblin or human slaves can easily do the work for you.

"Do you live near here?" I asked, making myself comfortable on the rocks.

"Yup. Mum and Pap have a cave just up the gorge. Prob'ly waitin' supper on me right now." The ogre nodded his head lugubriously, turning his neck as if to look around but wincing from the sudden pain caused by the movement.

Again I wondered at the creature's strange behavior. Most ogres would have been furious at being stuck in such a predicament and would have striven to kill anyone who came within reach out of sheer viciousness. This fellow Badswell was clearly a unique example of his race.

"You're a very interesting ogre," I noted by way of an

opening.

"I'm only half an ogre. Mum's a human," the big fellow said after a momentary lull.

I nodded thoughtfully, thinking that this explained a lot. Badswell was not a full-blooded member of his savage clan. Then I pictured another, frightening thought.

"Your Mum—she lives in a cave with your Pap?" I asked, suddenly shivering at the image of savage captivity that was conjured in my mind.

"Yup." Badswell Lummoff nodded proudly. "All my life, and before then, too. Ever since Pap brung her up here from the town long time ago."

My nostrils flared in outrage at the thought of a helpless maiden dragged into the wilderness by a brutal monster, no doubt horribly used, forced to live in the ogre's squalid cave, to tend his needs—even to bear his child! I had to draw several deep breaths just to calm myself, and only then did my own reaction register as a surprise. After all, although kidnapping and slavery were clearly great wrongs, I typically would not have viewed them as my problems unless I was the one being kidnapped or enslaved.

Yet somehow it seemed as though Badswell's—and especially his mother's—situation made a difference to me.

"She's still there?" I asked casually, wondering whether the brutish ogre kept her chained to the wall, or perhaps forced her to languish in some sunless pit, no doubt sealed by a boulder only her vile master could move.

"Sure. That's where we live! Lived, I guess—I'm gonna die purty soon."

For the first time, I remembered that I might have the ability to help this poor fellow, who seemed a remarkably decent sort when one considered his ancestry. My hand closed around the stick of wood in my pouch, and I leaned forward to get a look at the fellow's leg.

"A bad break," I allowed.

"Sure 'nuff. Fell right down the cliff. Never thunk I could be so clumsy."

"I might be able to help you," I said hesitantly. "That is ... I'm kind of lost. If I could make your leg better, do you think you could take me to your cave, let me meet your Mum?" The ruse of dishonesty was troublesome to me, but far less so than the mental image of that helpless human female. Then I comforted myself with the reflection that, when I thought about what I had said, I hadn't really lied after all.

"Why, sure! But how kin you help? I kin see you don't got a new leg for me!"

"Maybe I can make the old one better," I suggested, suppressing my smile. Badswell clearly had a rather limited education, which wasn't surprising given the enslavement of his mother and the doubtlessly ruthless and brutal nature of his father.

I took the stub of ebony and placed it against the broken leg. In seconds, the swelling subsided.

"Wow! You got a good stick there!" Badswell exclaimed, rising and experimentally placing his weight on the leg. "It works."

"Healing magic," I explained modestly.

The half-ogre ambled across the ground in a rolling gait that showed no signs of a limp. I hadn't fully appreciated his size until he stepped up to me, looming like a mountain overhead.

"Whyn't ya come with me? Meet Mum and Pap?"

Again I pictured that dark lair and the helpless human

female imprisoned within.

"Sure," I agreed. I felt a twinge of reservation when I scrambled down from the rock to stand beside Badswell Lummoff, realizing that my shoulder was about the same height as his knee. Still, I had already made up my mind.

Badswell started to lead me over the tangled ground at the base of the cliff. Surprisingly we made good time, and I realized that the half-ogre followed a regular network of paths and ramps formed by the fallen trunks of huge pines and the crests of monstrous boulders that had tumbled from the precipice since ancient times. The route allowed us to avoid the jagged rocks and weathered stumps that made a tangled obstacle course out of the ground itself.

Curiously, my sense of direction matched exactly the route that Badswell took, as if I had been headed here since leaving Oakvale. I began to sense the rightness of the destiny that took me toward the ogre's lair. With each step, my outrage grew. I imagined, in vivid and horrifying detail, the captivity that must have been the lot of the half-ogre's mother for the last several decades. In fact, I was amazed that she had even been able to survive.

Badswell himself didn't seem like such a bad sort. He held back his pace to accommodate my shorter legs, and often turned back to lend me a hand over a high obstacle or across a wide span of space. On these occasions, his face was invariably bent into a tusk-baring leer that I gradually recognized as a guileless, friendly smile. Doubtless the influence of his human mother had tempered the vicious brutality of his low-browed sire.

Before I knew it, we were scrambling up a narrow ravine, hopping up a series of flat rocks arrayed very much like a stairway. Bads stepped easily from one to the next, but I was puffing and sweaty by the time we reached the lip of the limestone bluff.

"Here's cave," he said helpfully as I stared upward at a moss-draped hole leading into the blackness of the rising ridge beyond. The tang of bitter smoke was thick and acrid in the close air of the ravine. A massive beam framed each side of the door, supporting a huge lintel of granite. That upper stone merged into the rock of the hillside, looming ominously over the entryway and holding back a significant tonnage of loose boulders.

The sense of direction that had guided me through the wilderness rose to an acute level, indicating the dark aperture of the cave was my destination. Perhaps it was only right that I rescue this woman, I thought. Certainly the feeling was an urge that I found increasingly difficult to ignore.

"Does your Pap keep your Mum in there?" I asked, cautiously eyeing the gloomy aperture. At first nothing was visible within, but gradually my vision adjusted and I began to perceive a few details.

A trail of smoke drifted through the air, near the flat ceiling of the passageway. From the rough walls and irregular floor, I could tell that the cavern was natural for the most part, though the ogres had done some work to smooth and widen it. I tried to imagine the plight of the poor human captive, supposing that she was chained to the wall somewhere in the lightless depths. The very thought sent a shiver of outrage down my spine, and my fingers clenched around the hilt of my short sword in a conscious gesture of grim determination.

I had decided against asking Badswell for more information. Though he seemed none too swift, I was taking no chances on alerting him to my intentions. Even though the half-ogre himself had made no overt moves against me, I had to regard him as a potential enemy. It seemed far safer to approach the task of his mother's rescue with stealth and secrecy, at least for the time being.

"Bads! You bring supper?"

The cry screeched from the depths of the cave as we passed through the entrance. I would not have been surprised by the bellow of a bull ogre, but the high-pitched nature of the cry contradicted my initial anticipation.

Then a hulking brute charged from the darkness with startling speed, rushing like a lumbering buffalo. The fellow's torso was round-shouldered, the face tusked and bestial, feet broad enough to set the ground pounding. My first instinct was to flee, but then I noticed that the creature wasn't even aware of my presence. Instead, he looked over his shoulder, and I got the distinct impression that it was the *ogre* who was fleeing.

The monster was huge, larger even than Badswell, and dressed in a tattered rag of bearskin. Those tree-trunk-sized legs pumped furiously, and the rasping sound of the ogre's breathing whooshed like a blacksmith's bellow. The screeching voice followed him from the darkness as he bore down on me.

"You call this firewood? I want some *dry* logs! Something that'll burn without blowing your fool breath all over it!"

"Certainly, luv!" barked the ogre, charging through the entrance of the cave. The round, tusked face swiveled around, staring wildly over the brute's shoulder, and I got the distinct impression that his features sagged with relief as he made his escape.

Then a bulky shadow loomed inside, approaching the cave mouth, and I wondered if that person could possibly be human, never mind a helpless, kidnapped maid. She looked more like a giantess as she gestured us curtly forward with an arm the size of a bear's foreleg.

"Git in here!" she demanded in the face of our hesitation, and I had the sickening feeling that I had made a very terrible mistake.

CHAPTER 8

MUM AND PAP

"Well? Don't jist stand there. Git in here and let's see what you got." The voice rumbled from the shadowy figure within the cave, the question as palpably hungry as the glare of a ravenous spider-wolf.

"Uh, sure, Mum," Badswell grunted, taking me by the hand.

Though he still towered over me, the half-ogre seemed smaller than he had before. His shoulders slumped, and his head dipped awkwardly forward in a posture that made him look slightly off-balance. "Come on—you don't wants to keep her waitin'!" he hissed from the side of his broad mouth.

Actually, at this point I was ready to keep "Mum" waiting for a very long time. My doubts about the hastily conceived idea of a rescue had grown into full-blown misgivings. Still, Bads had me pretty firmly by the arm, and there was the matter of my peculiar direction sense, the feeling that I was *supposed* to go into this cave.

"What do we have here?"

The shrill voice dropped to a whispered hiss that was, if possible, even more frightening than the shrieking cries that had echoed moments earlier. I saw the dim shape moving forward, and as my eyes gradually adjusted to the pale light of a fading fire, I had trouble believing that the woman before me was in fact human.

She was certainly the largest person I had ever seen, male or female. Lumbering on legs that made Badswell's limbs look like twigs, she scowled from a face creased by numerous wrinkles—or chasms, more accurately, since her skin resembled the relief map of a mountain range. Squinting her bloodshot eyes, she leaned down to regard me, and her bloated face broadened into a hideous smile, revealing gums that provided home for only a few scattered, blackened teeth.

"A halfling, huh? Bads, ya done good."

"T'anks, Mum," said my newfound friend, beaming. "Dis's Kip. He fixed my leg."

"Oh, 'e did, did 'e? What a nice little fellow. Now you come here for yer reward, I'm bettin?"

"Uh, no, ma'am," I replied before bowing as politely as I could with Badswell's hand still gripping my arm. Sheepishly he let go, and I sensed that he'd been holding me more for his own comfort than my security. It was easy to understand why: His mother was undoubtedly the scariest creature I'd ever seen.

Then I remembered the spider-wolves that had killed Saysi, and modified this realization: Mum was only the *second* most frightening being I had beheld.

"I'm Bertisha," declared the woman, with a gurgling attempt at gracious hospitality. "Bads don't got the manners of a stableboy, so he prob'ly din't tell ya that. Whyn't ya come over here and have a seat?"

The big woman seized my shoulder in a calloused paw and whisked me across the cave before plopping me onto a hardened stone bench. "Supper won't be for a while yet. Oakgnar, that fool husband of mine, brought a bunch of green wood for the cookfire!" As she said this, her voice dropped to a rumbling growl, and I actually felt sorry for the bull ogre I had observed moments before.

For the first time, I noticed the source of illumination in the cave: a large firepit, lined with glowing coals. Much of the smoldering blaze was obscured by a massive caldron suspended over the blaze. With a growing, sickening certainty, I suspected that the iron kettle figured prominently in the dinner plans.

"Um, thanks a lot, ma'am," I replied as graciously as I could, considering that my heart was lodged somewhere in the middle of my throat. "But I really have to be going."

I started to sidle toward the entrance, but Bertisha reacted with startling speed. She reached out and touched me with something hard, sneering wickedly as I tried to twist away. Immediately my limbs felt sluggish, as if they were mired, trying to push through thick mud. I spun, ducking my head and leaping toward the cave mouth, when I realized that several seconds had passed and I was still in the midst of my first step. My right foot finally padded to the ground, but before I could raise the left to take another step, Bertisha seized me by the scruff of the neck and plopped me down onto the bench.

"Stay there!" she barked, her face inches from my own. I gagged, realizing that if it hadn't been for the sweetening effects of plenty of onion, her breath would have almost certainly been toxic.

When I tried to squirm in place, I found that the invisible mire remained close around me. Miserably I understood that some kind of magic spell had been worked on me, an enchantment of slowing that virtually ensured I would be caught if I tried to flee. I've always hated being ensorcelled, and I struggled desperately in the invisible, but very real, grip of the spell. No matter how hard I strained, every move I made was enacted in excruciating slow motion. I kicked my foot, and it was like pushing the limb through a pile of soft sand.

"He *helped* me, Mum!"

Badswell fiercely confronted the bloated hag, and I had a sense that standing up to his mother was not something he did casually.

"His mistake, then," Bert replied, turning her back to her son as she regarded me with those wicked, piglike eyes. "But our good fortune."

"Whattaya mean?" grunted Bads.

"You've never had the taste, boy, but halfling is a rare delicacy." Bertisha nodded ominously at the big pot. "Those plump legs are lined with good, sweet meat. Boiled for a few hours, then sliced thin like I've tried to show yer Pap, it'll tickle yer tongue better'n good venison."

She fastened those eyes upon me again, starting to drool at the prospect of the meal she'd just described. Apparently worried that the spell of slowness might not be enough to hold me in place, she rummaged in a pile of junk and came up with a length of ratted rope. With a few quick twists, she pulled it snug around my wrists and tied a crude knot to keep me pinned to the bench.

Her words—not to mention her breath—were making me thoroughly sick. Yet despite my increasingly frantic struggles, I moved far too slowly to do anything effective.

It was then that I noticed the object dangling from a thong around her neck, remembered the touch she had administered—the touch that had slowed me down to turtle speed.

A dark stub swung from the leather strap, suspended on her huge, round belly. I saw that the object seemed to be made of the same black wood as the healing stick that I carried. Indeed, there were curious patterns and indentations on both ends of Bertisha's stick, and I got the distinct impression that the piece might match the opposite geometrical facets carved into my own talisman.

In a flash of insight, I recalled my sense of direction and knew that it wasn't the cave nor the woman that had guided my path.

It had been that little piece of stick.

Already I could see that her ebony stub was slightly longer than mine. It also differed in that it had the strange carvings at both ends, while my own piece was perfectly blunt at one terminus. Furthermore, although it was clearly magical, it had a completely different effect. Obviously the strange black stick was the source of the spell that had mired me in this cocoon of invisible mud.

A shadow darkened the entrance, and Oakgnar shuffled in, his arms filled with dried limbs of hardwood. Without looking at his wife, he sat on a boulder and commenced breaking the logs over his knee, quickly forming a pile of firewood. Bertisha stumped over and began to feed the smoldering fire, which slowly grew into a crackling blaze.

"But Mum," Bads tried again, "he fixed my leg! I asked him to come here so's you could meet him and say thanks!"

"I will say thanks!" Bertisha replied, smiling wickedly. "I'll be grateful for each delicious mouthful!"

Bads slumped miserably in the corner, looking at me with a pathetic expression, as if to say "I tried." I shrugged, unwilling to hold his mother's villainy against him. Once more straining to rise from the bench, I determined that the spell of slowness still held me in its sticky grip.

A low growl rumbled from the mouth of the cave. Bert, Oakgnar, and Badswell all spun to gape in that direction. I tried to whirl around, but my motion was more of a slow twist than a rapid spin. It seemed as if ten seconds passed before I could see what was going on.

Crouching low, hackles bristling, a large hound crept forward. Mournful eyes fastened upon me with familiar, remembered sadness, and I realized that the dog from Oakvale had found me again.

"Hound! Good dog! Come here!" I cried, my words dirgelike and slow under the effects of the spell.

The forlorn gaze turned toward the ogre-wife as the dog, with apparent reluctance, bared her teeth in a low, rumbling growl. The animal's mouth suddenly gaped, revealing sharp white teeth as she barked explosively.

"Kill it! Kill it!" shrieked Bertisha, seizing a long club from the corner. I thought she was going to bash the animal herself, but instead she clouted poor Oakgnar on the shoulder, then jabbed the crude weapon into his hands. "Kill it!" she repeated, her words echoing shrilly in the enclosed confines of the cave.

Oakgnar rose to his feet and lifted the club. The hound stood stiff-legged, floppy jowls drawn into a menacing snarl, staring at the ogre but making no move to advance or retreat.

"Mebbe it'll go away," declared Oakgnar, without a great deal of conviction.

The dog looked at me again, and I sensed some sort of plea in those bright eyes. I had a peculiar notion that the animal was trying to communicate with me. Why had she returned? More to the point, could she help me get out of this mess?

Frantically I wrestled with the knot binding my hands. Of course, as wildly as I struggled, I was still mired in the cocoon of slowness, so my efforts remained maddeningly retarded. The ogre family's attention remained fixed upon the big dog, though I saw Bads flash me a quick look. He saw my hands working at the knot, but said nothing.

At the same time, a whitish glow slowly suffused one wall of the cave—the rocky surface directly behind Bertisha—and my heart sank in grim certainty of what was coming. Redoubling my efforts, I felt one end of the line slowly slip through the loosening knot. Ignoring the rasping pain against my skin, I pulled one hand, then the other, free of the bonds. Goggle-eyed, I watched the cave wall change, noticing that Bertisha and Oakgnar's attention remained fixed upon the barking, bristling dog.

Light suddenly spilled into the cave from the surreal opening, and Oakgnar turned, gaping stupidly at the transforming surface.

"Look out for the dog!" shrilled Bertisha, stepping forward and snatching the club from her husband's nerveless hands.

The hound still made no move to attack, but when the hulking woman advanced with upraised club, the animal skirted to the side, staying just out of range of the heavy stick, teeth bared, dark eyes regarding Bertisha with almost palpable sadness.

"Mum—look!" Bads grunted, pointing at the back wall of the cave.

The ogre-wife showed no inclination to turn away from the hound, even as the opening grew more distinct. Again I saw the long tunnel, flanked by the white pillars or tree trunks. The first lupine monsters, their arachnoid bodies scuttling grotesquely forward, charged into view. More of the horrific creatures raced behind, a half dozen of them closing fast.

With a growl, Oakgnar picked up several large stones, stepping to the mouth of the aperture in the back wall of the cave. With remarkably effective aim, the ogre pitched one of the rocks, striking the leading spider in its wolfish head. The animal fell, stunned or dead, but several of its fellows leapt over the motionless form, hurtling toward the cave with shocking speed.

Bertisha turned finally, gaping into the unnatural tunnel, jabbering inarticulately in fury and fear, and the hound picked that moment to spring. The animal smashed into the burly woman's back, driving her to her hands and knees. Growling with frightening savagery, the dog's fanged jaws closed toward the back of her neck.

I winced, expecting a gout of blood, but instead the snapping fangs severed the leather thong tied around the obese throat without so much as breaking Bertisha's skin. The piece of black stick clattered across the floor as the monstrous woman shrieked in rage, spinning on the floor, raising her club against the snarling dog.

The hound pounced away, crouching before me, facing the gaping, lighted opening in the wall of the cave. I rose to my feet, still moving like thick molasses, instinctively groping toward the thong and stick that lay a few feet away.

"Pap! Look out!" cried Badswell, charging toward Oakgnar as the ogre pitched more stones into the magical tunnel. Another spider-wolf went down, but the next one pounced forward, slavering jaws striking toward the bull ogre's face. Oakgnar tumbled to the floor, grappling the creature with his powerful arms, but when those wolflike jaws ripped into his cheek, the ogre bellowed in unworldly pain.

Oakgnar's back arched reflexively, his eyes all but bulging from his face. Drool spattered unnoticed down the ogre's cheeks as the venomous bite stung him, sending almost visible rivers of agony through his convulsing body. In another moment, he lay utterly still, and the spider ripped into him with cruel fangs.

Bertisha shrilled unspeakable rage, hurling herself at the murderous monster. With a blow of her massive club, she drove the spider-wolf to the ground, then crushed its skull with a single bash of her fist. More of the hideous beasts crowded through the opening, howling, snarling, and yelping, but for a moment, the berserk female held them at bay, slashing the heavy club back and forth like a cavalier wielding a feather-light rapier.

My hand finally fastened around the thong attached to the black stick, and I pulled it up with agonizing slowness. Jamming it into my tunic, I turned toward the mouth of the cave, taking one plodding footstep after another. I heard the hound barking behind me and knew that she had joined the fray.

Bads raised a club of his own, bashing the monsters away from Oakgnar's ravaged body, his half-ogre face filled with agony. Tears brimmed from his eyes as he looked toward his mother. Bertisha dropped another of the spider-beasts but was forced to take a step backward, allowing more of the monsters to spill into the cave.

"Take them—seize them!" growled one of the monsters in a surprisingly clear voice. The command, with its deliberate enunciation, chilled me as much as the appearance of the savage creatures. The speaker had a pair of gruesome arms, covered with bristling hairs, growing from its shoulders. One of those limbs gestured, pointing directly at me.

"Come on—*run!*" I urged, my voice as thick and slow as my body. Badswell shook his head, and at that moment, his mother screamed in pain. Looking back, I saw two of the spider-wolves shoot tendrils of sticky web, erupting from the bloated abdomens, spiraling outward to encircle the ogre-wife's feet. As she tumbled backward, the monsters leapt upon her massive body, their cruel fangs tearing into her flesh.

At the same moment, I stumbled headlong toward the door, as if I had been leaning against a door that had suddenly swung out of the way. My feet kicked free, and I knew that the slow spell had passed. Sprinting toward the cave mouth, still clutching Bertisha's stub of black stick, I cast a backward glance at Badswell, silently pleading for him to follow.

The hound barked savagely, leaping at the nearest spider-beast, driving the thing to the ground and sinking long teeth into its lupine neck. With a crushing bite, the hound twisted its head, and I heard the snap of bone as the monster fell dead. Silently the dog raced toward me, with Badswell lumbering hastily behind her.

Several spider-wolves milled around inside the supernatural doorway, growling, worrying the bodies of Badswell's Mum and Pap. With a gesture of its hairy arm,

115

the monster that had spoken in that clear voice gestured toward us and repeated its command.

"There they are, my kakkuu! Take them!"

Immediately the howls and yelps rose into the cacophony of the hunt, the spider-wolves lunging toward the cavern mouth in response to their leader's cry. I saw a single chance to save ourselves from the creatures.

"Here—knock one of these down!" I panted, hurling myself against one of the pillars beneath the massive granite lintel.

Fortunately Badswell got the idea and swung the big club against the sturdy column. Stones and dust crumbled down on us, but the support remained intact. The half-ogre tossed the club to the ground and lunged at the post, driving his shoulder into the solid block of stone.

I dived through the cave mouth and skidded onto the ground, turning around to watch, silently urging the big fellow on as a trio of wolf-spiders scrambled toward him, bloody jaws gaping hungrily.

Then boulders began to tumble free, bouncing beside Badswell, and a split second later the pillar of stone toppled outward. The half-ogre lunged backward as tons of rock smashed into the entrance of the cave, crushing the deadly attackers. More chunks broke free, tumbling with ground-shaking force, sending a great cloud of dust billowing into the air and completely concealing the entrance from our taut observation.

Yet we both sensed that there was no purpose in further flight. If the cave-in failed to seal off the ogre lair, we might as well die right here as in the trackless woods of the ravine. The hound stood between us, panting, ears upraised as she, too, studied the wreckage, waiting for the dust to settle.

In seconds, the collapse had ceased rumbling, and the billowing cloud began to thin. I finally got a good look, enough to insure that no passage remained. Taking only a moment to confirm that observation, I turned toward the woods and hurtled myself down the steep slope into the ravine. The hound, ears flopping, bounded after me, while Badswell picked his way, more slowly, behind us.

Skidding down to the bottom of the gully wall, I scrambled onto a log and jogged away. In the full sweep of darkness, the forest was ominously still around us.

Finally, minutes later, we paused to catch our breath, straining to listen over the sounds of our own gasps for any sounds of pursuit. Behind us, the night echoed nothing more than a growing circle of grim, ominous silence.

CHAPTER 9

TRAVELING COMPANIONS

Dawn found Badswell and me in the depths of track-less wilderness, blundering wearily along. We had left the gorge hours ago, making our way across a thickly wooded forest floor. Warm air sifted through the ancient trunks, carrying a hint of moistness and decay. Or perhaps the stench was just a result of my mood.

Finally, exhausted, we collapsed amid a grotto of lichen-encrusted boulders, sipping water from a clear spring that bubbled up from the ground. I caught my breath and allowed my heartbeat to slowly settle, strain-ing once again to listen. Now, at least, birds chirped in the overhanging greenery, heralding the arrival of day as they had each dawn for countless centuries. Their music offered no balm to my pain, but the song eased my fears slightly. I felt certain that if any of the hideous spider-wolves had been nearby, the birds would be unlikely to make the slightest peep.

"Mum and Pap—d'you think they're kilt?" asked Bads miserably, turning his dark eyes toward me. Water from the spring drooled across his protruding chin, and he carelessly wiped it away, shifting his gaze back to the direction from which we'd come.

"I'm afraid so," I said, surprisingly saddened by the acknowledgment. Bertisha had been a hateful creature, but it was hard to feel that even one such as she deserved that horrid fate. Furthermore, Oakgnar, I now felt certain, had paid many times over for his crime of kidnapping the human woman.

"What was those things?"

"I . . . I don't know," I admitted. "I saw them once before. . . ." Memories of Oakvale's plaza, of a bloodstained shred of green silk, overcame my efforts to speak.

"And that dog—you called her like she was yours."

"Not mine . . . but I saw her before, when the monsters attacked me for the first time." With that thought, I whirled around, looking for the floppy-eared hound that had fought so bravely. The animal had padded after us as we plunged through the woods, but now there was no sign of her.

"Must've wandered off," Badswell concluded. "Too bad. She was a good dog."

"The best," I agreed fervently, wishing I had been more alert as to the hound's presence. Still, it wasn't as though I would have tied a leash around her neck. The dog was free to come and go as she pleased.

I was struck by another thought. Pulling the chip of wood and broken thong from my tunic, I extended it toward Badswell. He took it as I removed my own piece of stick from my belt pouch. "I'm afraid those monsters have something to do with this—or *these*."

Indeed, it seemed almost certain as I looked at them together that the two pieces of wood were in fact part of the same longer shaft. "Where did your mother get that?"

"I dunno. I guess she found it in the cave jist a few days back—asked me if I brung it there, then thumped me when I told her I hadn't."

He looked at me, a plea for understanding in his guile-less face. "But it was the *truth!*" he insisted. "Me an' Pap din't know how she come to get it, but there it was. She even used it to slow me down so she could catch me and whup me."

His eyes misted, and he looked at me, speaking through a choking voice. "What am I goin' to do now?"

I shuddered, remembering my early intention of rescu-ing the hapless human woman from the clutches of the brutish ogre. Still, though Bertisha might not have been much of a mother, she was the only 'Mum' Bads had ever known, and it grieved me to see his agony.

"You can come with me," I said, without even thinking of the future ramifications. "At least, till I get . . ." My words trailed off.

"Where's you goin'?"

"Well, to tell you the truth, I don't know."

"What was you doin' when you come along to find me yesterday?"

Good question, I thought, but then I remembered the answer. "It's that stick of your mother's, I think. The one that I'm carrying seemed to be attracted to it somehow. At least, it made *me* attracted to it. I sensed where it was and had a general idea of going that way."

"They're the same color, huh?" Bads squinted at his chip of ebony, then looked at the piece I held.

"Yup. And these patterns here—see the way they're

carved? Like some kind of matching puzzle piece." I had a sudden idea. "Let me have that one for a moment. I want to see if they fit together."

Bads looked strangely reluctant, holding the piece next to his chest as if he thought I'd snatch it away from him. At first I was irritated at his distrust, but then I realized that the ebony talisman was probably the only memento he had of his mother.

"I promise I'll give it right back," I pledged seriously.

"Well . . . okay."

He handed me the piece and I looked at it closely. As I had earlier observed, it was slightly longer than my own and perceptibly thicker toward one end. Taking one segment in each hand, I raised them before my face, trying to determine which end of Badswell's stick seemed the best match for my own. I brought them toward each other—and the larger piece abruptly vanished from my grip.

"Where'd it go?" demanded the half-ogre, glowering with barely contained anger.

"I—I don't know!" I stammered. "It just . . . went away! It simply vanished!"

"You took it!" The anger in Badswell's voice took on a generous hint of menace.

"No!" I declared forcefully. I was shaken by the abrupt disappearance, but my mind raced for an explanation. The fact that my companion could have squashed me like a bug if he decided to do so was something I had to factor into my hypothesis.

"We already know these are magic sticks," I told him. "Mine heals; yours causes that slow spell. There's some kind of other enchantment that took effect as soon as I brought them close together. One of them just disappeared!"

"Not 'one of them,' " Bads retorted with distressingly effective logic. "*Mine* disappeared."

"Look," I said, forcing myself to remain calm, "you can search me if you think I took it. But we're *partners*, Bads. I wouldn't cheat you or lie to you!"

It was the truth, too, though I realized with a trace of guilt and chagrin that I had cheated and lied to other partners before, without a noticeable twinge of conscience. Yet now, somehow, I had changed. I only hoped that Badswell could be made to see that.

Despite his dim-witted appearance, the half-ogre seemed to grasp that fact. He stared at me, still scowling, then nodded slowly.

"How will you get it back?" he demanded, shattering my illusions as to his understanding.

"How should I know?" I shot back. "I tried to tell you—it just disappeared!"

"You said that little piece helped you know where my Mum's piece was before. Why won't it do it again?"

I was about to make another sharp retort when I realized what he was saying and immediately regretted my assessment of my companion as 'dim-witted.' He had perceived something that I had been too agitated to understand.

"Let's see if it'll do the same thing again," I declared, suddenly very hopeful. Indeed, it seemed terribly important, somehow, that we find the other piece of the stick, if only to improve Badswell's mood.

I stood up in the little grotto and started to walk in the direction we'd previously been traveling. Immediately I felt that I was making a mistake, and veered my course toward the right. By the time I'd climbed out of the rock-lined depression, I had turned ninety degrees off our previous route and found myself starting down a long, gradual slope.

"I can't be sure," I said, trying to contain my excitement. "But I think it's somewhere in this direction."

"Let's go." Badswell lumbered to his feet, then paused and scowled at me. "Wait—I'll take yer stick till we get mine back."

Panic surged at the thought of losing the little chip of ebony. "Why?" I asked, stalling for an excuse to change his mind. I wanted desperately to hold on to my piece.

"Make sure you gets me mine, all right?"

"Well, I can't find yours unless I carry mine—right? I promise I'll stay close to you. I won't go away."

I was telling the truth, though once again I wasn't entirely sure why I did so. Perhaps I felt somewhat responsible for the big lug. In any event, I had no intention of abandoning Badswell to his fate.

The half-ogre thought for a second, but apparently he believed me. "Okay," he agreed, and he followed me from the clump of rocks. We walked side by side as we started to make our way along the forest floor.

The gradual descent of the ground held firm. As we walked through the day, I sensed the moistness of the air against my face, smelled the growing stench of stagnant water. At the same time, I felt utterly certain that we were going in the right direction—that my piece of ebony did, in fact, convey the course to the stub Bertisha had owned.

We had passed into an open woodland, and fortunately the walking was easy. The ground at the base of the trees remained grassy and smooth, the grade too gentle to require much attention. As we strolled along, I groped for an explanation of these peculiar ebony-black segments.

More to the point, I began to guess that the two chips were in fact parts of the same magical device. It had somehow been snapped in two, and the strange geometric patterns had been inscribed as a means of showing how it linked together.

Another thought occurred to me: Since the larger of the two pieces had been carved at both ends, perhaps the original device even continued into a third piece. This made sense, at least when I considered past experiences. During the course of my adventures, I had encountered a variety of magical wands and staffs, and even the smallest had been bigger than our two pieces of ebony placed together.

My mind turned toward the grotesque spider-beasts that had twice attacked me. Those things were a worry, to be sure, and with that thought, I swiveled my head, peering into the woods on both sides and behind us, momentarily fearful that another one of those white tunnels might open up.

"Whoops!" declared Badswell, abruptly grabbing me by the collar.

"Hey! What's the big—" I started to object, then looked down and realized that, lost in my musings, I'd been about to step off the lip of a steep precipice that suddenly yawned in the forest floor. The cliff dropped into a deep gorge, with an opposite face of rock rising to our level about thirty feet away. Down below—far, *far* below—I saw a tangle of jagged rocks lining the bottom of the chasm.

"Um, thanks," I murmured, shuddering at the vision of the fatal fall I had so narrowly avoided.

"Anyone kin fall down," he said with a grim chuckle, pointing to the leg I had healed for him yesterday. "Just try not to drop so far."

"Right," I agreed, still shaken by the narrow escape. Still, it was good to see some sign of humor from the big half-ogre; I was glad to see that he might break out of the bleak mood that had taken him since our flight from his home.

"We got to go that way?" He cocked a quizzical eyebrow at the far side of the gorge.

Following his gaze, I saw that the chasm extended as far as we could see in either direction. At the same time, my sense of direction, as strong as ever, indicated that we had to get to the other side.

"Yup. We've got to keep going."

"How we gettin' across?" wondered Badswell.

My eyes fell upon a nearby tree trunk, fallen amidst the living trees sprouting from the forest floor. The timber was dry, but when I walked over and kicked it, it proved solid and unrotted. Furthermore it was fairly straight, and at least forty feet long.

"D'you think you can move this?" I asked, somewhat skeptically.

"Sure. Want me to throw it into gorge?" Badswell was agreeable if, once again, somewhat dim.

"How about stretching it *across* the gorge—you know, like a bridge?"

His face lit up and he nodded, regarding me with an expression of deep respect. "That's a good idea!" he declared heartily.

I tried to help, but as the half-ogre reached down and hoisted the log, I had to duck to avoid getting knocked into the chasm. The most useful thing to do, I realized, was to get well out of the way and stay there. Badswell hoisted the heavy timber off the ground, swinging it about, positioning the trunk with the narrow end extending over the chasm. Stepping sideways to the very brink of the precipice, he heaved the log with a grunt, and the end came to rest on the far side. With a few rocking motions of his powerful hands, he set the trunk firmly in place.

"That's the fastest bridge-building I've ever seen," I acknowledged, impressed.

"We cross now, hey?"

"Yes . . . but one at a time, perhaps?"

Badswell was agreeable, so I started across, balancing by extending my arms, carefully stepping around the occasional stubs that jutted upward from the beam. Fortunately the half-ogre had placed his makeshift bridge with care, and it didn't even rock or wiggle underneath me.

Waiting until I had safely reached the far side, Bads started across. The log sagged alarmingly under his weight, but once again showed no signs of dislodging, and in moments he had joined me.

As we turned to continue through the woods, I reflected on the display of strength I had just witnessed. Even Benton, the strapping barbarian warrior, would have seemed a weakling beside the brawny half-ogre. Not only was he strong, but Badswell had displayed remarkably good balance as he followed me across the gorge. Now his round face and its double-tusked mouth was creased by the traces of that smile he'd shown moments earlier. The tips of his lower tusks barely showed as he looked back at his handiwork, then turned to regard the woods before us.

"This way?" he wondered.

"Sure enough," I agreed, falling easily into step beside him.

By late afternoon, the fatigue of our nightlong flight caught up with us, and by mutual consent, we looked for a place to camp. I found a bower of grassy turf in the midst of a dense grove of evergreens, and Badswell displayed a new skill as he quickly built us a small smokeless fire. While my half-ogre friend gathered some wild tubers, garlic, and mushrooms, I visited a nearby stream and, with neither net nor hook, soon returned with several plump trout.

"Betcha tickled 'em, like my pap taught me," Badswell guessed, his eyes growing misty at the memory of Oakgnar. "Ya just reaches yer hand in and grabs 'em by the belly. They pops right out."

Acknowledging his correct guess, I started to clean the fish.

"Did yer pap teach you how ta tickle fish?"

"Yes . . . I guess so," I admitted.

"Where is yer pap?"

I sighed, realizing that the half-ogre was in the mood to pry. "He died, back when I was just a youth. My mother, too. There was a bad disease that came through Colbytown. It took many of the older folks."

"Colbytown, huh?"

"Yup. That's where I lived, until I couldn't stand it anymore." All of the reasons that I had left that little town came back to me: the boring predictability of life there, the lack of excitement, the peace and quiet that seemed as if it would suffocate me by the time I reached adulthood. It's funny, but none of those things seemed that bad now that I recalled them from the rude comforts of this wilderness camp.

An hour later, as sunset painted the sky in lavender and rose, we devoured a delicious meal of roasted trout flavored with mushrooms and wild garlic. As the first stars popped into view, I laid my head on the makeshift pillow of my boots and spare cloak. I thought of Saysi. I missed her a lot, but for the first time since her loss, I had at least a small sense of hope and purpose about the future. We would find Badswell's piece of the black shaft, and it felt good to know that I was doing something for a friend.

I found my thoughts returning to the mysterious hound. Before bed, I had left out a little of the fish from our dinner in an effort to draw her to our camp. After all, I reasoned that the animal must be somewhere in the woods.

Yet there was no sign of that loose, wrinkled pelt, and even when I called "Hound—come here, girl," a few times, nothing rustled in the trees. I missed those mournful eyes more than I thought possible, and before I drifted off to sleep I offered a silent prayer to Patrikon, hoping that our former canine companion was safe somewhere.

CHAPTER 10

THE VASTEST BOG

For three days we made our way through the wilderness, following a gradually descending slope that, not infrequently, rose to block us with steep ridges or bluffs. In these places, we scrambled up and over precipitous hills and crests, but thankfully the heights became less frequent with every mile's advance in our steady, relentless march. With each mile, it seemed that we were getting steadily lower, descending from the highland wilderness into a part of the world I had never visited before. The air became thick, moist, and pungent with the taint of decay.

The lofty trees of the highlands gave way to patches of scrub pine and buckthorn, through which we pressed against needlelike prickers and spiny thorns. Fortunately these thickets were interspersed with broad, grassy meadows, open swaths that allowed us to make up for time lost in the passages of tangled undergrowth.

Furthermore, the generally descending grade also helped us to make good time.

Badswell never let me out of his sight, or indeed out of the reach of his long arms. He wasn't belligerent or bullying, though, and seemed quite content to follow my directions regarding the missing piece of stick.

I remained nervous about the eight-legged attackers, remembering in particular the beast with the hairy, bristling arms sprouting from its shoulders. Whenever I closed my eyes, I saw that snarling wolf face and heard the clearly articulated words spoken by the monster. When I looked around again, the day seemed colder and more oppressive, a feeling brought on by the vivid and unpleasant memory.

Finally the forest and the descending ground ended at the edge of a broad, brownish-green marsh. The flat expanse of wetland extended to the far horizon, and probably for miles beyond. The odor of rotting vegetation had teased our nostrils for the last several days, growing stronger by the mile. Now we saw the source amid intense wafts of swamp gas, and it was not an encouraging sight.

"You sure we got to go there?" wondered Badswell, his sloping brow creased by a scowl of concern.

My own instinct, guided by the chip of ebony, was to march right into the swamp. "Yup," I replied resignedly. "At least, if we want to find the other piece. I'm pretty sure it's out there somewhere."

"Pap told me about a place around here called the Vastest Bog. D'you think this is it?"

"It sure could be," I replied, my heart sinking at the appellation.

"Mebbe my stick's on the other side," speculated the half-ogre.

The flat, soggy terrain extended to the right and left as far as I could see, and to the limits of the horizon before us. Patches of open water were covered with green algae or dense lilies, while numerous thickets of reeds or mangroves clumped here and there on the flat surface. Whether this marsh led to a sea or lake, or rose again into high, dry ground at the far side was a mystery. Still, to judge by the view to each side, the prospects of successfully finding a route around it were very poor.

"Could be, but I'm afraid not. I can't tell how close we are to your piece of the stick, but there's no way to say that we'd have any luck trying to find a way around."

"Let's go then," Bads declared, with a shrug of resignation. He took a step forward and sank to the knee in gooey muck. Laboring to free his foot, he pushed forward for several steps while I watched in dismay. When my companion looked over his shoulder at me, his own concern became apparent.

"Too deep for you," he realized.

"It'd be up to my neck," I agreed dejectedly, trying to imagine the work involved to travel even a hundred steps through this morass, not to mention the miles that we might have to traverse.

"C'mere—I'll carry you." Badswell extended his arms, taking a step closer to shore, and I reached out and allowed him to hoist me up to his broad shoulders. With no more effort than I might use to lift a baby halfling, he settled me with my legs straddling his thick neck before turning back to the stretch of swampland.

Grabbing the fringe of his bearskin tunic, I struggled to hang on, surprised at the speed with which Bads negotiated the dank, soggy terrain. Tirelessly he lifted his feet from the mud, plopping a heavy boot before him and then lurching slightly to pull the other foot free. He rocked back and forth, almost staggering, drawing breaths in great, snorting gulps of air, then bulling forward as if the swamp represented a personal affront to his pride.

After a few hundred yards, he reached a stretch of more solid ground—a sandbar, covered by a few inches of stagnant water, but firm and unyielding beneath his feet. The solid bed extended in the same direction as our course of travel, so for a few minutes the big half-ogre padded along more quickly, splashing his boots easily with each step. Soon, however, the sandbar petered out, and Badswell once again slogged into the muck. Clumps of brush and reeds jutted upward in frequent clusters, and we made minor adjustments to go around these, all the while maintaining our direction into the midst of the stagnant flat.

Once I cast a glance over my shoulder, seeing that the forested slope of dry land had receded surprisingly far to the rear. Our trail was for the most part indistinguishable, though in a few places, broken bushes or a wedge of flattened reeds showed where Badswell had forced his way through.

I listened for the sounds of birds, thinking that such creatures—ospreys, gulls, or terns, perhaps—would flourish in such a marsh. Strangely, there was no audible sign of these feathered denizens. Nor, when I looked into the sky, did I see any sign of vultures or birds of prey soaring in the lofty heights.

Perhaps there was nothing for them to eat here, I speculated. Yet it seemed hard to believe that no frogs, muskrats, fish, or snakes dwelt amid the reeds and brush. The lack of animal life began to weigh upon me, an absence that was oppressive in the extent of its void.

Finally Badswell drew closer to a rounded hummock of terrain, a muddy, thicket-covered spot that was not a hill by any stretch of the imagination. Still, it domed slightly above the surface of the stagnant water, and that at least was a relief. Gratefully I let go of the half-ogre's tunic and slid down his broad back to come to rest on dry ground once again.

"This hump might not last so long," Bads warned, indicating the surrounding stretch of marshland.

"I can always climb up again," I said, stretching my cramped legs. "But I think both of us can use a little break."

"Yer not heavy," he said with a shrug, dropping down to his haunches so that I could climb back aboard if I wanted to.

I was about to reply—something about trying to straighten my permanently twisted legs—when an instinctive sense of fear jolted through me. Badswell, too, widened his eyes in alarm and started to rise.

"Hide!" I hissed, seizing his thick forearm and tugging sharply downward.

Bads reacted with encouraging agility, throwing himself flat on the ground as I crouched amid a thick cluster of cattails. Every nerve in my body jangled with terror, though I still saw nothing dangerous.

Before our eyes detected any sign of danger, we heard a steady splashing of water, as if the muck were being parted by a large object. I wondered at first if the sound might mark the approach of a boat, but the noise seemed too irregular, more like a monstrous swimmer stroking with fins or powerful arms. Small waves sloshed through the reeds, washing onto the shore of our little island, and I knew that a large presence pushed through the mire, not terribly far away.

Gingerly I reached out and separated a few of the reeds, then tried vainly to bite back a gasp of apprehension. A snakelike neck of inky black, topped by a scaly, reptilian head, jutted from the swamp a mere stone's throw from our island. Crimson eyes, wickedly cruel and evil, glittered coldly from the lofty face, and I sensed that a massive, unseen body surged beneath the surface, driving the monster forward with relentless power.

The beast approached us at an oblique angle, reaching the island just a short distance off to the side. Two mighty forelegs emerged from the stagnant muck, and I saw feet, studded with hooked talons, leathery webbing connecting the toes, seize the firmament and easily pull the rest of the immense serpentine body from the mire.

The creature advanced smoothly and with supple grace, but it still took that sinuous form a long time to emerge. I saw slime-slicked wings tucked against narrow flanks, rear legs even larger and more powerful than the fore, and a long, snakelike tail. The whole body, except where it was coated with lime-green algae or tendrils of muddy seaweed, was black, as pure and lightless as solid obsidian.

My experience with the great wyrms of any kind or color was admittedly limited. Once or twice I had fled, panic-stricken, from the distant presence of a mighty dragon of red or green, without getting—or desiring—a real good, up-close look at the creature. Still, the resemblance between the serpents of different colors was significant, and from the leathery, folded wings and long, supple neck to the trailing and snakelike tail, it was impossible to mistake this creature for anything else. Though I had never seen its like before, I recognized the monster as a black dragon.

Casting a look at Bads, I was impressed to see that, though he remained pressed to the ground, his head was up and his eyes followed the dragon's advance with no sign of panic.

The ground of the island shuddered underfoot as the monster shook itself, casting a rain of stagnant water and algae through the underbrush. Neither Bads nor I made any move to wipe ourselves off as the misty drizzle showered us with goo. Timber crashed and snapped as the huge body pushed its way through the thicket, and as the tip of the serpentine tail vanished from view, I realized that I'd been holding my breath.

"Black dragon," Bads declared, nodding his head as if a mental picture had been confirmed by reality.

Mutely I nodded. My limbs shook, and I felt a twinge of nausea. Still, I was pathetically grateful that the monster had passed us by without taking note of our position. Carefully I rose from my crouch, trying to stem the trembling in my arms and legs.

Then an even more chilling knowledge hit me with the force of a thunderclap: The dragon had disappeared in the same direction as Bads and I had been traveling. Even without reaching a conscious conclusion, I had the sickening sensation that the second piece of the ebony stick and the black dragon's destination were indisputably entwined.

"We follows him, right?" Bads whispered, as if he had sensed my own suspicion, but without the apprehension that accompanied my thoughts. Indeed, for the first time, I seriously considered turning around and forgetting about the stupid piece of magical wood.

Of course, it was Badswell's segment that we were

after. "Yes," I agreed, rising to a sense of duty that had never propelled me before.

My affirmative reply contradicted my fears, and I didn't really know why. Perhaps Badswell's own courage shamed me into agreeing to continue our quest. More likely, it was that strange sense of purpose, of the *rightness* of our mission, that compelled me to continue.

Creeping cautiously, we moved through the undergrowth on the low island. In places, water pooled between the trunks of the small trees or turned a flat place into a sticky mess of mire. Fortunately, because of the trampled underbrush, the dragon's trail was easy to follow. Furthermore, the beaten state of the greenery served to muffle any sounds that our passage otherwise would have made.

In a short time, we came to a place where a wide swath had been cleared. Obviously the dragon traveled here a lot, for the gap was just the right width to accommodate its bulk. A reptilian stench lingered in the air, nearly gagging me, as we tiptoed gingerly along the edge of this path. The center of the well-used route was wide and clear of obstruction, but also thoroughly muddy. Though neither Bads nor I felt in any way fastidious, we were both leery of walking somewhere where our tracks could be so easily observed.

Instead, we skulked along the edge of the dragon's walkway, probing through strangely still woods, looking for any sign of ambush or trap. Though the trees were scrubby and small, they nevertheless arched high enough to meet over our heads, casting this wide path in perpetual shadow and no doubt concentrating the acrid stink of the black dragon.

After about ten minutes, the pathway spilled into a

wide clearing, surrounded on all sides by tangled trees draped with moss and vines. The open area was itself a mass of thornbushes and burdock gathered around a small hill that domed upward to a low crest in the center of the gap. Still following the fringe of the dragon's walkway, we tried to avoid the thorns as much as possible, creeping cautiously to the foot of the gently sloping rise.

Dropping to our bellies, we wormed across the mucky ground, inch by inch drawing closer to the rounded crest. At the top, we discovered a circular opening leading straight down into the ground. Square stones, like monstrous bricks, surrounded the opening, apparently as prevention against erosion. The pit plunged into utter blackness, a lightless shaft into the heart of the swamp. The sides were black, moist dirt, with roots and vines dangling from the earthen embankment. A few of these trailed for a long distance downward, vanishing into the dark, while a smell of rich soil, tainted by that familiar, unmistakably reptilian stench of decay, rose from the hole.

I was not surprised to learn that the dragon had gone underground, but the fact nevertheless proved considerably disheartening. Once again I briefly thought about abandoning our mission, but Badswell knelt boldly at the edge of the hole and peered inside.

"We kin climb down," he said. "Vines like ropes hangin' all over in there."

"Great." My reply was spoken without enthusiasm, but Bads seemed to take no notice of my reluctance. The half-ogre turned his back to the hole and, without hesitation, dropped to his belly and slid his feet over the edge. Cautiously he lowered himself, seizing several of the vines and supporting his not inconsiderable weight as he eased himself down the side.

One of the ropelike tendrils slipped in a cascade of dirt, and I gasped, holding my breath in apprehension as Badswell reached out and grasped another vine. In seconds, his grip was secure, and he continued downward until he was swallowed by the shadows.

I realized that, for the first time since leaving his home, Badswell had let me get well out of his reach and his sight. Still, I gave no thought to abandoning the big fellow. Instead, muttering reluctant questions under my breath, I found a sturdy vine and began to lower myself after him. My bare feet slipped along the muddy sides of the pit, and the circle of sky grew ever smaller as I descended.

Shortly we stood together on the muddy ground at the base of the deep, sheer-sided pit. Dim light filtered downward from the sky, and I could make out a pair of looming apertures, black holes of stagnant darkness, leading in different directions into the lair.

Badswell sniffed cautiously, his broad snout testing the dank air. "Dragon went that way," he concluded, pointing to one of the two tunnels.

I touched the chip of ebony and my spirits brightened, at least a little. The compulsion was as strong as ever, and for once, it didn't seem to lead straight to disaster. "We should go down *that* one," I replied, indicating the other tunnel, stepping forward with a display of fearlessness.

Shadows cloaked the damp, muddy corridor, closing like flowing ink across walls and ceiling and floor. My bare feet padded softly against moist dirt, and I sensed the breadth of the passageway extending far to either side. Perhaps the dragon wouldn't be able to fully spread its wings in here, but it would otherwise have no difficulty in the large passageway.

Soon the darkness was so complete that I couldn't see my hand in front of my face. I hesitated, but Badswell touched me on the shoulder, steering me with a steady hand. "I kin see a bit," he whispered.

We passed around a long, gradual curve. I felt pressure against my toes and sensed that we were descending a very gentle slope. Shuddering, I reflected that each step took us farther and farther away from the air and marsh above. The Vastest Bog might not have been a paradise, but it was a pastoral picnic ground by comparison to this lightless lair.

In the absence of illumination, other senses took over. Most notably, my nostrils seemed to become exceptionally keen. The moist, stagnant air seemed to stroke my skin, probing into every recess of my lungs. The reptilian stench of the dragon remained pervasive, but now it was masked by a more vile and steadily growing presence. It might have been rotting flesh or offal; whatever caused the stink was a physical force that seemed to drag me down with each step. Eyes watering, blinded by the stink as much as by darkness, I groped relentlessly forward. Despite the noxious surroundings, there was no reduction in my compulsion to find the missing piece of stick.

Abruptly I could see again, and I realized that we had come around another curve in the depths of the black dragon's lair. Drooping wedges of fungus grew, mosslike, from the walls of a wide circular chamber. The lichen glowed with a natural phosphorescence, light enough to barely part the stygian shadows. Water trickled down the walls of this dank cavern, gathering in a shapeless puddle of muck in the center of the circular floor. My eyes detected more subtleties of the greenish light, and I realized that the passageway we followed continued onward. The circular chamber was a side cavern, with no other entrance visible.

I started past the diverging entrance, but felt a tug of mental resistance. Badswell, his hand still on my shoulder, felt my hesitation.

"In here?" he asked, skeptically eyeing the stinking chamber and its puddle of nameless goo.

"I—I'm not sure," I said. In fact, for the first time since starting out, I felt confusion over which way to go. Part of me wanted to continue on, but there was something compelling about this dank and oppressive room. "Maybe I'd better have a look."

The half-ogre's hand lifted from my shoulder, but I took comfort from knowing that he held his heavy club ready behind me.

Hesitantly I advanced, now feeling—and fighting—a strange compulsion to hasten into the room. The murky liquid in its dark pool was singularly uninviting, but I couldn't bring myself to turn away.

Something odd disturbed the surface of that brown muck, a circular spot distinctly brighter than the surrounding ooze. The strange sight drew me like a moth to a lantern, calling me on a level I found impossible to resist. This was not a segment of black stick, but still it was something that pulled me closer, luring me . . . *wanting* me.

A thrashing movement drove me back before I even registered the danger. Slashing past my face, a blunt tentacle smashed into my shoulder, knocking me to the side. I tried to twist away, but the gummy tendril clutched my upper arm with a deathly grip, pulling me down helplessly. I splashed into the murk and felt the soupy liquid closing over my head, but even in my frantic terror, I couldn't break the iron grip that threatened to drown me.

My lungs burned as I squirmed in the forceful clasp, inexorably drawn toward the center of the pool. Still underwater, I kicked and thrashed and punched, but the powerful tentacle only squeezed me harder.

Something seized my bare foot, tugging hard, and with that twisting grab, I came free, spluttering to the surface to see that Badswell had waded into the gooey mess. The half-ogre, holding me upside down, lifted me free of the pool and then tossed me to the shore as a hulking monster flailed closer.

Gulguthra! Although I had never encountered one of the dung-eating horrors, the beast's reputation was well known to every adventurer. I saw the distinctly circular mouth with its ring of wicked teeth, the two powerful tentacles thrashing outward from the bony shoulders.

Now those ropelike tendrils had fastened around Badswell. The big fellow planted his feet, but still the monster pulled him steadily closer. Two round, luminous eyes gaped soullessly from the blunt body above that horrific maw.

"Bads! No!" I cried, splashing into the pool, hacking Goldfinder into one of the ropey strands. The gulguthra merely bashed me aside with a powerful blow. Once again brown water closed over my head and, choking and retching, I scrambled toward the shore.

I lurched to my feet, sobbing and cursing, watching as Badswell's club was plucked from his fist by the return swipe of the slapping tentacle.

The half-ogre rolled out of sight, buried by the bulbous, three-footed shape of the dung-eater. Two mighty fists rose from the scummy liquid, bashing against the monster but growing weaker with each blow. The blunt face remained underwater, the big body pressed down by the even greater bulk of the bony-shelled dung-eater.

"Badswell, you can't die!" I cried shrilly, leaping onto the back of the grotesque monster. Repeatedly I stabbed my blade through that chitinous shell, driving steel deep into the vile innards. I lost track of how many blows I had struck, but some moments later I realized that I was the only one moving in this dim chamber. The gulguthra, slain, lay still in the midst of spreading gore. More frighteningly, the only sign of the half-ogre was a limp fist lying alongside the dung-eater's body.

I seized that hand and pulled, my eyes blinded by tears, my small body infused with desperate strength.

"Come *on!*" I cried, my voice choking. I pulled again, knowing this was the most important thing I had ever done. Too many friends, too many loyal companions, had fallen beside me through the years, and I knew that I couldn't let that happen again.

Slowly the big body came free, the corpse of the gulguthra rolling to the side, settling into the nameless murk of the pool. I waded around Badswell's shoulders, reaching down, seizing his head to lift it free from the liquid. Bubbles frothed from his lips as he choked out a cough.

Those big, sad eyes remained closed. Frantically I pulled, until the half-ogre's head and torso were free of the pool. His chest rose and fell raggedly, each breath accompanied by a bubbling gurgle.

My fingers found the stick of healing in my pouch, and I held the chip to Badswell's mouth, pleading and crying, praying to Patrikon and begging for my friend's health to be restored.

Finally he coughed explosively, spewing liquid over me, and I laughed out loud.

"Get up!" I cried. "You're going to be all right! Come on, Badswell, sit up! It's me, Kip!"

Fear for the half-ogre set my heart to pounding painfully. As I worked my hands up and down on his chest, I was surprised to realize how much I'd come to care for the big galoot. I offered up another prayer to Patrikon, pleading with Saysi's deity for whatever protection and comfort he could offer my oversized friend.

Gradually I felt the half-ogre's awareness return. With a soft sigh, Bads pushed himself to a sitting position. "Lots better," he declared quietly.

"I—I was terrif—" I tried to talk, my words choked off by uncharacteristic emotion. "I'm—I'm glad you're okay."

The half-ogre touched me, very gently, on the shoulder. "Where's my club?" Shaking his head groggily, he lumbered back into the pool of muck, feeling around until he lifted the heavy, knobbed stick from the mud. "Got it."

"D'you think you can walk?" I began to have a strong feeling that we shouldn't waste time. Without speaking, Badswell nodded and pushed himself slowly to his feet.

"Which way?" wondered my companion.

Still holding the piece of stick, I turned toward the dark tunnel leading deeper into the lair. The sense was undeniable now. Somewhere in there we would find the missing piece of ebony. Wet muck slurped under our feet as we started ahead. Without success, we tried to muffle the sounds of our passage, but even when we moved against the wall of the cavern, the ground was soft and sloppily yielding.

A sudden sound rustled through the dank tunnel from the opposite wall. I froze in panic, until a gentle whine settled my fears.

"It's the hound," I whispered, delighted to see the animal, then immediately puzzled as to how she could have gotten down here. The sheer shaft was far too steep for any dog to climb down. For that matter, I had to wonder how she had followed us through the swamp.

Bads, too, stiffened and then relaxed beside me. He reached down and patted the dog on the head. "Good girl. But why you come here now?"

Abruptly I knew the answer, understood what the dog's presence meant—the same fact heralded by her last two appearances.

"It's a warning! More of those spider-wolves must be coming!" I hissed urgently, striving to hold my voice down. Immediately I looked around, seeking, dreading the shifting of reality that, twice before, had resulted in attack by the savage spider-wolves.

"More trouble." Bads, his tone strangely matter-of-fact, indicated the depths of the cavern. I couldn't see anything in the darkness, but I heard low, rasping breaths and the sound of a large body moving through the muck, advancing toward us. "Dragon's comin'."

Obviously Bads's eyes were better than mine, at least in the darkness, and I wasn't about to argue with him. At the same time, the all-too-familiar whitish glow rose in the cavern wall across from us. The solid dirt of the dragon's lair faded, turning milky white and casting soft illumination through the cave. That surreal tunnel, flanked by the unnatural pillars of white, led directly from its unknown origin to this dank hole in the ground.

CHAPTER 11

ACYDIKEEN

The black serpent's eyes glowed like embers, emerging from the darkness as the monster advanced along the corridor. At the same time, turning my head to the side, I saw the hideous shapes of the arachnoid spider-wolves charging rapidly down their white-bordered tunnel. Drooling jaws snapping, shaggy heads straining forward from the bloated bodies, the monsters advanced as a whole pack, more of the beasts than I had ever seen before. In that ungainly but speedy gait, they scuttled down the path toward the milky opening.

Another whimper reminded me of the hound, and I looked around to see the animal trotting toward one side. Though I had thought the wall behind us was solid, the dog vanished into a darkened alcove I hadn't previously discerned. Pressing back against the wall, I felt a gap; a quick look showed me a good-sized niche in the tunnel's side.

"In here!" I urged, taking Badswell's big hand in both of mine.

Willingly he followed, ducking his head below a low, moss-draped beam that supported the ceiling of the alcove. Silent now, the hound padded after us, spinning to regard the outer tunnel with upraised ears and alert, still mournful eyes. The niche wasn't deep, but it provided at least some shelter, and we huddled against the back wall, turning back to stare helplessly at the onrushing pack of eight-legged monstrosities.

I noticed that the leading spider-wolf was the same type as the creature that had spoken in Oakgnar's lair, that had seemed to command the pack of attacking monsters there. This one was larger than the others and covered with scraggly, bristling hairs of the same blue-green color as the body of a plump carrion fly. It scuttled like the others on eight gangly but well-coordinated legs, and like the previous leader, it had a pair of additional limbs jutting from its neck. As the monster raced closer, I saw that these were like human arms, but tipped with hooked talons and layered with shredded flesh.

Hideous eyes bored through the darkness, freezing me in place. Snarls and growls resounded, echoing through the tunnels, vibrant with menace. The monsters' corrupt, unspeakable hunger was a physical force in the air, and in that instant, I knew the beast's very mind was reaching out to me, touching my consciousness, paralyzing me with terror.

The spider-wolf pounced through the opening of the surrealistic tunnel. Drool spattered from the wolf fangs, and a black, vile-looking tongue draped between gaping jaws. Other beasts, howling, animalistic lackeys, followed obediently, a dozen gathering behind the leader. The pack advanced into the corridor and formed a half-circle to block Badswell and me in the hollow niche.

"Ah, mortals . . . again you draw us—for the last time, I trust," declared the commander in that melodious, smoothly articulated voice.

I raised Goldfinder, ready to fight, while beside me, Bads hoisted his makeshift club, preparing for a battle that could only end one way.

The blast of searing, steaming liquid came from the left, from the direction of the black dragon, as a spray of death that showered through the confining tunnel. A drop struck the back of my hand, burning like a bee sting, while other splashes spattered around us, smoking and hissing on the dirt floor.

The great mass of the corrosive stream gushed across the gathered mass of spider-wolves, sizzling through carapaces, eating away flesh and fur. Howls and shrieks rang from the doomed mass, a cacophony of agony as arachnoid monsters whirled about in a futile effort to reach the white-walled tunnel. More crumpled beneath the shifting stream of killing acid as a gout of liquid spurted again, soaking the panic-stricken mass. Most of the spider-wolves collapsed where they'd been engulfed, flipping over, sometimes kicking sporadically as jaws worked in yelping pain, other times perishing instantly, like spiders crushed by the step of a heavy boot.

The grotesque spider-wolf that had led the attackers ducked under the initial blast of the dragon's acid, cowering against the wall of the cavern beyond our hiding place. Its crimson eyes burned from the narrow, wolfish face, fastening upon the dragon and glaring with hatred and fury.

"Servant of chaos, *cease!* You threaten the will of one

who is mistress to us all!" cried the spider-wolf, again enunciating in that deep and powerful voice. The monster rose into the air, rearing onto its four back legs, flailing with its forelimbs. The two humanlike arms spread wide, a beseeching gesture that seemed no more bizarre than the creature's appearance or its smooth and cultured voice.

Another blast of acid spewed, catching the pleading spider-wolf directly in the face, smashing it onto its hard-shelled back. Fumes rose thickly, the stench of corrupt flesh seething and billowing through the corridor. I covered my nose and mouth, striving not to gag as the grotesque spider-wolf withered under the corrosive attack.

Bads and I stared in horror and awe at the scattered refuse of dead, still-dissolving monsters. All of the arachnoid intruders had been slain by the blasts of dragon breath. The magical gate was already closing, fading into an improbably mundane wall of moist dirt beyond the gruesome remains. Monstrous flesh continued to bubble and seethe across the floor as the remnants of the acid worked its destructive power. Occasionally one of the arachnoid forms twitched or wiggled, an effect of collapsing support as legs and bristling, hairy carapaces were eaten away by relentless corrosion.

A stinking, billowing fog filled the corridor, burning eyes, savagely stinging the membranes of noses and throats. I tried desperately to restrain the sounds of choking, leaning weakly against the wall, holding my breath until I grew dizzy, then exhaling with slow, painful deliberation. Gratefully sucking air, I heard Badswell, too, stifle any audible sound of our presence. The hound still squatted between us, eyes wary and watching, but apparently suffering no discomfort from the vile fumes.

Slumped against the wall of our niche, praying that the dragon didn't advance far enough to see us, I recalled the peculiar sound of the spider-wolf's voice—and its words. The monster had spoken to the dragon as a servant of chaos, as if the two beings were some sort of allies in a universal cause, an alliance that had done nothing to gentle the dragon's violent response.

Badswell and I waited in utter silence, allowing the heartbeats to pass with excruciating tension. We heard no sound, and finally I started to hope that the dragon had returned to the depths of its cavern. We crept cautiously out of our niche, striving to move silently, fully terrified of the monstrous master of this lair. Skulking in the shadows near the wall, gingerly putting one bare foot in front of the other, I tried to avoid the corroded corpses of the spiders and the small pools of acid that lingered here and there, smoking and bubbling dangerously.

The hound growled softly, a bare whisper of sound that brought us up short. I felt Badswell stiffen beside me as my eyes strained to penetrate the inky shadows.

Then I didn't have to see, as a voice deep with menace and droll with cruel amusement rumbled from the depths of the tunnel before us.

"I see you, little rats."

Now I discerned the head rising in the darkness, cruel eyes blazing down at us as a forked tongued flickered between rows of serrated fangs. Again the powerful voice boomed. "I have eliminated the minor distraction. Now you will be kind enough to tell me—quickly—why you are here."

My mind groped for excuses—anything I could tell this dragon that would postpone the blast of acidic breath that was certainly imminent. But what could I say—that we'd been out for a little stroll and lost our way? Or we were explorers, perhaps, looking for a good path through the Vastest Bog?

"We came here to find a piece of stick, much like this one," I explained frankly. Somewhat surprised by my own forthrightness, I nevertheless pulled the chip of ebony from my pouch and held it up for the dragon to see. "The other one belongs to Badswell, here . . . only it disappeared a few days ago. We aren't sure where it went, but we think it's around somewhere, in your lair."

If I was startled by my own explanation, I was astonished by the dragon's reaction when I showed the black stub. The monster reared back, hissing loudly, fanning those dark wings in the constricting corridor. Wincing against a gush of air, I cowered away, expecting the blast of fatal acid that would conclude our adventure.

But more surprises were imminent. The dragon dropped to its forepaws, glaring at us with crimson eyes. Midnight jaws gaped, revealing those sharp teeth again, but still the creature didn't spew its deadly spray.

"You got my stick?" Badswell asked bluntly. If his legs were as jellied, his guts as churned as mine by the monster's presence, the half-ogre did a fine job of concealing it. Now he planted his hamlike fists on his hips and glared at the serpent.

The hound stood between the two of us, staring with interest at the great wyrm. Neither cringing nor bristling, the dog seemed more curious than anything else.

"Take it! Take it and begone!" spat the dragon with a dart of its head that startled me backward onto the floor. The hound merely blinked, then turned to regard me with a gently impatient expression, as if to ask what I was waiting for.

"Wh-where is it?" I managed to blurt, looking upward from my seat in a pool of mud.

The blood-red eyes bored into us as the wyrm moved silently and deliberately backward into the depths of its lair. Bads hoisted me with an easy tug, and the two of us followed cautiously after the retreating dragon. The hound padded along, frequently turning her head to sniff interestedly at the shadowy corners of the muddy lair.

I couldn't quell the palpitations of my heart as the dragon's shape became clearly outlined against a pale source of illumination. This close, the monster towered overhead, more like a building than a being. The serpent backed into a large domed chamber, and I saw that the entire room was suffused with a pulsing, shimmering glow.

"Patrikon have mercy!" I gasped when I passed through the door. The gentle light rose from the myriad brilliant gems scattered across the floor, shedding glows of emerald, ruby, turquoise, and sparkling diamond. Among these precious stones, other sources of brightness were larger, and pure white. Scanning the chamber, I counted one mighty sword, at least three smaller blades, a shield, and some sort of pike. Silvery metal cast a moon-like glow from the blades of magical weapons, and the rainbow spectrum of glowing gems shimmered in a multitude of magical colors, while the entire, vast chamber seemed to be carpeted in a layer of silver and gold coins.

In short, it was a treasure trove such as I'd never seen. Bads stood dumbstruck in the arched entry, if anything, even more astounded than I. The dragon sidled off to the side, looming over the doorway that seemed to be the only point of access to this big cavern.

Taking several steps forward, I realized that I had unconsciously started for the center of the room. The chip of wood was smooth and heavy in my hand, and there could be no mistaking the source of my urgency.

Badswell followed me for a pace or two, and the serpent lowered its sinuous neck behind us so that its head blocked the entry tunnel. "Hasten!" the monster commanded curtly.

The half-ogre suddenly turned and regarded the wyrm, his jaw jutting stubbornly barely an arm's length from the black, scaly snout. "You keep lots of stuff. Why you so happy to give away my stick?"

"Fool!" sneered the wyrm. The baleful gaze swept to include me. "You are dealing with powers you cannot hope to comprehend, powers that cause even me, Acydikeen, to know fear!"

"You weren't afraid when them big spiders came," Badswell noted.

"The spyder-fiends invaded my lair. They fully knew the risk of such intrusion. They merely paid the price."

I wondered silently if we would have to pay the same price. If so, I had to ask at least one question first "What powers are we dealing with, Acydikeen?"

"Do you know of the immortal mistress of the spyder-fiends, the Queen of Chaos?" it demanded.

"I've always made it a practice to leave the affairs of the gods to themselves," I explained, silently asking for a moment of forgiveness from Patrikon and wondering why the minor dishonesty should bother me.

The dragon's reply was a laugh, chortled to convey even more menace than a thunderous roar or sibilant whisper. Anything that this dragon found humorous, I sensed, was bad news for my companion and me.

"The queen herself—she of glorious disarray and all-powerful cruelty. She commands legions of spyder-fiends, kakkuu, and lycosyds, and others who number among the greatest of all tanar'ri. Even the mighty raklupis, rare and potent as they are, fear her wrath and obey her commands without question."

Tanar'ri I knew by reputation; the word sent an icy spear through my belly. Powerful magical denizens, purveyors of hatred and evil, these beings of colossal villainy served horrible gods and pursued murderous goals with tireless vigor. Tanar'ri could appear at will, attacking suddenly and without mercy, striking in ever greater numbers until they achieved their inevitably hurtful objectives. Now that I thought about it, that pretty well sounded like the spyder-fiends.

"Touch it but carefully," Acydikeen warned. "You know by now that its use can bring more of the fiends?"

I was stunned by the news, though I decided I didn't have to admit that to Acydikeen. Yet, once again, much was explained: Every attack of the spyder-fiends, I suddenly realized, had followed a use of a segment, such as to heal Saysi or Badswell or, when Bertisha had used it, to magically slow me.

I remembered another thing, in a timely fashion for once. We didn't want to put the two pieces of the rod too close together, or we risked having the larger one disappear in an instant. "Badswell, why don't you pick up your piece?" I suggested, as still more questions popped into my brain. I turned to confront the wyrm as my companion advanced.

"You never told us why you're so anxious to get rid of it," I stated.

"It is law, and I am chaos!" hissed Acydikeen. "It came to rest here between two of my prized gems, polluting them with its rigid essence. I fear it shall seep through all my baubles if it is not removed."

"And it's pollution to you, too," I guessed. "So you don't dare touch it?"

"Take it and begone!" the dragon snapped, drooping leathery lids halfway across crimson eyeballs as it studied me appraisingly.

Badswell, meanwhile, crossed the chamber and quickly saw the black stick. He picked it up, looked at it, and nodded to me.

"You said these are segments of law," I pressed, turning back to the serpent. "But *what* law?"

"Nothing less than an artifact of many planes—a cursed thing that has now descended upon our world. The Rod of Seven Parts, it is called, and woe befall the one who bears too much of its load. Now, take it and flee, while I deign to spare your miserable lives. Go!"

Acydikeen swept its great wing toward the tunnel. Bads and I needed no further encouragement, and both of us sprinted into the darkness. The hound, ears and tongue flapping, gamboled along behind us. We retraced our steps toward the base of the plummeting pit, stepping gingerly around the partially dissolved bodies of the spyder-fiends and avoiding altogether the cesspool of the slain gulguthra.

Only when we reached the sheer, vine-draped shaft leading to the surface did another problem occur to me. I turned from the steep wall, looking for the big dog that had panted easily at Badswell's heel while we ran. The animal was nowhere to be seen.

"Hound?" I called, urgency raising my voice.

"Where'd she go?" Badswell scratched his head, peering

curiously into the darkened tunnel. "Ain't there."

"Come here, dog—hound. Where are you?" I shook my head in frustration, pained by the animal's disappearance even as I realized that there was no way we could have lifted her up the wall of the shaft.

"Mebbe she's got a different path," Bads suggested. "She got down here somehow."

I was forced to agree. "Well, maybe we'll meet her up on top, then," I said hopefully. At the same time, I wondered something else: The dog would certainly have had to swim in order to reach this island, yet her coat had been as smooth and dry in Acydikeen's lair as it had been on the two other occasions the hound had appeared. Indeed, the animal must have been living in the wilds for days, yet somehow managed invariably to appear moments before the arrival of the spyder-fiend attacks.

We had no time to ponder mysteries, however. The dragon's imperative would allow no delay. Taking care to find only the sturdiest vines, I led the half-ogre up the side. Foot by panting foot we strained upward, clutching the ropelike tendrils with white-knuckled fists, kicking and clawing with our feet to aid the ascent.

Finally we crawled over the flagstones at the rim and collapsed, gasping and sweating, on the ground atop the pit. The air of the Vastest Bog—a stagnant and oppressive miasma hours earlier—now seemed a breath of freshness, breezily wafting away the stench and rot of the depths.

Quickly we started across the tangled island. This time it was Badswell leading the way, and he trampled the thorniest bushes into a flattened path. When we reached the edge of the wetlands, I climbed onto his shoulders again, and he waded without hesitation into deep muck and through stagnant, lily-tangled pools.

Only as we pressed toward the distant shore did I reflect on the half-ogre's purposeful flight, realizing that we left the bog by a different direction than we had come here. Reaching a conclusion of my own, I nevertheless asked him about the fact.

"I dunno," he admitted, finally pausing to catch his breath. With a blink of his pouched eyelids, Badswell reached into his pocket and pulled out the piece of stick that looked so much like an extension of my own stub. I thought of a third piece of this mighty rod, an extension of the two small portions we held, and I knew that Badswell was thinking the same thing.

Then his eyes rose, turning toward the east, the direction we had started. He spoke with unusual deliberation.

"I only know that we *have* to go this way."

CHAPTER 12

MEETING IN THE FAR PLANES

Spots of bobbing light filtered through the spaces between lofty pines, surrounding the lone traveler's camp with a ring of sparkling, enchanted illumination. The pearly baubles might have appeared random at first glance, but careful observation would reveal a precise and measured cadence to their stately march.

The softly feathered trees formed a nearly perfect ring about the grassy clearing, and a tall, naked figure occupied the very center of that roundel. Arquestan stood as still as a pillar of stone over his fire ring of flat rocks arrayed in a precise circle. Within that shallow pit, embers glowed pale red, visible only because the rest of the night had descended into realms of absolute, utter blackness.

The wind duke was uneasy. A long and dangerous road had brought him here, to a world he had visited often in the past, a parklike realm of pastoral solitude that had offered him respite from many a more chaotic locale. Yet now he watched flares of lightning ripple through the sky beyond the distant horizon, growing more powerful with each passing minute. He heard the distant rumbles, felt the vibrations in his chest, and knew that the queen flexed her power, sending ripples of chaos through the planes.

The cause, Arquestan felt certain, was her growing desire for the Rod of Seven Parts. The queen's agents sought the artifact desperately, and as long as that quest was thwarted, her fury would grow ever more disruptive and deadly. The outcast thought about the scattered segments of the artifact, and he was deeply afraid.

Against the cosmic disquiet in the distant sky, the sparkling lights drifted nearby, placidly circling, floating in a steady procession through the verdant evergreens. Drooping limbs, far-reaching and thick with needles, masked enough of the woods that the enchanted, luminous sentinels were for the most part hidden from the central clearing. Still, the glowing spheres became clearly visible each time they floated from the shelter of one tree to the next.

"Enough of your pacing, my pack; come join me beside such coals as remain."

Arquestan spoke quietly, sensing the restless forms of his hounds as they emerged from the ring of pines. Soon the baubles of pearly light gathered to him, coming to rest as they would on the ground or upon the nearby rocks.

As each hound settled, brightness faded with the changing of its shape. At Arquestan's feet, the first glowing bubble shifted form and, with a flop onto a lean flank and the thumping of a gray, shaggy tail, rested on the ground. The sleek wolf that was Terril looked to his master with loving eyes, long tongue lolling between jaws that, despite their array of sharp fangs, remained fixed into an eager smile.

"Ah, Terril, how is my brave one . . . the elder of my pack?" The wind duke's face split into a smile, white teeth showing bright against black skin and the framing curls of hair and beard. With an easy gesture, the outcast reached down, brushing smooth fur with his fingertips.

The wolf, in reply, thumped its tail more enthusiastically. Arquestan's eyes rose to regard the other hounds of law as they gathered, settled, and shifted around the quiet camp. Beyond the fire to the right were Kalis and Fuyrree, the two speckled terriers sitting upright, staring curiously at their master. And Dulthap, the bucolic bloodhound, and Challis, the burrow-delving corgi, gathered in the darkness to the left. Challis sat upright, the short-legged dog perched upon a round boulder to enhance her otherwise diminutive height. She licked her lips and turned a keen, intelligent gaze toward the wendeam while Dulthap, with a lugubrious look at the darkness, curled around and began to lick himself indecently. Arquestan suppressed a chuckle, then turned to observe the last arrival of the group.

The final bubble settled, flickered for a moment, and then Borath, the staghound, sat directly across the fire from the outcast wind duke. With serene, comprehending eyes, the shaggy animal looked at his master. Borath sat up in a properly alert position as the circle of hounds and vaati was completed.

The wind duke sensed question and concern in that look, emotions he shared with Borath in full. "I know . . . she is in danger, but Bayar is smart and brave and swift,"

Arquestan said softly. Borath whined in response, then settled to the ground, head resting upon his outstretched forepaws.

For a moment, the outcast's mind focused on the missing hound. If any member of the magical pack could anticipate the attacks of spyder-fiends and move to warn the potential victims, the clever and courageous Bayar would be the one. Still, the knowledge that he had sent her upon such a dangerous task was a heavy weight in the back of the vaati's awareness.

Abruptly the big staghound raised his head, dark eyes probing the shadowy woods. A pale light glowed there, and the big dog whimpered once, the sound eager, even joyful. The other dogs turned, too, ears upraised, sniffing the faint breeze for a clue. Even the outcast stared, his own keen senses probing the darkness. Finally Arquestan allowed himself a glimmer of joy.

"Ah . . . she comes back to us." The vaati's broad smile mirrored Borath's joy as the big dog bounded to his feet and barked sharply.

Another bubble of light drifted into view, circling tentatively, then bobbing closer to the fading fire. Gradually the newcomer came to rest on a soft patch of grass, and then the jowly, floppy-eared hound with the skin that was many times too large stood there. Tail wagging, Bayar stepped forward, chuffing softly under the touch of the wind duke's gentle hand, then circling the coals to lie beside her mate. Her head collapsed wearily onto her paws as she leaned against Borath and allowed the big staghound to gently lick her nearest ear.

With several more flops of her heavy tail, Bayar signaled her contentment. Then her melancholy gaze turned upward, staring into Arquestan's golden eyes. The wendeam concentrated, nodding his head and speaking softly.

"I see . . . this is interesting news indeed. A halfling . . . and an ogre spawn. Their endeavors are not without promise. Well you have served the cause of law, old girl."

Bayar wrinkled her brow and whimpered softly.

"We share your fear," Arquestan replied gently. "And, yes, chaos is abroad among the planes. See those storms on the horizon? Never has this world been wracked by such. The queen's power is great, and she seeks to reach out into every realm."

Wind sighed through the limbs of the trees, and Arquestan abruptly sat upright, while Borath and Bayar sniffed the air and Terril growled softly, their sounds too quiet to carry beyond the circle.

"Be still, my pets . . . this is not the surge of chaos. Rather, we may welcome the coming of a friend—or at least an ally."

With a crescendo of groaning and wailing, the wind grew, sighing through the trees, whipping the heavy limbs back and forth. Shortly a vortex of air spun into sight, rising as high as the tallest trees, gliding forward with easy grace.

Nearing the fire, the whirlwind dispersed without fanning or scattering the coals. Arquestan regarded the naked figure standing where the funnel cloud had twirled away, a figure whose black skin was even darker than the outcast's.

"Greetings, Xathwik. You do well to find me here in the distant planes."

The sturdy vindeam, his scalp shaved close and smooth, shuddered, looking at the encircling darkness as he moved closer to the fire.

161

"It was a matter of all the vaati wizardry—vindeam, rudeam, and even the grideam. In the end, in fact, it was the grideam Farrial who divined your location. He and Balka have discovered some rather urgent news, and we thought it important enough to try to reach you. They merely directed me where to go and how to travel through the trackless ether."

Arquestan chuckled, the sound soft and pleasant within his long rib cage, white teeth flashing in the tangle of his black beard. He settled himself to a stump again and gestured for the other duke to have a seat.

"Farrial should have come himself," Arquestan noted teasingly. "He needs to see the worlds beyond Aaqa every once in a while."

"You know that's impossible!" snapped Xathwik, appalled. "The grideam are bonded to the land; all of their power and knowledge comes from the sanctified ground of our valley. Farrial could no more travel here than he could rip out his own heart."

"I know . . . it saddens me, but I know."

"It's hard enough for we vindeam to make a journey," continued Xathwik, looking at the surrounding trees with a shiver of discomfort. "Everything is so . . . *disorderly* here among the wilds."

Arquestan shrugged. "One merely has to make his own order, and then it's not so bad. Witness the circles of my campsite and fire. Even among the wilds, one can find, or create, places of order and precision."

"But the storms! I see lightning walking along those ridges. Can chaos become any more real, more deadly?" Xathwik's tone was tremulous as he looked at the looming storm clouds.

"True, there are things in the worlds that one cannot

control," conceded the outcast. "Yet perhaps that is the greatest danger of Aaqa's isolation. You have come to believe that everything is subject to the purview of law, and such is not the case."

"But this—?" Xathwik squinted at a brilliant, pulsing display of lightning. Seconds later, thunder rolled through the campsite, a basso trembling the two vaati sensed through the soles of their feet.

"Chaos waxes strong, here and in other worlds. This is a disturbing trend, and it grows stronger by the day, even the hour."

"That bears out the substance of my news," Xath declared solemnly, nodding his smoothly shaved head.

"I know that you are ill at ease, so I will not make waste of your time. What do you have to tell me?"

"Farrial has been studying the activities of the queen. She grows restless, desperate with the knowledge that segments of the rod have been discovered. In her rage, she flexes her power and sends ripples of chaos through the worlds of law."

Arquestan's brow creased into a frown of concern. "This is not entirely a surprise. Has the grideam learned how strong the effects are thus far?"

"Minor, to begin with. Still, even the early manifestations of chaos can be frightening to the mortal population of a world. Imagine awakening to find that a once-blue sky has become red, or that a vast swampland has been rendered into desert!"

"Or storms in a sky that has always been calm," mused the outcast, turning his eyes toward the bright, flickering surges of power.

"The queen's might is great. We are far from the Abyss, yet still she reaches us."

"We must act quickly to forestall her," declared Arquestan. "Is there confirmation of the whereabouts of the seventh segment of the rod?"

Xathwik's voice lowered an octave, and he looked around nervously as if he expected that the woods themselves could hear. "Your guess was as accurate as we could have hoped. Using his arcane formulae, Balka has tracked that segment. The task was not easy, but his powers extended into the very portals of the queen's palace."

Arquestan nodded, not surprised. "From there she has sent it to Pandemonium, has she not? That it may be guarded by Miska himself?"

"How did you know?" The vindeam's eyes widened.

"It is the only thing that makes sense. She could not abide the presence of such law within her own palace, yet she will desire that it be well guarded until her agents can gather the other pieces. I am correct, no?"

Xathwik nodded curtly as Arquestan closed his eyes in meditation. Faced with his companion's silence, the vindeam glowered in growing annoyance. "This was a wasted trip. I traveled to the very gates of chaos, and you already knew the information I so determinedly brought!"

"Not wasted, my friend," replied the outcast. "I needed your confirmation before I could move."

"Move? In what way? Where?"

Arquestan drew a deep breath before answering. "I intend to carry the sixth segment as far as the Oasis of the Planes. The mortals should be able to reach me there, bearing other segments of the artifact."

"The oasis?" Xathwik was appalled. "But how will they survive? Will they not be battling chaos the whole way?"

"No doubt. But from what Bayar tells me, these mortals are ingenious. Perhaps more to the point, they seem to have good luck."

"May we be blessed with the same," offered the vindeam devoutly.

"Aye. And if you fear a wasted trip, you should know, my cousin, that it is good to share the company of a kinsman."

Xathwik harrumphed stiffly, but then his expression softened. "Aye. I'm glad to sit beside your fire for an hour, to see you in the life you have taken on. But there is something more as well."

Deliberately, conscious of his own drama, the vindeam magician pulled the hilt of a mighty sword from his small belt pouch. The haft was followed by a blade the gleaming yellow of pure gold, the massive weapon slowly emerging, far larger than the magical sack that had contained it. Xathwik turned the sword, taking the keen blade in his hands and extending the hilt toward the outcast.

"This is a weapon fit for a great hero, forged in the smithies of Aaqa. You are to take it."

"A fine blade indeed," Arquestan said, impressed. "But it is too heavy for me. I am happy with my twin swords."

"I understand. But you are to grant this golden blade as a gift to a hero who, in your judgment, will bear it with courage, honor, and the steadfastness needed of a champion of law."

"I will seek such a hero." The outcast nodded, remembering Bayar's message. "I know of several mortals who already possess portions of the rod. Perhaps I shall find a champion of law among them, should they be smart and fortunate enough to reach the Oasis of the Planes."

"If they do that, one of them shall certainly be worthy." Xathwik closed his eyes and sighed. For a long time, silence lay between the two vaati, and then the vindeam stood.

"Perhaps next time we shall meet in Aaqa?"

"You know that will never happen," Arquestan replied, a hint of sadness in his voice as he, too, rose to his feet and stretched.

"Yes . . . I suppose that I do."

Silence again settled like a comfortable blanket around them until, abruptly, the outcast kicked out the fading remnants of his fire.

Before he summoned his whirlwind, Xathwik turned to regard the towering figure of the wendeam. "I—I know that we have had our differences . . . that some of those schisms run very deep indeed. I want you to believe me in this one thing: I wish you the best of luck." The sturdy, valley-bound wind duke sighed. "How ironic it is that the future of our race, of all the planes where a proper order of life is cherished, has come to depend upon one we have labeled an outcast."

Arquestan smiled, without humor. "Your wishes of luck are well received . . . as to the irony, let us wait to see how I fare before we offer any thanks."

CHAPTER 13

ARGENPORT

"There it is," I declared, gesturing into the valley below us. "Argenport . . . city of a thousand delights, more or less. We'll be through the gates in time for a late breakfast!"

We stopped on the shoulder of the mountain road to take in the view. Only a mile or two of descending track remained before Badswell Lummoff and I could finally fall into civilization's embrace.

For a week we had followed the nameless compulsion that guided Badswell toward the third segment of the rod. Pressed through trackless wilderness, our path had ultimately brought us to this pass and would soon enter the city that sprawled in ghostly, tenuous magnificence below.

Argenport rose from the dawn mist like a mystical paradise in the clouds. Low walls and buildings were lost in a dense layer of fog, but towers, peaked roofs, and high

167

gates rose above the vaporous blanket to sparkle in the rising sun. Sprawling through the width of a flat-bottomed valley, Argenport was a vast network of streets, walls, buildings, and towers, filling every space of level ground on the valley floor and climbing onto the steep slopes, clustering on valley shoulders like lichens clinging to mountains of rock. Banks of white mist filled the streets and alleys, burying the lower buildings, leaving mansions and manors and the numerous, lofty watchtowers to jut upward into the early morning sun. The fog stretched beyond the city as well, resembling a flat, formless plain extending to the far horizons.

"Beneath that fog is nothing but ocean—past the city, I mean. You'll be able to see it when the fog lifts."

"How big is it—the ocean?" wondered the half-ogre.

"*Real* big. Goes all the way to the end of the world, so I've been told. Matter of fact, I've killed a certain amount of time on those docks, looking out to sea. . . ."

In fact, the waterfront of Argenport and the ocean that rolled away from it were the scene of several pleasant memories. Most meaningfully, I recalled with an all-too-familiar pang of grief, the first time I kissed Saysi. It had been on an evening walk along a quiet, deserted pier on that very shoreline. The color of her coppery hair under the full moon had never been more lovely; even in my memory, I saw it shining. Swallowing the lump that was growing in my throat, I sniffled, then angrily shook my head.

All of a sudden my feet seemed terribly sore, my throat parched by an agonizing thirst. The city was looking better and better by the minute.

"Let's go. All the comforts of civilization await!" I started eagerly forward, taking several steps before I realized that the half-ogre had remained in place.

"I dunno, Kip. . . ."

Bads looked dubiously at the expanse of city and slowly shook his head. "Mebbe I'll just go back to the hills."

"Guess you've never been to a place like this before, huh?" I asked. Bertisha and Oakgnar could not have prepared him very well for an experience such as we were about to have.

He nodded grimly, his expression locked in a scowl of stubborn suspicion.

"Cities aren't so bad," I counseled. "Just think of it as a forest with animals all over the place. Only here all the animals can talk."

"And carry swords and shackles," the half-ogre declared morosely. "My Pap told me about shackles."

"Don't worry. I know a thing or two about shackles myself," I assured him. "You're not likely to get locked up as long as I'm around." After all, I could pick locks, couldn't I? Actually, the notion of surreptitious burglary caused a prickle of conscience to move along my spine.

Still reluctant, Badswell reached a hand into his pouch. I knew he touched the chip of ebony, no doubt sensed the compulsion that had brought us across miles of wilderness, through bog and thicket and over mountain ridge.

"The next piece is down there somewhere," he allowed. "I *want* to go."

"Let's go, then," I encouraged him. "I can show you around, just like I showed Saysi. . . ." My words trailed off as the memories returned, as powerful and painful as ever. This was the city of our first meeting, of many happy times in the last year. Again I longed for her, an ache in my heart as the wind brought a gentle waft of sea breeze that reminded me of that romantic stroll along the waterfront.

"I like her . . . Saysi," Badswell mumbled.

I looked at him in surprise.

"I mean, from hearing you talkin' 'bout her. She sounds nice," clarified the half-ogre, clapping me roughly on the shoulder.

"You two would have gotten along fine. She'd have liked you, too," I replied, painfully aware that this was wasteful talk, something that could never be.

Badswell finally nodded, lowering his head to start resolutely down the road. By the time we approached the valley floor, much of the fog had burned away, revealing a city considerably less pristine than it had appeared from the heights. A dozen or so drunks lay in an uneven pile off to one side of the gateway, stinking, snoring derelicts who had been haphazardly tossed there the night before. A salt-flavored breeze swept inland across the city, but the stench of human filth and garbage far overpowered any lingering odor of fish or seaweed. The stink was far worse than I remembered from any previous visit, and I wondered if it had anything to do with the fog that still lurked in the lower alleys, extending in misty tendrils beyond the unseen waterfront.

We passed through a gateway in the midst of a file of farmers bringing the day's goods into the city. The gate was flanked by stone towers wide enough to accommodate a pair of huge wagons or a block of men marching fifteen or twenty abreast. A heavy portcullis dangled overhead, and twin slabs of iron-strapped gates stood to either side.

Guards lounged listlessly on either side of the gates, some watching the file of people entering and leaving the city, others conversing, gambling, or bickering among themselves. A few scowled at Bads, who kept his head down and simply plodded on through. None of the well-armed watchmen made any move to accost us.

The maze of streets within the gates further belied the city's grandiose facade. No fewer than five routes led from the small courtyard within the gates. None of these was more than ten or fifteen feet in width, and each quickly twisted out of view amid a mess of shacks and shanties. The mansions and towers we'd observed from beyond, it seemed, did not extend to these reaches around the city's fringe.

"Which way?" Badswell asked.

"I . . . um, let's try this way," I suggested, surprised by the constricted nature of the place. "I guess I was remembering the High City, which is through the second wall. The streets are wider there." Again I was struck by a surprising feeling of distaste. Argenport was far more dirty, ugly, and generally unpleasant than I recalled.

"I like this part okay," Badswell allowed as we started forward once more. "What'sit here—Low City?"

"Yup. This is where you'll find the thieves and harlots, beggars and barterers. Good thing we don't have any money. We'd have to keep a real close eye on it around here."

Nodding sagely, the half-ogre stepped along behind me as I started down one of the stinking, winding alleys. Picking our way along the littered path, we stepped over unidentifiable refuse and nameless derelicts. At least one or two of the latter, I suspected, had ceased to breathe hours or even days earlier, although I didn't take the time to bend down for a closer inspection. Again I was struck by the fact that Argenport seemed strangely squalid and depressing, far more so than on any of my previous visits.

Tiny doorways, for the most part set within dark, hooded alcoves, led to small and windowless buildings. Shadowy figures moved here and there, darting between covered doorways and concealed alcoves behind us. Fortunately Badswell's size proved a significant deterrent to any potential thief, and I was increasingly glad of this fact as I sensed hostile eyes peering from narrow cul-de-sacs to the left or right.

"Big place," Bads commented as we moved into a crowded square. Hawkers of trinkets cried out, waving fistfuls of tin bangles. Fruit vendors hoisted melons and citrus, carefully holding the produce to conceal the bruises and scuffs that marked it as inferior goods. An old woman raised a colorful parrot in her gnarled fist, and the bird squawked and shrieked at us, batting broad, powerful wings. Plunging through the crowd, we left the throng behind, taking our choice of several narrow streets departing the other side of the tiny square.

"Argenport is the biggest city I've ever visited," I admitted. Always before I'd had the company of experienced companions, such as Barzyn, Dallzar, and Benton. It worried me slightly that this time I was the knowledgeable leader, my partner depending upon my experience to see us safely through the maze of civilization. Perhaps that was why the city seemed so much more dangerous than before. At least, I tried to make myself believe this was the case.

A scream echoed from a small structure at the end of a winding alley—a man's voice, full of shrill terror. We heard an angry outburst from another speaker, jabbering in a strange tongue, and then a groan of pain accompanied by a sickening gurgle. Hastening along, we moved past sounds of weeping from another shack. Arguments echoed from numerous directions as the sun rose higher and life stirred in Argenport's slum.

"Should we help?" Badswell asked as some truly piteous wailing rose from a nearby hovel.

"Help who?" I asked, flinching under the growing fear that chaos reigned everywhere in this vast city. "We've no way to know what side to take—don't you see?"

Badswell looked unconvinced as another cry, thrumming with fear, echoed from a side street.

"Keep going," I urged at a narrow intersection. "Which way?"

"Here," declared Badswell, indicating one street, touching his own segment of the rod as confirmation.

Finally the alley opened into another courtyard, and we saw another, higher wall rising at the far side. A gate, guarded by men in gleaming, silvery plate mail, stood open. Beyond stretched a sunlit plaza, and a suggestion of elegant, flowered balconies extended above a wide avenue between alabaster facades of marble.

"The High City," I explained, pointing through the gate. "Where the money is."

"That's where more of the rod is, too," Badswell replied. "You can feel it?"

"Just like all along. Strange magic, but we keep goin' this way."

Privately I reflected that if anyplace needed an artifact of law, it was Argenport. Thuggery, fear, and squalor all seemed to be running wild in the place.

A crowd of people moved toward the High City gate, including several robed women, a slave-borne litter occupied by a bejeweled merchant, and several fruit merchants hauling two-wheeled handcarts. I noticed that the latter offered wares that were fresh and well ripened, not like the bruised goods offered in the Low City market.

Badswell stopped abruptly, scowling. "Wait," he said. "The third piece—it's movin'. Goin' this way." He pointed back toward the slums.

The crowd filed steadily through the gates in both directions. Abruptly the half-ogre turned, looking across the small gatehouse square, then pointing toward another alley leading into the slums. I saw a half dozen men, unshaven fellows dressed in dark cloaks and tattered leggings, skulk into the shadows there. With a few furtive looks behind, they gathered into a huddle.

Seconds later a girl followed them, waiflike in a blue skirt and bare feet. I felt a flash of irrational recognition, something in the child's easy, undaunted gait that almost caused my heart to stop beating. Surely she was too adult, too confident to be a youngster. Angrily I told myself that I was dreaming, I must have been mistaken.

"Hey, stop that!" the girl's voice piped up, indignantly directed at the suspicious-looking fellows gathering in the alley.

When I heard the high-pitched voice, my doubts were dispelled with absolute certainty. "Saysi!" I cried, starting across the square with the startled Badswell lumbering behind.

The girl apparently didn't hear me cry out. She marched up to the biggest thug and confronted him with a determined planting of her fists on her hips, a stubborn gesture that I knew well.

"What is it, brat?" The man's voice, a guttural, menacing threat, emerged from the shadows of the alley and made my heart hammer in fear. Beyond that blue hood, cruel, leering features glared down at the angry girl. "You stole that old lady's apples, and her money, too!" Saysi—it *had* to be her—accused tartly.

In response, a chorus of men's voices joined the sneering character who had questioned her. "We let her live, didn't we?" chortled that villainous thief. "'At's more'n might be said for you, wee lass!"

I charged into the narrow confines of the alley as the leather-cloaked boor made a grab at the feminine figure. Still with her back to me, she ducked away, but the thug's paw caught hold of her hood and ripped it from her cloak. In a flash of coppery curls—hair like spun metal, flaming brightly in the dawn light—I knew Saysi was alive, right here in front of me!

Alive for now, at least, but for how much longer? The slight figure tumbled to the ground, four burly thieves looming over her. Goldfinder in my hand, I plunged ahead, desperate to call out, to offer some kind of encouragement. Yet I held my tongue, knowing that my only chance was to take these bullies by complete surprise.

That, and to hope Badswell wasn't too far behind me.

In another second, I reached the nearest of the thieves, a scrawny fellow who had sidled around to block Saysi's retreat. Darting past him, I jabbed with my blade, slicing keen metal through his hamstring. He went down with a shriek of pain as I leaped into the air, slashing my weapon across the face of another thug. Then I crashed headlong into the brute who had reached down to clench the tiny priestess by the shoulder.

He went down in a tangle of curses and punches, squealing rather like a pig when my blade ripped into his soft belly. Rolling free, I bounced to my feet to see several more of the ruffians closing in. Saysi—it *was* Saysi!—

regarded me with wide, panic-stricken eyes.

"Kip?" she gasped, in the most delightful sound I had ever heard. She smiled with such a sudden sense of contentment that it would have melted my heart, if not for the deadly fight raging a sword's length away.

"Run!" I cried, gesturing toward the mouth of the alley.

In response, she picked up a piece of stick that lay beside a nearby shack, whipping the makeshift club around to smash a thug in the knee.

A hulking shape loomed suddenly, and Badswell was there. Fortunately he didn't stop to ask questions. Instead, he plucked a hefty thief up by the shoulders and pitched the fellow into a darkened corner of the alley, leaving him sprawled insensate on the muddy ground. Another man went down under the hammerblow of Badswell's mighty fist, and two more staggered dizzily after the half-ogre bashed their heads together.

Darting to Saysi's side, I took her hand and pulled her back toward the street.

"Kip! How did you . . . what's—who's that?" she asked, standing dumbfounded between Badswell and me.

"Later!" I cried, spinning to face the half-ogre. "Follow us—and that was real good work, Bads!"

We raced out of the alley. With a guttural growl and a glare that froze the bandits—those who were still conscious, at least—in their tracks, Bads retreated slowly after us.

"That poor old lady!" Saysi said, stopping suddenly. She marched back to the thug who was in his death throes from my stab to his stomach. While Badswell glowered at the other thieves, she reached for the wretch's belt and pulled away a small purse, while the other thieves looked on malevolently. One or two made a noise to object, but when the half-ogre smacked his lips and growled, they quickly reconsidered their boldness.

"Come *on*," I repeated, tugging at her arm. "Let's get out of here!"

"Well, it was *wrong*," she told me righteously and as firmly as if we had never been parted. "They stole her money, and I'm going to give it back."

"I know you always despised thievery," I replied, looking nervously over my shoulder as we moved down the street. Fortunately nobody appeared in the alleyway; Badswell had thrown a pretty good scare into the band of thieves. "But don't you think that's carrying it a little far? Those guys would have killed you without thinking twice!"

"It was still wrong," she repeated.

I laughed. "You know, it really doesn't matter. The important thing is, you're alive!" I embraced her, feeling her arms close around me in return, forcing myself to speak around the lump that grew solid in my throat.

"I—I thought for sure you were dead. I looked for you in the alley, back in Oakvale. One of those monsters, the kakkuu, came out, and you were nowhere to be seen."

"I went down a manhole," she explained cheerfully. "The bite of that . . . kakkuu, you called it? It made me kind of dizzy. I passed out down there for a while, till well after sunrise. By the time I came out, the monsters were gone, but so were you. I was afraid that you'd been eaten or captured or something!"

"No," I admitted miserably. "I just left. By Patrikon, I should have waited. I should have looked more carefully!"

"Don't say that," counseled Saysi. "We're together again now, and I'm sure we have lots of adventures to talk about. First, tell me, who's your friend?"

The half-ogre bowed with elephantine grace as I made the introductions and described my meeting with Badswell. "His mother had another piece of that black stick, like a part of the one I bought in the Red Garter. Bads has his mother's piece now, and we've been traveling together ever since. We came to Argenport to try to find the third piece."

"You mean this?" asked Saysi, pulling a stub of familiar-looking ebony from a pocket of her robe. Dumbfounded, I saw the geometric patterns on both ends, recognized the sheen of perfect obsidian blackness. Sure enough, the piece was a trifle longer than Badswell's and seemed to continue the trend of getting wider at the end away from the tip.

"How did you get that?" I was astounded by her possession of the piece, amazed at the pattern, the strange sense of order that seemed to be falling into place.

"I found it. It was on the ground in the middle of a bandit camp, near the road out of Oakvale. All the bandits were dead . . . killed by some kind of disease, I think. But when I saw it, I remembered the one you got in the dragonfire game back at the Red Garter." She looked at me, her eyes misting as she gave me a quick hug. "I guess I took it because it kind of reminded me of you."

"That's great! You've got the third piece of the rod!" I cried ecstatically.

"Can we stick them together?" the halfling priestess wondered.

"No!" Bads and I barked in harmony.

"That is," I explained, "I don't think that would be a good idea." I told her of the disappearance of the second part when we had tried to do just that.

"We came to Argenport because we sensed that was

where the next piece of the rod was. Each piece, it seems, lets you know where the next bigger one is," I continued, then paused as I was seized by a sudden thought. "But what brought you here to the coast?"

"I . . . I don't really know," she said, her curved brow creasing into a very attractive frown. "It was just sort of a feeling I had, as if I should be going in this direction. Say, you don't think . . . ?"

She looked at me quizzically, letting her question hang in the air.

"That the fourth piece is here, in Argenport?" I concluded excitedly. "I'm *sure* that's it!"

"And I know just where," she continued breathlessly. "I found this place in the High City. It's like a grand mansion, surrounded by a wall. Almost a fortress of its own, with square corners and lots of towers. Every time I wandered around the city, I found myself drawn to the place. I'd just stop in the street, standing outside and staring at it. I didn't understand why I kept going there . . . until now!"

"This mansion—can you take us there?" I pressed.

"Sure. As I said, it's in the High City," she said, and then a look of concern clouded her otherwise perfect face. "Do you have someplace to stay in the city? I've been staying at the temple down near the waterfront. The high priest let me have an apprentice's cell for as long as I want to stay."

"We don't have lodgings yet, but let's see this mansion first." Urgency compelled me to haste.

"Okay. I have to give this money back to the old lady, but she was in the High City anyway."

Saysi started toward the gates that led to the wealthier portion of Argenport. Bads and I fell into step behind her, and my mind churned with a whirlwind of new discoveries—Saysi's presence, her possession of a piece of the rod, and the hope that a fourth piece might be found just around the corner.

CHAPTER 14

PARNISH FEGHER

"About Badswell," I whispered to Saysi as we approached the looming gates leading to the High City. "Do you think he'll have any trouble from the guards?" I remembered that the upper-class district of Argenport had been considerably more diligently guarded than the slums.

Saysi shook her head, turning to look affectionately over her shoulder. The half-ogre ambled along a few steps behind, giving us a chance to walk arm in arm in privacy.

"I don't think so. Before, sure, it seems they would have been alarmed by someone like him. But have you noticed? Argenport seems, somehow, kind of *wilder* than before. Like the laws don't mean much to anybody."

I nodded grimly, but decided not to say that I had reached the same conclusion. "About this mansion, the place where you think the fourth piece of the rod is. How often have you gone to look at it? Have you seen anyone going in or out? Do you think you've been observed while you were there?"

"First, I don't *think* the piece is there, I *know* it is," she replied tartly.

"Of course."

"And I don't know how often I've gone there, but I've never seen anyone going in or out, so naturally I don't think anyone has seen me."

As she led us onward, I looked around, remembering immediately that the High City was much nicer than Argenport's outer quarter. The streets were wider, lined with plants and bright with blooming flowers, and the scattered drunks much more well dressed than the ragged beggars we'd encountered outside the lofty walls.

"Here's that fruit seller." Saysi crossed the street, extending the small leather purse to a stooped, frail-looking woman who stood beside a cart of apples. The elder's wrinkled and toothless face broke into a disbelieving smile as she took the purse, nodding thanks as the priestess turned back to join us.

"Bless you, child!" called the vendor as we started once again along the street.

"That was nice," Badswell said, looking back at the woman, then over to Saysi. "You helped her good."

For the most part, the people on the streets kept their eyes downcast or looked furtively after us as we passed. No one seemed inclined to accost anyone, or even acknowledge a stranger's presence. Armed guards paced before the gates of several stately houses, and when a patrol of the city watch tromped by, we stepped to the curb. From the protection of their tight formation, the guardsmen's eyes watchfully probed each alcove and alley.

"Why don't they post more men at the city gates?" I wondered aloud. "Then they wouldn't need to send half a regiment out on marching patrol."

"I don't know," Saysi replied. "But you're right. It doesn't make sense."

We started on as the receding footsteps of the patrol faded away down a connecting street. "The sea's down there," Saysi said, pointing along a broad avenue we were crossing. "Remember when we walked there and saw the ships from all over the world, and the big temple to Patrikon down near the water? As I said, that's where I've been staying."

I nodded at the memory of the granite, square-walled edifice. Like most of Patrikon's holy places, it had resembled a fortress more than a place of worship. I hadn't spent much time there, but I recalled that the vast chambers had seemed unusually quiet, almost like abandoned ruins amid the bustle of Argenport's streets.

"What about the rod?" Once again our mission began to take on a sense of urgency in my mind.

"Right here," she said as we entered a broad, paved plaza. An outdoor dining area, shaded by large, fat-leafed bushes, occupied one side of the square, while across the open expanse rose a high stone wall.

"Behind that?" I asked, indicating the barrier.

Saysi nodded. I looked upward, over the few people moving across the plaza, studying the top of the wall and anything I could see beyond. The turrets and gables of a building within were visible and suggested a square pattern for the occupant's house. The tops of lofty pines and spreading oaks also extended above the wall, and from these, I guessed that the trees on the enclosed estate had been planted in a very regular pattern.

"Wait here," I suggested, indicating the nearby tables of the café. "I'll go have a look around."

"What about shackles?" Badswell asked, frowning at the walled enclosure and the small fence surrounding the outdoor inn.

"Don't worry. You and Saysi should just act like you belong there," I said breezily. After our experiences thus far, I didn't think it likely that they'd be bothered by guards. In fact, there were people sleeping in the open around the fringes of this very plaza, a circumstance that would never have been tolerated in Argenport's High City, so far as I could remember.

In a slow, deliberate circuit around the fortified mansion Saysi had identified, I noticed a number of unusual features. Perhaps most dramatically, the compound was laid out in an absolutely regular pattern: an octagon of high walls, with identical towers jutting up from each of the eight corners, and four solid, closed gates in the middle of the north, south, east, and west walls.

I saw no sign of the owner's identification, no coat of arms or herald emblazoned on the walls or gates. Indeed, none of these portals seemed any different from the others; nothing suggested one as a main entrance or front door. Nor had I seen any flags or pennants flying from the turrets that had been visible above the surrounding wall. Still, the very size and splendor of the place denoted that some kind of nobleman, or perhaps a very wealthy merchant, dwelled within.

Small plazas or marketplaces faced several of the compound's walls, while the others were skirted by wide streets. These avenues were littered with garbage and refuse, though none of the waste had been allowed to collect along the wall around the stately mansion. I completed my circuit and returned to the small café where I had left my two companions.

I found Badswell and Saysi at the table on the outdoor patio of the inn. This early in the day, the place was mostly empty, but it served our purposes well because it provided a splendid view of the walled enclosure.

"Did you notice? There's no one sleeping near the place," Saysi remarked as I made my way between the tables to rejoin her and Badswell.

"That, and the streets are clean around the wall—cleaner than anyplace else I've seen in Argenport."

"*Too* clean," Badswell muttered, clearly uncomfortable with his bulk wedged into a small chair. "I like Low City better."

"But even in the High City, there are drunks flopped all over the place, and beggars squatting on just about every corner," Saysi observed.

"Every corner but those around here . . ." My eyes were drawn again to the rigidly organized compound, to the towers and the ranks of regimented evergreens arrayed within the walls. "I'm betting it has something to do with whoever lives there."

"You're sure the next piece is in there?" asked Badswell, scowling as he followed the direction of my gaze.

"Sure as I can be," Saysi replied. "You've both carried pieces of the rod. You know how that direction sense works. It drew me all the way to Argenport, to the High City. Then, when I walked around that place, every instinct in my body told me that I should try to find a way to get inside—that that's where the fourth piece of the rod is."

"Let's go get it, then," Badswell muttered, shuffling his feet.

"Shouldn't we have some sort of plan?" I asked, laying a restraining hand on his big arm.

"Any ideas?" Saysi wondered.

"We could try knocking on the door," I suggested reluctantly. The idea sounded too much like walking into a trap for my tastes.

"What'sat?" questioned Badswell, pointing to a square of parchment that had apparently been nailed to the gate in the nearest wall of the compound.

"That wasn't there before—at least, I didn't see it when I walked around the place!" Given the extent of my earlier reconnaissance, there didn't seem to be any way I could have missed the yellowed sheet. I felt absolutely positive that it had been posted since my circuit of the octagonal compound's walls.

"I didn't notice it either," concurred the priestess. "But I didn't see anyone putting it up just now."

"I can't say that I like this much," I groused.

"*Somebody* put it there." Saysi's logic was irrefutable. "Maybe it says something useful."

"It could be a trap." The situation still smelled of treachery as far as I was concerned.

"We just gonna stand here? Let's look." The half-ogre was clearly growing impatient.

"I'm with Badswell," Saysi declared. "We've got to do *something*."

I was tempted to suggest that "something" could conceivably include abandoning all thought of the Rod of Seven Parts, turning our back on this place, and getting on with the rest of our lives. Saysi had returned, as if by a miracle, and it would have been very easy to wander off with her in search of further, safer adventures. The business of potent artifacts, of age-old strife between law and chaos, was clearly nothing but trouble.

Yet in my heart, I knew that turning aside now was an unsatisfying notion; something strange, deep, and compelling made it essential that we try to locate the next piece of this ancient artifact. The others agreed. Only later did it occur to me that, as we made up our minds, each of us reached down to touch our individual stub of ebony.

"Let's go see what the sign says," the little priestess suggested.

"I don't know. . . . It seems too obvious, somehow, to just walk over there. How about having a look at the other gates?" I suggested. "Maybe each of them has a sign now. The one to the left, at least, was a lot more private than this one across the square."

We made our way casually along the street leading from the plaza, following the high wall of the compound around to the left. Going around another corner, we were on a stretch of street that had earlier struck me as the least traveled section of the compound's environs. Trying to be surreptitious, I yawned and stretched, tilting back my head and allowing my eyes to sweep along the crest of the wall. It was crenellated, suggesting a platform for fighting or observation behind it, but I still saw no sign of a guard or any other inhabitant.

Walking along the side of the street opposite the wall, we drew near the western doorway. Like the others, this portal was a heavy stone archway, with a door of massive oaken planks banded with bolts of iron or steel. There was no aperture to suggest a window or even a speaking hole in the barrier; the door seemed, to all appearances, like a very solid surface indeed.

As on the gate in the plaza, a sheet of parchment,

187

curled slightly at the lower corners, had been nailed into the middle of the door. From this distance, we could see several tiny symbols scrawled on the sheet.

"The writing's too small to read from across the street," Saysi observed.

"But who put it there?" I demanded crossly. "I couldn't have missed two of these signs, could I?"

"It hasn't been there for long," deduced the priestess. "The first rain—or even a strong wind—would rip it right off."

"Maybe somebody 'spects us to come along," Badswell declared dryly. "What's it say?"

"Only one way to find out," I muttered.

I looked left and right, glad to see that there were no other pedestrians in sight. Trying to maintain an elaborately casual air, we sauntered across the street and gathered in front of the oak-paneled door. Saysi and I craned upward, reading the words on the sign and looking at each other in surprise.

"Say it out loud," gruffed Badswell.

"Sorry." I had forgotten that the big fellow had no doubt never learned to read. "It says, 'If you are the bearer of the key, you *must* enter here! My command is etched with all the power of the law.' "

"Who says?" The half-ogre glowered to all sides, ready to argue the point.

"Does it matter?" Saysi asked. "Try the gate."

I pushed at the door. I wasn't surprised to find that it was in fact very securely locked.

"What key? Does it say that?" Badswell pressed.

"No," Saysi replied, as her hand fished into the big pocket of her gown. It emerged, pink fingers clenched around an object of glossy black. "But I have an idea."

"Do—do you think that's a good idea?" I wondered, suddenly hesitant.

"I don't know what else to do," she said. "And, yes, I think it's the right thing to do. After all, this sign doesn't seem to be a threat or a warning. It's more of an invitation, and it invokes the name of law."

This didn't seem like a good time to mention that a threat could easily be concealed as an invitation. Besides, despite my misgivings, I was forced to agree with Saysi: Trying to open the door—lawfully—seemed like the right thing to do. That command was phrased in terms of the undeniable rightness of law, and I believed in law. If we had the key, then we had no choice but to enter.

There didn't seem to be any kind of keyhole, so Saysi simply raised her stub of the rod, touching the door just below the parchment.

I was beyond surprise when the portal swung soundlessly open, revealing a straight walkway of crushed gravel between sentinels of lofty pines. The path connected directly to a door in the manor house that came into view as we passed hesitantly through the outer gate. I gulped back my apprehensions as I heard the barrier swing softly shut behind us. Part of me wanted to turn around and make sure that it would open for us again, but—perhaps because Saysi advanced with unhesitating courage—I quelled that notion, proceeding abreast of my companions along that inviting walk.

Stone crunched softly under Badswell's boots, while Saysi's and my bare feet barely disturbed a single chip of rock. Beside the walkway was a lawn of precisely trimmed grass, broken by the verdant umbrellas of pine clumps and the stately, solitary oaks. The lofty trees were arranged with care between stretches of smooth lawn, broken by several swaths of brightness that were clearly small, formal gardens. Not surprisingly, the garden on the left was a virtual mirror image of the one we could glimpse to the right.

Birds chirped and squawked, adding to the pastoral gentility of the surroundings. I saw a pair of robins hopping on the lawn, and a male woodpecker, his crimson head vibrating, hammered at the limb of a tall oak while a brown female perched watchfully nearby.

Without discussion, we advanced toward the great house, looking upward at the great structure with growing awe. The lower fringe of the building was made of uniquely matching fieldstone, a gridwork of perfectly matched hexagonal pieces. The upper walls were paneled in dark timbers and crossed by grids of heavy beams. Several windows were visible in the upper floors, though neither movement nor light suggested the presence of anything or anyone alive or moving up there.

"Look! Another sign on the door!" Saysi pointed, her voice tightening in excitement and tension. A yellow sheet was nailed prominently in place, bold script proclaiming something that we couldn't read at this distance.

Once again I wasn't surprised, but neither was I reassured. We climbed three marble steps to the landing of the house, discovering that the front door was every bit as solid and windowless as the gate in the compound's outer wall.

I immediately saw that the message was similar to the one we had seen outside.

" 'Ye who would serve the law *must* enter here, for only thus may the tides of chaos be held at bay!' " Saysi read the words aloud and, before anyone could object, reached forward with her chip of the rod.

"Wait!" I gulped, pulling her hand back before it made contact. "Are you sure . . . ?"

She looked at me, her brow creased in a clear invitation for me to offer a better suggestion. When I said nothing else, she nodded—a touch smugly, I thought—and pressed the stub of the rod against the door.

Immediately the portal swung smoothly open, revealing a corridor leading into the depths of the mansion. A floor of black marble gleamed as if freshly waxed, and walls of sleek mahogany reflected the marble's glow with a sheen of their own. Overhead, several crystal chandeliers led into the distance; from each of these a few candles flickered, the minimal illumination proving more than ample when reflected by the glossy surfaces of wall and floor.

"Well, no point stopping here," Saysi said, stepping boldly forward.

Feeling far less bold than the priestess looked, I nevertheless accompanied her. Badswell kept pace, and together we marched into the depths of the strange house. I was not surprised to hear the door click softly shut behind us.

"I'm worried," I said in a low whisper. "I'm afraid this might be a trap."

"Well, take a look around," Saysi retorted. "You used to be pretty good at finding traps. See if you see anything that worries you."

I moved into the lead, conscious of my companions following close behind me. My eyes roved from the ceiling, which was lost in shadows except around the chandeliers, to the walls and floor. The mahogany paneling was smooth and flawless—I saw no sign of any irregularity that might have indicated a hidden door, peephole, or anything else out of the ordinary. Still, I couldn't shake the feeling that I wasn't doing this right. I was missing something, or forgetting to look for obvious clues.

We had progressed for more than two dozen steps when I saw the first unusual feature: a small metal lever in the wall, with one of the ubiquitous parchments nailed to the wall just below it.

" 'You *must* pull this lever, for the law compels you,' " I read aloud as I stepped up to the unusual feature. Without thinking, I reached out, took hold of the handle, and jerked it sharply downward.

The rattling of chains gave us a split second's warning—enough to panic, but not to move. Metal crashed with an ear-shattering clang, the sound resonating down the long corridor. By the time I took a step, I met the bars of a heavy cage that had dropped from the ceiling to completely enclose the three of us.

"I think you found a trap," Saysi declared wryly.

"Why did I pull it?" I groaned, cursing my thoughtless stupidity.

"Because of the rod—you carry an artifact of law," she replied, her tone surprisingly gentle, considering the circumstance. "When you saw the instructions, you did the right thing—the *lawful* thing—and followed them."

"Catching you all very neatly, I observe."

The new voice emerged from the depths of the corridor, spoken in a man's well-modulated tones. Bitterly I looked for our captor, watching as a door slid open in the side walls of the corridor, farther down than we had progressed.

"This should prove to be a very profitable encounter . . . very profitable indeed."

The speaker came into view then, and I was surprised

to see a man of relatively diminutive status. Somehow the voice had made me expect someone much taller. He wore a red silk jacket of impeccable tailoring, and his clean-shaven face was smooth, though the gray in his hair suggested that he was past middle age. Still, his steel-colored head was carefully, even immaculately groomed, with not a hair out of place. Eyes that were dark and piercing flashed with keen intelligence from behind metal-framed spectacles, and though he smiled as he approached, I saw no trace of humor in anything about his appearance.

"Welcome to my humble home, travelers. I have been expecting you."

"You knew we were coming?" Saysi blurted.

"Well, not *you* exactly, but I've been expecting at least one visitor. You see, I possess something that has attracted you. By the fact that you have come through my doors, I know that you possess that which I seek."

"You have the fourth part of the rod," I accused, having no patience for vague games.

"Ah . . . I see that you are aware of the nature of the precious segment you bear. Perhaps you are not as unworthy as appearances might indicate." With careful dignity, the gray-haired man stroked his smooth chin.

"Your supposition is correct. I have the fourth piece. And I know that you have the third." Abruptly his forehead creased more deeply, then brightened with an anticipatory smile. "I should say, at *least* the third. But there are three of you. It occurs to me that you might have the first and second pieces as well."

None of us replied to his statement. Recognizing the truth, I suspected that we wouldn't have the segments of the artifact for much longer.

"Rathentweed! Come here, my good gnome!" cried the

man, clapping his hands together. "Come and meet our visitors."

Moments later a short, stocky figure with round cheeks, a flowing brown beard, and a colossal nose bustled into view, entering through another panel in the hallway that slid aside to reveal a secret door. That portal, I saw with chagrin, was located on one of the walls I had already inspected. Though I had noticed not the faintest irregularity, the aperture revealed was as broad and high as a normal door, dwarfing the little fellow who stepped through and now stood, blinking curiously, tugging on one of the tassels that dangled from his floppy hat as he regarded us.

"Oh, dear," the gnome muttered, gulping audibly as he looked up at the glowering form of Badswell. "This is a *very* large one—and worse, not man, and not ogre. Dear, dear me! He seems a very chaotic mix of the two."

"Leave him alone!" snapped Saysi, confronting the gnome through the bars of our cage. She was as tall as the stocky little fellow, who blinked and stammered awkwardly, taken aback by her firm stance.

"Now, now," declared the man, stepping forward until he stood just beyond the bars on the opposite side of the cage. I momentarily considered a quick stab, Goldfinder snicking through the grid, but discarded the notion—at least for now. After all, this fellow might be able to tell us something useful; he might even let us out of the cage. It didn't help my plan that he seemed to be watching me carefully, obviously anticipating some sort of aggressive move.

Even without his observance, however, I'm not sure I would have attempted violence. There was a quiet competence about this man that gave me pause, so I decided to wait and see what happened next.

"Allow me to introduce myself. I am Parnish Fegher, your host in this house of law. As long as you are capable of following a few simple rules, I think you'll find that we shall get along quite nicely."

"Do you always trap your guests in iron cages?" Saysi snapped.

"Heavens, no! Only my most important visitors, I should say. Isn't that right, Rathentweed?"

"Oh, quite," the gnome declared, bobbing his head eagerly. His pointed beard bounced enthusiastically, and his tasseled hat flopped around with a ludicrous motion that would have been amusing under other circumstances. I found it hard to believe that anyone could walk around with a nose like that; it seemed that the weight must certainly topple him forward onto his face. "That is, he caught me the same way when I came here with my piece of the rod!"

"He let you out, then?" Badswell deduced.

"Certainly—as soon as I gave him my piece of the rod. You see, he already had the fifth. That's what drew me here. And I gave him the fourth. Now it's your turn! That's all he wants . . . well, mostly, anyway."

I began to sense that this situation might not be completely disastrous. If we just had to give up the stubs of the black artifact before getting out of here, perhaps I could bring myself to do so.

"Why do you want the Rod of Seven Parts?" Saysi asked with her typical lack of reticence.

"My dear, the rod is the artifact, the symbol and embodiment, of ultimate law. There is nothing else like it among all the planes. It represents power beyond belief."

I was not pleased to hear Parnish talking about worlds

and planes and such. It reminded me too much of those white gates and the attacks of the spyder-fiends that had grown so distressingly frequent.

"Surely you know that throughout the world there is a great surfeit of chaos," continued our determined host. "Why, you can see it in the wretched refuse that clogs the streets and alleys of my own city. Thieves and whores and drunkards abound, committing debaucheries beyond comprehension, and well beyond the bounds of law."

"We noticed," I stated dryly. "Argenport seems to be a little the worse for wear."

"It is the coming of chaos! The power of the queen is abroad in the world!"

"And you plan to stop her?" I couldn't help needling a little bit.

"I shall try, using the power of the rod," replied Parnish, without a trace of irony or amusement. "Nothing else, anywhere, embodies the rigid framework of order as purely and as potently as even the tiniest piece of this mighty artifact. And the one who can assemble the pieces will be the wielder of power unlike anything known for a thousand years! A reign of true law will commence, an order superior to any the world has ever seen! Wrongdoers will face their deserved punishment, and the tides of chaos will be held firmly at bay."

Privately I smiled at the prospect of his attempting to join the pieces, almost hoping that we'd see Parnish try to stick two of the black sticks together. Well did I remember the sudden disappearance of Badswell's stub when I had tried to do the same thing.

"Of course, this assembly is not a thing done quickly or casually," Parnish continued, quickly quashing my momentary amusement. "Only a fool would try to do that.

No, one must prepare the spells, the hieroglyphics, the arcane symbology and incantations that will allow the pieces to be properly fused. Now, if you will be kind enough to hand over your pieces, I will see that the cage is removed."

Sighing in resignation, Saysi pulled forth her stub of the rod. Badswell and I did the same, though, for my part at least, without the reluctance that the little priestess displayed.

Parnish Fegher's eyes glinted avariciously as he took each of the pieces, carefully stowing it away before touching the next one. I noticed that even when he tucked them away, he kept them a good distance away from each other: one in a shoulder pouch, one in a purse hanging from his belt on the opposite side, and one even stuck into the upper cuff of his leather boot.

"You talk very proudly of the law," Saysi observed sharply. "Yet that didn't prevent you from taking us captive nor from stealing our possessions!"

Silently I willed her to be quiet, sensing that this wasn't a good time to be angering our host—not when we had just relinquished our only bargaining chips.

"My acts are well justified by the very law you would invoke," Parnish replied smoothly. "The profit to the entire world must be weighed against the possessions of a few. The risks and the debits are great. You should know that, sooner rather than later, someone or some*thing* would have taken these from you. It is far better for the world, and I daresay for you, that they have come to me."

"That's what *you* say!" Saysi declared heatedly.

"That's what I *know*. Now, if the debate has concluded, I shall release you."

"The debate has concluded," I declared, with a stern

look at the unrepentant priestess.

"Very good," our host said with a benign smile. He muttered a word and pointed. My skin prickled at the sensation of magic all around me as the metal cage, which must have weighed many hundred pounds, lifted into the air without a perceptible strain on the part of Parnish Fegher.

Immediately I knew that our captor was a wizard, and no slouch of a one to judge by the ease with which he levitated the cage. I congratulated myself privately on the discretion that had prevented me from trying to stab him through the bars. If I had, I suspected that right about now I would be hopping around in the form of a frog or something.

"Thanks for getting the cage off—and you're welcome to my part of the rod!" I snapped peevishly. "Now, if you'll just open the door, we'll be on our way."

"The door? Heavens, no!" Parnish objected.

"But you promised—" Saysi began, before he cut her off with a curt gesture.

"My dear, I promised to let you out of the cage. And I have done so, I'm sure you will agree. After all, I never go back on my word."

"But you won't let us out of your house?" I demanded.

"No, no. That would be impossible. You will remain here as my guests—my pupils, if you will—and I hope that you will be apt students."

The wizard appeared distracted for a moment, as if his thoughts had just traveled far away. Abruptly his eyes flashed onto mine in a smile that was both observant and empathetic—much in the same way that a hungry snake might stare at a mouse.

CHAPTER 15

TALE OF THE WOLF-SPIDER

I have been imprisoned on several occasions during the course of a long and eventful life, once spending the better part of a year in a dank, flea-infested hole at the rear of a giant's lair. At other times, I've been locked up for various periods in a king's dungeon, a sheriff's cell, and even a storage room behind a gem cutter's shop. By the standards of all those previous captivities, the surroundings of Parnish Fegher's mansion were admittedly not too bad.

After he removed the cage, the wizard ushered us through a luxurious anteroom and down a long hallway. Polished marble columns flanked the door at the far end. Plush carpeting layered the floors, and every wall we had seen so far had been paneled in smoothly finished planking.

"We have only a few matters to discuss before you get settled," our host informed us.

"What kind of matters?" I asked suspiciously.

He ignored my question. "By tomorrow, serious work will begin. I hope you will have no difficulties making yourselves comfortable before then."

"Our host's accommodations are splendid," Rathentweed declared enthusiastically. "You will be right at home. Even you will have a large enough bed," he assured Badswell.

"A bed, huh?" The half-ogre nodded thoughtfully. Obviously he wasn't terribly distraught about our imprisonment. As Saysi looked around in wide-eyed amazement, I realized with disgust that I seemed to be the only one who was upset about the involuntary nature of our stay.

Accompanied by our captor and the fussy gnome, we entered a large sitting room. Eight chairs stood in pairs around the chamber, facing a fireplace—currently cold—and a craggy limestone hearth in the wall opposite the door. A large chandelier sparkled brightly after one word from Parnish, shedding light throughout the room. There were no windows, and I remembered from my outside observations that the entire first floor of the manor had been enclosed by a solid wall.

The wizard promised us that we would have private rooms—"chambers," he called them—and servants to tend to our needs. Indeed, no sooner had he made these explanations than several liveried young men appeared with tape measures, pins, and samples of cloth material.

"We have certain standards of dress here," Parnish explained. "Of course, you didn't know that when you arrived, so your initial breach of etiquette will be forgiven. However, as soon as garments can be prepared, you will all be expected to follow the rules."

He sniffed audibly as he looked over Badswell, whose

ragged breeches showed the strain of our weeks in the wilderness—not that they had been spectacular to begin with. I had maintained myself a little more carefully, but even so the patches at my knees and elbows were wearing thin. The wizard looked archly down his nose at me, sneering through his spectacles as he pinched my threadbare collar until I angrily pulled away and, with a great show of dignity, straightened my clothes as much as possible.

Only Saysi, who had managed to keep her skirts and robes clean, drew a slight nod of approval. However, she was still included as the tailor and his apprentices stood us straight, then measured arms, legs, feet, shoulders, and all sorts of other dimensions. The clothiers bustled around in silent concentration, the only sounds the scratching of quills on parchment as they noted down innumerable figures.

"What you do need *that* for?" I asked once as I was being very thoroughly measured for an inseam. I had always preferred loose-fitting garments and made a point of saying so, but the apprentice, a young man, merely looked down and scribbled a note onto his sheet of parchment.

"Can't these guys talk?" I demanded as the servants continued to ignore our questions and comments.

"They can, but they won't," Parnish said. "It's against the rules."

"What rule is that?"

"The rule that bars the servants from speaking. Violation means instant dismissal, but it has been years since there has been an infraction."

"You mean that none of the servants in your house are allowed to *speak?*" I asked, dumbfounded.

Parnish nodded calmly. "I have found that the servant-to-master relationship is more profitable that way. Of course, they're permitted to converse normally once they have left the bounds of my estate."

"Why in the world do you have a rule like that?" pressed Saysi, looking sympathetically at the small army of bustling, mute tailors.

"Profit and debit, as I intimated earlier," Parnish declared with a touch of impatience. "Servants are necessary to my comforts, and as such are a worthwhile investment of my money. Their presence is 'profitable,' in a word. However, the gossip and innuendo—not to mention the simple wasting of time—that results from servants who spend their time gabbing instead of working creates a clear impediment to that profitability. A debit, or loss, if you will. You will find that I have many rules designed to insure just such efficiency."

I'm sure you do. I didn't voice the sarcastic response, but I was getting pretty tired of hearing about Parnish and his rules.

"*We* get to talk, though?" Badswell asked, scowling suspiciously. He had fidgeted through a fitting by no fewer than three tailors, and his temper was clearly foul.

"Of course. You're guests. In fact, allow me to provide a tour of your accommodations."

"You will find them delightful," Rathentweed repeated, nodding his head and setting that pointed beard and ridiculous nose to bouncing again. He bustled ahead and opened the door with a flourish. "Everything here has its place—a very comfortable situation."

"We will begin with the library." Parnish preceded us through several wide corridors, stopping at a pair of large oaken doors that terminated the hallway. With a single soft knock, he touched the wooden panels, and both heavy doors swung silently inward. He repeated the magical command he had uttered in the sitting room—it sounded something like *illictus*—and four crystal chandeliers blossomed into white light.

We followed the wizard into a massive room, outlined in an apparently perfect square. A walkway of carpeting led straight across the floor and was intersected halfway through the room by a perpendicular strip; the flooring served to divide the library into four even quarters. Each of these was illuminated by its own chandelier and contained a large, square table flanked by sixteen chairs.

The walls of the room were lined with many shelves, though the wooden frameworks were interrupted in a number of places—sixteen, I realized almost instinctively. In each of these niches between the shelving, a single oil painting was prominently displayed. Even from a distance, I could see that the works were of exceptional quality, tending to portray vast scenes of landscape, battle, or council.

My curiosity was aroused in spite of myself, but before I could start across to the nearest painting, the sound of a deep chime rang through the manor.

"It's noon!" Rathentweed declared excitedly. "Time to change out of our morning attire." He looked at us, his chubby cheeks pouting in a frown of exaggerated concern. "But your clothes aren't ready yet!" he squeaked.

"These'll do for another few hours," I snorted, not sure whether I was amused or annoyed by his officious manner.

"Rathentweed is right." The wizard spoke, and there was no trace of humor in his bearing or his voice. Instead, he glowered unpleasantly, and I bit back more sarcastic remarks. "I have forgiven your breach for the morning, but I was hoping that would be the only time."

Parnish drew a deep breath, as if he were reluctantly arriving at a very painful conclusion. "However, the rules require *some* sort of clothing—nudity would be an even greater affront. Since these are what you have, you will wear them until your new clothes are prepared."

"*I* shall change immediately, my lord," declared Rathentweed, making a deep bow, then sniffing contemptuously as he bustled from the library.

"Where did you get these paintings?" I asked, trying to draw the wizard's attention back to his earlier topic.

"I painted them," he declared. "They are benchmarks in a great strife, a conflict that has been waged since the dawn of time."

Apparently I was onto something. Parnish turned with animation toward the nearest piece of artwork, a battle scene that had caught my eye as soon as I had seen it. I walked over to the canvas. Unconsciously my pace slowed as I drew near. The strident colors and vivid sense of motion visible from a distance had not prepared me for the graphic and horrifying detail of the painting viewed up close. I shuddered at an unspeakably monstrous image in the center of the scene, instantly pulling back to observe the piece as a whole.

The artist had captured a battle in a moment of furious, savage climax. I recognized a host of spyder-fiends, the arachnoid horrors swarming in countless hundreds around their monstrous leader, the grotesque giant that had so deeply affected me upon my first look at the painting. The beast resembled a monstrous version of the spyder-fiends, but towered over the lesser monsters in an even more terrifying aspect. The huge monster had three heads, with a humanlike face in the center, flanked by a pair of sleek, lupine snouts. The visage of the man-head was upraised, as handsome and aloof as any proud king, except for the light of cruelty that the painter had somehow captured in the wide, staring eyes.

Each of the wolf-heads loomed massive and evil, with a maw large enough to engulf a kakkuu in a single bite. White fangs gleamed in the long jaws, and I saw that one of the heads had seized a victim in its fangs. The naked, manlike corpse, ebony black in color, drooped lifelessly, blood trailing in slick rivers down its back as the monster crushed the life from it.

Only then did I look at the forces arrayed against the arachnoid horde. They were tall warriors, similar in appearance to the bleeding corpse in the monster's maw, naked and handsome and dark-skinned. Despite their nudity, I couldn't tell if they were men nor women; they lacked the features of either sex. Savage and determined fighters, they stood in close ranks against the swarm of tanar'ri, bearing swords and spears of keen, gleaming steel.

A series of whirlwinds, like small tornadoes, formed a backdrop to this valiant army. Staring at the motionless images in the picture, I could clearly sense the tension of an imminent charge, and I realized that the funnel clouds were in fact chariots, vehicles of spiraling wind that stood ready to bear the tall warriors forward to victory or death.

"You have a perceptive eye," Parnish declared, having stepped unnoticed behind me. "This is perhaps my finest work, a painting that cost me dearly to create."

"What is the scene?" I asked, mesmerized. Each second brought new details to my eye. There was a kakkuu, spitted upon the spear of one of the black, manlike defenders;

here a band of the warriors stood in a ring, holding against a pressing circle of merciless jaws.

"It is the Battle of Pesh, the finest legacy of the wind dukes," Parnish said, his voice thick with emotion. "It was the greatest victory of the vaati, but a tragic triumph in the end. The cost decimated the warriors of Aaqa beyond recovery."

"Pesh?" I wondered. "Never heard of it."

"The battle was waged countless centuries ago, on a world very far from our own. Indeed, the time was in such distant past that even the greatest sages have lost track of the real date. Nevertheless, the effects of its outcome are still felt in the worlds today."

"What do you mean?" Saysi asked as she and Badswell came to stand beside us. I heard her gasp as she, too, felt the impact of the scene. Her fingers wove into my own hand, clenching tightly as she sought courage in the face of the horror.

"That . . . *creature*—" the wizard spoke with almost physical loathing, and without looking, I knew he meant the three-headed monster commanding the spyder-fiend army— "is Miska the Wolf-Spider, consort of the Queen of Chaos and the greatest threat to law ever to menace any world."

"His army wins?" Badswell observed curiously.

"They are destroying the wind dukes and their champions, the captains of law. If not for the arrival of a mighty weapon, Miska's forces would have prevailed and chaos would rule all the cosmos. Our lives, and the lives of our forefathers for countless preceding generations, would be nil, snuffed out before they had a chance to begin."

"What mighty weapon?" I asked, scanning the ranks of the dukes. Abruptly I saw it: In the background, surprisingly small by the standards of a "mighty weapon," was a shaft of midnight black, borne by a tall, solitary wind duke.

"The Rod of Law, as it was known," Parnish explained. "When the last of the dukes were trapped and surrounded, a great captain took the rod and pierced Miska's body with it. The power of ultimate law met absolute chaos, and the battlefield was riven by natural violence. The rod shattered into pieces, an amount equal to that most chaotic of numbers—seven. But even as the pieces of the rod disappeared, so ultimately was Miska banished to his prison. There, in the wild realms of Pandemonium, he remains to this day."

"But why did the pieces of the rod show up now?" Saysi wondered.

"The question should be 'why now and why *here?*' " admonished Parnish Fegher. "Through the centuries, they have appeared frequently among the known worlds. Always they are scattered by apparently random pattern, and always on a world where law and chaos remain in strife."

"And the Queen of Chaos wants to gather the pieces?" I guessed.

"Indeed, for if she can assemble the rod, she can free her consort, and Miska will once again be unleashed across the planes. Any world in his path would be riven by chaos, countless lives destroyed, histories lost, entire peoples obliterated."

I gulped at the bleak description. Even the arrival of a few spyder-fiends had been enough to disrupt my life of relative peace and quiet. It didn't take much imagination to picture what an entire army of them could do to a place like, for example, Argenport. Or, even worse, Colbytown.

"You talk of worlds," I said. "I've come to realize that this cosmos is a pretty big place, but how many different lands or realms can there be?"

"No one knows," Parnish Fegher replied, "possibly because it is impossible to count that high. Suffice to say that there are countless worlds beyond our own, many of them quite similar, but others so different that to merely draw a breath there would cause instant death."

I shuddered at the prospect, not so much of a fatal atmosphere as the very idea that there could possibly be a countless number of worlds.

"And every one of those worlds would face danger—mortal peril, in fact—should the Queen of Chaos and her foul consort gain control of the rod."

Parnish glared at me, apparently wondering if I was convinced. I nodded to reassure him, realizing that he had outlined a very large problem. At the same time, I was liberated by the sensation that it was no longer *my* problem.

"What are you doing about it?" Saysi asked bluntly.

"I intend to assemble the rod before the queen can retrieve the pieces. When all seven parts are brought into proper conjunction, it is an artifact of absolute, ultimate law. As such, I shall wield it to drive chaos into abeyance."

Nodding silently, I privately wished him luck. At the same time, I decided that it would soon be time to get as far as possible from Parnish Fegher's reign of "ultimate law."

"Ah, here's Carrall. I believe your clothes are completed," declared the wizard.

I turned to see the elder tailor bowing, mutely, of course, in the door to the library.

"He and Rathentweed will escort you to your quarters.

You may rest for the afternoon, or peruse my library as you will. I have many preparations to make myself, but I will see you all for dinner."

With that, Parnish spun about and stalked from the chamber by a different door than we had entered.

"This way," declared the officious gnome, leading us back into the hall. We followed him up a wide stairway flanked by railings of polished ebony, and we were pleasantly surprised as he led us into an area of airy rooms, with soft furs on the floors and several large windows providing a view of the well-ordered estate grounds within the octagonal wall.

"Rathentweed," Saysi asked as the gnome bowingly showed us each a private bedroom. "Parnish said that seven is the most chaotic of numbers. What did he mean? How can one number be more chaotic than others?"

"It should be obvious!" He clucked disapprovingly at our ignorance, but nevertheless launched into an enthusiastic explanation. "The more well ordered a number, the more evenly it can be broken into components. Numbers such as eight—and, by extension, thirty-two, one hundred and twenty-eight, and so forth—are precisely reached. They are numbers of nearly perfect law. Numbers such as six, or thirty, for example, are neutral. They can be broken into equal components only so far, for they are based upon a chaotic root such as three or five. Seven is the most vile of these, for ever have the servants of chaos used it as their talisman."

"I see," I muttered hastily, having heard far more than I wanted to about law and chaos and numbers and worlds. Opening the door to our chambers, I waited for the gnome to depart.

Badswell merely grunted, looking at his fingers. "Two

and two . . . that's four. And two fours, makes eight. But seven is two of nuthin'."

"Splendid!" Rathentweed beamed up at the hulking half-ogre. "I can tell that you will be a very apt pupil."

"Not to interrupt schooltime, but perhaps you'll give us leave to change into these splendid garments?" I reminded the gnome of his purpose in showing us the chambers.

"Of course!" he said, bowing deeply. All but pushing him out the portal, I closed the door behind him.

"Did you see what I noticed?" Fixing my eyes on Saysi, I spoke in a whisper as soon as the gnome was out of earshot.

"What?" she wondered.

I pointed at the big panes of glass. "Windows! We can get out of here . . . escape! I'll break one if we can't find a way to open it!"

"Escape?" She surprised me with a look of befuddlement. "Why?"

"What kind of a question is that?" I shifted my attention to Badswell. "Don't *you* want to make a run for it?"

The surprises were not over for the day. The big half-ogre scowled in an expression of deep thought, though the question was clearly not that complicated. "I dunno," he muttered finally. "I think mebbe not right now."

"But we're *prisoners!* Trapped here against our will! Parnish even stole our pieces of the rod. Surely you must want to get away from him!"

"I think maybe he can put the rod to far better use than we could have," Saysi said—with irrefutable logic, I had to admit. "But can't you see, Kip? We're involved in something terribly important here! I think I'd like to see it through to the end."

I couldn't believe my ears. "Law and chaos aren't

affairs that concern us! Freedom or imprisonment—*those* are important. And I want to be free!"

"Free in a world that succumbs to chaos and dies?" Saysi retorted sharply. "You saw that painting. Is that what you want for the world?"

"No, of course not! But how can I change what's going to happen?"

"You can help! Each of us had a piece of that rod, and I don't think it was an accident. Patrikon knows there are patterns beyond things that you or I can discern, and I think we're seeing some of those effects right now! Kip, chaos is the *enemy*—not just of Parnish, or of Patrikon and his followers, but of everyone! I'm not about to run away when I could do something useful—perhaps even make a real difference for once in my life."

"You make a *big* difference—to me!" I objected. "Come with me. We'll get away from here. We—we could even get married!" I blurted out the idea before I realized what I was saying.

Saysi looked at me archly. "Is that supposed to be some kind of irresistible *bribe?*"

"No! I mean, we can go where you want to . . . do what you want. But we should be together!"

She sighed heavily, then looked at me with those melting-chocolate eyes. "You can do what you want. I know you will, regardless of what I say. But I'd really like you to stay here with me."

"Stay with *us*," Badswell noted firmly. He looked out the window, at a vista of blue sky and pleasant greenery. "We can always run away later."

"If we're still alive," I groused.

Sulking, I went to my room and sat on the bed. Beside me was an array of colorful, shiny material, where the tailors had laid out my new clothes. Intrigued in spite of my mood, I decided to try them on. Silken trousers fit perfectly, and a matching tunic and jacket added a dashing cut, I thought, to my trim figure. Satisfied, I looked in the full-length mirror, turning this way and that. As a gesture of independence, I ignored the supple moccasins that had been provided. I wasn't about to change a basic fact of halfling life merely to accommodate someone's rules.

Feeling a little better, I emerged to find Saysi resplendent in a blue silk gown that swirled about her shapely legs. Tight at the waist, it swept upward to the fullness of her small breasts and seemed to bring a healthy glow to her round cheeks. She blushed as I looked her over, and I privately concluded that maybe it wouldn't be too bad to stick around here and see what happened next.

I was glad to see that Saysi, too, had rejected the slippers that the tailors had made for her. When a mute attendant arrived and escorted us to the dining room, Parnish looked disdainfully at our bare feet, but, somewhat surprisingly, decided to make no comment.

Dinner was served on time, naturally. Silent servants brought out platters of veal and vegetables, no doubt in precisely measured portions. Fortunately for Badswell, the cook factored the size of the various diners into his equations, so the half-ogre got a serving adequate for his bulk. We halflings were content with human-sized portions and grateful that the cooks had considered the fact that, though our stature is only about half that of a man's, our appetites are every bit the equals of our larger cousins.

"Tell us more about the Rod of Seven Parts," Saysi asked as she delicately lifted a forkful of peas. Badswell and I, sensing the wizard's disapproving eyes, vainly tried to mimic the little priestess's table manners.

"You will be learning much in the hours to come," Parnish said mysteriously. "As I indicated, it is an artifact of almost unlimited power. It is said that it can even be used to bring a person back from the dead, though that creates such a drain on the rod's power that it would almost certainly shatter, again casting all the pieces loose into the worlds once more."

"Now you have five pieces here?" I inquired. "Do you know where the others are?"

"No, alas. As you know, the power of the rod is such that the bearer of a piece will almost certainly *feel* the direction to the next larger piece."

Saysi, Bads, and I nodded; we had all experienced the uncanny sense of direction. The wizard continued with his explanation. "But with the fifth piece in my hand, I received no such indication. This leads me to believe that it is somewhere very distant, perhaps even on a different plane."

"Or destroyed?" I suggested.

"No—by all the worlds, *no!*" roared the wizard, turning furious eyes upon me. "Each piece is indestructible! It has existed for eons, and it shall outlast each and every one of us—and our grandchildren, and their grandchildren as well!"

We finished in awkward silence, but Parnish seemed to have recovered his temper as he excused us from the table and preceded us to another chamber of his house, a place we had not seen before.

Entering a circular room with a high, domed ceiling, I noticed that several benches had been placed near the walls. Flickering, reddish illumination sputtered through the area, originating from a pair of torches set in wall sconces. To my memory, this was the first room in the mansion not lit by the ubiquitous chandeliers.

Parnish bade us sit upon the benches while he stalked to the center of the chamber. Several heavy stone tables had been arranged in a row there, and upon each sat a chip of ebony—five tables and five pieces of the rod. They had been arranged with the smallest—formerly my little curing stick—to the left, progressing to the largest at the other end. That segment, I guessed, was not quite a foot long.

"I must insist upon absolute silence," Parnish Fegher said in a voice that would brook no disobedience. For once, I was not inclined to argue with the magic-user. In truth, the somber preparations had left me a little awestruck. The black stubs of the rod seemed so ominously potent, so mysterious and frightening as they rested on their slab tables, that I was happy to be quiet and inconspicuous.

Abruptly the torches died, flames sizzling into steam, as if an unseen hand had capped them. The smell of smoldering wood filled the room, which was completely, utterly dark. My hand found Saysi's, and I sensed her staring—as was I—toward the place where we had last seen Parnish Fegher. We heard him chanting, speaking strange words in a deep voice, pronouncing each foreign sound with a precise and rhythmic cadence.

A dim glow slowly appeared, an aura expanding to surround the smallest of the rod's segments. In the pale illumination, I saw that Parnish had etched a series of hieroglyphic symbols onto the stone surface of the table. Now these sigils flickered with bluish flame, forming a circle of cool, silent fire around the ebony stick.

Gradually, one by one, the other four pieces began to

glow, wrapped by the gauzy cocoons of mysterious fire. When all five segments were shrouded within these auras, the light was barely bright enough for us to make out the form of the wizard, now standing near the middle of the row of tables. Parnish Fegher's eyes picked up a flash of reflection as he stared fixedly at one after another of the rod's pieces. Turning my head to the side, I sought some sign of Saysi, but the illumination didn't reach this far; if it hadn't been for her hand in my own, I wouldn't have known she was there.

Parnish barked a word, the sound cutting like a knife, sharp and forceful in the tense, darkened room. I couldn't suppress a gasp of astonishment as I saw the smallest piece of the rod slowly rise into the air. Still outlined by that peculiar glow, it hung suspended, a foot or two above the table. One by one, in ascending order, the other segments levitated until all five dangled in the air.

They lined up perfectly, as far as I could tell, and slowly began to drift closer together. Remembering the way Badswell's piece had disappeared, I surprised myself by hoping that Parnish knew what he was doing. Perhaps this was only because I didn't want to have to face his rage if he was thwarted, but deep inside I admitted that I, too, wanted to see the pieces successfully joined.

Slowly the segments drifted closer, until no more than two feet separated each part from the nearest neighboring pieces. Now they ceased their movement as the blue fires on the tables flared upward with increasing brightness. Parnish continued to chant bizarre words, sending shivers of apprehension along my spine as I sensed his casting building to a crescendo.

Ultimately the wizard's voice rose into a commanding bark, and faster than I could follow, the five pieces shot through the air—or rather, the four largest moved, arrowing in line toward the smallest segment while the latter remained fixed in place.

With the *boom* of a nearby thunderclap, the second piece touched the first; three more explosions rocked the room in quick succession as the next parts of the staff came together. My ears rang, and I heard Saysi gasp in fright beside me as sound continued to reverberate, echoes rumbling like fading thunder through the room.

I felt a sense of shocking disorientation as a wash of cool light spilled toward us from all around. When I swiveled my head, I saw that the walls of the room—indeed, the entire *mansion*—had disappeared. Instead, we were surrounded by a ring of towering, startlingly regular peaks. In the shadows from the foot of the mountain range, I sensed many powerful beings watching, and vaguely guessed that these were the wind dukes.

But how had we come to be here? Where was this place? Where were *we?* I saw Parnish Fegher standing before us, the segments still floating, now as one black stick about three feet long. Then the mountainous horizon began to fade, and I saw another being lurking in the darkness.

I recognized the handsome head flanked by the two snarling wolves that I had seen on the painting. Miska the Wolf-Spider watched us through a film of gauzy haze, three pairs of eyes glittering with hatred and fury. I wanted to crawl away and hide, but, paralyzed by that hideous and omnipotent gaze, I was unable to move a muscle. The beast stood upon the platform of a lofty castle, with a great chasm yawning beyond and a sky of whirling colors storming above.

Then, beyond Miska, rose an even greater, more horrifying figure, a mountainous image of evil and chaos. I saw a grotesque bloated face, green eyes flashing hatred, mouth twisted into a sneer of cruel anticipation as tentacles lashed and twitched around the creature's vast torso, slurping wetly across the slick smoothness of floor . . .

And I knew that the Queen of Chaos was watching as well.

CHAPTER 16

A JOURNEY COMMENCES

I didn't remember walking back upstairs to our apartments. Somehow I found myself embracing Saysi before one of the big windows in the common room of our chambers. A vast bank of stormy thunderheads rose in the distance, darker by far than the night sky. Silent flickerings of brightness, yellow and orange and red, pulsed across the crests and slopes of the billowing cloud mass.

The nearby sea lay below those clouds, I knew, yet the air seemed uncommonly dry, brittle and electric with distant energy. Unconsciously I curled my toes against the floor, seeking a solid grounding against the vaporous and unimaginable might of the distant storm.

I heard a clattering sound and gradually realized that Rathentweed's teeth were clacking together like castanets. The little gnome stood at a nearby window, hunched miserably beside Badswell. The half-ogre, looming like a pillar of rock in the shadows, reached out a brawny paw to pat Rath's shoulder. Gradually Parnish's assistant overcame his terror, though he turned his back to the window, clearly unsettled by the violent and unnatural storm.

Memories of the last minutes fell into place, more like the jumbled remnants of a wine-sotted dream than recollections of actual events. My ears rang, and I felt nearly as jumpy as Rathentweed, twitching as a new burst of lightning flared in the clouds, watching the brightness sustained like a massive celestial bonfire for several heartbeats.

At least the rod was out of sight. Parnish had snatched up the artifact as the vortex of chaos had still whirled around us. The wizard had stalked from the chamber while Rathentweed, Badswell, Saysi, and I slowly regained our senses. The gnome, pale and trembling, willingly accompanied the three of us back to our guest apartments.

"Saysi . . . where *were* we?" I asked, still trying to convince myself of what we had seen.

"We never left the mansion . . . but at the same time, I think we were very far away."

I felt her trembling and pulled her close. Badswell turned his broad face to us. I could see the glistening saucers of his eyes and the white points of his lower tusks in the starlight that filtered into the room. He seemed surprisingly unperturbed by the events that had shaken the rest of us.

"Chaos . . . it *is* growing," Rathentweed muttered, grimly shaking his head. He clapped his black hat to his scalp, his hand trembling, and squinted sternly at us over the bulbous knob of his nose. "The danger is very real."

"Real, mebbe. But not right now," Badswell suggested.

"If you want, I'll walk wit' you to your room."

The gnome nodded stiffly, with a little sniff of disdain, but the relief was visible in his eyes. He actually smiled slightly as he bowed to Saysi and me, bidding us good night. The two companions, one gigantic, one diminutive, departed to the mansion's hall.

"There's something comforting about seeing them together like that. It gives me hope." Saysi spoke quietly, almost to herself.

I wrapped both my arms around her; her face rose toward mine, and in moments we were kissing, lost in the comfort of each other's embrace. A long time passed before we broke apart, gasping for breath. I was acutely conscious of my pounding heart, sensing Saysi's own emotions raging as strongly as mine.

"Come . . . come here tonight," I said quietly, gently taking both of her hands, pulling her toward the door to my bedroom.

She took a step, then halted, though she made no move to release my hands. "No, Kip . . . it would be wrong. I can't."

I wanted desperately to change her mind. This was a discussion we'd had before, many times, but surely things were different now. We weren't the same people who had wandered around, carefree, accompanied by Barzyn and Hestrill and other bold companions.

"We're in this together, all the way," I told her. "I'll stay here as long as you want. . . . I know that the rod is a real threat, and perhaps an opportunity as well. Just remember, it's not the *only* thing that matters. It's not *everything*."

"Kip . . . I know." Her voice was soft, as silken as the strands of coppery hair that I stroked with my fingers.

I pulled her close, drawing her fully into my arms. "You're the most important person in the world to me, Saysi—now and always, for the rest of our lives. It's only right that we share everything and stay together forever!"

"Why, Kip . . . are you actually proposing to me?" she asked coyly.

"Yes! By Patrikon, yes, I am! I want us to get married as soon as this is all over! Will you?"

She pulled back, her eyes shining in the starlight as she stared intently. "I do believe you mean it, you rascal."

"I do—more than I've ever meant anything before!"

"I'm touched . . . I really am." Her tone was strangely hesitant.

"What's—what's your answer?"

"I—I have to think about it," she said. "It's kind of unlike you to do this, you have to admit."

"Can you think about it in there?" I asked, gently pulling her toward the door of my bedroom.

"I want to," she replied. "Really, I do. But it's not the time, and certainly not the place. I *can't!* Don't you see? It would be wrong, a violation of the order of law. I can't allow that!"

Privately I reflected that now and then a little chaos in a person's life might not be a terrible thing. Yet I sensed the determination in her voice and her posture, and I knew that any attempts to press my arguments would have exactly the opposite effect that I desired.

"Stay here with me for a while, won't you?" she whispered as I started to pull away. Reluctantly, biting back my frustration, I allowed her to lead me back to the window.

Looking at the sparkling array of lightning, I felt a

sense of awe returning. "There's chaos and law out there, together." My voice came out as a rasping croak. "There's no pattern, Saysi. It's like *life!* We have to make of it what we can, take what joys are offered to us."

"You know I can't believe that, Kip," she said, speaking far more gently than I probably deserved. "Patrikon has put me here for a reason, and that reason has to be found in the ordering of lives, of worlds. I know that's hard for you to understand, but it's *real* to me. I can't change it any more than you can change the fact of who you are."

Who I was? Right now that was one very randy little halfling. Yet as my frustration seethed, then settled back, I suddenly realized that there was an undeniable sense of security and comfort in standing here with Saysi, knowing that my presence was important to her—as hers was, even with her stubborn sense of morality, to me.

We kissed again, as the lightning flared and raged overhead. A few minutes earlier, I might have felt their blazing pyrotechnics as a threat. Somehow, in the warmth of Saysi's embrace and surrounded by the whispered, almost inaudible chant of her evening prayer, I felt the celestial display was a benign presence. When at last Saysi broke from my arms and we each turned to our own rooms, my frustration was all but forgotten, replaced by an aching memory of her sweetness and a growing determination to stay with her, to protect her from anything this life could offer.

Still, as I drifted toward sleep in the feathery softness of my lonely mattress, that same thought returned: A little chaos in one's life was not necessarily a bad thing.

Morning found Saysi and Badswell bustling around our apartments before I even crawled out from beneath my covers. Dressing in the morning robe that the tailors had delivered after dinner on the previous night, I joined my two companions in descending the ebony staircase to find Parnish and Rathentweed arriving for breakfast at precisely the same time.

"I trust you slept well?" inquired the wizard, clearly in a good humor.

"As well as possible, under the circumstances," I retorted, annoyed by his cheeriness—and then guilty as I saw a look of pain flicker across Saysi's face.

"Quite, quite," declared Parnish, ignoring my mood. He sat at the head of the table, and I noticed that he had the black staff of the assembled rod, at least the five parts in his possession, at his side. He placed the stick between his legs as he drew his chair up to the table, and kept his left hand on the shaft as he took a seat.

Five or six servants entered in a silent file, bearing plates of cooked eggs, fresh bread, and a variety of fruits. Parnish watched the serving of the food, bouncing the rod back and forth between his hands with unconcealed excitement. When the last of the servants had departed, he cleared his throat, sweeping his stern gaze around the table to make sure that he had our undivided attention.

"I have some rather exciting news," he declared suddenly, his tone ebullient.

"What is it, my lord?" inquired the gnome, his own eyes sparkling.

"I have learned where the sixth part of the rod may be found. With the five segments assembled, I settled down to meditate during the night and was rewarded by a vivid sense of direction—the knowledge that we can proceed in continuation of our quest!"

"Really?" Saysi was too enthusiastic at the announcement for my taste, but I couldn't very well silence her. "Do you think it was the melding of the five segments? Did that increase your sensitivity?"

"I really don't know, my dear. In truth, perhaps not. It feels more as though the sixth piece of the rod has been brought closer, to somewhere we might have a chance of reaching it."

I didn't like his repeated use of the word "we," and I had a rather sickening feeling about what was coming next.

"My sense of direction confirms that it lies somewhere beyond the ocean shore—doubtless an island, or one of the distant realms over water. In any event, we shall depart tomorrow morning in search of the next segment of the rod!"

"Why not leave right now?" I asked, my words well leavened with sarcasm.

"Impossible." Parnish missed, or chose to ignore, my tone. "Any trip requires planning and preparation. Sudden departures lead to chaotic journeys; it's a maxim that's been proven time and time again. No, we shall depart promptly following tomorrow's breakfast."

"You got ship?" Badswell asked suspiciously, as if he expected that Parnish would make us swim.

"Not personally, no. But we shall have little difficulty hiring passage. I have already sent a solicitation to the waterfront and will no doubt interview several captains during the course of the day. There are many reliable sailors operating out of Argenport, and I don't doubt that one of them would welcome the chance to make a profitable voyage."

"What about the end of the world?" I had to ask, as long as nobody else brought the matter up. "Don't you sail off of it if you just set out blindly from land?"

"Myths and fairy tales, I assure you," declared Parnish dismissively. "And, besides, we shall have the rod to guide us."

"Straight into trouble," I muttered underneath my breath, drawing a kick to my shin from Saysi.

The wizard looked at us, blinking solemnly behind those wire-framed spectacles. If he gave any thought to the notion that one or another of us might not be wild about joining him on this quest, he made no acknowledgment of the fact.

"You have the day to make your own preparations," he continued. "You should have all your clothes by now; my tailors are nothing if not speedy. Pack them in the crates that the servants will provide for each of you. It is well to remember that standards of dress will not be relaxed merely because we are aboard ship."

After breakfast, we tried on our traveling clothes, and I was forced to admit that even Badswell looked rather dapper in his polished boots and long jacket. Rathentweed, in a black silk hat, struck a properly officious air, and Saysi was a fairylike vision in a lace-trimmed dress of emerald green.

Although Parnish had granted us the day to make our preparations, we three prisoners in fact had very little to do. Badswell, accompanied by Rathentweed, poked about the mansion and grounds, while Saysi and I browsed the extensive library.

We soon discovered that the vast majority of Parnish Fegher's volumes dealt with the Rod of Seven Parts—the artifact's violent history, its mighty powers, and its uncertain destiny. One source had detailed descriptions of the spyder-fiends, from which we identified the ferocious kakkuu and soft-spoken lycosyds that had attacked us. We also learned of an even mightier version of these creatures called the raklupis. This powerful tanar'ri was particularly deadly because it could appear in any guise. It spoke with such seductive allure that a victim could be easily deceived into regarding the deadly horror as a friend.

The wind dukes, or vaati, were described in most passages with terms approaching homage. We learned of their rigid standards of law, of the different sects such as vindeam and rudeam, the two wizardly orders, or the nature priests, the grideam. Each order had unique powers and distinctive roles in this highly regimented society. Most intriguing to me were the wendeam, or outcasts, who spend their almost immortal lives in a ceaseless search for the Rod of Seven Parts. Sworn foes of the Queen of Chaos and her tanar'ri, all vaati lived in fear of her gathering the pieces before they did, knowing she would seek to use the artifact to free her beloved Miska.

Saysi found several detailed passages about the grim, tentacled goddess whose image we had doubtless observed the previous night.

"The Queen of Chaos is the ruler of a realm called the Steaming Fen," she explained to me. "It's in a plane called the Abyss, which sounds like an all-around awful place. Her influence is strong on many worlds, depending on how thoroughly chaos prevails there."

"Worlds? Planes?" I could only shake my head. "I'm happy enough to stay right here, thank you."

We saw Parnish again at dinner, but he provided no further information on our upcoming journey except to say that no sea captain had responded to his bid for services. "We'll have no trouble booking passage at the docks in the morning," he declared confidently.

After the meal, a brawny servant appeared with a

226

leather-wrapped bundle.

"I noticed that you lacked a weapon suitable to your size," the wizard explained to Badswell. "My smithy has created something for you. I hope you will find it suitable."

Frowning, Bads unwrapped the leather covering to reveal a massive battle-axe, a double-bitted blade of steel supported by a massive hardwood shaft. His tusked mouth drooped into a grin, and when Saysi elbowed him, he even remembered to say "thank you" to the wizard. Impressed, I reflected that the weapon seemed very suitable indeed.

When Saysi and I retired for the night, I made no further suggestions of intimacy, knowing that her opinions on the matter would remain the same as on the previous night. In the morning, we dressed for travel and, following breakfast, departed the wizard's estate on foot. Our luggage would be delivered to the docks when our bookings had been arranged.

Parnish led the way, with Rathentweed in tow and Badswell, wearing his splendid battle-axe at his belt, right behind. Saysi and I held back, enjoying the feel of the outdoors again. With Goldfinder at my side, I felt good enough to put a little swagger into my walk as we passed jauntily through the streets of the High City.

Those avenues and byways were already crowded, though shoppers and merchants alike stepped quickly aside when they spotted Parnish leading our small procession. The hawking of vendors, the shouts of parents chasing their children, made the city seem like a raucous and untamed environment after several days of sedate and well-ordered surroundings. On the other hand, I found the streets a breath of fresh air following the admittedly luxurious prison of Parnish Fegher's compound.

However, I no longer entertained any thoughts of escape, and not just because I didn't want to leave Saysi behind. I found myself vaguely curious about our destination, and since I had never sailed aboard a ship before, the prospect of that new experience was also rather intriguing.

The drinking and revelry that had distinguished Argenport earlier seemed to continue unabated. Indeed, people danced and wove along some side streets as if they had been at it all night, and didn't slow down a bit with the coming of dawn. We saw a surprising number of people who seemed to be extremely drunk. One brawny warrior swaggered forward as if to challenge Badswell to a fight, but a glowering look from the smooth-faced wizard sent the fellow cowering back to his alley like a whipped dog.

Unfortunately I had trouble with my traveling clothes almost as soon as we stepped beyond the walls of Parnish's compound. One of my cuffs popped open, and the neck felt uncomfortably tight. Just my luck, I decided glumly. Badswell got that nice axe, and I apparently received clothes made by some clumsy apprentice tailor.

We started on the descent toward the waterfront, walking along a wide street that was relatively uncrowded compared to the throngs elsewhere. An expanse of mist blanketed the flatness beyond the last building, much as it had covered the sea on the day of our arrival, and I found it hard to imagine the breadth of ocean beneath that cloudy camouflage.

"The temple of Patrikon should be just around this corner," Saysi said as we neared the waterfront. "That's strange," she said a moment later. "I thought I remembered that it was right there."

I looked at the place she indicated, which was occupied by a dingy tavern, apparently a hangout of scruffy sailors and other disreputable drunkards.

She shrugged, looking around, perplexed. "I guess I lost track of where we are. It must be that this street looks just like the one going past the temple."

Passing through the gates of a large walled compound at the base of the hill, I expected to find dockyards and ships arrayed at the stone quays. Instead, the flat ground was just bare dirt, with many fences, corrals, and barns just beyond. Parnish looked around in confusion as the mist rose, drifting away in the morning sun and the light breeze off the sea.

Another button popped off my vest, and I was glad that I had resisted the suggestion to wear boots or other footwear. My feet were the only part of me that didn't feel as if they were getting strangled. All my clothes seemed to be shrinking around me.

"Where is it? Where's the sea?" Saysi asked, fingering her amulet. Her eyes were wide, her expression full of increasing alarm.

As the mist slowly dissipated, I looked to the east, observing a vast steppeland of grass. "It's gone." The fact didn't seem surprising to me.

"We're supposed to get a ship!" the halfling priestess insisted.

"No, you are mistaken!" Parnish declared insistently. "There are no ships, for there is no water. It's a matter of utter, lawful logic! There is land before us; thus, we shall travel by land."

"But once there was water, a whole waterfront." Saysi whirled to face me. "Kip, you remember. We walked along that waterfront! It's the first place you kissed me."

"Well, sure." The night had been one of the most romantic of my life; again I pictured the full moon setting her copper hair alight. I looked around, seeing nothing that resembled the setting of our walk. "But . . . that wasn't here. Was it?"

Parnish, after looking the area over, had ceased to listen to our debate. Grimly the wizard started across the yard, seeking a silk-robed merchant standing before an enclosure. As we followed, I was intrigued by the large gray animals in the corral behind the vendor.

"How can I help the esteemed lord?" asked the merchant, bowing low before Parnish Fegher.

"I wish to purchase elephants and supplies for an overland journey."

I didn't pay attention to the rest of the conversation, since I heard Saysi gasp in astonishment. Before I could try to calm her down, I was abruptly annoyed by the loss of another button. It popped right off of my vest, and when I tried to pull the garment shut, I found that my chest was too broad to be enclosed.

CHAPTER 17

THE STATURE OF A CHAMPION

The steppe lands, Parnish said these were called. I thought the name inappropriate, because in my mind "steppe" meant "stairs," and stairs meant going up and down. As far as I could see in any direction, there wasn't the slightest hint of an increase or decrease in the surrounding elevation.

And from the back of my elephant, I could see pretty far. The creature lurched along with a gait that snapped my head backward and forward with each lumbering step, forcing me to grasp the railing that surrounded the enclosure—it was much more than a saddle—where Badswell, Saysi, and I rode. Before us plodded another of the great, gray-skinned beasts, this one bearing Parnish Fegher and the gnome, Rathentweed.

The animals themselves, I was forced to admit, were magnificent. Great ears flapped like sails in the hot air, creating a bit of a breeze along the elephants' flanks—

and over us passengers as well. The creatures seemed tireless. On this, the day we departed Argenport, they had lumbered along for more than eight hours without any sign of faltering and complaint.

In fact, the only distressing thing about the journey so far was the vague memory of disquiet—that, and Saysi's constant declarations that we were supposed to be crossing an ocean.

"How can you *not* be upset?" She started in on us again as the sun plunged toward the flat western horizon. "We went to the waterfront to book passage on a *ship!*"

"There *was* no waterfront!" I retorted, growing increasingly peeved with her irrational insistence. "How can you book a ship to cross a grassland?"

"Elephants are kind of like ships," Bads, the peacemaker, suggested. "And this flat ground is sorta like a sea of grass, don'tcha think?"

"Sure," I agreed, anxious for an explanation that didn't mean Saysi was losing her mind.

"Kip, we walked along that waterfront together," she said quietly. "Near the temple of Patrikon—the temple that wasn't there."

"We did that, I know," I replied. "But . . . things change. Sometimes there are differences after a time."

" 'Things' don't change as they did today!" Saysi smacked me across the back of the head in her frustration. "Last night we all talked about it. Parnish was going to talk to a *sea* captain about getting on a ship!"

"Ouch! Hey, stop it!" The little priestess was impossibly stubborn and, when I turned around to glare at her, not the least bit apologetic. Her tiny fingers clutched the jade amulet at her neck, and she met my stare with an equally belligerent look of her own.

Furious, I whirled around to face the front, then winced as I felt another line of stitching give way, this time down the right side of my splendid tunic. Already one shoulder had torn, and several buttons had popped off both my trousers and my shirt.

"*Now* see what you made me do!" I sulked, though the air that washed against my skin was actually rather refreshing. Still, that was the third tear today, and the sleeves felt so tight that I wondered if the clothing made by Parnish's tailors was actually shrinking on my body.

Instead of a sharp reply, Saysi remained silent, though I could feel her eyes on my back. Still, her emotion didn't seem to be anger; rather, it was a sort of deep concern that made me worry more than ever about her sanity. She had always been a trifle rigid, but it seemed to me that she was having a very hard time adapting to ... adapting to what? Had things really changed?

I was starting to get a headache, and I didn't think it came from Saysi's slap.

"This just makes it all that much more important that we succeed—that Parnish can assemble the rod," she declared, as if expecting me to argue.

"Well, of course," I concurred, anxious to find some grounds for agreement. "That's where we're going, to find the sixth part."

The caravansary agent in Argenport had provided us, or rather our elephants, with large casks of water in addition to a normal outlay of provisions, and as we began to look for a place to camp, the reason became apparent. It occurred to me that we had gone through the entire day without sign of so much as a creek, swamp, or watering hole. Our camp would be made, obviously, at some featureless point on the featureless terrain, amid grass tall enough to conceal Saysi and me from view.

But the lush vegetation proved not to be so deep as I had imagined when Parnish finally indicated a halt and I slid down the rope ladder we unrolled from the elephant's shoulder. The carpet of plantlife proved to be only neck-high to me as I held the base of the ladder steady and waited for Saysi to descend.

She let go at the end and tumbled a surprising distance to the ground, rising to look up at me from amid the grass. Her face was startlingly pale, her eyes wide with fright.

"What is it?" I asked, spinning to see if something behind me had frightened her.

"Y-You're *growing*," she stammered, clasping a hand to her mouth as she blinked several times in disbelief.

"What do you mean?" I countered, distressed by this sign of further confusion. I planted my hands on my hips, looking down at her, knowing that I had always been taller than she. Hadn't I? But had it been by a full head? No . . . she was right. The memories came to me through a dim haze. . . . Once there had been a time when we'd been practically the same size.

"Chaos!" she declared in a whisper of horror, her brown eyes wide with fear. "It's changing *everything!*"

Another seam ripped in my clothes as, this time, my breeches let go down the left leg. I realized that the cuffs of my blouse had crept halfway up my forearms, while at some point I had discarded my leather belt. I tried to convince myself that my garments were shrinking, but in the face of Saysi's assertion, such delusion proved increasingly difficult.

"But how?" I asked stupidly. "I grew up a long time ago. I've been the same size for years and years!"

"I tell you, it's chaos!" declared the little priestess, glaring at Parnish as the wizard and the gnome came over to join us. "It's increasing in strength, affecting us all."

"That's impossible," snapped Parnish Fegher. He clutched his portion of the Rod of Seven Parts in both hands, brandishing it against the air as a fighter might wield a pole arm. Eyes wide, he glared around us, as if chaos was some hideous monster waiting to attack.

"Kip's growing. He's added half a foot or more since we left your estate, just today," Saysi declared bluntly.

The wizard looked at my shredded garments, then reached out a hand to touch the top of my head, as if to confirm my actual height. "Nonsense!" he snapped. "His clothes are shrinking. My tailor must have cut his costs by purchasing inferior materials! It'll cost the wretch his job!"

"Can't *you* see?" Saysi demanded, turning to Badswell.

"Kip's always been pretty small—still is," declared the half-ogre with a noncommittal shrug.

"Of course!" Rathentweed declared, tottering toward me and tilting his head to peer up into my eyes. "It's just the clothes!" he insisted.

Stomping her foot in agitation, Saysi clutched her amulet, looking angrily at the others. When she turned to me, I felt the heat of her emotion as a strangely disturbing force.

"Maybe—maybe they're right." I saw from the set of her rounded chin that these were the wrong words, but I blundered ahead. "I mean, it could be that you just don't remember. . . ."

I sensed the truth—that it was *we* who didn't remember—but how could that be the case? I admitted that my memories of Argenport, the seaport city, were increasingly vague. . . .

Too many thoughts were conflicting with each other in my mind, and the result was a terrible headache. Turning my back on Saysi, I helped unload the big cargo satchels from the elephants. The massive leather sacks were lowered, still clasped shut, by slowly releasing the straps that bound them in place. When they were on the ground, we could flip them open and have easy access to all our belongings.

With no firewood for dozens of miles in every direction, we ate a cold supper and had a lightless camp. Still, the night breeze remained balmy, and the black vault of the sky was brightened by more stars than I had ever seen in my life. So clear and brilliant were the multitude of these diamondine specks that the familiar constellations—the bear, the shield, and the spider, among a few others— were fully masked by shining newcomers. It was as if the gods had decided to speckle the heavens with a million new stars.

"Kip?" Saysi sat next to me as we stared upward in wonder. "Do you remember this sky? These stars?"

"Sure . . . well, not all them. But of course I do. I mean, this is the same old night sky, just a little more clear than we're used to."

"I . . . I hope you're right. I really do—even if it means that I'm losing my mind." I wrapped an arm around her, sheltering her easily against my side, and held her until her gentle breathing indicated that she slept. Only then did my own eyelids close as the stars beamed down on a peaceful night of rest.

One thing about camping in the desert, I learned the next morning, is that sand gets into *everything*. Awakening slowly, I spat the tiny granules from my parched lips, rubbing them into crumbs from my eyelids before I could even begin to see. Badswell, Parnish, and Rathentweed slept nearby; like myself, they were partially drifted over by miniature dunes that had blown across us during the night.

Fortunately my cloak had kept Saysi—who still slept, curled in the crook of my arm—relatively free from the sand. Thus her discomfort surprised me as she opened her eyes and looked wildly around.

"It's all right," I said soothingly. "The wind blew some sand over us, but you were covered pretty well." Lifting my arm, I drew back my large cloak and gestured at the expanse of rolling dunes. "And it appears it's going to be another nice day," I added encouragingly, as if we could have experienced anything else on this long, sandy trek.

"D-D-Don't you *remember?*"

Saysi was pale and trembling, looking searchingly into my eyes as she touched her amulet and stared wildly around our desert camp. "The steppes? The flat ground extending forever, covered with tall grass?"

"Yes, sure. . . but that was a long time ago . . . before we moved into the desert. Remember?"

That headache was getting started again.

By this time, Parnish had risen. Holding his assembled segments of the rod, he stalked briskly back and forth, prodding Badswell and Rathentweed. "Up, up! Time to get back on the march!"

"And what about the elephants?" Saysi demanded, pulling away from me and standing to glare at all of us. "Don't tell me that none of you remember them. Riding on top of those big animals?"

"Yes, that was really something." My memories were clearer on this point. "Nice way to travel. But it was a long time ago."

Standing, I tried to shake the sand out of my loose and billowing cloak. I clapped the half-ogre on the shoulder, then leaned down to smile encouragingly into Saysi's concerned face.

"Look out!" Badswell shouted suddenly, scrambling to draw his big axe.

Something large loomed against the skyline, a four-footed creature with a gaping, tooth-studded maw. The beast rose from behind a nearby dune and lumbered toward us. A second monster, like the first as big as a small house, charged just behind its mate.

Goldfinder, feeling about as dangerous as a toothpick, gleamed in my hand; I pushed Saysi behind me and stepped forward to stand beside the half-ogre. Twin visages of gaping mouths, each lined with drooling tusks, rushed closer. The beasts loped quickly on large, padded feet, thudding heavily, each step lifting a puff of sand into the air.

One of the monsters roared, a bellowing explosion of thunder like the rage of some monstrous lion. In fact, there was something vaguely catlike about the broad feet, the wide skulls with raised foreheads and keen, hungry eyes. Yet the long tails lashed with supple control, more like tentacles than feline appendages, and the mouths were grotesque and unnatural. Circles of fangs, they flexed open and closed like the sucking maw at the center of an octopus's body.

"Where'd *they* come from?" I wondered aloud as Badswell swiped his axe, sending the nearest of the monsters rearing backward. The other circled to the side, and I skirted around to face it. Parnish, holding his five-sevenths of the rod in both hands, stepped forward to face the beast on the other flank, while Rathentweed scrambled through the sand in a desperate effort to get away.

I stabbed upward with my short sword, but the weapon, which was little more than a dagger in my brawny hand, failed to connect with the bristling jaws of the nearest sand beast. For the first time in my memory, I found myself wishing for a more deadly weapon. Goldfinder was just too damned *small*. Those sharp fangs clicked audibly as the monster snapped, sending me tumbling down the side of the dune as I leapt away.

Badswell boldly stepped into the creature's path, slashing with the gleaming battle-axe, and the huge, catlike body once again reared back, thwarted in its pursuit. Standing again, I shook sand from my hair and clothes, wiping a hand across my face as I whirled to confront the second of the gargantuan attackers.

The monster crouched, sinuous tail lashing, creeping forward on those massive feet. Even in its squatting position, it was as large as a big horse, and considerably bulkier. Through the sand, I could feel the impact of each heavy step, a series of quaking thuds that grew more pronounced as the beast padded closer. Baleful eyes of gleaming yellow blinked from beneath hooded lids, enhancing the vaguely feline appearance of the monstrous being, though I had never seen a cat even half so large.

We backed away, through the dip at the base of the large dune, staying together as we retreated carefully up the slope on the opposite side. Saysi and Rathentweed went first, with the wizard, the half-ogre, and me falling back carefully below them.

Showing no inclination for a sudden rush, the hulking monsters came slowly after us, as if content to observe our fearful retreat.

Douglas Niles

"Cease, beasts!" roared Parnish, suddenly stopping on the side of the dune and holding up his staff of ebony in both hands. He bore the rod horizontally, peering over its smooth black line as he stared first at one of the monsters, then the other. "I bid you—*cease!*"

Surprisingly, the creatures seemed to understand. In fact, they halted their advance at the base of the dune, looking upward at Parnish with expressions as bland and unthreatening as any cud-chewing cow's.

Looking around tensely, I searched for some sign of a threat. I held Goldfinder ready in my big hand, and saw that Badswell, too, had his weapon raised. The half-ogre looked at me with a scowl of confused frustration.

"Where'd they go?" I asked, not entirely certain what it was we had been fighting.

"Dunno. Only thing I see are the camels," he said, slipping his axe through his belt with an embarrassed shrug.

"Bad-tempered animals," I agreed. "But not dangerous."

I was a little confused, then, trying to remember where I had left my turban and spare cloak. Once again that persistent headache nagged at me, shooting brief stabs of pain from my temples to my forehead.

"Best get mounted," declared the wizard, striding boldly down the slope of sand. "Daylight's wasting, and we have a long way to go today."

Parnish's words made sense, so I went along with him, returning to our sandy camp. The two camels waited placidly while we pulled the heavy saddlebags from the drifts of sand, dusting them off and securing their heavy leather flaps for another day of our dry crossing.

Rathentweed and Badswell helped to secure our belongings. Only Saysi remained distant, staring down at

240

us from the heights of the dune, her wide, fearful eyes shifting back and forth from the two great, shaggy camels to her four companions.

"What happened?" she cried finally, shambling down the dune to confront me.

"We're packing the camels!" I declared crossly, looking down at the little halfling with increasing annoyance. "You could help a little, you know."

"*What* camels?" she demanded, with the committed persistence of the truly insane.

"Are you blind as well as crazy?" This was getting to be too much. The massive, double-humped animals stood side by side, no more than a dozen feet away from us. A shift in the desert winds even brought the pungent and familiar scent of the animals wafting past us.

"By the gods, Saysi, surely you can at least *smell* them!"

"Of course I can! But can't you, *any* of you, remember that yesterday we didn't have any camels? And just a few minutes ago they were fanged monsters, ready to gobble us up for breakfast!"

My anger melted, replaced by the all-too-familiar concern. One of the camels chewed meditatively, working its long jaw from side to side and revealing a glimpse of several worn, yellowed molars. There was nothing even vaguely resembling a sharp tooth in the animal's admittedly disgusting maw.

"What about the monsters?" Saysi pressed again. "Do you remember them? We were retreating up the dune, fighting for our lives, until Parnish changed them into camels!"

"Law will ever triumph over disorder, my dear," declared Parnish. "But to suggest that I have the power to transform hideous monsters into useful beasts of burden is going too far."

Saysi glared up at me so angrily that for a moment I wondered if she planned to smack me in the stomach, which was directly in line with her angry eyes. Instead, she settled for spinning on her heel and stomping away through the sand, kicking puffs of the dry granules into the air with each step.

I finished cinching the saddle and duffel onto the big brown camel. Badswell pulled himself up onto the beast's narrow back, while Parnish and Rathentweed mounted the second camel. Deciding that I would start the day on foot, I took the reins in my hand and plodded after Saysi.

In the morning hours, the sand was still relatively cool against my bare feet. I fell into stride beside Saysi, following the course that Parnish indicated from his lofty vantage. The priestess said nothing, tugging her hand away when I reached down to try and take it in my own. Once again my emotions were more concerned than angry. She was clearly disturbed, and there didn't seem to be any way that I could get through to her.

As the hours of the morning progressed, the relentless assault of climbing temperatures began to take its toll. Waves of heat rolled across the sand, rising from the dunes, descending from the sky, increasing with each blast of the wind. The savage gusts of air were in no way refreshing. Instead, they were part of the overall searing onslaught. Sometimes stinging needles of sand swept along the ridges and crests of the dunes, coursing downward to strike with pinpricks of pain against every exposed inch of skin.

Those inches became progressively more elusive, however, as we pulled our robes tightly around ourselves, leaving the barest slits over our faces, gaps just wide enough to allow us to see. Each breath was filtered through a gauze of the cloth, but even so, grains of fine sand found their way into mouths and noses. Our eyelids were caked with the stuff, and a simple blink became a gritty, painful experience. I found myself postponing for as long as possible each momentary closing of my eyes.

Though in stature I towered over Saysi, my feet were as tough as a halfling's, and thus I was not terribly troubled by my steps over the abrasive surface. By midday, however, the sand was so hot that even our fur-covered soles became sore and sensitive to the searing granules.

Badswell announced that he needed to walk for a while, halting his camel and sliding from the saddle to stand on the scorching sand. His heavy boots, fortunately, would give him protection from the sunswept terrain, and I gratefully prepared to mount the camel in his place. Lifting Saysi by clasping her tiny waist between my hands, I hoisted her over my head to set her on the fore saddle at the camel's shoulders. Then I took the stirrup of the high mid saddle and pulled myself into position between the animal's humps.

The camel's gait was a lurching stagger that would have done justice to a blinded drunkard. Within minutes, my neck was sore, snapped back and forth as it was by each plodded footstep. Saysi, apparently numbed by her own confusion, sat quietly, holding on to the lip of her saddle and refusing to meet my eyes when I solicitously inquired as to how she was faring.

We stopped frequently to take sips of water from the large skins carried in the camel's saddlebags. The amazing beasts seemed unfazed by the heat, simply waiting patiently while Badswell splashed a thin trickle into his mouth. Smacking his lips, the big half-ogre handed the waterskin back to me, and I stowed it as we once again resumed our march across the trackless expanse of sand.

The late afternoon hours brought no relief from the heat. If anything, it became hotter than ever, as if the sinking sun were determined to sear us with its most savage rays before seeking inevitable banishment below the western horizon. Our course, guided as always by the wizard's sense of direction to the next piece of the rod, took us generally southward, so at least we didn't stare directly into that fiery orb as it drew near to setting.

Then, for the first time all day, I caught a glimpse of an irregularity in the featureless terrain: trees! A glimpse of green fronds peeked over the rim of a distant dune, and as we lurched over the next rise, I saw more and more of the leafy palms coming into sight.

"An oasis!" Parnish declared excitedly.

We all shared the wizard's anticipation. Even Saysi's eyes brightened as she looked ahead, watching as we came over the last dune to see a green-speckled valley spread out below us. The lowering sun reflected a haze of orange and red rising from an expanse of crystal clear water, as beautiful as any sight I'd ever seen. The camels picked up the pace, lumbering eagerly down the descending slope until they were striding through a fringe of tall grasses.

Soon the palms rose around us, casting merciful shade and cloaking us in a cocoon of cool, moist air. The scents of fragrant blossoms filled the air with lush perfume, while insects buzzed lazily along the fringe of cool water.

It was with a sense of profound relief that we halted the camels. By the time I slid down and assisted Saysi and Rathentweed from their high saddles, Badswell already had his boots off and his feet immersed in the water, while an expression of serene, almost ecstatic pleasure softened the edges of his broad face.

Only Saysi's mood remained worried and tense as she stared around fearfully, even at me. I stood protectively near her, looming high over her tiny form, determined to defend her from any and all threats, including the delusions of her own madness.

CHAPTER 18

A RIDER FROM THE PLANES

We feasted on dates, citrus fruit of varied and tangy flavors, and roasted fish, the latter netted from the pond by Rathentweed with an ingenious strainer system of his own invention. During the few minutes while the rest of us set up our camp, the industrious gnome collected no fewer than a dozen plump panfish from the crystalline waters of the spring-fed pool. Though reeds and lilies enclosed much of the shoreline, the gnome found a sandy spit extending into the water; he claimed that the fish were so thick they all but jumped into his nets.

Even the air seemed cooler around the oasis. Though logic suggested that the breeze was the same harsh wind that had scoured the desert all day long, something about the surrounding greenery, the fragrance of many thousands of blossoms, and the moisture of the life-giving oasis changed that abrasive current into a pleasant, balmy breath of air.

Only Saysi's mood darkened what would otherwise have been a delightful meal. She remained sullen and silent, casting frightened glances up at me every time she felt my eyes upon her. When I tried to talk about mundane things, such as the food or our sleeping arrangements, she was disinterested to the point of rudeness. Shifting to a discussion of our beautiful surroundings, I was startled when she burst into tears, leapt to her feet, and ran from our little circle to disappear amid the brush of the oasis.

"Best let her cool down a bit, young fellow," Rathentweed counseled when I rose to follow her. "She's obviously not used to traveling. Even the most seasoned adventurer can find the steady change of scenery unsettling. Perhaps she feels a touch of homesickness."

Privately I was skeptical. After all, Saysi had never displayed anything remotely resembling homesickness before. Too, I had a hard time picturing the fussy gnome as much of a "seasoned adventurer," and this couldn't help but make me suspicious of his opinions. Still, there was a kernel of wisdom in there somewhere, enough so that I acknowledged that this might indeed not be the best time to go talk to her.

Instead, I stayed with the others and ate like a horse. My brawny legs crossed beneath me, I gathered fronds of palms on my lap, tucked my loose-flowing robe around me, and concentrated on the food. As I devoured bite after bite, I couldn't help but admire the strapping muscles of my arms. Stroking my fingers over my square, firm chin, I pondered the tufts of fur on my bare feet, wondering at the incongruous note; they were the only part of my body that didn't look as though they belonged to the mighty warrior I knew myself to be.

By the time we had finished our splendid repast, however, Saysi had still not returned, and I decided to seek her out. Walking across the lush grasses, making my way between lofty palms, I marveled at the display of heavy blossoms, watching as fat bumblebees dipped and danced from one to the next.

I found the little priestess sitting at the bank of the pool, watching fish weave between floating lilies. She didn't meet my eyes as I came up beside her, but she scooted to the side as if to offer me a place to sit. Flopping to the ground, I let my bare feet trail into the water, relishing the cool wetness on my fur-covered toes.

"Look at your feet," she said calmly after a few moments of this soothing balm.

I did. They were good feet, if a little large. The tufts of fur common to many halflings were smooth and silky, and as I had many times before, I wondered how it could be that humans and dwarves and so many other creatures felt compelled to restrain their feet within shoes or, even worse, heavy boots.

"They're *halfling* feet, aren't they?" Saysi asked pointedly.

"Of course they are." I was willing to humor her. In fact, I was glad to hear that she had now controlled the tremors of anxiety that had quavered in her speech before.

"But now look at you," she said quietly, looking up as I, even while relaxing casually, loomed over her. "You're not a halfling anymore!"

"What?" I was taken aback. "Of course I am. You yourself just said so when you looked at my feet!"

"Stand up." Saysi rose while I studied her. Standing beside my sitting form, her eyes were even with mine.

When she planted her hands on her hips, I knew that she was stubbornly determined that I follow her instructions. With a heavy sigh, I obeyed.

Her head, with its framework of pretty copper curls, came barely to my belt. "*Now* do you see what I mean?" she asked. "You're as tall as any human—I daresay taller than most of them."

"So?" Her words were giving me a headache again, but I tried to follow the line of her reasoning. "Lots of halflings are kind of tall."

"Not like *you.*" She gestured at my arms, at the cords of sinew that bulged beneath my skin, rippling as I moved.

"But Saysi . . ."

She looked up at me, bravely blinking back the tears that started to swim in her eyes. I looked at those soft brown orbs, remembering things about her: the soft and voluptuous curves of her feminine body, the coy way in which she had resisted—fortunately, not always success-fully—my kisses, the sweet smile that had lighted up my life in the months we had been together.

With those memories, an explosion of burning guilt surged upward in my mind, searing through my head like a lance of agonizing pain. What had I been *thinking?* How could I have entertained romantic thoughts toward one so sweet, so pure, so . . . so *small?* With a groan, I slumped back to the ground, refusing to look at her.

"Kip . . ." I felt her tiny hand on my strapping arm, and despite my effort to pull away, she retained her grip with surprising strength. She didn't say anything more, and I told myself that she couldn't have known about my dark desires.

"No . . . I'm all right. Thanks," I said weakly.

Of course, Saysi would no doubt find a proper halfling

mate . . . marry someday, perhaps bear children . . . but why did that prospect fill me with such mournful sadness?

"We don't have to talk about it anymore," she said quietly. "I can see that things are . . . *different*, for all of you. Maybe it's my amulet, or my faith in Patrikon that puts things into a clearer light. But let's just remember that we're friends. We should help, not hurt, each other."

"You're right," I agreed, my headache already beginning to fade. "Friends forever . . ." But why did this pledge feel so empty, as if I needed something more?

"Look there!" she declared suddenly, pointing across the water toward the red-lit horizon toward the west.

At first I thought she had spotted a small cloud, a lonely wisp of vapor in the clear evening sky. A dark object rose like an inverted cone, perched upon a point and looming some distance into the air. Upon further examination, however, I saw that the thing was moving, advancing with surprising speed.

"Is it a tornado?" The resemblance was undeniable, but even as I asked the question, I discounted the possibility. The sky was otherwise clear, with no signs of any kind of storm brewing.

As it drew nearer, I began to hear sounds, like a strong wind blowing in the distance, listened to from a position of shelter. The swirling shape was indeed a cloud of sorts, for the piercing rays of the sunset actually passed through the cyclone, casting it in fiery translucence.

But the inverted cone moved with startling precision, clearly under firm control. The cloud spun along the crest of a nearby dune, kicking up a plume of sand around its base, behaving like nothing so much as a fast chariot pulled by strong, eager horses. Indeed, twin shapes reared before the tornado, wispy manes flowing in tendrils of cloud, and it seemed that there *were* steeds pulling hard in their traces. The ethereal animals guided the tornado-like shape, now descending from the heights of the sandy ridge, gliding swiftly closer.

Remembering the painting in Parnish Fegher's library, I felt a growing, awe-inspiring belief that this was a wind duke, riding the cyclone of his chariot. I was not surprised to see that the comparison was truly apt, for this chariot did indeed bear a passenger. A tall figure, ebony black and sternly regal in posture, stood alone atop the cyclone. The whirlwind reached the greenery of the oasis, passing between the palms, setting the long grass to waving back and forth. Yet the effect of the winds seemed controlled and very local, for the tops of the palms didn't flutter to anything other than the steady evening breeze, nor did the grass that was more than a few paces away from the whirlwind's base.

The cloud spiraled across the surface of the glowing water, splashing ripples into a wide wake without losing a bit of its steady speed. I could see the passenger clearly now, and the sight confirmed my initial deduction. A tall, manlike figure, with skin as black as ebony and a grim, even haughty demeanor, stood tall and straight atop the whirling cyclone. Like his skin, the vaati traveler's beard and mustache, his long, tightly curled hair, were of perfect blackness.

Parnish, Badswell, and Rathentweed had obviously noted the arrival of the whirling wind, for they emerged from the grove to join us at the bank of the pool. When he caught sight of the regal figure standing atop the spiraling cloud, the wizard uttered a gasp of amazement, then fell to his knees, pressing his face to the ground in a ges-

251

ture of utter devotion.

"Kneel, fools!" he hissed to the rest of us. "Kneel and show homage in the presence of a wind duke!"

The command in the wizard's voice was too assertive to ignore, and furthermore the newcomer's arrival was so spectacular that we naturally shared the awe that was so vibrant in Parnish Fegher's voice.

Nevertheless, I was not so overwhelmed as I knelt that I didn't keep an eye on the whirlwind as it swept across the waters of the pristine pool and came to rest on the bank beside us. Like a wisp of smoke borne away by an evening breeze, the cone of swirling air and its magical, ethereal horses dissipated, vanishing into the atmosphere after slowly, gently, lowering the tall passenger down to the ground.

"Rise, mortals," he said, in a voice that was deep with resonant power, yet calm and direct, full of dignity and compassion. "I thank you for the honor you display, but it is you yourselves who are truly worthy of esteem."

"Great lord, your arrival is a blessing beyond any of our hopes," declared Parnish, slowly lifting his face from the ground.

I was somewhat taken aback by the sight of this powerful wizard bowing and scraping like the most miserable of serfs. At the same time, I took the example as a cautionary note, reasoning that anyone who could fill the magic-user with such awe must be a person of power, influence, and stature. Remembering my reading, I wondered if this was a wendeam, one of the wind duke outcasts who traveled among the worlds, constantly tracking the whereabouts of the Rod of Seven Parts.

Rising, stepping protectively before Saysi, I studied the vaati traveler. He was taller than I, nearly equal to

Badswell in height. Though his body was slender, his black skin moved with supple, almost fluid grace as he bowed, gesturing smoothly with his right hand to include us all in his greetings. He carried a long pole of smooth wood in his left, leaning on the staff with casual ease.

Somewhat startled, I realized that the visitor was virtually naked, except for the thin strip of a leather belt, from which several pouches and scabbards dangled. I thought of him as a male, no doubt because of his voice, and the full beard and mustache that encircled his chin and cheeks. However, because of his nakedness, I saw, with a twinge of embarrassment, that his body seemed utterly sexless.

Only then did I notice a trailing formation of floating lights, like bubbles of shimmering gossamer, each containing a bright firefly. These specks of illumination bobbed and dipped in the air, forming a small circle around the wind duke's head. I counted about a half dozen of the obviously magical baubles, which reminded me of a will-o'-the-wisp that had once almost lured me to doom in the depths of a fetid swamp. Nevertheless, there was nothing threatening in the appearance of these magical lights; instead, they seemed more like loyal followers, even bodyguards, of the wind duke.

As the vaati traveler stepped closer to us, the bubbles of light bobbed along in precise formation, maintaining a vague halo about the fellow's tall, proud head.

"I am Arquestan," he declared, bowing again. "I have watched you, wizard, and know your efforts on behalf of law. You should realize that your staunch labors have not gone unnoticed in the Valley of Aaqa."

"My Lord Arquestan, I am overwhelmed and certainly unworthy of such praise," declared Parnish Fegher, with another gasp of awe.

"Please do not be. Every world needs its heroes, defenders of truth and law. These times are fraught with peril. Even with all your efforts, and the courage and righteousness of your brave companions, danger lurks very near, and our success is far from assured."

"Do you know where we are?" asked Saysi boldly.

"Aye, my lass, daughter of Patrikon. You are one who sees the truth, even as chaos grows. To answer your question, this is the Oasis of the Planes, and it is fortuitous indeed that, through the shifting dunes of chaos, you have all survived to reach here."

"It was the lure of the rod, the sixth piece, that drew us here," Parnish explained.

"Aye—this segment." Without ceremony, the wind duke opened one of the pouches to remove a piece of black stick, one that we recognized very well as an extension of the pieces that Parnish had already succeeded in joining.

"It is!" Parnish declared. When Arquestan offered the piece, the wizard removed one hand from the shaft of five segments, carefully, reverently, accepting the sixth piece and holding it up to the sky.

"And with the sixth, we will know the way to the last, the final piece!" I realized, strangely excited by this dramatic progress in our quest.

"Aye, though that will be precious little help," Arquestan noted, looking at me with a raised eyebrow. "For the final piece is in the hands of the queen's own agents. She has taken steps to deliver it to her foul lover, the wolf-spider, so that Miska may guard it and gain possession of the rest of the rod when you take it into his fortress."

The wind duke's words sent a shiver of apprehension

through my body, but at the same time, it brought my heart to a pounding pulse of excitement. I remembered the image of Miska, the three-headed giant, and his terrifying visage of horror and hate. Our quest was nearing its end, and the conclusion could well bring us into battle with that foul force of ultimate chaos! My earlier thoughts of abandoning the task, of going back to my old life, were distant memories, the fears and weaknesses of another person. I wanted nothing so much as the chance to strike a powerful blow, to make a difference in furthering the cause of law.

"You are Kip Kayle," Arquestan said, again addressing me. His words formed a statement, not a question, so I merely bowed my head in acknowledgment.

"A tall halfling," declared the wind duke with a hint of irony, "one who stands at the brink of becoming a great champion of law."

This time Arquestan's words sent a jolt of awareness through me. Though I had never thought anything of the kind, I sensed that he spoke the truth, feeling in my grim determination that I *had* become such a champion. My days of thieving, of wandering with the impulse of a given day's winds, were a thing of the distant past. Now my future held epic strife, perhaps a contest with the wolf-spider himself!

"A champion such as you deserves a weapon worthy of your powers." Arquestan reached to his belt again, this time drawing a mighty sword from a scabbard that had been partially concealed behind him.

"Behold the Vaati Blade, forged in the smithies of Aaqa, imbued with all the power wind duke mastery can bestow."

Now it was my turn to gasp in awe as our visitor

extended the weapon, hilt first, toward me. The blade was pure gold in color, with a pair of brilliant diamonds gleaming in the hilt. The handgrip was big, suitable for clasping in my two brawny fists. Overall, the weapon was even longer than Saysi was tall. Slowly, feeling a strange anticipation mingled with apprehension, even fear, I reached out and took the leather-wrapped hilt. Arquestan released the weapon, and the sword floated like a feather in my clenched grip.

"Wh-why?" I stammered, still awestruck. I sensed a foolish smile growing across my face as I looked toward the wind duke for an explanation.

"You shall prove yourself worthy," Arquestan replied simply. "In some ways, you already have, and in others you will be tested, sooner perhaps than any of us might wish."

CHAPTER 19

CHAOS SWARM

"Nice sword." Badswell lumbered over and, with a tusk-baring grin, leaned down to regard his reflection in the pure gold of my blade. With a blunt fingertip, he touched the keen edge, grunting in pleased confirmation as he raised the bleeding digit to his mouth.

I raised the mighty weapon, swinging it easily through the air. The blade was supple and light, yet I sensed it was stronger than any mortal steel. And it had been bestowed upon *me!* For the first time, I felt competent to stand against the queen's tanar'ri with some chance of defending myself and my friends. With the coming of the wind duke, I suspected that we would not have long to wait before my blade, and in fact all of our weapons, would be put to use.

My attention was distracted by the bizarre globes that had arrived with Arquestan. Glowing even against the remaining daylight, the spheres scattered, as if to inspect our camp. One of the bubbles floated past me, circling my head, then drifted over to Saysi and Badswell. I wondered if the wind duke was telepathically controlling the sphere, but I glanced over to see Arquestan in conversation with Parnish, paying no attention to his glowing attendants.

The bubble, which seemed to contain a small, glowing spark, settled to the ground, shimmering slightly. Abruptly I found myself staring into a pair of familiar melancholy eyes. Ripples of loose skin cloaked a lean canine body, and a shaggy tail wagged in affectionate greeting.

"It's the hound!" I declared, tugging at Badswell's arm. "The dog who warned us about the spyder-fiend attacks! She disappeared in the dragon's lair, remember?"

"Guess she musta floated outta there, huh?" suggested the half-ogre with an affectionate chuckle. He bent down to pat the hound's head, and she leaned against his leg, grunting with contentment as her tail wagged through a wild circle.

"Ah, Bayar remembers you," Arquestan declared with a deep, resonant chuckle, looking toward us. "She . . . described some of your adventures to me. You both impressed her with your quick thinking."

"She *talks?*" I asked.

"Not exactly, no. But I have a close empathy with the hounds of law. Often we share our knowledge without the use of words."

I had no trouble believing further testimony of magic, having just witnessed the animal's dramatic shape shift. Only then did I realize that an assortment of dogs now lolled about our grassy shore—a couple of terriers, a short-legged, fox-faced animal with the body of a much larger dog, a morose-looking bloodhound, a wolf, and a massive staghound.

"My hounds," Arquestan said by way of introduction. "The sole company of the wendeam. They provide steadfast accompaniment for me in my journeys through the planes." He pointed to the long-legged, shaggy staghound that had watched our attentions to Bayar with interest. "This one is Borath, the leader of my pack and the beloved mate of Bayar."

"Arquestan, you said that you're a wendeam, and I know that means an outcast. But why? Are you exiled?" Saysi asked with her customary forthrightness.

"In a sense. It is because I, like others of the order wendeam, travel beyond the rigid sanctity of our valley," Arquestan explained. "And when exploring those other worlds, probing the reaches of distant planes, it is impossible to attain the kind of order that most of the wind dukes require."

"The legacy of Pesh," Parnish Fegher suggested in a voice husky with awe.

"Aye, my human friend. With Miska contained after that epic strife, most of the dukes retreated into Aaqa. There they remain to this day."

"But you wendeam spend the years in search of the rod, do you not?" inquired Rathentweed.

"Indeed—our years, and our centuries," Arquestan replied. "Which is why this is such a momentous meeting today."

"Why come here?" Badswell voiced the question that was in my own mind.

"I came because the Oasis of the Planes is the one place we could meet without subjecting you to passage through the gates or to potentially chaotic teleportation between the planes," the outcast answered. "It is an intersection of worlds, a place where you, Parnish Fegher, could feel the summons of the sixth part of the rod."

"Indeed, the sense of direction was unfailing," Parnish admitted. "Even during the many days when trackless steppes or endless desert surrounded us."

"Days or hours may blend when one is passing through the storms of chaos," cautioned Arquestan. "How long do you think you journeyed from Argenport to the oasis?"

The question was simple, but the answer hard to recall. My memories of the long journey were hazy and unclear. "I'm not certain," I admitted. "Three weeks, perhaps?"

"Tsk, tsk. No," interjected Parnish curtly. "It was a month at the very least."

"And your estimate?" With a tight smile, the wind duke turned to Saysi.

"Two days." She looked almost apologetic as my eyes widened in surprise.

"Saysi was having some . . . problems in recollection," I mumbled quietly, trying to speak privately to Arquestan. Surprisingly his smile grew wider.

"The priestess is correct," he replied, than continued, speaking to the wizard as Parnish stared in speechless surprise. "It is true that your directions guided the party, but it was the priestess of law who held the disruptive forces at bay. Without her, you would still be wandering among the sands of chaos."

Saysi's tone was pensive. "I thought I was losing my mind. . . ."

"But it was your faith in Patrikon that allowed you to discern the disruption. So pernicious is the ripple of chaos that your companions might have mistaken your perceptions for madness."

"He's right, Saysi . . . I'm sorry." I recognized myself in our visitor's words. The priestess merely hugged me, her arms barely enwrapping my sinewy waist.

"Are we out of danger, then?" wondered Rathentweed, with a nervous look around. "Is the oasis safe from the queen's tanar'ri?"

"Alas, no," Arquestan replied. "On a mortal world, they can only be drawn by the use of a segment of the rod. In the sands, however, they can roam at will."

"That's the second time you mentioned 'the sands.' And you called this the Oasis of the Planes," I pressed. "Where exactly *are* we?"

"This is a place between worlds, where the ether and the astral meet amid sand and air, water and fire. From this spring, trails lead to a multitude of worlds, including your own and hundreds more."

"If we're not safe here, is it not best, then, that we leave immediately?" pressed the gnome.

"I think not. Take advantage of such time to rest as you have. I think I can assure you that, where we are next bound, the surroundings will be considerably less comfortable."

I really wanted to ask him about that, but right then Borath rose and growled, hackles bristling across his sturdy shoulders. Bayar stepped beside the staghound, echoing his growl with a rumbled warning of her own.

"It may be that we are already too late," the wind duke admitted. "Wizard, perhaps you should use the staff."

"How, my lord duke?"

"I suggest you bestow the power of the third segment upon our champion."

I looked on in mystification as Parnish nodded, then turned to me. He extended the tip of the staff, touching

my shoulder as his fingers circled the middle of the artifact. There was a sensation like a tiny spark where the
rod met my skin.

Abruptly I felt keen energy flaring through my nerves,
a tingling sense of quickness that brought my surroundings into clear, sharp focus. I reached to touch Saysi's
shoulder and was startled as she recoiled, then realized
that my intended normal movement had whipped my
hand out like the blur of a striking snake. Taking a few
steps back from my companions, I found that I had darted away in an eyeblink of time.

"The rod has hastened your movements. The effect will
last for only a short time, but I suspect it will be needed,"
explained the wendeam. "You will find that the enchantment of haste can be quite beneficial during battle."

In fact, the wind duke's speech seemed dramatically
slowed. When Badswell stepped over for a closer look at
me, he appeared to move like one struggling through
molasses, each step sluggish and deliberate. Bemused, I
sensed that Arquestan was right. My movements seemed
at least twice as fast as before, yet with as much precision
and control as ever. Only then did I think of the rest of his
remarks and wonder, What battle?

One of the camels answered my question with a terrified bellow, rearing as it uttered a shrill, panic-stricken
cry, then stomping down again with a ground-shaking
thump. Ripping its tether, the wild-eyed animal plunged
past us, galloping through the lush grass of the oasis. The
second camel roared its own terror, tugging furiously at
the leather thong that held tight against the pitching
beast, lashing the hapless creature to a stout palm.
Barking dogs added to the din as the whole pack milled
around, each hound facing the brushy cover around the

spring.

The Vaati Blade raised, its golden metal gleaming in the setting sun, I looked for the as yet unseen enemy. Badswell, his axe poised in his big hands, joined me in squinting at the surroundings of our camp.

"Over there!" Saysi declared, pointing a steady finger toward the palms beyond the tethered camel.

The first kakkuu spilled into view, scuttling from the tangled grove beyond the pitching, bucking beast of burden. Wolfish howls resounded through the peaceful glade, ringing from the surrounding dunes with furious intensity, mingling with the frenzied barking of the hounds.

Two of the eight-legged monsters leapt at the tethered camel, bearing the big animal to the ground, biting and snarling, then lifting bloody jaws from the beast's gored belly. More of the tanar'ri pounced over the still-twitching corpse with prodigious leaps, racing toward us. Howling like ravenous, rabid wolves, the spyder-fiends scuttled as fast as charging horses, encircling our party at the water's edge.

"Look out on this side!" cried Saysi, yanking my attention to the rear.

More of the hideous spyder-fiends rushed from thickets along the other shore of the oasis! Badswell bellowed a challenge, bracing himself with his keen, double-bitted axe upraised, while I brandished my golden blade and faced the first kakkuu to appear. Energy tingled through my body, and I felt an urgent desire to counterattack, to rush these beasts in a whirlwind of speed and killing force. Only the need to protect Saysi held me in place.

Lupine jaws gaped and snarled to the right and left. Holding the hilt of the Vaati Blade in both hands, I flicked the blade back and forth with an agility that would have

Douglas Niles

astounded me if I had wasted a precious second in reflection. The sword a blur in the air, my magically hastened movements whirled the keen edge against one tanar'ri, then the other, without an elapsed blink of time. With desperate, precise violence, I lopped the heads from each kakkuu, ignoring the bodies that thrashed on the ground, spewing blue-black gore.

Another lunge carried my weapon into a tanar'ri skull, and two quick slashes cut into a pair of the monsters charging to either side. A dozen spyder-fiends halted just out of reach of my blade, growling and slavering. The wolf heads swung low, eyes bright with menace, but apparently the sudden deaths of five of their companions had given them some small measure of caution.

Flames crackled amid the lush palms, searing leaves into instant blackness, hissing and sputtering around the bodies of spyder-fiends as Parnish Fegher's fireball spell caught a cluster of tanar'ri in its deadly sphere. Immediately the wizard chanted more arcane commands, his voice clear and calm above the chaos of the melee, and in seconds, a massive lightning bolt blasted through more kakkuu, violently rending the monsters as they scrambled over the torn body of our unfortunate camel.

A weblike strand of silk shot from the body of a snarling kakkuu, wrapping my ankle like a tentacle, but a flick of the golden blade severed the line like a razor slicing thread, then bit into the head of the web-spitter. Hisses of rage exploded from a nearby tanar'ri, and I whirled to face one of the grotesque monsters that commanded the kakkuu—a lycosyd. The humanlike arms jutting from the monster's shoulders met above its head, terminating in hands that clutched a huge gray-bladed sword.

"Your fight is futile, champion of nothing!" the spyder-fiend said with a sneer, the human speech incongruously emerging from the grotesque wolf jaws. The sword whistled toward my head. "In the end, chaos must prevail!"

I raised the Vaati Blade with the instant of thought, deflecting the crushing blow with a ring of metal. The monster's insult flamed my temper, a passion as surprising as my apparently instinctive skill with this mighty blade. Smashing aside the lycosyd's next hacking chop, I skipped away from the snapping bite of venomous fangs, drawing back like a mongoose evading a cobra. With crushing force, I brought the golden weapon down onto the monster's chitinous back. The keen edge sliced through the bony plates, the lycosyd shrieking in agony as gore spilled from the gaping wound, bluish-black ichor staining the body and the ground as the creature died.

Yet my sword, as I whirled to seek the next foe, remained as gleaming gold and pristine as ever. It occurred to me that this unnatural cleanliness in the midst of such gory work was odd, an unusual effect of the weapon's potent enchantment.

Borath roared into the fight, teeth sinking into a kakkuu's flank. With a wrenching twist, the mighty staghound threw back his head, pulling the tanar'ri off its feet. Yelping, the eight-legged monster tumbled away, falling to lie on the ground, twitching in the throes of death. Bayar, as ferocious as her mate, leapt to protect Borath's flank, driving back another spyder-fiend with fang-baring fury.

Badswell, his axe coated with dark tanar'ri gore, stood before Rathentweed as the gnome guarded his back, jabbing and thrusting with a long-bladed knife. Parnish stood just to the side, casting a volley of sparking magic missiles, while Arquestan raised his smooth pole and bashed it right and left with crushing effect.

Suddenly, shockingly, a pair of kakkuu blinked into sight a few feet in front of me and just a step away from Saysi. I had encountered teleportation before, but the tactic was so startling that I gaped in momentary, nearly fatal, astonishment. The little priestess raised her club, swiping at the first of the nearby monsters while the second lunged, jaws slashing toward her pixie face. Finally I reacted, springing in a blur of muscle and golden metal. The Vaati Blade slashed, slicing the kakkuu in two just before its cruel fangs could rip into Saysi's cheek.

Whirling around, snarling furiously, the second kakkuu barely had time to crouch before my blade sent the wolfish head tumbling to the ground. Without pause, I rushed at another one of the monsters, dropping it with a double strike, one blow to the flank and a follow-up slash, as its head snapped around, to split the hateful skull. In fury and desperation, I turned to a new target, slaying and chopping mightily in the midst of the swarming tanar'ri.

The monsters snapped and snarled around me, lunging from all sides. Aided by the magic of the rod's haste power, I slashed back and forth amid deadly jaws. My blade cut here, stabbed there, then swirled back in a murderous, decapitating swipe. Three kakkuu fell in the blink of an eye, and before the bodies lay still, I hurled myself at the next spyder-fiends.

I caught a brief glimpse of Arquestan, who was armed only with that long, straight pole. The wind duke smashed the weapon onto the head of a massive kakkuu, crushing the monster to the ground, then whirled on the rebound to drive back another kakkuu and a lycosyd that had popped into view behind him. The sleek wolf guarded his master's back, darting and snarling back and forth in a whirlwind of snapping fangs. The kakkuu were larger than the enraged wolf, but the tanar'ri still hesitated and ducked away, reluctant to face those slashing teeth.

More of the spyder-fiends converged along the shore of the once-pristine pool, and I rushed over to protect the wind duke's back, pushing Saysi into the relative shelter between us. Nearby, the two terriers barked frantically, darting and lunging among the kakkuu. Borath and Bayar pounced through the fight, protecting each other as they bit into tanar'ri flanks and legs. The little fox-faced dog lay still and dead, ripped nearly in two by kakkuu jaws.

Even with my golden sword in their path, the monsters tried to duck past me, to rush at the black-skinned wind duke with fanatical, even suicidal, passion. I chopped and hacked and slew, leaving a pile of shattered, leaking bodies scattered around me, but still the beasts tried to reach Arquestan. My awe grew as the tall figure, armed so simply, flailed to all sides with incredibly deadly effect, smashing chitinous backs and legs, crushing wolfish skulls with his hard, straight staff. At the same time, I realized that anyone who could arouse such hatred in the vile tanar'ri was one well worthy of my respect and admiration.

The hounds of law howled and snarled in the midst of the melee. Now Borath and Bayar fought at my side. The big staghound charged like a bull, bashing a kakkuu backward and then sinking long teeth into the tanar'ri's throat.

On the far side of the oasis, I saw two kakkuu turn upon one of their human-armed masters, ignoring us in favor of tearing the lycosyd to pieces. In other places, kakkuu broke from the attack to turn, snapping and howling, attacking members of their own ranks. The tanar'ri in the rear of the attacking ranks seemed to strike out anywhere in a chaotic, leaderless frenzy. If one of us wasn't in range, they often turned against their own kind, as if in desperate need to attack *something*.

Parnish, his spells depleted, struck a kakkuu with the partial Rod of Seven Parts, sending the monster scuttling for cover. Badswell still hovered protectively over Rathentweed, smashing with his axe in the midst of swarming monsters, while Parnish fell back to limited protection between Arquestan and me.

"Hold!" cried the wizard once, using a—to me—previously unknown power of the artifact to freeze a leering lycosyd in place. The monster struggled and yelped, unable to move any of its eight feet. More tanar'ri pressed close, and I saw sharp teeth cut into Parnish Fegher's leg. Badswell hacked the monster's head off, but as he did, another spyder-fiend chomped into the half-ogre's thigh.

"Over here!" I urged Badswell. Battling against a press of drooling jaws, I couldn't rush to the half-ogre's aid without exposing Saysi to terrible harm. Instead, I cried out to him again, and my big friend, snorting with determination, bashed his way through the ring. Rathentweed, poking right and left with the long dagger, hurried behind him as they joined Arquestan and me. The half-ogre, wind duke, and I formed a triangle of deadly weapons as the priestess and Rathentweed turned their ministrations to Parnish. The wizard was bleeding from several gory bites to his legs and had slumped to the ground with a groan of agony.

Badswell, too, had been wounded. I glanced at him in

dire concern as he staggered like a drunk, wielding his axe with great, wild slashes. The toxin of the spyder-fiends, I feared, would soon bring the mighty half-ogre to his knees.

Again I killed a kakkuu, splitting the creature as it crouched for a leap. My blade whipped free of the gory mess, still pristine and clean, as bright as any burnished gold ornament. My movements remained unnaturally quick as I darted to the side and blocked a pair of tanar'ri that crouched for a leap at the wind duke.

A yelp of anguish rose above the din, and I spun back to see Borath go down, his gut ripped open by a lycosyd's sword. Bayar howled in fury, hurling herself against the spyder-fiend. The tanar'ri whipped its blade around, but in that eyeblink of time, I raced over and blocked the blow directed toward the loyal hound. In a flash, my own sword cut down, driving deep into the spyder-fiend's torso.

Arquestan raised his voice in a high, ululating command. "My hounds—hounds of law! Come to me, my pack!"

Dancing globes of light materialized above the melee, bobbing and weaving among the spyder-fiends. The tanar'ri, as a pack, seemed driven to a frenzy by the ephemeral spheres. Kakkuu growled and lunged in desperate attempts to strike at the baubles of magic as they floated, just out of reach, to their master's side.

Badswell toppled, but I reached him before he struck the ground. Bearing my sword in one hand, I hoisted the beefy half-ogre over my shoulder, staggering back to rejoin my companions.

Abruptly my vision was obscured by a whirlwind of water, mist, and sand. I heard the roaring of an airy vortex, felt myself lifted from the ground by a force that I hadn't anticipated. Still clutching my immaculate blade, I saw that Badswell, Rathentweed, Parnish, and Saysi were secured with Arquestan and me in the cradle of his whirlwind.

Like a speeding chariot, the cloud twisted away from the battle, soaring across the waters of the pond while the howling, snapping spyder-fiends raced along both shores. I counted dozens of the monsters in one quick glance, and watched as more and more of them popped into sight.

Finally the whirlwind rose from the ground, carrying us away from the fight. In seconds, gray mist surrounded us, a maelstrom of noise raging against our ears, and I knew that the wind duke carried us away from the oasis, from the desert . . . and from the world.

Only then, as I gaped at a vista of swirling, cloaking gray, was I seized by a fatigue more numbing than any I had ever known. Unable even to force myself to stand, I felt my legs go numb beneath me. Helpless, I gave way to utter, numbing unconsciousness.

CHAPTER 20

PANDEMONIUM

For a long time, I languished in the blackened well of unnatural fatigue. Eventually, when I groggily opened my eyes, I thought I had merely progressed into a nightmare. Everything was chaos. Thunderous sound roared, vibrating my body with pulsating force. Vaporous wisps of cloud whipped in a dizzying spiral overhead, as if we were in the middle of a thunderstorm, yet I felt no wind against my skin. Several glowing bubbles of light drifted just overhead, apparently unaffected by the gale.

Then I felt Saysi's fingers on my brow, turned to see her melting-chocolate eyes regarding me with concern. Those pearly spheres were the hounds of law, I remembered, and with these points of reference, I began to recollect the struggle at the oasis, and our flight in the wind duke's whirlwind chariot.

The cyclone surrounded us with solid walls of air, as secure a compartment as a framework of hewn oak. The area was circular, enclosed by a rim about waist high. Saysi relaxed her touch as I rose, suddenly eager for a look at our surroundings. For a long time, I stood hypnotized at the rail, staring at a formless vista of mist and fog whipping past with shocking speed. Yet within the cyclone, there was not the faintest breath of breeze. Still, this chariot of air was so fast, so unspeakably powerful, that I imagined myself as a bug caught up in the fury of a tornado.

For all that power and violence, Arquestan's funnel of wind was also a thing of sublime control and smooth, rapid movement. The wind duke stood tall and silent in the center of the circular platform, eyes open but focused on some distant place. We all sensed that he concentrated upon the guiding of our magical conveyance, and no one made any move to disturb him. Five baubles of light circled his head, and I felt a pang of grief at the knowledge that two of the courageous hounds had been left behind. The fox-faced little dog and the mighty staghound, Borath, had both been fatally rended by tanar'ri fangs.

I walked the circuit of the curving wall, which rose only as far as my waist, looking outward, trying to understand what I was looking at. Thick mist gathered in swirls and wisps. Gray fog was everywhere, masking visibility beyond the near reaches of the spiraling chariot, and within that short distance, there was nothing to see.

For a time, it was easy to imagine that we swirled through a bank of heavy cloud, an overcast that had suddenly blanketed the desert and perhaps the entire world. Yet I recalled what Arquestan had said: the Oasis of the Planes was not a thing of my world. I had a pretty clear idea that we had traveled very far indeed. For one thing, the sky had been perfectly clear when we rose from the oasis, yet I knew that this fog had embraced us within moments of our departure.

Abruptly all doubts were dispelled as we emerged from the clouds to discover a landscape of orange and red, in shades far brighter than the reflection of the setting sun at the oasis. But this was not a place cast in the extremes of sunset. In fact, the colors were those of tree and grassland, an expanse that sweltered under the glare of a hot sun, a sun that now stood near its zenith! On the flat ground, strange beasts galloped away in all directions, fleeing the sudden arrival of the whirlwind. These were creatures like none I had ever seen, or even imagined, the most common a herd animal with six legs, a pair of snaky, prehensile tails, and a blunt skull with three long horns jutting from the forehead. The beasts ran with a horselike gallop, veering to the left and right with bellows of panic, crushing brittle crimson grass with the force of their stampede.

In another instant, we plunged once more into the fog, and who could say how much time passed in gray mist? Then we emerged over a seascape of purple waters pulsing in long, rhythmic breakers. A great scaled head rose from the sea, poised for a moment on a serpentine neck, then darted upward like a striking cobra, reaching a hundred feet or more into the air. I jumped back from the edge of the compartment, instinctively reaching for my mighty sword, but Arquestan simply dipped his head to one side, and our airy chariot veered smoothly away from the threat. Trembling, I watched the creature tumble back to the waves and send cascades of dark, sheeting spray in every direction.

By the time the bizarre liquid had settled, we had once

again plunged into that misty barrier of cloud, the vaporous overcast that I knew was far more than the stratus barrier that so had often blanketed the world where I had spent all my years. The mist was very thick, yet strangely dry, and it lacked entirely the damp smell and moist feel of fog, or rain, or dew.

Rathentweed nervously stepped to Badswell's side, looking around in astonishment and barely concealed fear. "This can only be the ether," he whispered in a tremulous voice, continuing when I looked down at him in mute question. "The barrier between the planes—and the stuff of raw chaos. Give me four walls and a good book any day!"

"Stay close, little fella," counseled the half-ogre. "We'll git through here okay."

I didn't argue with the gnome's identification, though neither did I share his fright. If this journey brought us closer to the seventh piece of the rod, if it helped to hold the chaos of Miska the Wolf-Spider in abeyance, then I was more than happy to take part.

Stationing himself at the wind duke's side, Parnish glared about the small compartment. I wondered privately if, like Rathentweed, the precise and orderly wizard was terrified by our traverse and perhaps found it easier to keep his attention directed at the interior of the spiraling cloud in order to avoid confronting the evidence of chaos and confusion that reigned beyond. I realized another thing: If the wind dukes were the ultimate servants of law, then it wasn't a mystery why one who chose to expose himself to such a torrent must be considered an outcast by his less adventurous brethren.

Like me, Badswell stood at the side of the whirlwind's platform, looking at the barrier of ether and the sweep of worlds beyond. More places passed in quick succession: first a snowy wasteland extending to the far horizons, though no chill reached into our magical conveyance. Next we emerged into a blue sky over a pastoral realm of lakes, forests, fields, and castles. For a few heartbeats, we flew over this world, and then once again plunged back into grayness.

When Rathentweed came to join Badswell, the big half-ogre hoisted the gnome to his shoulders, and both of them stared in wonder at the expanse of colors, shapes, and movement. Catching a glimpse of Rathentweed's face, I saw that the little fellow remained pallid and wide-eyed, yet he seemed unable to take his eyes off the panorama of unbridled chaos.

It occurred to me that Saysi might desire a similar vantage, but when I looked around, I saw her huddling against the bulkhead of air. Her hands were clutched before her, and her face was turned down, staring disconsolately at the deck.

"What do you think?" I asked, settling my large frame beside her. "Would you like to get a view of what's going on?"

She turned a misery-filled expression to me. "Aren't you frightened, even a little? Don't you wonder if we'll ever get back home again?"

Truthfully, I hadn't thought about that, and with equal candor, I acknowledged to myself that I wasn't particularly worried if I ever saw our world again. I tried to think of my village, Colbytown, but my mental images had little meaning and no clear definition. It was a storybook place, and it belonged in the realm of myth and legend.

This was such a ride, the surroundings so fantastically

impressive, that I knew I would be content to explore and travel as Arquestan's escort for as long as it might be necessary.

As long as Saysi was there, too, that is. That fact struck me like a thunderbolt, and all my concerns about her dwindling sanity, her growing uneasiness, returned with a relentless chill.

"Home, for me, is where you are, Saysi. But I want you to be happy. I want *us* to be happy together." For a moment, I forgot the difference in our sizes, my mind drawn by habit to a consideration of her as a partner in more than just travel and adventure.

"How can you *say* that?" she said, practically wailing.

"What?"

"You're so *big!* I never told you this, but there was a time I thought about that, too, about the two of us, together! I liked the way you tried to take care of me. It made me feel warm, safe. . . ."

"I can still do that—better than before!" I asserted, flexing my brawny arms. At the same time my mind wondered why this was different from the way my life had always been. I had always felt protective of the little priestess. My great size and strength had seen to that. Wasn't that the reason? Surely it must have been!

"Will I ever get you back?" she asked plaintively.

"I'm here!"

"Kip, don't you see? It's not enough for you to stand around like a big hero, always ready to save me! Remember, *I* used to help *you*, too. To make you see things that didn't always seem obvious to you right away. And you were *learning*. . . ."

"But—" I was starting to get that headache again, and it was hard to think of sensible, logical arguments.

"You're too big for me now! Whatever made you like this—it has to be some kind of chaos, a chaos so deep and terrifying that you, Parnish, Badswell, and Rathentweed didn't even see it happening right in front of your face! And then Arquestan came, and suddenly you're a champion of law! Do you realize that your *sword* is bigger than the Kip Kayle I first met?

"You know," she went on between sniffles, "I wish now that I hadn't been so stubborn when you tried to seduce me all those times. I wish, at least once, that I'd given in to you when we had the chance."

"No!" I was shocked, appalled. "You're too good for that, Saysi—too pure! It's you who's given me the strength to see the rightness of law. You kept me on the right track, guided me away from the course I was on . . . a path that could only have led to chaos and destruction!"

"Would it have been so wrong?" Saysi stared at me intently, a trace of her old humor questioning me from those chocolate-pool eyes.

"Of course!" This whole conversation was making me squeamish. Once again I felt like some kind of pervert, wondered what kind of lustful chaos and evil seethed, barely checked, within the darkness of my soul.

She chuckled quietly, sadly. "It's funny how I would have longed to hear you say those words, to feel this way, just a few short weeks ago. And now I want to slap your face, to wring that thick neck of yours, for feeling like I used to *want* you to feel!"

"But it's *right*," I pressed, more than a little stung by her words.

"Sometimes right and wrong get hard to distinguish," she replied quietly. She stood then and looked into the space beyond our chariot, and I felt the distance between

277

us grow much broader than the single arm's span between our bodies.

"We are on the approaches to Pandemonium. Behold the heart of chaos itself."

For the first time, Arquestan spoke, his strong voice carrying easily, gently, over the storms of the whirlwind. "These are the tunnels of doom. In the distance rises the Fortress of Law, the prison of Miska the Wolf-Spider."

I didn't know how many places, how many different environments and worlds, we'd passed through while Saysi and I conversed, but when I stared over the edge of the whirlwind, I knew that we must have traveled an incomprehensible distance by any scale I had ever known. This time I hoisted the little priestess in my arms so she could have a clear look, and numbly we observed surroundings that seemed to defy any attempts at understanding.

A great flat plain extended on one side of—not below—the whirlwind. Although our chariot felt firm and solid underfoot, the picture of this flatland was disorienting in the extreme. Ground extended straight up and down, as if it were a cliff wall of impossibly huge proportions. Yet the plain seemed to be flat, for I could see creatures walking around on it, mere specks at this range, but visible nonetheless.

The landscape was broken in several places by irregular openings, like sheer-sided pits that plunged into the black, limitless depths below. I counted at least three of these gaping holes, and as we flew past one, I saw pale, bluish light emerging from a great distance within. The illumination allowed me to see that the shaft was not in fact a tunnel plunging straight down, but rather a winding passageway of immense proportions. Many miles away, it curved far enough to block the farthest reaches from our line of sight; it was from around this bend that the azure light originated.

Reeling under an assault of dizziness, I turned away and was confronted by the mouth of a gaping tunnel, a thing so huge that it could have engulfed Argenport and the surrounding farmlands in its maw without the slightest difficulty. The pits marring the plain, though huge, were dwarfed by this massive aperture. The rim of the tunnel's mouth was vaguely circular, yet I got the sense that one could have walked all the way around the walls without falling, as if there were no ceiling but merely a tubular "ground" that somehow knew no up and down.

I was not surprised when Arquestan inclined his head, and the whirlwind rushed toward that gaping maw. Looking back, I caught a quick glimpse of a mountain range that seemed to be floating on a base of cloud and a sea of blood red that curved upward and away, as if it lined the inside of a great bowl. The vistas everywhere defied logic, challenged any attempt at explanation, and yet they looked as real, as solid as any fundament that had ever supported me in my own world.

For a fleeting moment, I shared Saysi's apprehension, wondering if I would ever see familiar places again. With a growing pang, I thought of Colbytown, that quaint little halfling village where . . . what? I knew the place had some significance to me, but once again my mind was thick and unfocused, my memories vague. Two plump halfling maids came into my thoughts, each surrounded by a brood of little ones . . . Hallie and Berdeen they were called, somebody's sisters. . . .

Suddenly I treasured green hills, blue water, white-capped mountains, and sandy beaches with a poignancy that took my breath away.

I realized that Saysi was crying, and I pulled her close, cradling her in my brawny arms in a vain effort to offer shelter from the surrounding chaos. Casting a quick glance at Arquestan, I saw that the wind duke's face was set in an expression of grim, total concentration. His teeth were clenched, chips of white in the blackness of his tightly curled beard, and his dark eyes stared into the depths of that vast tunnel as if they attempted to penetrate the very depths of Pandemonium.

"Put me down . . . please," Saysi declared in a tight, controlled voice. I obeyed, and she turned to the wall of our airy chariot, clutching her jade amulet and avoiding my concerned, inquiring gaze.

Curiosity had begun to get the best of my fear, and I watched in awe as we swept into the vast, cavernous expanse. Lifeless landscapes of barren desert, cracked and broken mountains, and dry, eroded hills covered all the sides. I forced myself to resist the notion to think in terms of floor, walls, and ceiling, since there seemed to be no difference in the pull of gravity in any direction.

Unwilling to disturb the wind duke's concentration, I turned to Parnish, who glowered as I stepped to his side. Looking down into his smooth, clean-shaven face, I was not reassured to see that the wizard's jaw was clenched, his eyes, wide with fear, staring through the steel-rimmed spectacles.

"What *is* Pandemonium?" I asked quietly, not wanting to alarm Saysi any further.

"A place of terror and disorder, one of the most chaotic, wildest, and most miserable of the Outer Planes," he hissed through clenched teeth, words expelled with staccato precision, as if it required a great force of will for him to make any sound at all. "Home to chaos of all forms, and to the fortress prison of the wolf-spider in particular. The wind duke takes us to his very doorstep!"

"Do you know why?" I asked, turning to look at Arquestan, who still guided his whirlwind with that impassive expression of concentration.

"There can be only one reason—the seventh part of the rod. I can feel its presence now, which I was unable to do at the oasis or indeed since we began to travel the ether."

"It is time for your spell, wizard. Any further delay and she may learn of our presence." The wind duke spoke grimly.

"Very well." Parnish removed the long segment of rod that Arquestan had given him at the oasis. I saw by the markings on the black surface that at some point during our travels the magic-user had marked it with the blue sigils such as he had inscribed on the first five pieces prior to joining them in his mansion.

The assembled portion of the rod had been marked in preparation for the conjunction, in thick and dramatic script near the wide end, trailing into tiny, faint hieroglyphics near the almost pointed terminus that had once been the smallest stub of the great artifact. When I recalled carrying that lone healing stick with me upon embarking on this grand adventure, it was with vague and hazy memories, almost as if I remembered the substance of someone else's life, like tales told around a smokey and fading campfire or recalled from the depths of a sleep-shrouded dream.

Rathentweed came forward at some unspoken command from the master wizard, taking the sixth piece and holding it before his large, rounded nose. Parnish took the already joined segments and lifted the staff until the two portions were carefully aligned, though with a gap of several feet still precisely maintained between them.

The wizard began to chant, and it seemed as though the whirling air within the chariot grew very still. Only when I glanced around did I see that Arquestan had brought our airy conveyance to a complete halt, obviously waiting for the magic-user's enchantment. In words that grew into a harsh, brittle crescendo, Parnish harnessed the forces of law, channeled them into a mastery of this artifact.

In a sensation that was very different from my initial, reluctant participation in the ceremony of adjoinment, I eagerly watched the bonds of magic grow between the two sections. Sparks of white light crackled there, and Rathentweed closed his eyes, scrunching his bearded, big-nosed face in an effort to avoid the compelling power. Badswell gaped in awe, a trail of drool hanging unnoticed from one of his tusks, and then he, too, clapped his eyes shut. Even that wasn't enough; the half-ogre abruptly whirled, averting his entire face from the crackling power that swept outward to envelop the rod.

Saysi, I saw with a quick glance, hadn't even raised her head from her knees. If she was even remotely aware of the ceremony enacted only a few feet away from her, she gave no sign.

On the other hand, I found the entire procedure compelling. I couldn't have turned my eyes away if I had wanted to. Raptly I watched as the lone piece in Rathentweed's grip rose into the air, hovering on its own as the gnome snatched his hands away. With a pounding, thunderous explosion and a white flare of sputtering brightness, the wandlike terminus shot directly toward the adjoined segments in Parnish's hands. The wizard reeled backward as the sound of thunderclap resounded through the small compartment of the chariot. Lightning etched him in a silhouette of crackling brightness, and the acrid scent of ozone stung my nostrils. The smoke wafted away, and the magic-user's ever precise hair stood on end, sparking and flickering with bright power.

After a few seconds, the sparks died down, and the wizard held a seamless staff that had grown by the length of the sixth segment. Perhaps four feet long now, the artifact was taller than Saysi or Rathentweed, its ebony darkness fully as black and as pure as Arquestan's skin.

The wizard reeled dizzily, and I reached out a hand to steady him. Parnish's eyes were glazed, but slowly came into focus—and when they did, his stare widened in terror and awe. Following the direction of his gaze, I, too, looked beyond the chariot, and my hand went involuntarily to the hilt of the Vaati Blade.

A vast fortress had arisen before us, separated from the chariot by the gulf of a deep canyon, a chasm that seemed to extend around the full circumference of the vast, circular tunnel. Above, below, and to all sides, the "ground" plummeted into a haze of blackness and smoke, sometimes illuminated by distant fires of crimson fury, in other places fully obscured by the mists and fogs of chaos.

But the fortress itself stood in clear relief, proudly capping a pinnacle of white stone, a promontory so high that it jutted nearly to the center of this vast tunnel. Twisting towers rose from beyond walls of slick black, with crenellated battlements circling all the spire of rock, enclosing structures of smooth stone within.

Parts of the fortress were the same white stone as the alabaster pedestal, while others—such as a huge, narrow keep rising from within high walls—were as purely black as the Rod of Seven Parts. I saw bridges of crimson stone connecting some of the upper towers, and one of the walls was the same pale blue as the sky that had formed the upper boundary of a distant and pastoral world—the only world I had ever known until the beginning of this journey.

There seemed to be no way for a land-bound creature to reach this fortress. The spire supporting it was at least four or five miles high, with sides as sheer and featureless as the smoothest glacier-scoured cliff.

Only by looking very carefully did I notice a haze, like a film of mist in the air, that seemed to encircle the entire place. It apparently rose from the bedrock of the white-colored spire, swirling into the air, expanding to enclose all of the towers, every wall and bridge and building within the lofty fortress, then coming together to form a pointed peak in the space above the castle's highest tower.

"The cocoon of law," whispered Parnish Fegher as his own eyes followed mine in tracing the outline of the pale mist. The barrier was so faint as to be almost invisible, and it certainly did not provide any obstacle to our attempts to view the castle.

"Indeed," Arquestan declared in his deep, rumbling voice. "It looks tenuous, but it is stronger than steel, and it imprisons Miska, prevents him from departing the castle."

"What is the threat in one monster?" Badswell asked. "How can he make worlds end?"

"He does it by leading, by mastering the forces of chaos," Arquestan explained patiently. "The servants of the queen are, for the most part, incapable of working together. If there are more than a dozen or two of them in one place, they almost certainly start fighting each other.

Yet Miska is able to lash many thousands of them to his will, to lead them on campaigns of unceasing fury and destruction."

"And if he is freed . . . ?" I wasn't sure I wanted to have the answer spelled out, but I needed to ask the question.

"He will certainly commence another war, spreading chaos across all the planes. Indeed, his frustration, coupled with the queen's fabled impatience, would probably lead to the initiation of an attack within hours of his escape."

"Can he travel through planes like you?" Saysi wondered.

Arquestan smiled dryly, but without amusement. "My kinsmen consider that a curse—that we wendeam, the outcasts, can find the paths that lead between the planes. "But you are correct. One such as Miska can follow those paths as well, even make his own roads. That is one reason we made certain to imprison him so completely after the incomplete triumph of Pesh."

"Why have you brought us here?" I asked, already knowing the answer and feeling a strange thrill of anticipation, when all my rational mind told me that I should be completely, desperately afraid.

The wind duke regarded me shrewdly, clear eyes narrowed, white teeth bared in an expression that might have been smile or snarl. Tilting his head slightly, he encompassed all of my companions in his gaze; I noticed that even Saysi raised her head, regarding Arquestan with an expression mingling apprehension and awe.

"Because within this fortress prison, guarded by Miska himself and no doubt also protected by the watchful presence of his tanar'ri bodyguards, there shall you find the seventh and final piece of our artifact of law."

CHAPTER 21

HALLS OF THE RAKLUPIS

"Use the rod," Arquestan told Parnish. "Only thus may we pass the cocoon of law." The whirlwind was poised a stone's throw away from the fortress, and we mortal passengers stared in awe at the bleak edifice.

The wizard did as he was told, standing at the very edge of the whirlwind chariot, raising the ever-growing staff out before him, and reaching it toward the lofty fortress that by now loomed forbiddingly close.

Arquestan pointed to one of the nearest towers, a squat block of stone that rose straight from the precipice of the stone pillar. "When we reach that tower, I'll float in the space just beyond the fortress wall. You must all quickly leap to the platform. Seek the seventh piece within the structure."

"*We* must?" squeaked Rathentweed. "What about *you?*"

"The wolf-spider knows me. He would sense my approach. I must await you outside, or he shall certainly intercept us. As it is, I shall try to distract him by luring him to the opposite corners of his prison."

The misty barrier of the cocoon became visible as a filmy membrane, apparently made of air. Parnish extended the rod, and the artifact made a soft tearing sound as it sliced through the tenuous layer. The whirlwind angled slightly, though the deck remained solid and flat under our feet, and with a slight strain, Arquestan guided us through the gap and poised his airy chariot beside the battlements of one of the fortress's largest towers.

"Go!" he urged, and Badswell and Parnish leapt from the compartment, perched on the rampart, then jumped down to the surface within the cocoon. Rathentweed stood at the edge, trembling, but he seemed utterly incapable of flinging himself into space.

"C'mon, little feller," urged Badswell, turning to the gnome. "I'll catch ya!"

Finally Rathentweed closed his eyes and hurled himself outward. With an easy grab, Badswell proved as good as his word, snatching the gnome out of the air and setting him safely onto the platform.

I stood ready to jump, then looked back to see Saysi staring grimly at me from her position beside the whirlwind's far wall.

"Come on!" I urged, holding out a hand.

For a second, I thought she was going to refuse, but then she rose and came forward, taking my hand.

"If this will help me get you back," she said, "then I'll try!"

Together we leapt the narrow gap, landing easily on the wall. She shook her head despairingly as we stepped down to join our other companions on the white stone floor of the battle platform. The tower top was a large circle surrounded by the battlement. Beyond, space plunged into a deep court-yard, from the center of which the black, imposing monolith of the keep rose into the chaotic sky.

Arquestan and his chariot, still within the cocoon of law, began to rise away from us with a gusty motion that set Saysi's copper curls lashing across her face.

"I'll stay nearby, moving around the outside of the palace." The wind duke spoke briskly, electric tension conveyed by his rigid posture and the intensity of his piercing stare. "Miska will sense me, and that should give you a bit of a diversion. Also, realize that there will certainly be a raklupis or two about. In the old days, they formed the wolf-spider's most trusted, fanatic bodyguards."

"What about these raklupis? Are they like the other spyder-fiends?" I inquired.

"They're worse. A raklupis can appear in any guise. Should you meet anything within, human or elf or drooling horror, there's a good chance that it will be one of these potent tanar'ri. Remember, suspect *everything*."

"Good luck!" I called as the spiraling cloud rose and then zoomed quickly around a corner of a castle tower.

Swiftly we crossed the platform, anxiously watching for signs of defense. The courtyard appeared empty, and we quickly discovered that a long bridge spanned the distance from our tower to the keep. With no better route before us, we started across the span, drawing steadily closer to the vast edifice of black stone. The bridge terminated in an entryway that was secured by a very strong-looking door.

Parnish strode up to the barrier, which was a heavy, iron-banded structure in a wall of bright blue stone. The portal seemed to be the only way to get off this rampart, and even from my vantage across the way, I could see the outline of a massive iron lock.

"I'll smash it down," I declared confidently, drawing the gold-bladed sword.

"Kip!" Saysi hissed with an urgency I couldn't ignore. "Just pick the lock! That's how you always get into places you're not supposed to be!"

"I can't do that!" I protested, shocked that she would suggest such a thing.

"No," she replied bitterly. "I suppose you can't. That wouldn't be lawful, would it?"

"You should know that as well as I!" Surprised by the anger in her tone, I decided this wasn't the right time to argue about it.

The door had a large iron clasp, securing it solidly against my attempt to pull it open. The locking mechanism was primitive by comparison to some I had seen, but since I didn't have a key, it might as well have been the most advanced in all the worlds. No matter, since one bash of my heavy-bladed sword reduced the door to splinters, and I stepped through the shattered barrier with the Vaati Blade raised before my face.

Badswell and Saysi followed right behind, with Rathentweed chasing after and Parnish Fegher, staff held in both hands, bringing up the rear. Though the hallway was dim, I had no difficulty seeing, and I realized that the illumination seemed to be everywhere. It wasn't just the outside light spilling through the doorway.

Walls of blue stone extended into the middle distance. The floor was clean, and the ceiling . . . well, it was nonexistent. I looked upward into a mass of swirling, bluish smoke. The vapor was thick, suspended in a dense layer well above my reach, even when I raised my sword and tried to touch the stuff with the end of the blade.

I started forward without hesitation, striding purposefully down the hallway in long steps. The far end of the corridor was shadowed to either side, suggesting that additional passages broke to the left and right. The distance didn't look particularly far, but it took a surprisingly long time for us to traverse the length of the hall. I had counted something like a hundred steps before we drew near the branching corridors.

As we approached to within a dozen paces of the intersection, I was startled to see a woman step into view from the opening to the left. She was clad in a gown of dazzling blue silk that did little to conceal full, voluptuous features. Her face was stunningly beautiful, framed by high cheekbones and hair of shimmering gold.

"Hello, warrior," she said in a voice of melodious perfection. "I am grateful that you have come."

"So—so am I," I stammered, taken aback by her appearance. She fastened a look upon me that all but caused my knees to buckle. Certainly I had never seen a person of such consuming, immaculate perfection. I felt a growing desire and a certain knowledge: This woman would indulge my every desire, would please me as no other female ever had. She was the perfect complement to a champion of law!

"Kip! Beware!" The words, barked by Parnish Fegher, had no effect upon me. My sword clattered to the floor, unnoticed, and I took a step forward.

"Who are you?" I asked, certain that I had found the love, the perfect beauty, who would complete my life.

"I am *yours*, warrior." She raised her arms to embrace me, and I stumbled senselessly toward those perfect features, reaching, driven by a desire so strong that everything else was forgotten.

Badswell hit me from behind, his bulky form smashing me to the side, both of us crashing into the wall with a force that drove the air from my lungs. I drove my elbow backward furiously, resentful of every second's delay before I could enjoy that anticipated embrace. My friend grunted as I hit him hard and low, drawing a deep and ragged breath, but Badswell's strapping arms and beefy fists still held me tightly imprisoned.

"Wait!" I croaked, reaching, straining to touch the gorgeous creature who had recoiled a step or two after Badswell's sudden attack. Her eyes were no longer upon me, and the sight of her looking past me, down the corridor toward my companions, filled me with blinding, jealous rage.

The streak of lightning flashed past me before I knew that Parnish had cast a spell. With explosive force, the bolt struck that vision of fabulous beauty between her perfect breasts, an assault of cruelty that sent outrage shivering upward through my body.

With a roar of animal rage, I bounded to my feet, casting Badswell aside, reaching for the gold-bladed sword I had earlier dropped.

"Kip, *look!*" screamed Saysi, pointing past me, her eyes wide with awe and horror.

I shook off the warning, blinking through my rage, seizing the Vaati Blade and seeking the wizard who had stricken my newly discovered love.

"Warrior . . . help me. . . ."

That melodious voice, full of pain and inhuman suffering, drove me to a frenzy. I rushed at Parnish, who, like Saysi, seemed more concerned with staring at the woman behind me. My sword was raised, ready to slash through the wizard's immaculate vest.

"Kill him! Avenge me!"

In my fury, I didn't notice that the woman's voice had taken on a harder edge, cruelty rising through the sounds that had been so gentle a moment before. Blindly I raised the weapon, forcing Parnish to step backward as he realized I wasn't about to turn away.

Then Saysi was standing there, blocking my path to the hateful wizard. Beside myself with fury, I almost brought the blade down on her copper-curled head. Only some inner reserve of sanity brought me up short.

"Move!" I snarled. "Move, and let the wizard die!"

"*Look!*" she repeated again, her tone strangely calm in the midst of my storm of fury.

Something, some lingering memory of who she was, of who *I* was, stayed my hand. The blade remained level, suspended in the air over her head; her chocolate eyes pleaded with me, strained to penetrate my madness. Slowly, deliberately, I turned my head and followed the direction of her pointing finger.

"Warrior, please . . . avenge me . . . *save* me."

But the woman was gone. In her place was a scuttling, crablike horror, a thing that I knew was a spyder-fiend, though a type I had never before encountered. There were the eight legs, the wolfish head with drooling jaws. Unlike the kakkuu, however, the fur on this monster's lupine portion was sleek and clean, bluish black in color. The back was covered in a shiny carapace of the same color, and three parallel rows of spines ran along the body, extending backward from the leering head. Two human arms emerged from beneath the shell, reaching, beseeching from either side of that awful head.

"Warrior . . ." Again came the alluring word, the melodious voice; the sound was like an angel singing or the breathy endearment of a lover.

But it emerged from those black, carnivorous lips.

Seeing her ruse shattered, the monster—a raklupis, I now knew—darted at Badswell, driving its cruel fangs toward the half-ogre's arm. Bads chopped with his axe, forcing the creature's charge to the side—but not far enough. Teeth scraped his skin, and he howled with pain as he staggered back against the wall.

Now, cursing my lateness, I responded. Head down, I charged, flailing with my mighty blade. The spyder-fiend tried to block my blow with one of those humanlike arms, and I lopped it off at the wrist. Screeching in pain and rage, it cowered backward, moving with the scuttling quickness of its kind.

But my vengeance would not be denied. I leapt after it, chopping savagely, cutting through the skull and drawing a spill of black liquid that gushed to the floor. My sword raised, I stepped in for the kill, bringing the weapon down with crushing force against a wounded and, I thought, helpless target.

My weapon clanged to the floor with hand-numbing force, and I pitched forward, skidding through the black ooze and barely retaining my balance. Only then did I perceive that my enemy was no longer there.

"Teleportation," Parnish muttered, stepping past Saysi to look down the two adjoining corridors. "The battle was lost, so the monster escaped to fight again."

"Teleported?" I demanded, panting, furious with myself as much as with the treacherous enemy. "To where?"

"There's no way to know, unless you can follow tracks through the ether," the wizard declared dryly. "The next time we try to tell you something, I suggest you pay closer attention."

"How . . . what happened?" I asked dizzily, shaking my head against the confusion. "She was so . . ."

My words trailed off in shame. Surely she had been beautiful, but since when was mere beauty enough to drive away my sanity? I looked at Saysi, realizing the risk she had taken in stepping in front of the wizard, and my guilt brought a choking shame to the surface.

"Don't," she said gently, seeing the agony on my face. "This was a thing of chaos, of potent magic. There's no shame in failing to realize it immediately."

"No brains in that failure, either," declared Rathentweed tartly. The gnome had crept forward and now joined the rest of us.

"How badly are you hurt?" asked Saysi, kneeling beside the panting form of Badswell.

"Not hurt . . . I guess . . . kind of . . . sleepy," grunted the half-ogre. He looked at me from beneath hooded lids, and I sensed him straining to cling to consciousness.

"Poison!" she whispered, bending to examine the wound. Though the monster's fangs had barely grazed Badswell's wrist, the wound was angry and inflamed. The scratch had already raised a large welt, and I could imagine the potent venom creeping up his arm toward his heart.

Taking a tiny hand and wrapping it around her jade amulet, placing her other hand over the sinister wound, Saysi murmured a quiet prayer. The rest of us stood silently, watching, except for Rathentweed, whose eyes darted back and forth around the intersecting corridors. No doubt he expected a rank of raklupis to charge into view at any moment.

"Patrikon grant me this power, the touch of your benign hand. . . ." Her words trailed off as the prayer of healing took hold.

The little priestess winced suddenly, then wrapped her tiny fingers even more tightly around the half-ogre's big wrist. I sensed her magic flowing, perceived the magical touch of Patrikon through the vast distances of the planes.

Abruptly Badswell snorted and blinked, smacking his heavy lips as his eyes flickered open. "Wakin' up now," he acknowledged, though he winced when he put his weight on the wounded limb in an effort to rise.

"The staff!" Saysi said insistently, turning to Parnish. "My spell halted the spread of the poison, but the power of the staff is needed to cure the wound."

The wizard stepped to the half-ogre's side. Impatiently Saysi tugged the narrow end of the rod, the part that had once been my lone stub of ebony, toward the wound. At the touch, the swelling subsided visibly, the skin closing over the angry-looking gash. All that remained was a scar of red flesh. Saysi wrapped a clean cloth around his wrist, and finally Badswell stood, strong and steady and once more ready to move.

Rathentweed turned back from looking up and down the adjoining corridors, addressing Parnish. "Can you tell, my lord, where we are to go from here?"

With both hands on the nearly assembled staff, the wizard closed his eyes behind the wire spectacles. I could sense his concentration as he sought the subtle emanations of the seventh and final segment. "My feeling leads me upward," replied Parnish Fegher after a few moments' reflection. He indicated the divided hallway. "Either direction might be as good as the other."

Wordlessly I stepped into the lead again, determined that my mistake in judgment would not be repeated.

Choosing the left corridor, perhaps because that was the direction from which the raklupis had approached, I proceeded along the passageway. Badswell held his axe easily in one hand and came along closely behind.

Once again we made our way through the fortress prison of the wolf-spider. I lost track of how long we spent wandering the halls, taking guesses at each intersection, climbing marbled stairways wherever we found them. Sometimes the walls around us were the same pure blue as those that had flanked our initial entry; on other occasions, we walked between panels of black or white, and once we found ourselves in a stretch of the maze where our surroundings were blood red.

In many places, rubble was strewn throughout the passages, great pieces of rock ripped from the walls with blows of singular violence. Boulders bigger than Badswell's head appeared to have been hurled into corners, chipping away massive wedges from the walls. I could only imagine at the fury of the confined wolf-spider that would drive him to tearing at the foundation of his fortress during his long eons of captivity.

We reached a steep, narrow stairway and found that many of the steps had been bashed away, battered by a barrage of rubble. Here we were forced to scramble up with the aid of our hands, like scaling a small stretch of cliff. With me at the top and Badswell hoisting at the bottom, we easily passed the other companions to safety. Then, grunting from exertion, the half-ogre himself scaled the sheer barrier.

There was no discernible pattern to the layout of hallways and floors—nor, I realized after an interminable amount of time, did there seem to be any actual rooms. Perhaps they were concealed behind the walls, accessed by secret doors. There must have been *something* other than the corridors, for these halls were long, the intersections infrequent. Yet as far as we could tell, the rest of the fortress might have been solid rock. Several times Rath paused to tap against the walls, which invariably resulted in a thud as solid and free of resonance as any mountainous bedrock. Of course, that would have also been the case if the walls were merely very thick, so we couldn't draw any real conclusions from this experiment.

The only encouraging feature of our exploration was that we did seem to be able to work our way, very gradually, into the higher reaches of the keep. The stairways were generally no wider than the halls, and they varied in length from about a dozen steps to one long, spiraling circuit of no less than one hundred. Finally one of these flights—it must have been the fifth or sixth that we encountered—seemed wider, more grand, than the steps that had led us to this point, and as we embarked upon this climb, I allowed myself to hope that we were drawing nearer to our goal.

The walls in this part of the fortress were of a green as pure as the most beautiful emerald, and the floors matched this color in a darker, more opaque hue. The ceiling remained concealed by misty vapor—naturally, here it was a viridescent green in color—and likewise the upper reaches of the wide, straight staircase were masked by the brightly colored mist. Perhaps because this time it blocked our view of what lay ahead, I began to see that mist as a sinister thing, a concealment for ambushers or a seething cloud of poisonous mist that might float forward to enwrap us all in a shroud of death.

The steps were at least thirty feet wide, and we all climbed abreast. Saysi took the left flank, I noticed with a pang; since I was beside Parnish, near the right, this left Badswell and Rathentweed between us, and I feared that her distancing was intentional. Still, I focused on the climb and tried to see through the cloaking mist that screened the upper reaches of the steps.

That obfuscation seemed to actually rise before us. At least, it seemed that it remained a constant distance away, even as we made steady progress upward. After uncountable minutes of climbing, we paused to catch our breath, still in the midst of this eternal stairway.

"Look—can't see the bottom anymore," Badswell observed, turning to look behind.

The half-ogre was right. Green vapor had seeped into the lower reaches of the stairs, masking the flight about fifty or sixty steps below—the same distance, approximately, that we could see above us.

"Do you still feel the lure of the seventh piece?" Rathentweed asked Parnish, and the wizard nodded curtly in reply.

Having caught our breath, we once again resumed the ascent, plodding through the seemingly endless series of steps, approaching the upper reaches of the keep.

"Listen . . . hear that?" It was Badswell who spoke, raising a hamlike fist to halt our ascent.

"No," I replied as the sounds of our walking faded away, leaving the great fortress in a well of silence as deep and all-encompassing as death itself.

"What is it? What do you hear?" Saysi asked worriedly.

Without replying, Badswell sprang ahead, all but sprinting forward, leaping up the steps as fast as his tree-trunk legs could carry him.

"Wait!" I cried, bounding after him. The others followed, but couldn't keep up with me—and I couldn't catch

Badswell, who ran with a grace and speed that I had never before observed in the big fellow.

Finally the mist dissolved, parting around Badswell's lumbering form like seawater breaking around the prow of a fast ship. I saw the upper terminus of the stairs, a wide landing with passages extending straight ahead and to either side. Bounding up the last steps, the half-ogre didn't pause before he veered to the left, skidding on the slick floor, and charged into the hallway.

His turn carried him out of my sight, and I renewed my efforts, leaping up the last dozen steps, darting after my friend. Desperately fearing for his safety and sanity, I caught a glimpse of him once more, well ahead of me. Badswell lumbered steadily, showing no signs of tiring as he lowered his head and charged along. Now, at least, I was able to close the distance. The half-ogre planted his boots and darted around another corner, but by this time, I was right at his heels. I darted around the corner, crashing into Badswell's back as he abruptly halted.

Finally I heard the singing, and I knew that this was the sound that had drawn my friend into his impetuous advance. Two female creatures stood there, eyes closed, voices raised in a faintly musical song—more of a chant, actually, but then that was fitting, given the grotesque appearance of the singers.

Both were huge, nearly seven feet tall, massively muscular. They were humanlike, but not quite human. I realized, with a grimace of dismay, that they, like Badswell, were crossbreeds of ogre and human! The nearest, her head surrounded by a thick cascade of dark black hair, opened her eyes to meet Badswell's adoring gaze. The tip of a dark tongue slid between her meaty lips, tickling between two dainty, blunt tusks. She smiled, and my friend took a faltering step, reaching out, falling toward the arms extended to embrace him.

I reacted without stopping to think, shouldering Bads aside and driving my sword into the creature. The golden blade stabbed home, drawing a shriek of unworldly pain from the monster I had instinctively pierced. She staggered back, pulling free of the blade, and I chopped once more with a vicious sideswipe, lopping the head from those brawny shoulders.

"Kip—*no!*" Badswell's voice was a wail of grief and fury, emotions I remembered all too well from my own confused encounter with the deceitful raklupis.

The heavy body fell to the floor, flailing reflexively, as the head thumped nearby. Already the tusked feminine features were changing, the jaws extending, the head sprouting smooth black fur as it transformed into the horrific lupine image of a raklupis. Twisting and writhing, the body ripped under internal pressure, legs sprouting to right and left. The two humanoid arms remained, clutching at air, while the heavy ogre legs became bent and arachnoid. Six more legs, three from each side, tore free, and as the corpse finally grew still, it was the body of a giant spider that lay, stiff and rigid, on its back.

Hoping the half-ogre would retain enough of his sanity not to stab me in the back, I turned toward the other half-ogre female. This one had pulled a long dagger and used the weapon to deflect my first crushing attack. Instead of striking at me, however, she darted past, driving the blade toward Badswell's broad chest.

"Wait . . . what . . . ?"

The big fellow gaped stupidly, making no move to raise his axe. Desperately I spun, bringing the Vaati Blade around to chop the female half-ogre in the back of her neck. She went down, twitching and flexing, and I stabbed her again, then stepped back as the transformation distorted the already grotesque features, pulling them into the gruesome image of a lifeless raklupis.

Badswell blinked back his tears, looking at me without comprehension. "She was so *beautiful.* . . . Why did you kill her?"

"Look at her!" I demanded. "It was a trick, just like they tried to trick me!"

Shaking his head, snuffling loudly, Bads made a cursory glance at the two corpses, then turned about with a wounded expression. Irritated with his stubbornness, I sheathed my still-immaculate blade, then stepped out of the alcove to rejoin him. Saysi and Parnish had arrived by this time, and I briefly explained the situation.

Still blinking, Badswell looked at the bodies and scratched his head. I got the feeling he was beginning to piece together the events that had drawn him here and the fact that I had saved his life.

"Thanks, Kip," he said gruffly, and the matter was concluded.

"Where's Rathentweed?" Badswell asked suddenly.

"He was right behind me. . . . Now where did he scuttle off to?" Parnish muttered.

"I was fooled, and we left him behind!" groaned the half-ogre in dismay. He lumbered back toward the stairs, with me trotting at his side.

Feeling a growing tremor of fear, I turned with Badswell toward the stairs, then halted in shock before reaching the top step. "Here he is," I said grimly.

"Poor little guy." Badswell knelt, his voice choked with grief as he cradled the limp form of the gnome in his arms.

Saysi, following at a trot, gasped as she reached us. Kneeling beside the shriveled form in the half-ogre's arms, she reached for Rathentweed's wrist in what I knew was a vain effort to find a pulse. The gnome's eyes were wide open, his mouth locked in a rictus of soundless horror. The only visible wounds were a pair of punctures, revealed on his forearm when Saysi pulled back the torn sleeve of his shirt.

"Poisoned," she whispered sadly. "He must have died almost instantly."

"Another raklupis?" I guessed, looking around warily as Parnish came up to us.

"He died in the service of law. It is as he would have wished," the wizard pronounced, leaning down to regard the gnome's pinched, horror-stricken features. "He is a hero."

"My fault," wailed Bads thickly. "I shouldn't of—"

"No!" Saysi interjected firmly. She touched the grieving fellow's shoulder lightly. "Don't think that. It's a fate that could await any of us in here, and it's no one's fault!"

She was right, I knew as I blinked back a surprising level of grief. Perhaps Rathentweed had been a pompous fussbudget, but in the end, he had entered a horrible place with courage and faith.

Yet his was a fate that lurked around every corner, a possibility that each of us might have to face before this quest was through.

"Which way?" I asked gruffly, pulling Parnish's attention back to the task at hand.

"Up . . . still higher," he declared after a moment's reflection. "I can't be certain, but I think we're getting closer."

None of us knew how long we wandered after that,

finding more hallways, another set of stairs, always seeking a way to the top of the fortress. Once we reached a door, passing outside of the fortress, and followed a circling stairway from battlement to battlement while the vast chaos of Pandemonium lurked beyond the hazy barrier of law's cocoon. Atop the flight of steps, we followed a slender bridge toward one of the upper halls of the keep. There we came to a castle gate, and once more I smashed the barrier with a blow of my mighty sword.

Immediately within, we found another stairway, and Parnish led the way, bouncing forward with an eagerness that belied his years. Taking the steps two or three at a time, he all but jogged upward, forcing Saysi to scramble desperately to keep up. Badswell and I, with our long legs, followed with easy strides, casting anxious glances backward, remaining alert for any signs of pursuit.

At the top of this flight, Parnish had to decide whether to turn right or left, and as he turned toward the left, I saw him pause, then whirl back to the right with an expression of surprise.

"Rathentweed! My good gnome," he exclaimed in unmistakable delight. "You're *alive!*"

"No!" Saysi screamed as the wizard hurried out of sight. My heart was in my throat as I leapt up the last few steps, darting after the halfling priestess and the wizard.

I glimpsed a small figure limping toward Parnish. That big nose was unmistakable, though the normally flushed and cheery cheeks were pallid and sickly.

"Your Lordship! Thank the gods I've found you," groaned Rathentweed, falling to the floor, reaching up as Parnish stepped closer.

Saysi halted a few steps away, her hand locked around her jade amulet, her eyes wide and staring. Hearing my approach, she looked up and spoke with desperate urgency.

"Kill him!"

I had no choice but to trust her. Savagely elbowing Parnish Fegher aside, I brought my blade down, piercing the gnome's chest, drawing the weapon free and hacking again at the big-nosed face.

Something slammed me across the back, and I crashed into the wall, stunned, vaguely realizing that Parnish had struck me with the Rod of Seven Parts. Groaning, I looked up into the wizard's enraged face, then watched as rage gave way to shock, confusion, and finally grief.

On the floor, lying still and already fully transformed, lay the body of yet another raklupis.

Parnish Fegher whirled away, wiping at his eyes and stumbling in the opposite direction. I climbed stiffly to my feet, shaking the kinks out of my muscles. We advanced four abreast now, since the corridor was wide and danger obviously lurked all around.

In a few moments, we arrived at what promised to be a last stairway, which climbed a short distance and terminated in a landing and a door. I didn't hesitate to smash the barrier into splinters. Stepping through the wreckage, we found ourselves on one of the castle's highest battlements, soaring above vast descents to all sides. The bizarre sky of Pandemonium, filtered by the cocoon of law, extended far overhead.

But these features were minor compared to the thing that drew our attention toward a raised stone table in the center of the platform. On that slab of rock lay a wand of perfect black, longer than any of the segments we had found but clearly the ultimate object of our quest.

The seventh and final segment of the rod.

CHAPTER 22

THE ROD OF SEVEN PARTS

Parnish made the first move, darting forward before any of us could react to stop him. He was halfway to the stone table when I dived, wrapped my arms around him, and bore him to the floor.

"Wait!" I urged. "It's too easy. It could be a trap!"

"It's *mine!*" hissed the wizard, his tone wild with frustration. "You shall not interfere!"

"Of course it's yours," Saysi said soothingly, coming up to lay a hand on his perspiring brow. "And you'll have it soon. Just let us take a look around first."

"No!" The magic-user's eyes stared around wildly. Gradually, under the priestess's gentle touch, Parnish drew a few deep breaths and apparently settled down. "Of course . . . you won't steal it. . . . I know that."

"I promise you shall have it," I reassured him, startled by the need apparent in his posture and expression.

I helped the wizard climb to his feet. Saysi, meanwhile,

advanced to the stone table and walked a careful circuit around it. Badswell crossed to the far wall of the platform, leaning over the battlements to look down.

"Nothin' comin' this way," he announced, holding his axe with a determination that belied his confident tone.

"See if there's a trap around that table," Saysi urged me. "I don't like the looks of this."

"All right," I agreed, taking a step forward with instinctive confidence, then paused miserably, hanging my head with a groan of frustration. Seeking a trap should have been a simple thing. Hadn't I saved lives before, my own included, by spotting a cleverly concealed tripwire or hearing the hollow sound of a trapdoor? When I walked around the block of stone, studying it carefully, I saw nothing out of the ordinary, yet I had the peculiar feeling that I really didn't know what to look for. There could be a fireball trap ready to explode with a simple touch, but I doubted that I would see even the boldest and most obvious clue.

"I don't know *how* anymore," I declared in dismay. "I've forgotten!"

Saysi looked at me sharply, her eyes bright with excitement. "Forgotten? That means you remember that, at some time, you *did* know how?"

I felt one of those headaches coming on again but forced myself to concentrate on her question. "Yes . . . it seems as if I should know what to look for, like picking locks. . . . I used to be able to do that, too, didn't I?"

Her face softened into a smile. "You were the best damned lockpicker I ever tried to reform."

"I guess you succeeded," I said, wishing I could share her pleasure. More memories tickled at me, reflected thoughts of things that once had been: of myself as a small person, a true halfling, not a human-sized warrior with furry feet. I looked at my strapping arms, felt the solid weight of my sword, and for a fleeting instant missed the person I once had been.

But now I was a champion of law. The wind duke Arquestan had told me as much.

With that thought, I remembered that he might be nearby, and joined Badswell at the edge of the battlement. The "sky" of broken landscape within the vast tunnel of Pandemonium was a smoky mix of colors, muted only slightly by the gauzy barrier created by the cocoon of law.

"I myself shall check the table," Parnish Fegher declared, advancing slowly, then stalking a measured circle around the irregular block of stone. He muttered an incantation, waving his assembled portion of the Rod of Seven Parts over the solid platform.

I watched tensely as blue tendrils of fire flickered silently in the air. I wasn't sure if the brightness came from the rod or from Parnish's spell. The tongues of flame danced around the table, scouring little patterns on the sides, slowly working their way toward the flat upper surface.

Finally, like thieves sneaking past the guards of a treasure chamber, the blue flickers crept over the lip of the stone platform and began advancing on the ebony wand that lay in the middle of the space. I began to view the thing as not so much a table but an altar, and watched enthralled as the fires rose and commenced a rhythmic circle, twisting and bobbing about the black shaft.

The tongues of fire crept closer and closer to the stub of the rod, the seventh and final part of the potent artifact. This was clearly the biggest and heaviest of the segments. More than a foot long, it continued the tendency of the rod growing wider toward the end, terminating in a blunt stub that was easily a handspan across.

I continued to watch the dancing, bobbing figures of the wizard's flickering fires. As each neared the shaft, the little blaze left a scar on the surface of stone, etching hieroglyphic symbols very much like those Parnish had created when he assembled the five pieces in his mansion.

"Look," Badswell said softly, speaking to me alone.

I followed the direction of his pointing finger, out along the walls of the palace, still within the gauzy barrier of law, into the space enclosed around the lofty fortress prison. The whirlwind of Arquestan spun there, cruising easily along the side of the mighty palace, floating gradually lower along the lofty walls. Looking down at it, I saw the wind duke standing there proud and aloof, guiding his sky chariot by the mere will of his thought. His eyes met mine for a very brief instant before he looked away, diving more quickly now, maneuvering evasively, and I sensed his purpose.

"He knows we're close. He's trying to lead Miska away from here, away from us," I whispered to Badswell.

Recalling the image of the three-headed wolf-spider as portrayed in Parnish's painting, I could only hope that the outcast succeeded. It would take more than a champion with a golden sword, a half-ogre with a battle-axe, and a wizard to hold that horrific creature at bay should he discover our whereabouts and make up his mind to attack.

"It is ready." Parnish spoke in a strong voice, striding forward to stand beside the platform. "There are no snares, arcane or mundane, in place to inhibit our gaining of the seventh and final piece."

"How long will it take you to prepare for the linking?" I asked, glancing around nervously. Aside from the shattered door, through which we had entered the landing, there didn't seem to be any other way to reach this place short of flying. Still, I wasn't sure that would be a major deterrent to a creature as potent as Miska. For a brief moment, the hairs tingled at the back of my neck, another sign of warning that I found difficult to ignore.

"It is already done," Parnish informed me, indicating the sigils that had been scarred into the stone of the altar by the passage of the blue flames. "I have but to work the final enchantments, and the rod will be assembled."

"Be careful," I encouraged, probably needlessly. Sword clutched in both of my hands, I sidled over to the wrecked door, looking into the darkened hallway. Nothing moved there, but I resolved to stay ready. Saysi came to stand beside me, while Badswell remained on the opposite side of the platform, keeping his eyes on the vast space beyond the fortress walls. All of us looked anxiously from our posts back to the wizard and the Rod of Seven Parts.

Once we were in position, Parnish wasted no time in beginning the soft, muttered chanting of his spell. The words were audible, though indecipherable, but I recognized the patterns I had heard on two previous occasions—when he had linked the five parts in his mansion, and when he had added the sixth part in Arquestan's chariot. I found myself holding my breath as the seventh part of the rod was outlined in blue fire. Slowly it rose, levitating to float perfectly still above the stone platform. As the wizard's chanting approached a crescendo, the long black wand pivoted with the grace of a dancer, turning to angle toward the rest of the artifact.

Parnish Fegher held his own portion of the rod still,

horizontally before him, aligning the shaft perfectly with the floating segment. His words grew louder, the pace of the incantation faster. Bracing myself for the impact, I watched the wand, ready to see it smash against the rest of the ancient artifact.

The climax came so quickly that I didn't see the piece move. It seemed to disappear from my sight as Parnish staggered backward and a massive thunderclap echoed across the platform. My ears rang, and balls of lightning crackled outward from the artifact, rolling around on the platform, hissing and sizzling with angry fire. The stink of ozone, hot and acrid, immediately penetrated the air.

"It is complete!" cried the wizard, holding the artifact over his head, brandishing it at the sky. "Powers of chaos, behold your doom! Your ultimate destruction is upon you!"

I stared, elated and awed, as the faded impulses of lightning flickered around the gray-haired wizard. Parnish shook the staff at the sky in a frenzy of triumph, shouting his challenge, spinning around with wild, staring eyes.

Teleportation—that's the only way that the platform could have suddenly gotten so crowded, how a half dozen tanar'ri could suddenly be here, among us, sharing this space that had been ours alone a moment earlier.

In the instant of my recognition, a raklupis, its wolflike head growling, crouched between Saysi and me. Another snapped and bit at Badswell as the half-ogre swiped quickly with his axe, driving back the jaws that hadn't even been there a moment before. I started to turn, then froze, staring in awe and horror at the horrific beast that now crouched over the stone altar, leering at Parnish Fegher.

Miska the Wolf-Spider, master of the tanar'ri, consort of the Queen of Chaos, was far more terrifying in actual presence than he had been in the gruesome depiction of Parnish's painting. The creature was huge, looming larger than the elephants that had carried us from Argenport. The twin wolf heads snarled, baring fangs as long as swords, while the humanlike arms, as big as the limbs on any giant, reached for the wizard.

"Die, fiend of chaos!" cried Parnish, his eyes blazing behind his wire-rimmed spectacles. Hair unkempt, voice shrill, the wizard turned the rod like a spear, as if to cast it into the huge body. "Your time is past!"

"My *banishment* is past," declared the golden-haired, handsome head in the center of Miska's visage. The words were powerful, the sound booming like thunder, yet the voice was as calmly and clearly articulated as the gracious speech of a seasoned barrister. "I have had enough of imprisonment—and enough of mortal arrogance! As to impending death, that is but a proper fate for you!"

The giant hands reached forward and plucked Parnish from the platform, twisting the wizard so that he could flail the rod only at the air. One of the savage wolf heads snapped forward, jaws closing over the magic-user's kicking legs. I felt a surge of nausea at the sound, like the snapping of dry, brittle sticks, of breaking bones.

The other wolf head closed around Parnish's head, fangs piercing the all-too-mortal body, cascading gouts of crimson blood into a gory shower. The Rod of Seven Parts fell from the wizard's lifeless hands as the two monstrous heads pulled apart, ripping Parnish Fegher's body into ragged halves. The parts of the corpse flopped heavily to the platform, unrecognizable, as the black artifact clattered onto the flat paving stones between them.

311

"Kip, help!" Saysi screamed, drawing my horror-stricken gaze. The nearest raklupis leapt at her, forcing her back through the splintered doorway to the keep. She picked up one of the boards, bashing the monster's narrow snout, halting the deadly pursuer for a split second.

With a snarl of animal rage, I sprang at the monster's back, driving the gold-bladed sword with all my power. The weapon cleaved through the hard carapace, ripped into the monstrous body, and clanged off the hard stone floor. The two pieces of the raklupis twitched and kicked, trickling dark ichor, as the creature slowly perished.

Whirling back, I saw Badswell slash at another tanar'ri, and with Saysi in tow, I rushed across the platform to aid my hulking companion. The raklupis blinked out of sight as we reached the half-ogre's side at the castle parapet. The three of us stood with our backs to the rampart as five or six spyder-fiends, all raklupis, closed in slowly.

Miska himself loomed over us but took no notice of our fight. Instead, the monstrosity crouched above the rod, dropping a spiraling tendril of webbing from his bloated abdomen. A silken strand touched the rod, encircled it in a layer of shimmering web, and slowly began to lift the artifact upward.

Another raklupis reached beneath its belly, snatching up a strange, pale globe that had been affixed there. The monster tossed the ball with a humanoid arm, the object splattering onto the floor before me. I stumbled against the rampart, gagging on a rancid stench that rose like a stinking cloud into the air. My sword clattered to the flagstones, slipping from nerveless fingers. I desperately knew that I had to hold it, to wield it against these monstrous horrors, but my muscles refused to obey my will.

Wind swirled around us, and I was vaguely aware of a tall, dark form nearby. Arquestan, mounted on his whirlwind chariot, had soared to the edge of the platform and now stood ready to step across the gap. A gust preceded him, sweeping over us and starting to carry away the lingering cloud of the spyder-fiend's poisonous gas.

Badswell and Saysi gagged from the toxic stench, but the half-ogre managed to cling to his axe, slashing it toward the nearest raklupis as the monster advanced. Choking, still blinded by my own tears, I stumbled along the edge of the battlement in helpless retreat. Only the half-ogre kept us alive. Even as he choked and gasped, he managed to hold the snapping, snarling raklupis a step or two away.

"This way!" urged Arquestan. At last my vision cleared, and I saw Saysi scrambling to the battlement, then springing into the compartment of the whirlwind chariot.

Globes of light circled and floated there, but at least one of the hounds—Bayar, I saw—had resumed her animal form. The jowly dog, ears flapping, barked furiously from the compartment of the wind duke's platform.

Arquestan leapt with catlike grace, landing on the rim of the tower. Four globes, loyal hounds, circled his head as he reached low, scrambling for my sword. Miska himself grabbed with his giant-sized arm and snatched up the potent weapon, holding the mighty blade like a dagger in one of his monstrous hands. With an almost casual stab, he plunged it through Arquestan's chest, piercing the wendeam's mighty heart, driving the wind duke back against the rampart. With a groan, then a sigh of ultimate sadness, the outcast from the valley of Aaqa slumped to a sitting position before slowly toppling to the side.

Numbly I watched, giving way to a dull sensation of

utter hopelessness. I heard a sound nearby and knew that Saysi was crying; it seemed the greatest tragedy of my life that I couldn't go over and make her feel better.

Badswell finally connected with the lunging raklupis, splitting the creature's skull with a powerful blow of the axe. I heard a clattering of metal, saw that Miska had cast aside the Vaati Blade. Both wolf heads howled in triumph, the sound like the maelstrom of a hurricane, while the human face sneered with wicked anticipation.

Now the wolf-spider snapped up the webbing, with the Rod of Seven Parts clasped tightly in the coiled strands. Holding the black shaft in the strands of silk, Miska uttered a laugh of cold, utter cruelty. With a powerful cast, he flicked it outward and up, hurling the artifact like a spear.

The black shaft struck the cocoon of law with a force that reverberated through the air, driving the breath from my lungs, sending Badswell reeling backward to the floor. The rod stuck through the filmy barrier, then slipped slowly down to tear a long hole in the cocoon. I saw the vaporous barrier part, a wide rip running down the length of the gauzy cloud. Saysi, now alone with Bayar in the compartment of the whirlwind, drifted away from the keep—and toward the vaporous barrier.

With one last, sneering laugh, the wolf-spider lowered his head and leapt for the gap in the cocoon. Howling in glee as he escaped the bonds that had contained him for centuries, he pounced upward. A shriek of savage, furious joy echoed through the air, lingering in the depths of Pandemonium for long moments after Miska disappeared.

CHAPTER 23

PURSUIT THROUGH PANDEMONIUM

"Kip! Badswell! Get over here!" Saysi rode the wind duke's whirlwind, poised in space just a short distance off the rampart. The urgency in her voice was amplified by Bayar's frantic barking.

Reaching the parapet near her approach, I bent down to pick up my sword. The golden blade was marred for the first time, bright red with Arquestan's blood, and I stared at the weapon with something like horror. Only Saysi's shrill cry, repeated, broke through the numbing haze of catastrophe. I climbed to the edge of the battlement in numb, reflexive response as the half-ogre lumbered quickly after me.

Hesitating only a moment, I cast one backward glance, seeing Arquestan slumped in a wide pool of blood. His proud, black head lay tilted to the side, his eyes staring sightlessly. I didn't want to believe it, but there could be no doubt that he was dead. Of the four hounds, still in their dancing-globe state, two had been rent by raklupis, while the other two continued to bob and weave against their enemies, striking out with an occasional burst of bright sparks.

"Jump—right *now!*" Saysi sounded close to panic. "More spyder-fiends right behind you!"

Numerous tanar'ri, including several sleek raklupis, spilled in a tangle of arachnoid legs and wolfish heads from the broken doorway. More of the spidery horrors popped into view, teleporting onto the stone altar or suddenly appearing in different places on the circular battle platform. In a single instant, no fewer than two dozen of the howling creatures arrived, every one of them scuttling furiously toward Badswell and me.

Without another moment's hesitation, I flung myself into space, springing with all the strength in my legs to span the gulf of space and land in the compartment of the airborne chariot. Next Badswell flung himself outward, reaching with his big hands toward the edge of the cyclone. Though no less powerful than I, the half-ogre's weight proved a detriment, and his leap carried him barely to the edge of the whirlwind. His broad hands grabbed the edge of the chariot's compartment, but the solid rim was rounded and slippery, providing a very poor grip. He started to slip backward, huffing in frustration, until I seized both of his wrists, slamming against the side of the compartment as I took the full force of the half-ogre's weight. Grunting, straining, I gasped out a prayer to Patrikon, pleading for the strength to save my hulking friend.

Saysi ran to my side, throwing her slight form into the effort as Badswell kicked against the sides of the whirlwind, gaining a little purchase in the softly yielding surface of air. Slowly we lifted him until, with a groan of exhaustion, he propped his elbows over the lip of the compartment. In another moment, we pulled him in, the three of us collapsing on the deck.

Looking up, I realized that we had drifted some distance away from the battlement, where spyder-fiends now teemed in great numbers. Wolf jaws snapped and howled as the creatures surged back and forth, commanded by the cool, confident voices of the raklupis. Some of the tanar'ri turned to savage each other, while others clawed and climbed over their neighbors, howling and baying at us. A few dangled webs from the high rampart, scuttling down the wall, swinging outward in vain attempts to attack the whirlwind.

One big lycosyd tried to leap after us, but the monster plunged to its doom well short of our swirling chariot. I thought it fortunate that, for the time being at least, none of the raklupis showed an inclination to change shape into some winged form and fly to the attack. Then we passed through the gash in the cocoon of law and were safe from the immediate dangers of tanar'ri.

I turned to Saysi, and for the first time noticed the shaft of black she clutched in both of her hands. "The Rod of Seven Parts . . . but how . . . ?"

My words trailed off, my jaw slack with astonishment.

"When Miska tore through the cocoon, it was still falling downward. The whirlwind drifted over there. I certainly wasn't controlling it, but it was as if there were some kind of attraction. We were floating right there when it came past, and I just reached out and pulled it from the cocoon," she said, as if it had been as simple as retrieving an apple falling from a tree. "It seems to give me the power to control Arquestan's whirlwind."

At the mention of the wind duke's name, I groaned and looked back toward the fortress, which slowly receded into the distance.

"He's dead, isn't he?" she asked quietly.

"As dead as Parnish. By the gods, what a disaster!"

"That's not the worst of it," she said, turning a steely look into the depths of Pandemonium.

"I know," I replied, clutching the hilt of my sword with white-knuckled intensity. The stain of the wind duke's blood marred the golden perfection of the blade, but I had no desire to wipe it away. Instead, I raised the weapon, pointing into the distance of Pandemonium. "It's Miska. He's loose, freed from his prison."

"What kin we do?" Badswell asked, recovering his breath enough to stand beside us.

"We've got to go after him." Saysi and I spoke together, exactly the same words.

"Where'd he go?" The half-ogre posed the next, eminently logical question.

Slumping in dejection, Saysi turned tear-filled eyes toward the vast extent of Pandemonium's tunnel, the immense landscape spiraling away for an incomprehensible distance. "I don't know," she admitted. "He . . . he disappeared, became invisible or teleported or something. But *where?*"

The catastrophe was eminently clear to all of us: Miska's campaign of chaos could be unleashed against a hundred worlds as soon as he could raise an army of tanar'ri. The Queen of Chaos, no doubt, would be only too willing to help him raise his legions.

Abruptly Bayar rose to prop her forepaws on the rim of the circular compartment. The hound faced into the tangled depths of Pandemonium, whining urgently.

"D'you think she's tellin' us?" Badswell wondered. Turning her mournful eyes to me, Bayar stared with a clear plea.

"I think so—at least, I *hope* so." I spoke tentatively, but a feeling had begun to grow within me. Still holding that mighty sword, I squinted into the distance, trying to penetrate a mass of haze and chaos. There *could* be a trail there, a faint spoor lingering unseen, but perhaps marking a course of travel through the twisting coils and passages of this nightmare plane. We could only hope that this loyal hound could sense that ephemeral path, guiding us to a final confrontation with our immortal enemy.

"Let's try it." I pointed with the Vaati Blade, feeling more and more certain of Bayar's sense of direction. "Miska went that way. See if you can make us follow him."

Without further questions, Saysi inclined the Rod of Seven Parts, and the whirlwind quickly spiraled away from the fortress prison of the wolf-spider.

Swiftly the airy chariot built speed, until we soared faster than I could comprehend, shooting like a bolt of lightning through the winding tunnels of this abysmal plane. Abruptly we were surrounded by fog, the ether between the planes roaring with thunderous sound and spiraling, kaleidoscopic chaos. Bayar stood still, her quivering snout clearly fixed on a direction, and Saysi followed that indication.

With shocking quickness, we broke from the fog, emerging into a pit so vast that its very scope defied our understanding. Bayar again urged us forward, her jowly muzzle extending over the rim of the chariot. She regarded the depths of this bizarre and frightening place, guiding us with determined gentle whines.

Distant walls plunged downward, past wide shelves of

chaotic land masses. In a haze of volcanic eruption and surging, blood-red seas, I got the sense that each of these broad ledges was a world in itself, a nightmarish region in the vast chasm that could only be the Abyss. Well I remembered Saysi's description, read to me in Parnish Fegher's library, about this nightmarish confluence of chaotic power. Impossibly vast in scope, the place reminded me of the night sky, an array of fiery specks unreachably distant from where I stood.

"I know we're on the right track," I declared, my hand on the hound's flank. "This way." Bayar's tail thumped steadily in affirmation.

We watched mutely as volcanoes erupted a thousand miles away, stared in horrified silence as rivers of molten fire blotted out a vast landscape. Another realm held a sea of great size, surging liquid the crimson red of fresh blood. Those "waters" spilled into a vast maelstrom near the heart, a sucking whirlpool that looked as though it might swallow the moon or sun with little effort.

The priestess, following the gaze of the hound, guided us past these bizarre, doomed environments, angling toward a broad ledge on the wall of the Abyss, a place that dipped lower in the center than its outer rim to form a flat-bottomed bowl as big across as any continent. Air thick with the stench of rot and decay rose from this vast depression, coiling around us, stroking our skin with tendrils of festering horror.

"The Steaming Fen," Saysi declared as we plunged lower, beginning to discern far below a landscape of foul, rotting vegetation intermixed by sea-sized swaths of stagnant water and brackish mud flats. Still lower we dived, and now we saw movement as great serpentine shapes writhed through the muck, rolling in huge slimy coils.

I counted several of these great beasts, gradually observing that they all seemed to be swimming in the same direction—the direction toward which the hound guided us.

"What's that up ahead?" Saysi asked, her whisper dry with awe—or horror.

I saw it immediately, but at first couldn't answer her question. A great shape rose into the steaming, polluted sky, piled high on a broad base, climbing in shapeless deformity toward the blackened vault overhead.

"Mountain?" suggested Badswell.

"I don't think so." I began to discern tendencies in the vast shape—certainly nothing so orderly as a pattern or design, but nevertheless a vague symmetry and purpose to its creation. Some of the appendages angling outward from the massif resembled towers, twisted and malformed spires that jutted into space. A number of these were vertical, but others stuck out at oblique angles, and at least two that I could see were virtually horizontal.

As we zoomed closer, I detected movement on the fetid island surrounding the massive mound. At first it looked as though the ground itself crept like oozing mud, but I realized that the effect was caused by living creatures, thousands of them, all gathering toward the lofty pyramid.

"It's a fortress—as big as a mountain, yes, but it has been *created* by someone or something." In the back of my mind, a suspicion was growing, but I hesitated to utter the name. More of the great serpentine shapes coiled through the muck of the fen. I saw huge fins, like the dorsals of deadly, colossal sharks. These leviathans also swam toward the mountainous fortress.

The spiraling whirlwind of our chariot drew closer still,

and I saw gaping holes, black tunnel mouths that dotted the entire surface of the massive structure. We began to get a true appreciation of the place's actual size, and it was easy to see why Badswell had guessed it to be a mountain. Trying to judge perspective in the dim light and smoldering air, I guessed the fortress to be as high as the greatest peaks I had ever seen. Now it filled the horizon before us, yet still sprawled far to either side. The foundation was so broad that the overall slope of the blob-like mass was only a gradual, pyramidal incline. The tunnel entrances nearer the ground were choked by the throngs of creatures compelled, drawn forward, by some summons unseen and unheard by us.

"The horde of chaos," I muttered in awe. "An army that could destroy any world."

"Look—flyers," Bads said tersely, waving his axe.

Our course suddenly brought us into the midst of a flock of broad-winged horrors. Antlers bristled from the staglike heads of these creatures, but the monsters flew on the wings of great condors or vultures.

"Perytons—the heart-seekers!" Saysi declared in confirmation of my own guess. I raised the sword, eyeing the chaotic stag-birds warily. Fortunately none of them seemed to take any interest in our cyclonic conveyance.

Saysi dipped the rod, slowing the speed of our chariot and carrying us on a diving course below the flight of the gathering flock. Certainly the perytons had seen us, yet so single-minded was their response to the summons from that great fortress that not one of them veered to attack.

"An army gathers," deduced Saysi, mirroring my suspicions. "An army of chaos, ready to swarm across the planes at Miska's bidding."

"Their general freed, they gather for vengeance," I

agreed, the picture clear in my mind. Unless the wolf-spider could be stopped, the scope of potential destruction was unthinkable. No doubt the queen could open numerous gates such as the tunnels of white light that had guided her spyder-fiends on their attacks in search of the rod. Now, with the numbers gathered below and the commanding evil of Miska to lead them, teeming hordes would erupt from those interplanar gates, laying waste to any place they chose to assault.

"We kill him first?" Badswell suggested dourly.

"It's our only chance," I agreed, though the very idea made my stomach heave.

"How do we do it?" questioned the half-ogre.

"I don't know. Even Parnish and Arquestan couldn't stop him," Saysi answered before I could reply. It was clear from the tone of her voice that Saysi's determination didn't translate into optimism. "He killed them both, just like that." She snapped her fingers for emphasis, the sound precise and jarring in this vault of chaos.

"We have the rod and my sword. We'll have to get close, strike fast," I suggested, with an encouraging look at the priestess. "And leave the rest in the hands of Patrikon."

Bayar huffed softly, staring fixedly at the mighty edifice. Sniffing, with ears upraised, panting frantically, she turned urgent, pleading eyes to the three of us, willing us to understand.

"He's there in that palace somewhere," I confirmed with certainty. It was as though Arquestan stood behind me, a hand on my shoulder, his soothing voice strong and confident in my ear. "We've got to go inside."

"What about those black holes?" Saysi suggested. "Some on the higher towers don't seem to have any activity going on around them."

I watched as the perytons dived. Each of the antlered vultures tucked its wings, arrowing toward a yawning opening on the upper surface of the mountainous fortress. A trailing heart-seeker lowered its head, goring the black spikes of its antlers into the wing of the leader, drawing a shriek of pain and a cloud of feathers. As the stricken peryton tumbled from the sky, the treacherous follower assumed the primary spot, uttering a shrill cry of triumph as it swept into the vast dark entrance.

Other winged monsters shared the smoky sky with us, many of them arrowing for the same passageway the perytons had entered. Hag-headed harpies, keening their deceptively beautiful songs, swirled and squabbled, one by one vanishing into the depths of the palace. Dragons of black and white and green flew individually into the lightless maw, soaring out of sight, gathering to the commands of their queen.

The hound of law woofed and whined, looking toward the summit of the vast mound. Saysi steered, and Bayar's thumping tail indicated the dog's approval.

"There's one tunnel up near the top—nobody's gone there yet," Badswell observed, pointing to a dark, yawning pit near the summit of the massif.

"What about guards?" I wondered as Saysi tipped the rod, guiding the whirlwind toward the opening.

"Don't see any," the half-ogre stated—with a shrug that indicated he would take it either way. I, too, felt ready to fight and kill in vengeance for our slain companions, and for much, much more. I knew beyond any doubt that law was the bond that held worlds together, an order threatened by Miska and his horde of chaos. This was something I finally perceived with ultimate clarity, and I resolved to do whatever I could to protect that order.

"It looks as if everything is going inside the fortress," Saysi said. "That could mean we don't have much time."

"If we're not already too late," I muttered, suddenly chilled by that horrifying prospect. What if Miska had already commenced his attack?

We soared closer to the mighty fortress. Looking down, I recognized the mass of the monsters on the ground as spyder-fiends, marching like a parade of ants when viewed from our lofty elevation. Other beings of grotesque and monstrous appearance filled out the army of chaos. I saw things that looked like huge octopuses, bulbous bodies waddling grotesquely, lurching forward on eight tentacled legs. A bloblike shape, like a slug that was as big as a castle, oozed on no legs, leering with a visage that was surrounded by lashing tendrils, while six bright crimson eyes glowed from stalks on the upper portion of its wedge-shaped head.

Then the peak loomed high, blocking everything but itself from our view. The tunnel was a huge hole lined with stone walls of jagged blackness, leading into unseen depths. Abruptly the sides of the vast passageway encircled us as Saysi steered the whirlwind into the darkness. Acidic smoke stung my nostrils, but I cast aside worries about the air, ignoring the fact that it could prove fatally poisonous to mortals. Dim light, like the reddish illumination of fading embers, rose from somewhere far below, providing enough brightness to make out the dark stone walls on all sides. The shaft seemed to generally descend, and Saysi slowed our speed slightly to negotiate the winding turns.

Bayar still stared over the rim, her tail clocking slowly back and forth.

"We're on the right track," I whispered, fearful of attracting attention, though as far as I could see, the whole vast tunnel was empty except for us. The walls sped by, dark and slick and lifeless.

"Look." Saysi pointed, slowing our progress to a crawl as we approached a gap.

The passage opened into a vast chamber, a place so incomprehensibly huge that it was impossible to think of it as an enclosure. It was more like an entire realm surrounded by distant, mountainous walls. Obviously the center of the massive, mountainous fortress was hollow, and now we had penetrated to that grim heart.

The whirlwind hovered slowly, creeping close beside one of the black stone walls, gradually moving along a surface that at some point curved from our tunnel wall to merge with the ceiling of this cavernous chamber. Stalactites jutted downward from that upper surface, an inverted forest of spikes drooping like massive fangs.

Illumination rose from a fiery swath in the center of the floor, a vast lake of lava, molten rock bubbling and flaming, filling the place with furnace heat and spuming tongues of flame hundreds of feet into the air. The stench of ozone and other, more acrid, gases bit at my eyes and nose, and a smoky haze obscured everything, coiling in layers throughout the massive space.

Yet even through that haze, we could see that the floor of the chamber—all the space except that occupied by the flaming lake—teemed with the gathering horde of chaos. Countless thousands, perhaps a million or more, of the queen's minions thronged below, and more continued to spill into the chamber, swarming relentlessly forward from the dozen or so huge tunnels that broke the walls at the level of the floor.

Again it was Bayar who pointed with her nose, this time holding silent even as her body tingled with urgency.

She quivered, her tail straight, pointing at a shadowy corner near the vaulted ceiling.

"Here—this way," I urged.

Saysi steered us, still close to the ceiling. The massive spires of rock jutted downward everywhere, forming thickets of stone. We used this inverted forest for cover, crossing near one wall of the chamber, following the unspoken instinct of the hound. As with the flyers outside, the monsters below seemed utterly focused, unaware or uncaring of our presence.

I saw a pair of wide ramps circling upward from the floor of the great chamber, each following one of the cavern's lofty walls to converge on a high, wide shelf. Pillars flanked the entrances to this exalted balcony, and gouts of crimson flame erupted from cracks lining the far walls of the immense platform, breaking up the shadows that had cloaked the area when I first looked there.

"That's the place." I pointed to the ledge that, like a gallery, jutted outward from the wall, high up on the cavern side. A lofty dais stood there, and I could picture Miska mounting that platform to exhort his warriors. I cringed at the thought of the frenziedly howling tanar'ri that would follow his every command.

Saysi guided us through the thick shadows near a side of the ledge, at the upper terminus of one of the great ramps. Monstrous troops advanced along this incline, but as yet, the first of these were far below, drawing only slowly toward this great elevation. The little priestess said nothing, but through some definite command, the whirlwind dissipated, setting us gently onto a floor of slick black stone.

"Wait." Badswell whispered the word, then spoke to Saysi as we turned to look at him. "Should you touch the champion with the rod? Like Parnish?"

"The third segment," she remembered with a nod. Placing her tiny hand around the location of the piece, she touched the tip of the staff to my arm.

Again I felt that spark, the tingling of haste that caused everything else to slow down. Without a word, I began to walk, sword held ready before me while Bayar padded at my heel and Badswell and Saysi fell in behind. Stepping slowly and deliberately, so that the others could keep up, I skirted one of the pillars, which was as big around as a good-sized house. I saw that the flaming illumination rose from trenchlike grooves gouged into the floor. These depressions were filled with oil or some other flammable liquid, and the heat of the blazes grew uncomfortably warm as we slowly advanced.

Approaching a lofty arched entryway, I heard sounds of muted conversation from within the cavernous chamber beyond. As we drew nearer, the sounds became louder, the words spoken in a deep, throaty voice that was vaguely female. At the same time, the sound was clearly inhuman, a deep and resonant rumble so monstrously frightening that my hands began to tremble.

"Just a little longer, my pet . . . my beloved. It has been too long since I have known your embrace." The words gurgled outward, bubbling from something I pictured as a mountainous mass of flesh.

"Aye, my queen. But the army awaits, and vengeance demands that I strike." This reply came in the strong, masculine voice of the wolf-spider. I allowed myself a growing flicker of hope, fueled by the preliminary knowledge that we had at least located our target.

"There will be time, *eons* of time, for your revenge. Dally with me just a while longer."

The chill surging along my spine was all the confirmation I needed: This was the voice of the Queen of Chaos herself. "My pleasure has been denied for too long," she insisted, her voice dropping to a bass rumble, pleading and whining, yet also potent with an irresistible command.

"Or did you not yearn for me with the same fervor, with the unspeakable, unbearable passion that I longed for you?" A further note of sternness crept into the tone.

"Nay, Mistress. For too many centuries, I have been forced to rely only on memories, knowing always that such recollections cannot compare to the exquisiteness that is your being!"

We four intruders crouched like frightened mice in the thick shadows cast by the vast pillars flanking the entryway. Somewhere within lurked the two powerful beings, godlike immortals whom we dared to challenge. Yet I felt no hesitation in myself nor in my companions. I didn't waste time trying to predict what our fate might be after we dealt with the hateful wolf-spider.

"You take the rod," Saysi whispered, passing the artifact to Badswell. "You'll have the strength to drive it home, and Kip may need his sword to buy us time."

"Good idea," I mouthed back, then added another thought. "You stay here. Let Bads and me go ahead."

She gave me an expression that suggested she doubted my sanity, then fell in right between the two of us.

I concurred with a silent nod; the plan was as good as we could hope for, given the desperate nature of our task. The little priestess took hold of her jade amulet, murmuring inaudibly, and I knew that she sought strength and courage from Patrikon. I only hoped that the god of law would bestow his favor upon all of us.

We crept around the corner—the *last* corner. I found myself looking into a large room, with walls of burnished gold and a floor of immaculate silver. There was no light source that I could see, but the entire place seemed to glow with a dim but pervasive illumination. The chamber was featureless except for the two massive occupants coiled together within a stone's throw of the entrance.

The Queen of Chaos towered like a large building, rising from the midst of a nest of tentacles. Her body was a dark and shapeless blob, almost black in color, the upper portion resembling some grotesque, unspeakably foul version of a giantess. The form was vaguely humanoid and female, yet so bulbous and disfigured as to barely resemble anything like a woman.

Miska's human face was buried somewhere within the folds of the queen's monstrous body, but the two wolf heads were upraised and alert. One of them fixed me with a wicked glare, and I could have sworn that those lupine jaws curled into a grin of cruel amusement.

Things happened quickly then.

Realizing that I'd been observed, I raised the Vaati Blade and charged forward, hoping at the very least to distract the wolf-spider so that Badswell could approach and drive home the black artifact. Hastened by the rod, I sprinted across the silver floor like a bolt shot from a crossbow. Bayar barked bravely, charging after with a clattering of claws on metal.

Then the Queen of Chaos turned those malevolent eyes upon me, and my body grew weak with fear. I struggled, feeling my muscles become limp and helpless. Still I tried to attack, but now my feet seemed mired in glue, even frozen to the floor. With a groan of anguish, I found myself unable to take another step.

Bayar darted past me as if, with courage alone, she would rend both the foul queen and her grotesque lover. A black tentacle whipped outward, cracking into the brave dog's flank. With a plaintive yelp, the hound flew through the air, smashed into the golden wall. She slid to the floor and lay limp, like a bundle of brown rags.

"These are the champions of law, my queen," Miska declared, his mocking voice penetrating my wrenching grief. The wolf-spider's handsome human head rose to regard us contemptuously while the wolves sneered and drooled to either side. "It seems they have been kind enough to bring us a present."

"The rod?" The sound was a gurgling chuckle, menacing and amused at the same time.

"Of course," gloated the wolf-spider, turning to enjoy our discomfort. "Naturally the artifact of law would have been a great drain upon my power, should I have tried to bear it through the planes as I made my escape. Fortunately you mortal fools were available."

The vicious, manlike head turned back to his beloved queen. "They have brought it here so that you can store it safely out of reach of any of your enemies. It will never menace us again."

"Champions?" mocked the queen, sneering down at me from the height of a three-story mansion. "What sort of champion is this?"

I started to spit out a bold reply, some kind of brazen challenge to demonstrate my determination. But I was interrupted by the sound of my own sword blade dropping to the floor. Clutching the hilt, which suddenly seemed very large, I strained to lift the weapon. But it was too heavy for me to raise the massive thing . . .

Because I was only a halfling again.

CHAPTER 24

VENGEANCE OF A QUEEN

"Such precious little toys," gurgled the Queen of Chaos, looking down at Badswell, Saysi, and me. She clapped her hands with a remarkably girlish, yet terrifying, gesture. "How splendid that you have come to witness the end of your dreams . . . as well as the destruction of your world."

I looked up in helpless fury, my body that of a tiny halfling, still mired in the magical restraint of the queen's command. Helpless, I looked at Bayar's ragged form, shedding bitter tears for yet another companion I could not save.

"How ironic that the end of *their* dreams," echoed Miska, "should represent merely the beginning of *ours*."

"Yes, my pet. Still, we must be cautious. I would wager that the two little runtlings are no threat to us. Do you agree?"

"Aye, my queen. Yet the bigger one could be dangerous. He wields that axe with strength and skill."

Badswell glared impassively upward as the two horrible beings discussed our fate. The half-ogre's big hands clenched the solid haft of his weapon, and I imagined him evaluating his chances. Could he accomplish anything with a swift, violent attack? Somehow he had given the rod back to Saysi, I noted with a start. Perhaps he had foreseen this complication when our approach was first observed.

Don't try it, I urged silently, hoping that he would sense my plea. Certainly any overt move on his part could yield but a single inevitable result—one that was utterly, hopelessly suicidal. As to myself, though my nerves still tingled with the haste spell, I was incapable of lifting a hand in my friend's defense.

"Very well." The queen appeared to reach a decision, for she raised a finger and pointed at the mute half-ogre. The digit, which was the size of my whole arm, twitched once, and a tendril of blue-black smoke emerged from the tip.

I watched in speechless horror as the tentacle of vapor coalesced on the floor, coiling into a long, fat-bodied viper. The wedged head, with eyes of slitted evil glowing like fire, glared at the half-ogre while the sinuous body pulsed in a grotesque sidewinding motion. Badswell stepped warily backward, eyes fixed upon the serpent, axe raised defensively before his chest.

The strike came so quickly that, even magically quickened, I couldn't follow the movement with my eyes. One moment the serpent was poised, watching its intended prey, and the next it had flown through the air, stabbing like a spear against Badswell's chest. The half-ogre had no chance to react, not even to move the axe. The serpentine, scaly body flexed as I sensed venom coursing from its wicked fangs, piercing skin, swiftly driving into that powerful, loyal heart.

With a groan, Bads staggered backward, dropping the axe to the floor with a heavy clatter. His knees buckled as the snake remained pinned to his body. When he slumped forward, still and dead, the serpent evaporated into the dark smoke that had marked its creation. As the vapor drifted away, our bold companion twitched spasmodically, his head turning to the side, eyes open and utterly sightless.

"Badswell!" screamed Saysi, breaking from her trance and rushing to the lifeless half-ogre's side. "You killed him!" she shrieked, turning her dark eyes toward the queen, fury bringing her voice to a trembling pitch. My own despair rose in a wave of bleak helplessness, the grim foreknowledge that everyone who meant anything to me was going to be killed. Even the little priestess was doomed. The miracle of her survival from Oakvale was merely a brief reprieve.

"Of course I killed him," snapped the immense, grotesque creature peevishly. "Perhaps you are ready to share his fate?"

Again a bloated finger raised, this time aiming toward the little halfling priestess.

"No!" I cried, finally breaking free of the mire, forcing my own feet to move. I stumbled to Saysi's side, pulling her away from the corpse, and wrapped my arms around her as I turned back to the queen. "She's no threat. She can't hurt you!"

Pleading with the goddess, I squeezed Saysi—*hard*—in a desperate attempt to calm her fury, at least to the point where she didn't goad the queen into another deadly strike. My own heart was breaking at the sight of the poor half-ogre's body, but I couldn't let that despair drive our only chance away. As long as we lived, we still had cause for *some* hope, however slight. Fully small again, the same size as Saysi, I held her close and stared into her eyes, silently pleading.

The queen's attentions had already drifted to the massive ramps extending down either wall of the mighty cavern. Only one of these was in sight, but I noticed the file of creatures climbing there, marching steadily upward in answer to an unspoken summons. A mighty raklupis was in the lead, its sleek wolf head raised to regard Miska and the queen with an expression of adoring attentiveness.

Behind the Queen of Chaos, a white circle slowly took shape in the air, glowing with magical power, gradually gaining definition. It lingered there, a gate through the planes, though I could as yet see no sign of a destination through the large aperture. Still, I sensed that this was the invasion route, the avenue awaiting only Miska's command for the onslaught.

"My army gathers, poised to attack," murmured the queen, as if she couldn't quite believe the fact herself. "But where shall I commence the killing, the glorious supremacy of chaos . . . ?"

My heart stuttered as those cold eyes turned back to Saysi and me. "I have an idea," she declared with a sinister chortle. "Tell me . . . where is your home? Do you have loved ones there? I *do* hope so."

Resistance was instinctive, and I clamped my jaw shut in determination not to reveal anything. Suddenly I staggered backward, my head throbbing as though it had been ripped open. I could all but feel the queen's slimy tentacles reaching into the recesses of my brain, tearing out my thoughts as if she were plucking cherries from a bowl. Many of the morsels she cast aside, but soon, inevitably, she found one that she liked.

"Colbytown? A silly name, indeed. No doubt a bland and boring place, full of purpose and order. That shall change, and very soon."

"No!" I tried to cry out, but the word came out a rasping whisper.

"Oh, don't fret. Miska shall take his army to *lots* of places, and chaos will reign in them all. You should consider it an honor, of sorts. A pathetic little village of halflings, incapable of any significant boasts or accomplishments, shall be the initial point of destruction for your entire world. Indeed, I can't imagine why you're so upset."

The queen pivoted, the shifting of her tentacles making moist sucking noises on the slick floor. She addressed the raklupis that now stood atop the stairway. "Laak-ral, you will guard the captives, ensuring that they view the destruction of the first battle."

"Yes, my queen," declared the tanar'ri in an improbably genteel voice. The raklupis called Laak-ral stalked toward Saysi and me, positioning himself well to the side so that he could observe us and also have a clear view of the queen and the wolf-spider. Wolfish head lowered, the monster swung its attention back and forth between us and its master.

"Mistress of my life . . . remember the rod. It is still a threat, however small and pathetic its wielders." Miska's yellow eyes glared from the two wolf heads as his chiseled human features addressed the goddess of chaos. I sensed that the wolf-spider was tired of these games and would just as soon slay us instantly, then proceed with his long-anticipated offensive. "I would caution you to have them place it out of reach before we commence."

336

"A wise precaution, my beloved. You, the female runtling—bring the staff forward and place it beside that ridiculously oversized sword."

I looked across the floor, to where I had dropped the Vaati Blade when I had abruptly returned to my true size. How had I thought myself worthy of such a weapon? The question mocked me, increased my rage and frustration, but did nothing to overcome my utter despair.

Miserably I watched Saysi step forward, bearing the Rod of Seven Parts. Her head was lowered, as if she were unwilling to look at the looming horrors before her. Only as she passed did I see that her lips moved, that her face was locked in an expression of silent concentration.

Reaching the sword, she placed the rod on the floor, across the blade that was still stained with Arquestan's blood. Odd, I thought, how no other wound had left even the smallest blemish on that immaculate golden surface, yet the slaying of the wind duke had apparently created a mark of surprising endurance.

As the ebony artifact touched the keen blade, I heard a faint buzzing sound, like distant bees on a still summer day. Surely I imagined the noise. None of the others in the vast chamber seemed to take notice.

"Miska himself will lead the attack upon your world, commencing in this place . . . Colbytown." The queen spoke the name with a scornfulness that wrenched at my heart. I thought of my sisters, of the nieces and nephews who always greeted me with such enthusiasm on my rare visits home. Perhaps they would be gone, traveling somewhere, and avoid the initial onslaught of chaos. . . .

I all but gagged at the pathetic hope. What did it matter if they survived for a few days, cowering in terror as the force of chaos was unleashed across the world? No place would be safe from the spyder-fiends and their even more horrifying allies. Once the battles began, the ravages of chaos would be utter and all-encompassing.

The buzzing I had noticed before grew slightly louder, certainly more than merely my imagination. The golden sword itself seemed to be the source of the sound, and as I cast a glance from the corner of my eye, I fancied that I could see the weapon move slightly, vibrating with almost invisible pulsations.

The queen was speaking again, and I forced myself to listen, not wanting to give her any cause for hasty execution. I sensed that the longer she talked, the more time we gained for all the worlds unknowingly awaiting the ruthless onslaught.

". . . must be Miska himself, for only he can unite the horde that serves me, can bind these chaotic warriors into the kind of force needed to overwhelm whole realms, to devastate entire worlds."

I recalled Arquestan's words and realized that the queen had echoed the wind duke's explanation and our own decision: Miska was the key!

The queen looked at the gigantic eight-legged horror, her eyes shining with something resembling affection. The wolf-spider shifted back and forth, lupine jaws drooling, heads pivoting this way and that in eagerness to commence the war of destruction.

The bloated monstrosity that was his lover crowed, praising her demonic pet in glowing terms, but I had ceased to listen. My eyes remained surreptitiously glued to the Vaati Blade, certain now that it *was* moving, that the buzzing hum was caused by the resonance of the gilded weapon.

Abruptly the bloodstain vanished from the metal, hissing softly upward into a column of dark steam. Shifting my gaze, I tried to avoid watching, looking toward the raklupis Laak-ral and Miska instead. The tanar'ri was fascinated with his mistress's words, while the wolf-spider shifted with increasing agitation, turning his heads around to look at the space beyond the Queen of Chaos.

Following the direction of his gaze, I saw with horror that the whitish light denoting the gates between planes had solidified. I could clearly see the avenue of white pillars, a tunnel such as the spyder-fiends employed on their earlier attacks. I recognized familiar landmarks beyond that cream-sided tunnel—the millpond and stream of Colbytown, the quaint barns and silos dotting verdant hillsides beyond. Tiny figures probed along the shore, much as I had done as a youngster, and I grimaced at the thought of innocent little halflings fishing and frog-catching, unaware of the terror that was about to descend and shatter their lives and futures with cruel glee.

Tearing my eyes away, I looked back to the sword, and to the steam coalescing into a pillar above the weapon. Abruptly the blade itself became translucent, fading from view, while at the same time the column of steam grew solid and dark and recognizable. In the space of a split second, the sword was gone and the image of the wind duke Arquestan stood in its place. Laak-ral uttered a shrill cry of alarm, crouching to spring as the black-skinned outcast bent and snatched up the rod in a smooth gesture.

"Hold!" cried the figure who so resembled Arquestan, brandishing the artifact at the poised raklupis. With a screech of fury and frustration, the monster froze, locked in place by the power of the rod.

"You!" spat the enraged Miska, all three heads whirling

to confront this new danger.

"An old enemy, wolf-spider—one almost as hard to kill as you yourself."

It *was* Arquestan! That deep and resonant voice carried the confidence and courage that had been hallmarks of the wind duke's steady presence. Now he raised the Rod of Seven Parts, holding it over one shoulder like a javelin as he rushed toward the towering wolf-spider.

Miska's reaction took me, and apparently Arquestan, by surprise. The three-headed horror shrilled in panic, spinning away from the wind duke, attempting to dive behind the bloated form of the queen.

That chaotic monarch shrilled her own rage, lashing a tentacle across the floor with whiplike fury. Arquestan leapt over the whipping tendril in a smooth movement, closing on the scuttling figure of Miska. With a powerful stab, muscles rippling beneath his ebony skin, he drove the narrow tip of the staff against the wolf-spider's bulging abdomen.

Miska's shriek of agony was a sound unlike anything I had ever heard, an explosion of noise that tore at the very fabric of my flesh. I dropped to the floor, hands clasped reflexively over my ears, vaguely aware of Saysi tumbling beside me as the sound echoed through the chamber with crushing force.

But the wolf-spider pulled away before the artifact could be driven into his body. Spinning to face Arquestan, Miska lowered himself into a flat crouch, fury apparent in the slavering wolf heads and the demented features of the enraged man face. The wind duke wielded the rod in both hands, bashing aside the snapping bites of both pairs of jaws. He circled to the side, even though he exposed himself to the crushing attack of the wolf-spider's powerful clenched fist, a blow that sent the black-skinned outcast staggering, sparks crackling from the deflection he delivered with the rod.

Then I saw the reason for the tactic, as the queen rose to her full height, lashing and screeching in her fury. The wind duke kept Miska between himself and the enraged monstrosity, knowing that she would make no attack that would endanger her beloved.

Pouncing like a panther, the eight-legged wolf-spider leapt at Arquestan, desperately flailing at the rod with his humanoid arms. I noticed a trail of ichor spilling from the puncture in his belly, sensed that the monstrous being had been sorely hurt by the first stab of the rod.

With a deft feint, the wind duke started to the left and then darted back to the right. The huge wolf-spider landed where its foe had been, but now Arquestan had skirted two steps to the side. Muscles tense, bearing the rod like a long, slender sword, the outcast pierced Miska's body just behind the nearest wolf head. Driving the rod inward until only a handspan remained outside of the bone-shelled body, the wendeam gave the weapon a wrenching twist. Then he withdrew the gore-streaked rod, waving it over his head as the wolf-spider shrieked a cry of awful, ultimate doom.

Arquestan's bright eyes flashed and his white teeth gleamed in a grin of pure triumph as the wind duke brought the rod around again. Miska slumped to the floor, and once again Arquestan pierced him, this time shouting loudly in his clear, defiant voice.

"Back to your prison, hateful one! Again you are mastered by the Rod of Law!"

"*No!*"

The queen's shriek of rage was even louder than the

wolf-spider's cry of pain. Time seemed to come to a stand-still. Nothing moved except the blurring and fading of Miska's shape.

"Back to your prison! I banish thee!" cried Arquestan, standing tall and raising the Rod of Seven Parts over his head. The image of the monstrous arachnoid horror grew faint, misty, and then, in the blink of an eye, he was gone.

"You will die!" screamed the Queen of Chaos, raising both hands above her head, her voice a mix of incomprehensible grief and utter, consuming fury.

"Flee!" Arquestan turned toward us for the first time. He cast the rod through the air, and Saysi caught the artifact in both hands.

Lightning flashed and explosive thunder rumbled through the Fortress of Chaos. Bolts of crackling energy smashed into the bold, proud wind duke, driving him back with cruel force. Another blast echoed, and Arquestan's body was shattered by the killing power of the queen's vengeance, torn into shreds, the gory pieces cast across the high balcony.

Following the destruction with my eyes, I was startled to see the raglike bundle next to the wall twitch, to meet the gaze of mournful, yet *living*, eyes. Abruptly Bayar climbed to her feet, shook herself, and galloped over to us, barking urgently.

I gaped in awe at the courage and sacrifice of the noble hero, at the amazing recovery of the battered hound. Saysi chanted something behind me. Abruptly a swirl of wind swept me up from the floor. Bayar, very near to us, leapt upward to land in the whirlwind's compartment. The chariot moved fast, bearing us around the back of the Queen of Chaos. The bloated fiend's attention remained, for the moment, focused on the place where her lover had disappeared, and where the wind duke had died. Her cries of grief and rage thundered like a strong gale, sending her minions scuttling in a frenzy to flee back down the ramps.

Vaguely I realized that Saysi had used the rod to summon the whirlwind chariot. I tripped over something large, saw that she had gathered Badswell's stiff, blackened corpse into the riding compartment as well. Bayar, panting eagerly, rode with her forepaws on the edge, looking around with a rumbling, belligerent growl.

Saysi's goal was clear. The gate to Colbytown yawned before us. Already the edges of the circular hole grew faint, the power that had compelled its opening cooled by the chaos within the queen's palace. Though she had called the gate into being, the disappearance of her beloved Miska clearly was causing it to fade rapidly.

I saw the queen's eyes shift to the paralyzed, helpless form of Laak-ral, still frozen where Arquestan had held him at bay. She pointed, shrieking in rage, and the raklupis exploded into a cloud of gore under the monstrous and irresistible power of his mistress's vengeful rage.

The gate was closing faster now, the image of Colbytown fading like a picture viewed through gauzy cloth. Saysi tipped the whirlwind, compelling every ounce of speed from the spiraling chariot. Bayar barked eagerly, ears flapping, pink tongue extended as she stared keenly into the gate.

And then we were through, surrounded by blue skies and calm breezes, watching the shimmering hole slowly fade behind us. Below, the millpond rippled under the gentle wind, then swirled into a splashing wake as the funnel cloud of our chariot cruised across the water. I looked back, Goldfinder ready in my hand, to see the last, shimmering image of the gate closing in the green hillside above my village.

My knees felt strangely weak, and I wasn't certain we were actually safe. Slowly fear and awe subsided, replaced by a subtle but growing sense of elation. "Miska's gone—his army scattered, no one to unite, to lead it," I whispered in awe, realizing the consequences of our struggle and the sacrifices of brave companions.

"Arquestan . . . where . . . how was he still alive?" Saysi asked, shaking her head in disbelief.

The memory of the wind duke's return to life, and his subsequent death, cooled my initial feelings of joy. I tried to recreate in my mind what had happened. "His blood on the blade . . . it must have captured some of his essence, given the vaati weapon the power to make the transformation. When you touched the sword with the rod, it began to buzz, as if it were coming to life."

"It was," she agreed quietly.

Saysi set us down in the village square, and as the whirlwind faded to a gentle breeze, we stood over the body of our loyal half-ogre friend. Bayar sniffed the corpse morosely as diminutive villagers crept forward from the surrounding groves, pitchforks, staffs, and sickles in clear evidence as they scrutinized the new arrivals.

The door to the Big Tankard Inn popped open, and out swaggered the officious form of Burgman Deister, the mayor of my little hometown village. He blinked and rubbed his eyes, stepping hesitantly closer.

"Kip? By all the kegs in my cellar, is that really you?"

"Aye, Burgman," I said with a nod. I recognized Hallie and Berdeen, my sisters, as each rushed forward with a brood of little ones in tow. Even they halted a few steps away, sensing our grief.

Bayar whined plaintively, prodding at the lifeless half-ogre with her moist black snout. She padded with her forepaw, tail wagging expectantly.

My heart was heavy with grief, bearing a load more burdensome than any I had ever borne before. The loss of this bold and loyal companion was too high a price for any accomplishment. And all the others who had perished . . . Rathentweed, Parnish, and the nearly immortal wendeam Arquestan.

"Parnish Fegher told us of another power, a thing that the rod can do. Do you remember?" Saysi asked hesitantly, kneeling beside the body. The halflings of Colbytown remained in their circle around us, standing well back, as if they expected some sort of magical eruption.

That was a reasonable fear, I suddenly perceived as I understood what Saysi was proposing.

"It will probably scatter the rod again," I warned softly. "The artifact will be gone—all that power, all that *law*—out of our lives forever."

"I know," she said softly. The liquid, chocolate-colored eyes rose to mine, suggesting, persuading as she spoke. "You know we can't hold on to it, don't you? Sooner or later, someone—or some*thing*—will come for it. I know that *I* can't live with that knowledge, waiting for inevitable disaster . . . tomorrow, or the day after, or next year."

"You're right." I saw the truth clearly. "It would suit me if it scatters again, vanishes into the mists of the planes." My mind flicked to a memory of something Arquestan had told us about the rod's history. "Maybe it'll stay lost for seven centuries again."

When she started to speak, the beginnings of a twinkle

gleamed in the priestess's dark eyes. "Well, what are we waiting for?"

Saysi placed the Rod of Seven Parts over Badswell's still chest and rose, bowing her head in prayer. The gathered halflings took, in unison, about a dozen steps backward, leaving the two of us alone with the hound and our slain friend in the village square.

Whatever she said, Saysi's prayer took a long time. My mind reflected on the changes I had undergone, grateful that I was again small, again *me*. I remembered the places we had been, the dangers we had faced—and the little village around me had never seemed so perfect, so welcoming and comfortable.

Power began to build with a rumbling sensation, like the booming of very distant thunder. I felt the vibration through my bare feet, saw the Rod of Seven Parts begin to tremble, vibrating on Badswell's rounded chest. A searing flash crackled through the square, like lightning from the clear blue sky. A series of pops echoed sharply, a staccato pattern of seven loud, brief *cracks*. They happened quickly, but I was able to see the rod break apart, each piece vanishing with one of the explosive sounds.

The last to go was the tiny stub of ebony that I had first encountered in the lair of Scarnose Ogre. When that one vanished, I let out a sigh of relief and muttered a prayer to Patrikon that never again would I lay eyes on one of the shiny black segments.

Badswell snorted, like a loud, growling snore. Kicking his feet, stretching slowly and awkwardly as if awakening from a peaceful slumber, he sat up and blinked his eyes. The big half-ogre smiled at Saysi, then turned his eyes to me, mouth gaping in a grin that bared the prettiest tusks I'd ever seen.

EPILOGUE

Though we three travelers were virtually penniless, the occasion of my wedding proved to be one of the grandest extravaganzas Colbytown had ever seen. Burgman Deister donated many kegs of his finest brew, and my sisters and their husbands combined to prepare a magnificent feast.

A high priest of Patrikon traveled from a nearby temple to perform the ceremony, and Badswell stood over Saysi and me, scattering blossoms and offering drinks to whoever came by—and, this being a village of halflings, naturally a lot of people came by. Bayar sat beside us in a position of honor, though later in the evening, she amused the youngsters by shifting shape to her pearly globe, floating playfully just above the eager, clutching fingers of the children.

After a night of dancing, music, and revelry, the blushing bride and I retired to our quarters. In the intimacy of

347

a candlelit bedchamber, Saysi . . .

Suffice to say that some things are worth waiting for.

Weeks passed, and balmy spring gently merged into lazy summer. Our surroundings proved delightfully peaceful, pastoral, sweet, comfortable, predictable . . . in a word, boring.

By late summer, the three of us had decided to take to the road again. I still had Goldfinder, Saysi her jade amulet, and though Badswell had lost his battle-axe in the depths of the Abyss, he had fashioned himself a staff of solid rockwood, a local tree with timber so dark that it reminded us of ebony. I wondered aloud if the half-ogre was prepared to adventure, perhaps to battle for our lives, armed only with a pole.

"Seen it done before," he replied simply, and for a moment, the image of a tall black figure rose in all of our memories.

We left on a muggy dawn, the kind of day that promises sweathouse heat, after teary farewells from my sisters and promises to at least three dozen nieces and nephews that we would return with treasures and baubles—well, at least with a few interesting stories.

Bayar, ready to explore and adventure and travel, loped and gamboled in the lead. An archway of elms stood over the road, and as we passed beneath these, I knew that we would in fact be back, though it might take a while.

And if I had learned one thing, I knew that there could be no telling what road we'd follow to get here.